"Sometimes you run ⟨...⟩
Or the adjectives l⟨...⟩
What if I say that *Once i⟨...⟩*
brilliant, insightful, heartbr⟨eaking, enchanting⟩
what does that even mean anymore?
But this novel is BRILLIANT because the prose glows, sends off heat.
INSIGHTFUL because it allows us to see into a place that most
of us don't know about. HEARTBREAKING because you can feel
the situation that these characters are trapped in. And ENCHANTING
because it's told in the form of a fairy tale that lets us believe that,
somehow, these poor souls may be able to rescue themselves . . .
Laila Halaby has captured the human condition perfectly here."

—Carolyn See, *Washington Post*

"Set in the early days of post–September 11 America,
Once in a Promised Land draws its structure from Arabian folklore
and the western fairy tale, turning both inside out to illuminate the
mythic search for home and identity, the universal hunger of the soul
for the genuine, and the wounding yet redemptive nature of love itself.
In this timely and utterly original novel, Laila Halaby has crafted a
deeply resonant tale of our tangled and common humanity."

—Andre Dubus III, author of *House of Sand and Fog*

Once in a Promised Land

Once in a
Promised Land

⤙ A Novel ⤚

Laila Halaby

Beacon Press, Boston

Beacon Press
25 Beacon Street
Boston, Massachusetts 02108-2892
www.beacon.org

Beacon Press books
are published under the auspices of
the Unitarian Universalist Association of Congregations.

11 10 09 08   8 7 6 5 4 3 2 1

This book is printed on acid-free paper that meets the uncoated paper
ANSI/NISO specifications for permanence as revised in 1992.

Text design by Bob Kosturko
Composition by Wilsted & Taylor Publishing Services

Library of Congress Cataloging-in-Publication Data

Halaby, Laila.
Once in a promised land / Laila Halaby.
p. cm.
ISBN-13: 978-0-8070-8391-8 (pbk. : acid-free paper)
ISBN-10: 0-8070-8391-7 (pbk. : acid-free paper) 1. Arab Americans—
Arizona—Fiction. 2. September 11 Terrorist Attacks, 2001—Influence—
Fiction. 3. Arab Americans—Social conditions—Fiction.
4. Prejudices—United States—Fiction. I. Title.

PS3608.A5455O63 2006
813'.6—dc22
2006014841

The folktale "Nus Nsays" was translated by Laila Halaby,
based on a version published in Arabic by the
Popular Art Center, El Bireh, Palestine, in 1998.

A portion of the reading group guide, "Real People: A Web of Suspicion
Ensnares a Jordanian Couple Following September 11," by Margaret Regan,
was published in *Tucson Weekly,* February 1, 2007. Used with permission
of the author. Copyright © 2007. All rights reserved.

For Raik

Before

kan

ya ma kan

fee qadeem az-zamaan

They say there was or there wasn't in olden times a story as old as life, as young as this moment, a story that is yours and is mine. It happened during half a blink in the lifetime of the earth, a time when Man walked a frayed tightrope on large, broken feet over an impossible pit of his greatest fears.

It was a time when Man's throat was parched and dry, the earth's rivers too narrow and dirty to quench him, its lakes overflowing or drier than the bones from which his flesh hung. Many people clutched to the afterlife promise of *gardens beneath which rivers flow.*

More than anything, this is the tale of a man who delighted in the science of water and in word games (reshaping *water* to become *we art,* for example) and a woman with a penchant for numerals (Arabic, not Roman) and a taste for silk pajamas: a couple whose love for each other had parched around the edges, pulled up at the corners, so that air bubbles had separated adhesive from skin.

Our story takes place in the provincial American town of Tucson, Arizona, a locale with weather and potential (and very little water).

Our main characters are Salwa and Jassim. We really come to

know them only after the World Trade Center buildings have been flattened by planes flown by Arabs, by Muslims. Salwa and Jassim are both Arabs. Both Muslims. But of course they have nothing to do with what happened to the World Trade Center.

Nothing and everything.

Part One

Chapter One

One minute before Jassim Haddad's alarm was scheduled to hammer through the quiet morning, his eyes opened, and he lay awake in darkened silence for a few seconds before his naked arm stretched out to turn off the buzzer. Four days a week he woke up at this time, usually a minute or two before the alarm, so he could drive to the Fitness Bar, swim, come home, and still be able to spend morning time with his wife, Salwa.

Jassim delighted in the stillness the morning offered, a time before emotions were awake, a time for contemplation. This day was no exception as he got up, washed his face, brushed his teeth, and relieved himself, the beginning of a morning ritual as close to prayer as he could allow. His thoughts hovered over the internal elements of self and world rather than the external. Jassim did not believe in God, but he did believe in Balance. At five o'clock, with the day still veiled, Jassim found Balance.

He went to his bedroom once more to look at Salwa and to pick up the duffel bag he had packed the night before.

"Have a good swim, Father of Water Preservation," whispered Salwa.

"Thank you. Have a good sleep, Miss Pajamas." Sometimes he walked to the side of the bed and kissed her forehead, but usually he did not. Today he did not.

Outside, the darkness was almost warm, the desert's refusal to accept autumn. Though they had a garage, Jassim often parked his Mercedes sedan in the driveway, under an acacia tree, so that he could step out into the day before he got into his car. Radio off, he took a couple of deep swimming breaths before pulling off his property and looping down the hills in a silent nine minutes. Driving alone in the dark, alone anywhere, anytime, filled Jassim with peace and pleasure; driving was a secret drug, a secret god.

In a blink he arrived at the end of the road where the Fitness Bar was lodged, at the edge of a wash, a few breaths from the

3

mountains. He parked in the bright-for-safety lot, amazed as always by how many cars were already there.

ID approved by Diane, the early morning clerk, he entered, smiling politely, though believing that it was within decorum not to greet people at this time of day.

His goal was the outdoor Olympic-length pool at the heart of the gym; the building was U-shaped and the pool nestled within its inner walls. The east lanes were used by the faster and more serious swimmers (ex-competitors, he imagined, judging by the way they flipped when they came to each end), so while the west lanes were more apt to be subject to doubling, Jassim usually chose one of them.

Jassim put his duffel bag down at the end of lane #2. First he warmed up in his T-shirt and shorts: ten push-ups, ten sit-ups, twenty jumping jacks, which was just enough to start his blood pumping and get him ready for the water. He got out his goggles and towel and stripped down to his Speedo (*So deep*, he thought, liking the way the word broke down symmetrically).

Salwa hated his Speedo. "Why do you have to wear that? It's dreadful. Makes you look like clay."

"It's more comfortable to swim in. Besides, why would you mind? No one sees me in it."

"What do you mean no one sees you? You always talk about how full the gym is when you go."

"I mean no one we know. The only people there are people who are exercising, and people who exercise wear exercising clothes."

Goggles dipped in the water to avoid steaming, shaken out to make them clear, elastic strap stretched once before wrapping around his head, he was ready. Sitting on the lip of the pool with his legs dangling in the water, he breathed two swimming breaths, and then he was in.

The cold rush that surrounded his body stole his breath, forced his heart to speed up as his strokes sliced through the water. He stopped at the wall of the far end to catch his breath and then began to swim at a normal pace, as he had done for years and years. The crawl, breast stroke, backstroke, and crawl again, for a total of forty minutes.

Today, a day that changed everything, Jassim cleared his mind, forced away thoughts of work, of preoccupations, and relaxed for the last time for many years to come, letting his thoughts go where they wished.

—∞—

After his final lap, Jassim stood in the water and breathed heavily with his arms outstretched. Eyes closed, fingers reaching, palms facing the sky, head left, head right, slight rotation with each arm, and another deep breath to elongate his spine, face, and chest tilted toward the heavens. The city would now be waking up, but Jassim was drenched in that delightful contented state that exercise gives the body. He stood another moment, noting the swimmers in each adjacent lane, keeping in mind that he had less than five minutes to get out before his blood slowed down and he wouldn't be able to shake the cold. He had attained equilibrium.

Today, as on each day, he embraced his routine: climbed out of the pool, took off his goggles, shook them out, dropped them in his duffel bag, and dried his face with a thick hand towel, never having come around to using the giant towels that Americans loved. "They are as large as bedcovers," he had told Salwa when she bought a set for the first time.

"They are luxurious," she had countered.

And therein lay their differences.

He slipped into his shower shoes.

Footsteps followed him into the building.

"Have a good swim?"

Jassim turned and found an older man, perhaps sixty, with graying hair cut a quarter of an inch from his scalp, a young face, and an exceptionally lean, tan body. He too was wearing a Speedo, but unlike Jassim, he was dripping wet and had a white towel over his shoulder.

"Yes, thanks," said Jassim. "You?"

"Always. Don't know how people who don't swim manage."

Jassim nodded. They walked silently side by side until they got to the shower room.

"Name's Jack Franks," said the man, extending his hand.

"Jassim Haddad," replied Jassim, returning the strong grip.

He pushed open the red door whose white letters announced they were entering the men's locker (*rock semen, I* remainder), gestured for Jack Franks to precede him, and hoped that their conversation would end. Jassim liked to start the day with silence, required silence to cement the balance he had achieved by swimming. The shower stalls were lined up on one side, with benches in front of them. On the other side were lockers. Farther back were toilets and sinks. He dropped his duffel on a bench, got out a bottle of shampoo, which he placed on the shelf in the shower, and hung the slightly damp hand towel on a peg within arm's reach. Jack Franks had no bag, just hung his towel over a peg and got into the shower next to his.

Jassim stepped into the shower and pulled the curtain.

"You Iranian?" Jack Franks asked over the sound of water. He pronounced the word *I-ray-nee-in.*

Jassim turned the water on and stood under it, willing Jack Franks to be quiet.

"No, I'm from Jordan."

A hot five-minute shower after swimming was one of the few excesses that Jassim allowed himself, giving his muscles a chance to relax and his mind a chance to ready itself for the day. Not for the first time, Jassim wished that the gym offered outdoor shower closets that were open at the top so that he could bathe in silence and semidarkness, complete his morning routine, his meditation, his time for being in touch with the elements of the world, in peace, with no other stimulus.

"Jordanian? I went to Jordan once."

Jassim wondered if he could pretend he didn't hear. It wouldn't have made a difference, because Jack Franks kept talking.

"Followed my daughter there. She married a Jordanian. Not one like you, though. This one was from the sticks—or the sand, as the case was."

"I hope she was happy there," said Jassim, forcing his voice above the sound of the water and grasping for the uncontroversial.

"Hard to say. She converted. She's an Arab now. Probably still lives there. Don't know. Haven't talked to her for years. That's another story."

"I'm sorry to hear that." Jassim stripped off his Speedo and rinsed it out.

"Don't be sorry. It's not your fault. You have an American wife?" Though the room bubbled with the noise of the two showers and the hum of the cooler, Jack Franks's voice easily carried above it.

"No, my wife is not American." He pushed the soap dispenser twice, rubbed his hands together, and spread the lather from his neck down to his feet.

"She's from there, then?"

"Yes."

"She veiled?"

"No." Jassim poured a dollop of shampoo into his hand and lathered his head vigorously, then rinsed it out with his fingers rubbing at his scalp.

"Is she beautiful?"

This question went too far, and Jack Franks seemed to sense it.

"No offense intended. I'm just amazed by the beauty of the women there. Incredible. The hair, the eyes. No wonder you fellas cover them up. There's a woman at my bank, First Fidelity, who's from Jordan. Absolutely beautiful. Eyes like magic, the clearest, lightest brown you've ever seen, and thick, thick hair that never seems to move. Never seen anyone like her. Can never remember her name. Starts with an S and sounds like Sally, I think. You know her?"

Jassim let the water pound on his chest and stared at the tile wall in front of him, his serenity scratched. Salwa had a fan club. He didn't like that, didn't want to hear another man talking about his wife. Wished this man would go away and had an unpleasant feeling about him. Why had he never seen him before? "No, I don't think so," he finally answered, though it was not his custom to lie.

Jack had finished his shower and was drying off. Jassim tilted the showerhead up and closed his eyes, let the water pound at his face.

"Jassim, nice to meet you. You have a good day."

Jassim moved his head out of the water and watched through the gap in the shower curtain as Jack walked off, still wearing his

Speedo, with his towel over his shoulder again. "Take care, Jack."
Where would he be going, dressed like that? The sauna? But then
why had he taken a shower first? Jassim wondered. In all the years
he'd been going to this gym, Jassim had never been *buttonholed*
like that. People rarely tried to have conversations at this time of
day, and certainly not people who ran into each other for the first
time. That was something Jassim admired about Americans, something he had done his best to absorb for himself: they didn't allow
social constraints to get in the way of the day's plan. If you came
to exercise, you exercised, and you never let someone keep you
from it.

Water off, Speedo wrung out and deposited in the plastic bag
he always carried, his damp hand towel drying him from top to
bottom, bottom to top, he dressed again in his shorts and shirt.
Then he picked up his bag, held on to his keys, and headed out past
the front desk to the parking lot.

"Bye, Jassim."

"Bye, Diane. Have a good day."

"You too."

Jassim thought, as he often did when he passed the front gate,
that Diane wanted sex—not necessarily from him, rather that she
stood there in a state of wanting. Her obvious willingness disturbed
him and in no way appealed to him. So skinny, and still she poured
herself into pants that were stretched to capacity. Pale and blond
with a too-sweet smile, she was not a beauty, nor a turn-on, nor did
she seem interesting; her most outstanding feature was that she exuded availability.

He glanced at the clock on his way out. Five minutes after six.
On time, on schedule. Twelve minutes in the car and he would be
home (his return route added one stoplight and three minutes to his
drive). He got in his car, his high-performance machine, and sat for
a moment on the cool leather seat, enjoying the quiet.

Radio on, volume low, he headed home, not paying much attention to the news, his mind stuck on Jack Franks.

—◦◦—

For four days Salwa had looked at the tiny pills bubbled in their credit card–like container. She stared. They stared back. Tiny eyes. Tiny mints. Harmless-looking dots that could stop a baby in its tracks, keep it from ever greeting the world, keep it from ever being.

Women's tongues spat stories in Arabic and English of distracted women and absentminded mothers who had forgotten to take their pills, sometimes missing a day or two. True, a few weeks down the road often found them pregnant, which was usually the reason for the story to be told in the first place.

The first day Salwa pretended to herself that she forgot.

On the second day she couldn't forget, or pretend to forget. If Jassim were to look, which he wouldn't, but if he were to look, he would never believe that she had missed two days. One, maybe. Two, impossible. It was not her style. If she decided not to take the pill, she would have to throw it away and make it look like she had taken it on schedule. In other words, she would have to lie a Big Lie. And not a necessary lie that barely even counted.

This pill business was different. To tell Jassim that she took her pills when she had flushed them down the toilet was an out-and-out lie, the kind that slips into the waist of your clothes and slowly, slowly expands until you are so uncomfortable you think you might pop.

Lies of that nature rearranged entire lives, plunked people down where they didn't belong and left others out in the cold with no coat on. Lies like "I am going to visit my mother," the underbelly of which was "I am having coffee with a woman far more beautiful than you."

The interesting thing about lies was that if you found one, could pick out the one phrase that seemed too harmless and plain, and if you lifted it up by the corner, you would see its spectacular tummy with a rainbow of stories stitched in. You had to be an expert, had to be able to dissect conversation like a coroner or, better, like a surgeon, since you wanted everyone to be alive at the end.

Salwa's friend Randa was especially skilled at fishing out the lie, the one sentence that didn't quite fit. She would jerk up her fishing pole in just such a way—"Oh, I didn't see you buying cakes, and I was there all morning" (which might be another lie)—that you could see it for what it was, a brilliant creature dangling in the air, the kind that spent its day under rocks or in the deepest depths of the sea and hid its luster until it made a kill.

Salwa's Lie covered a glorious underbelly. It was not *I didn't take my birth control pill* but instead a much more colorful *For a few years now I've felt that I've been missing something in my life. That's why I got a real estate license. It wasn't enough, though. I think having a child will fill that void. I am going to try to get pregnant, even though Jassim says he doesn't want a child.*

But even Salwa didn't look at it that way, couldn't see its truth, could see only a vague hint of red as she succumbed to the frantic desire struggling within her.

Finish. She popped out the second pill that she was not going to take, held it between her fingers, and then dropped it down the sink's drain, which gave her an immediate truth if the subject came up: "I forgot one, and the next day's fell down the drain."

She then swore to herself out loud that she would take the next one.

It is as easy to lie to the Self as it is to Another. Twice tomorrow came and went, and no pills were swallowed.

Today, the fifth day, Salwa woke up with guilt at her throat. Sweetness and quiet usually filled the morning, but today deception soured the air. *What have I done, what have I done?* Salwa asked herself in Arabic, her language of thought and intimacy.

She lay staring at the guilty darkness as it pinned her down, kept her flat and immobile. In a sudden burst, she pushed it off and sat up. Sweet-smelling feet worked their way into satin slippers and slid across thick carpet to the bathroom. Without a thought, she pressed out a tiny tablet with her thumb. She dropped it in her mouth and ensured its destination in her stomach with a handful of water.

In another spectacular lie to the Self, she swore that there was no way she could have gotten pregnant in those four days. No way. It was done now. Four days that could change the shape of the world, not with war or torrential floods but by inaction.

Salwa glided back to bed, lighter and more honest now, and tucked herself under the cool covers. She smiled and the world was right again. The Lie was deflated. Her emptiness had been filled, and her need for a child could be rechanneled. That need had been so savage, so blinding, that for several months she had thought of nothing else and had not fought the evolutionary mandate to reproduce, just indulged it while she contoured her Lie.

Nestled there under cool covers, alone while her husband swam, Salwa found peace, a peace she would remember for years, as it would be scratched away within the hour by men whose culture was a first cousin to her culture, whose religion was her religion.

For now, however, Salwa slept in peace.

—◌ ◌—

"Who is it?" someone called down white stones.

"It is I, Hassan."

Laughter.

"Come in, It-Is-I-Hassan."

In the bright late Amman afternoon came the *slap, slap, slap* of imported shoes running up just-washed stairs two at a time.

"Hi, Um Siham. How are you doing today?"

"Thank God, I am well, Hassan. How are you? God willing, your family is well."

"Thank God, we are all well. My mother says hello." Greetings from down the alley where he had lived with his family for so many years.

"Please tell her hello from me and from our family. It is too long that we don't see one another." Reasons kept behind lips, under tongues.

"How is your health, Um Siham?"

"Praise God, it is well. God has given me the strength to do all that I need to. Come in and sit down, my boy. Congratulations on your engagement. God willing, you will spend a lifetime of happiness together and have many children."

"If it is God's wish."

"And when is your wedding?"

"In the late spring or early summer."

"God willing, it will be lovely and you will have many guests coming to celebrate with you."

"God willing."

"And your work? How is it going?"

"I'm doing fine and love what I'm doing. Our news shows are broadcast around the world. Those years in Romania have finally paid off. I hope everyone is well in your family."

"Praise God, we are all fine," replied the old woman, fully aware of Hassan's intention. "Siham is doing so well at the university, and her daughter has been accepted at the new private school. Thank God we have help from Salwa. If it were not for her, Mona wouldn't be able to go."

At last. "And how is Salwa?"

"Salwa is fine, thank God. She is working hard. No babies yet, but working like they do there. She is now a *real estate agent.*" She followed her heavily accented English with a giggle.

"*Real estate agent?* What is that?"

"It is someone who sells houses."

Land pimp, Hassan thought. "She likes this kind of work?"

"Yes, thank God, she does, and she is good at it."

"So she isn't working in the bank anymore?"

"She's still at the bank. But the other job offers quite a bit more money, so she does that on weekends."

He fought with himself to change the subject. "Um Siham, isn't it awful what happened?"

"What has happened?"

"You haven't heard? In New York. There have been explosions in New York. Also in Washington. Planes. Someone flew planes into buildings. Into the *World Trade Center.*"

"Flew planes into the buildings? Who?"

Hassan explained. Told her exactly what he had seen. Who they thought had done it. What they did and didn't know.

"God have mercy on those poor souls on the planes and in the buildings. God have mercy on them," Um Siham repeated. "I must call Salwa and make sure she is okay."

"Please go ahead."

"Stay here, so you can tell your mother that she is fine."

"As you wish."

"May peace be upon you," came a greeting from the hallway.

"And upon you peace. Welcome. Oh, it's my sister!"

"Um Siham, have you heard?"

"Yes, Hassan was just telling me. I want to call Salwa and make sure she is okay. And Selim? Have you talked to him?"

"Yes, thank God he is fine. He is in New York, you know," Um Selim said to Hassan. "He is fine. Um Siham, Salwa is too far away. She is fine. America is a large country."

"I'm calling my daughter." Um Siham left the room for a moment and reappeared with glasses and a tiny book. Her hands were shaking.

"Um Siham," said Hassan, "your sister is right. There is no need to worry. New York is on the opposite side of the United States. It is nowhere near Arizona."

"When children are far away, a parent always worries."

"A parent always worries," said Um Selim.

"That's true. That is true." Glasses on, Um Siham squinted at the notebook. "Hassan, help me here. I can't see."

Hassan sat by the side of the woman who was supposed to be his mother-in-law and read the number of his would-have-been bride. He read it aloud. And to himself he read the cellular number that was written in clear numbers beneath it. While he dialed the house number for Um Siham, he memorized the cellular number. Memorized the three-digit prefix and the seven-digit number. Hummed it to himself as Um Siham talked to Jassim (whose name, implying large stature and strength, seemed inappropriate for such an effete man) and made patterns with it as Um Siham talked to her daughter.

"Hassan has just gotten engaged," Um Siham finally said through the phone. She nodded and smiled at him, whispering, "She says congratulations." He nodded, pointed to his watch, waved, and got up. Um Siham waved and continued chatting. "Hamdan. Intizar Hamdan. She works where he does. Very nice girl." Though she had never met her.

When Hassan left Um Siham's house, he was still reciting the cellular number. When he got to the bottom of the stairs, he pulled out his own cellular phone and stored the numbers in his directory, tucked away among those of business contacts.

Hassan knew it was not a good idea to pull at the threads of an old love, but at this moment he couldn't help himself. Engaged for less than a week, he had gone to Salwa's house with the intention of asking after her one final time, of asking her sister frankly if Salwa was happy in her marriage. It was God's will that Um Siham had given him the key to speaking with Salwa directly.

Everything had been shaken up yesterday when he overheard Siham and his own sister, Huda, still close friends, talking. When he heard Siham say that she didn't think Salwa's marriage would last, that she thought Salwa should come home and live her real life with them.

Hassan's heart had thumped and thumped, his hands moist. For nine years he had done his best to live his life as though Salwa had never existed. He had left Amman for Romania to get a graduate degree. Had forced himself to focus on school so that he could work as he wished, deciding that if he could not have his country, was not to have the life he wanted with her, then he would create a new life and lose himself in it. Had come home and worked from morning to night in the production studio. And his hard work had paid off. He was now assistant producer for a daytime news program that was broadcast via satellite around the world.

During those long years, when Salwa's face came into his mind, he squeezed his eyes shut and forced it away, demanded that she leave him in peace. And when he had moved on and Intizar had suggested that they formalize their relationship, Hassan had gone with his mother to Intizar's house and asked for her hand in marriage, accepting that he would never love anyone as he had loved Salwa. Simple as that.

But here they were. Everything had now changed. For if Salwa was coming home, was she not coming home to him? She had tasted America and rejected it. He had always known he would lose her to the glossiness of the Western world, but he had thought it would be later. God's will that it had happened like this, after he had been able to prove himself to her father and she had gotten America out of her system. They would pick up where they had left off.

Part Two

Chapter Two

Awake before his alarm, Jassim got out of bed and went to the bathroom, hoping that movement would force the repeating images from his mind. His actions were automatic, but his brain seized on picture after picture, humans leaping from impossible heights, plumes of smoke filling the air and then charging down the narrow streets. He wondered what it smelled like. Ash? Dust? Burning steel? Were the smells of people drowned by the deaths of those two buildings? The buildings didn't actually die, though, did they? No, they were not living creatures. He doubted he would ever find out about the smell, nor would he see the images again of the people jumping, as it was considered too gruesome for the American public. Details rated X. Or was X only for pornographic images?

He walked through the dim house, relishing the embrace of darkness. He had been so distracted by the news on Tuesday that he had forgotten to empty the contents of his gym bag, which he found in the family room. Why was it called a family room? Were all houses with family rooms constructed with the intention that children would live in them? Or was it possible that a couple constituted a family? Perhaps it was an American attempt to create a thicker illusion of family, in much the same way that *living room* came to be used after the 1918 Spanish flu epidemic killed so many people and their bodies were laid out in what was then called the *parlor.* Someone, an architect perhaps, in an effort to bring some optimism to the world, coined the term *living room* as a way to express that this was a room in which people lived, not died, or so Jassim had read in one of Salwa's books when she was studying real estate.

With these thoughts filling his brain, he tiptoed back to their room and got a hand towel and dressed in his alternate Speedo, nylon athletic pants, and a shirt. Bag in hand, he went outside to his car. Did not kiss his wife goodbye. Did not look at her before he left. Did not even think to.

Once out of the house and in the car, he relaxed, looking up at the darkness of the sky. And the quiet. Cricket clicks and an occasional twitter, but other than that, silence. Looping down and down in his car, he did not think about the destruction of two days ago; it was not until he was in the pool and swimming that his mind wrapped around the pictures of those two massive buildings collapsing to the ground so neatly beneath the columns of smoke, that he returned to the impossibility of what he had seen. What entered into someone's mind to make him (them!) want to do such a thing? It was incomprehensible. And unnatural—human beings fought to survive, not to die. And had they, those many people who seemed to join together in crazy suicide, had any idea that they would cause such devastation? That both buildings would collapse? Lap after lap found him turning this over in his mind, the planning of destruction and the extent of that destruction. No, he was sure that they had wanted to hit the buildings but had not realized that they would destroy both structures in their entirety.

Drops of water seeped beneath Jassim's goggles and he stopped swimming to shake them out. The low stucco walls that surrounded the pool seemed to have no relation to the pictures in his head. Western American buildings were so different from those in the East, in that they were simpler, shorter, much more familiar, much more manageable. The one time he had visited New York he had been fascinated by the possibility of so much, so big, so high, but he had also felt claustrophobic from the grayness and the height of the buildings, which seemed to go up forever, lean together in conversation, and hide the sun from the streets below.

His body immersed in water again and moving smoothly, he saw the falling-down-an-elevator-chute style in which the two towers had collapsed. Somewhere he had read about the construction of those two buildings—that to make them so massive the architects had eschewed typical skyscraper protocol, if there was such a thing, and designed core steel tubes supported by narrower steel columns, putting the strength of the structure at the core rather than in the frame of the building, which allowed for large offices with expansive views. He wondered if that was the reason for the collapse. It would be interesting to see what architects and engineers said about this in the coming weeks.

Both his and Salwa's families had telephoned shortly after it happened, which was also beyond his comprehension. They were all intelligent human beings and knew that America was a large country and that New York was on the East Coast, and yet they had called to see if he and Salwa were safe. It was ridiculous, and he had told his father so. "Baba, we are so far away, there is nothing to worry about."

"You are far away from me, and I always worry."

Salwa had talked to her friend Randa several times as well, babbling about how horrible it was and how she feared for the repercussion toward Arabs in this country.

"Randa is worried about her kids, thinks someone might try to hurt them," she told him later.

"Why would anyone hurt Randa's kids? People are not so ignorant as to take revenge on a Lebanese family for the act of a few extremist Saudis who destroyed those buildings." He had promptly been proved wrong when a Sikh gas station attendant in Phoenix was killed *in retaliation.*

Salwa's outrage and sadness was immense. "What does a Sikh have to do with anything? People are stupid. *Stupid and macho,*" she finished in English.

"*Macho?*" he asked.

"*Macho.* You know, throwing their weight around if something happens that they don't like. Only it doesn't matter to them if they get the people who did whatever it is that they are angry about, just as long as they've done something large and loud. I hate to think what sort of retaliation there is going to be on a governmental level for what happened. Jassim, it's not going to be easy, especially for you."

Jassim said nothing.

"I think you might be right about Randa, though. I think the worst that would happen to her kids is other children saying unkind things to them. She worries too much about them, always thinking they are going to get kidnapped or hit by a car."

"Did you know that a child has a higher chance of having a heart attack than of being kidnapped?"

Jassim lost count of his laps. He had felt pleased with the statistic about children and heart attacks, as he thought Randa was irrational about her children. Why did otherwise level-headed, normal people believe the ridiculous stories about child snatching? And why did people become ridiculous when they had children? Children had been growing up for thousands of years and very few were ever kidnapped. In fact, judging by the population, most did just fine, so why was there all this impossible fussing?

He stopped, breathing heavily and not feeling relaxed. Glancing at the clock, he saw that he had at least ten more minutes to complete a half-hour, his minimum swim time, so he forced out a couple of slow laps and resigned himself to swimming more the next time.

At the end of all this, when he was completely done and enjoying the way his body felt, his mind leaped to his work, to Wednesday's meeting. The image that sat in his mind was that of the office girls at the end of the table. He carried them with him into the shower, standing naked under delightfully warm water with the three women from his office. Something had been wrong. Had he said something impolite? He couldn't imagine what, since he barely spoke with them. He'd probably not given them this much thought in the entire time he'd worked with them, and here they were in his thoughts in the swimming pool and in the shower. Why? Surely not because of what happened in New York? He had as little connection to those men as they did, and there was no way he could accept that anyone would be able to believe him capable of sharing in their extremist philosophy. No, he was not indulging this notion. He squirted shampoo into his hands, closed his eyes, and scrubbed his head, pulling at thoughts and the edges of ideas and letting them all fall into the drain in a clump of confused suds.

—◊—

That afternoon, driving up recently repaved asphalt to his nestled-in-the-hills home, Jassim pulled up his glinty Mercedes next to one of many identical expectant mailboxes, each painted a muted rusty brown. He lifted out the pile of mail and, without looking at it, dropped it onto the leather seat next to him, then pulled the car smoothly and silently over pebbles into his curved driveway and stopped under the acacia tree, whose canopy protected the car from the afternoon sun. The door of his car and the door of his house were across from each other, the steps he would take on an invisible line at a ninety-degree angle from both car and door. Briefcase, burdens, and mail in hand, leather shoes crunching over pebbles, he went up one, two, three wide brick steps and through the heavy wood door into an extremely cool house.

Salwa had forgotten to turn down the air-conditioning before she left. Again. He would have to say something. He stood for a moment, irritated at his wife's lack of . . . what? Compulsiveness? Responsibility? Ever since she had begun studying real estate on top of her job at the bank, she had had extravagant lapses like this, the worst being running a bath for herself and then forgetting about it, soaking their room in two inches of water that cost more than $500 to be suctioned out through the night.

Jassim had hoped that things would improve when she finally got her real estate license, but if anything they got worse. Initially she took several weeks' vacation to devote herself solely to the buying and selling of homes, to see if she was willing to commit to that professionally. But when her vacation concluded she went back to her busy and expanding bank job, accepting a position as a part-time merchant teller, which entailed more responsibility, more money, and marginally fewer hours, supposedly allowing her more flexibility to meet with real estate clients. She did that at least two days a week after work and also on the weekends, sometimes showing houses and being away for several hours. She was rushed to the point of distraction, and the times they used to share together (in the afternoons after work, in the evenings, on the weekends) now found Salwa busy, preoccupied, or gone. With the exception of the mornings, Jassim found himself alone quite a bit.

Today, in the quietness of the afternoon, in the coolness of his house, Jassim removed a gleaming glass from a glossy maple cabinet and filled it with the purest spring water money could buy, delivered biweekly up the hills by a gigantic complaining truck he never saw. He drank the first glassful in one slow gulp and filled it again, now turning his attention to the mail. He pulled the trashcan out from under the right side of the sink (the spot where 92 percent of Americans keep their kitchen trashcans, he remembered hearing somewhere, though he doubted the statistic) so that he could reach the recycling basket, into which he deposited a handful of direct mail and ads (except for Salwa's overpriced-underwear catalogue, which he took a moment to glance through, vaguely tingled by the varied exposures of toned and tanned breasts and bottoms). Salwa's two magazines (one with a cover not unlike the catalogue's, the other with a photograph of someone's pristine white living room) found themselves on top of the underwear catalogue; the bills were slit open with a steak knife and stacked.

Jassim pushed Salwa's tidy pile of house and body pornography to the corner of the counter and left it there with the bills, returning the trash and recycling baskets to their places under the sink. Taking his briefcase and his mountain spring water with him, he headed toward the tiny room they used as an office, which had a spectacular view of the city.

Today Jassim was glad to be alone, to unwind from a chaotic day of too many phone calls, one emergency staff meeting, one emergency consultation. Since Tuesday, his usually predictable job had been the focus of panicked people anticipating bombs and poison in their water supply. Demanding fluidity in service. Pleading for security.

At a meeting with city supervisors and their staff who had to field phone calls from a terrified public, he had tried to reassure them. "Tucson, like most big cities, has an elaborate network of water-quality sensors, detectors, and analyzers that are operated and monitored twenty-four hours a day, seven days a week." (He could never bring himself to say *twenty-four seven*.)

"Should we put security guards at certain places, put in more elaborate alarm systems? What are our most vulnerable spots?"

"It is impossible and self-defeating to physically guard the hundreds of miles of fenced but otherwise open canals," he replied.

Part of the problem, he recognized, was that he and his colleagues were meeting with people whose jobs had nothing to do with water; for them, the possibility of tampering was tangible, as it was based on the stretches their imaginations could take.

"If someone were to drop a vial of some potent agent—say, botulism—into the supply, could that affect consumers?"

"It's unlikely. To threaten the safety of the water system, an enormous amount of a contaminant would have to be added, and the systems in place would be able to detect it and remove the threat."

For hours, it seemed, the meeting had droned on and on, with people's worst fears (poisoning the supply, bombing wells) colliding with each other in irrational questions (Do you recommend posting armed guards around the clock? Locking down all the tanks?) that drowned out his answers, his patience. "Nothing has changed," he said. "Our water supply has always been vulnerable, and all the preparation in the world will not prevent someone who wants to do harm from dumping a large quantity of some contaminant somewhere in the water supply. However—and this is very important to note—any change in water quality, no matter how subtle, will be detected almost immediately, contained, and prevented from reaching consumers. So while it may be impossible to protect the water completely, the systems we have in place are so sophisticated that an attack, unless it is very large, shouldn't be able to affect the general public."

He watched staff members, their faces solemn, jot notes to themselves. The gaggle of office girls at the far end of the table from him stared and scribbled notes to each other. It was clear that he was the subject of these notes, and he had been tempted to tell them he knew that, to point out that this was a serious meeting and not a time for whispers and comments. And why had they been included? Corey, their business manager, had told him that he wanted the whole staff to be on the *same page*. But how could they get to the same page if they were starting with an entirely different book?

Now, in his cool home, Jassim felt a vague prickle as he reviewed his comments at the meeting, as he analyzed the dropped gazes of several of the staff members, the less than warm reception he had received from some of the city's engineers, a group who usually welcomed him with doughnuts and laughter.

"Finish," Jassim said aloud, refusing to entertain paranoid thoughts. Instead he leaned back in his chair and stared at the hills, which looked like home, before turning to his computer and reading the day's news.

—◌◌—

Salwa glanced at the clock. Five fifty-four. In a couple of hours she would go into her office to fill out forms and talk to clients. Her mother had called again yesterday, this time to thank her for the money she had wired on Wednesday. Fourteen thousand dollars was an enormous help for her family, and Salwa had felt so pleased, especially as it meant that aside from helping her parents, she could pay for her niece's tuition to private school. Her sister Siham was a recently widowed teacher who had just moved back home. Until now Salwa had been able to send only a few hundred dollars each month to help. Her mother had been surprised by the giant sum.

"This is what I made from selling two houses," Salwa explained. Minus a few thousand.

She should get up now and take her pill, but for the past four days, each time after she swallowed it, she felt like throwing up, something that had never happened before. Maybe her body needed to take a break from such strong hormonal interference. Somehow, as she lay in bed with her eyes closed, trying to keep the room from swaying, she allowed into her consciousness the fact that perhaps, just maybe, she was pregnant.

Her eyes opened. No, that would be impossible. She had stopped for four days. Started for four. Jassim had made love to her twice in that time. But she wouldn't feel the effects so quickly, would she? The sun heaved itself up over the horizon as Salwa lay silent next to her husband, secretly allowing in the sliver of awareness that she absolutely could be pregnant.

—◠◠—

Later that afternoon, as she and Jassim walked side by side in the mall with the mission of finding Lina, Randa's daughter, a gift for her fourteenth birthday, Salwa could feel the Lie between them, the Lie that only she could see, that kept trying to hold her hand, to remind her of its beauty and silvery color.

What if she really was pregnant? How could she possibly tell him?

Its voice was louder than Jassim's, and at times it completely drowned his words.

"Salwa, earth to Salwa. Where are you? Are you already in the intimate apparel section of Dillard's but forgot to take your body with you?"

Salwa couldn't look at him, resented the Lie which stood naked between them, and she had to turn away, hide her face. She ran her hands across some shirts that were displayed in front of a trendy store. "These would be cute if they weren't made to fit like skins."

"Maybe they're made for children."

"This is a women's store."

"Women who want to feel like children."

The Lie grabbed Salwa around the waist, shook her this way and that, demanding to be noticed. She wished she could give it a good hard kick and stand closer to her husband.

"Salwa, are you okay?"

"I'm fine. Feel a little funny, a little nauseated." Another lie. A baby to hold the hand of the Big Lie, the Original Lie. "It's the heat. I think I'm to the point where I can't stand it anymore." She stopped and looked around. "Let's go over there," she said, pointing to a large store whose music boomed into the corridors of the mall.

Salwa wandered around racks, with Jassim absently following her. "Do you think she'd like these?" she asked, holding up a pair of silver hoop earrings.

"Yes, and if things get out of hand, her mother can use them as handcuffs."

In front of a wall at the far end of the store stood a motorcycle on a pedestal. Jassim wandered over to it as Salwa continued to pick through accessories and then clothes.

A baby. She might have a baby in her belly. A lovely perfect baby who would grow to be a wonderful perfect child. She so wanted to share this with Jassim, and she would. She just needed to create a good atmosphere so that he would be more receptive. For just a brief moment, a surge of anger rose up within her—why should she have to create a nice atmosphere to tell him this most natural thing?

As quickly as it rose up within her, the anger subsided, and her thoughts danced here and there as she fingered tiny shirts and pants whose waistbands were designed low.

Salwa paused at a T-shirt with long sleeves. It had a picture of a skinny girl with a big head and said *baaaad girl* in cursive. Next to it was a tiny T-shirt that said *boys lie*.

Girls lie too, Salwa thought in English.

She had been circling each rack of clothes, focused on each shirt she looked at or dragged her hands across. Mostly polyester. *Yuck.*

Shopping was a soothing experience, allowed her to think while her body was engaged in something tangible. She circled rack after rack of hip clothing. Fake leather coats with faux fur. Fuzzy boots. Cling-to-your-body jeans. In one breath Salwa felt that she might explode if she didn't leave. She wandered out, expecting to see Jassim sitting patiently on a bench, but he was not, nor was he in the specialty food store next door. She walked farther down the mall, past the computer game store, past the accessory store for the person who had everything. She did not see him. She stood in front of the stores and looked toward either end of the mall. No Jassim. Then she went back into the corner store where they had started and saw him walking toward her from the back with an odd expression on his face, almost fear.

"What happened, habibi?" she asked.

"If you look behind me, you will see a woman with a walkie-talkie on her shoulder. She thinks she's Clint Eastwood. She's following me. Apparently I am a security threat. Maybe she thinks I'm going to steal all this fashion and climb on that motorcycle, which

I am then going to fly off its pedestal and into the mall. God give us patience."

Salwa's eyes were on her husband at first but glided over to land behind him on the security guard, puffed up and close to bursting out of her uniform. Her thick body turned toward a rack of the latest in teen fashion, fat fingers wandering over tiny shirts. Salwa glared.

"Is there a problem?" Salwa asked in English over her husband's shoulder.

"No, ma'am."

"Then why are you following my husband?"

"I'm doing my job, ma'am."

"Which is what exactly?" asked Salwa with open scissors in her voice.

"To protect the security of this establishment."

"And how are you doing that by following my husband?"

The woman said nothing, just stared at Salwa with a half-smile. "Ma'am, someone called security. There must have been a misunderstanding. I'm sorry for any inconvenience. You folks have a good day." She swung her gaze to the clerks in the back, turned, and walked out of the store.

Salwa's eyes followed her, iced and angry, and then rolled back to the clerks, two teenage girls who looked barely old enough to work, standing by the cash register, one tall, with soft skin and large eyes, and the other broomstick skinny, trying to appear busy.

"Salwa, I'm going out of the store. Please let it go." Jassim walked toward the door.

Snake anger crept through Salwa's body. "Excuse me, young lady," she said, walking over to the counter and standing in front of the busy broomstick girl. "Why did you call that security guard on my husband?"

The girl looked up, looked scared, which brought blood to Salwa's cobra face, venom to her words.

"Knock, knock. I'm talking to you. Did you think he was going to climb up and steal that motorcycle? Or perhaps run off with some T-shirts?"

When the girl finally spoke, her voice was ugly and nasal. "He was standing here and staring too long. He was just standing and looking at the motorcycle. It was weird." Her fingers fiddled with a small plastic hanger on the counter, and her eyes looked at the ceiling, at the floor, and at the other girl, who stood next to her.

"And what do you have to say?" Salwa's voice softened.

The girl looked at her fingers.

"Please look up. I won't bite you."

"He just scared me." Salwa saw that her eyes were enormous. "He just stood there and stared for a really long time, like he was high or something. And then I remembered all the stuff that's been going on." Here the girl stopped and looked at her as though she were checking to make sure her reference was understood.

The words slid into Salwa's understanding, narrowing and sharpening her anger. "I see. You thought he might want to blow up the mall in his Ferragamo shoes. Where is your manager?"

"She's in the back," Broomstick answered in a mouse squeak that forced Salwa a step closer under the thundering music.

"Please call her. And what is your name, Miss FBI?"

"Amber." Squeak.

"Okay, Amber. Please call your manager. What you two just did is illegal." Salwa stared at them, gigantic in her anger.

Amber's face changed in blotches. Something seemed to be building up in her, and she blurted, "My uncle died in the Twin Towers."

Salwa knew something like this was coming, had been waiting for the moment when it became spoken. "I am sorry to hear that. Are you planning to have every Arab arrested now?" She paused for just a second. "Do you not use your brains? This country has more than fifty million people in it, and you're worried about your tacky little store. But now you'll have a lot to talk about in school. You can say you saw a real live Arab and had to call security on him."

The other girl had tears at the edge of her eyelids, ready to fall, but Salwa's rage was still full and red and she showed no mercy.

"So you looked at my husband, a professional man in his forties staring at the motorcycle, and you thought that was suspicious?"

"Is there a problem?" interrupted a young woman with a clean face and green eyes.

"Mandy," Amber started to squeak, but Salwa's rage was larger.

"Amber," Salwa began, pointing at Broomstick. "Amber called security on my husband over there." Salwa pointed to Jassim, who stood in the doorway with his back to them and his hands in his pockets.

"Amber, did you call security?"

"I did, Mandy. He creeped me out. He was just standing staring at the motorcycle. He wouldn't stop. You told us to report anything suspicious, and I thought he looked suspicious."

Mandy turned toward Jassim again. "What exactly was suspicious about him?"

"I told you. He just kept staring."

Mandy turned her back to the two girls and walked with Salwa away from the counter. "Ma'am, I am so sorry. This all seems to be a big misunderstanding. I think people are a little freaked out by the idea that someone might try to blow up a mall here in Tucson. We actually have snipers on the roof today, if you can believe that. We were warned today to be on the alert for any odd activity. I guess odd activity is subjective. I'm really sorry." Mandy looked at Salwa and lowered her voice. "My grandmother is Turkish. I'm so sorry. Let me give you a gift certificate to our store as a goodwill gesture."

"No, thank you," replied Salwa. "Your Amber needs to understand that what she did is wrong."

"Believe me, she will understand. But come. Let me give you a gift certificate."

"No, thank you."

Salwa glared at Amber one more time and walked away. Jassim was sitting outside on a bench.

"Did you save my reputation?" he asked in Arabic.

"Her uncle died in the Twin Towers."

"What does that have to do with me?"

"You look suspicious, so she's avenging his death. The manager's grandmother is Turkish."

"Meaning?"

"Meaning she understands what we are going through. She offered me a *gift certificate consolation prize.*"

"Did you take it?"

"No."

"Why not? That could have been Lina's present."

"Jassim, you can't atone for the stupidity of people with things. *Stupid, stupid, stupid.*"

"*Stupid and macho,*" Jassim reminded her in English. "Once upon a time you thought they were just ignorant and you said they couldn't be blamed for that."

"You can blame them if they act on it."

"It probably wouldn't be so bad if we lived in a bigger city. Salwa, it's okay. She's just a kid. She's doing what she thinks is right."

"It's not okay, Jassim. Do you think this is going to get better? For God's sake, she called security on you in the mall, in a teenage clothing store." For all her rage, she could see that Jassim had shut off the part of himself that should be fuming, that he had accepted what had happened and allowed his thoughts to move on.

Salwa looped her arm through Jassim's. For the tiniest amount of time, the Lie was distracted by the War on Terror. For that slice of an afternoon, Salwa and Jassim were how they had once been: together.

"Can the present for Lina wait?" Jassim asked. "I think I'd like to go home now, before I get arrested."

"That's fine. Maybe I'll come back tomorrow."

They walked toward the exit, together, the Lie hiding somewhere—in Salwa's bag perhaps, or waiting for them in the car.

—⁂—

Back into the workweek, Salwa muddled through late-morning busyness when a knock on her glass wall startled her out of the most recent deposits for Hadrian's Liquor Store.

"Hi, Mr. Franks. How are you?" Instead of buzzing him in, Salwa stood up and walked to the door with her hand extended. "I've not seen you in quite a long time."

"Been busy. Took some trips." His hand gripped hers, could have lifted her into the air if it wished, spun her around like a helicopter rotor.

"Come in. Have a seat and tell me how I can help you today."

The security door clicked behind him and Jack Franks sat down, bent his tall, solid form into the blue upholstered chair across from her. "I want to make a deposit into my savings and I'd also like to know when my CD comes due." In his late fifties, Jack Franks (she always thought of him as first and last name) was a solid man, too big for his chair.

"Piece of cake." She turned toward her computer. "Let me pull up your account."

"Salwa."

"Yes?"

"I was just reading your name. For some reason I always want to say Sally."

"The first part is *el*, like *sell*, with a *wa* at the end, not a *ly*. Salwa." Her name sat in her mouth like a perfect strawberry.

"You make it sound so easy. Salwa."

Salwa said nothing, let her pale pink manicured nails click-click their way to Jack Franks's account while her name sat heavy on his tongue.

"I met a fellow from Jordan last week when I was swimming at my health club."

Salwa stopped typing. "Was he also swimming?"

"Yes, we had both just finished. I told him about Cinda." He breathed out loudly through his nose, expelling all the air that might have touched his daughter's name.

Salwa imagined Jack Franks plowing over Jassim's peaceful morning, bombarding him with the story of his daughter, bulldozing his peace. "What did he look like?"

Jack squinted his eyes, trying to squeeze out the last bits of Jassim's face. "Lean. Swimmer's body. Average height. Short curly hair. His eyes were large and I'd say very honest."

Salwa leaned back in her chair with her arms crossed and smiled.

"What, do you know him?"

She reached to the right of her computer screen and handed him a small framed picture. "Is this him?"

Jack took it from her with thick fingers, careful to touch only the frame. "Well, I'll be. That sure is him. Funny. I told him about you, but of course I couldn't remember your name right and he said he didn't think he knew you."

Salwa smiled. "Swimming for Jassim is like prayer. He tries not to talk to anyone in the morning."

Jack Franks handed the picture back. "Very nice guy. Good for you. For you both. How do you say his name again?"

"Jaa-sim. You stress the first syllable."

"Jaa-sim. What line of work is he in?" His elbows rested on the chair and his fingers interlocked in front of him. His head tipped forward to catch all of Salwa's words.

"He's a hydrologist."

"A water man."

"A water man."

Four years ago, when Salwa had been working as a customer service agent, Jack Franks had come into her office for the first time. "And where are you from?" he had asked before she could ask him how she could help him.

"I am Palestinian from Jordan," she had told him.

"Well, then I should tell you this story so it's out in the open," he had said, as though they were embarking on a personal relationship rather than a professional one. "My daughter, Cinda, met a fellow from Jordan back when we were living in Ohio. They got into drugs. Cinda was no angel, so it's hard to tell who started it. She ran off with him. I went all over the place trying to find them, even flew to Jordan and went to his godforsaken village. Never found them, but I did travel around your country looking, and it was very beautiful. The people were kind to me, as much as I wanted to hate every last one. I brought my kids up to be honest people. I don't know what happened to Cinda, where I failed her. The worst is not knowing what really happened."

"I'm so sorry," Salwa told him. "Did you ever find her or hear from her?"

"Nope. Never. It's as if she just vanished in thin air."

"That must be awful for you."

"It was. I try not to think about it too much. I thought you should know that."

"Well, I appreciate your frankness." And she had, though she had thought at the time there was something not quite right with his story.

Now the conversation moved to money, and Jack Franks left five minutes later.

—m—

That evening Jassim sat on a stool by the counter as she prepared dinner.

"I hear you met one of my customers."

"I did?"

"Yes. An older man, retired Marine. Years ago his daughter met a Jordanian from Zarqa. She went off with him and never came back. At least that's the story he told me the first day we met."

"Oh yes. I believe the words he used were 'She converted. She's an Arab now.' "

"Yes, those would be the words he'd use."

"He wanted to know about my wife, talked about beautiful Arab women. About how he understood why *you fellas cover them up*. I thought he was crass and arrogant. *A bull. A bulldozer.* He wouldn't stop talking while I was taking my shower. First time I've ever met him and he acts as though he's got the right to all my information."

"He said he asked you about me and you said you didn't know me."

"God, Salwa, he prattled on and on while I was taking a shower. I tried not to answer him at all. I just wanted him to go away. To keep quiet. Salwa, habibti, I was taking a shower, for God's sake, and he's going on and on about how beautiful his banker is. I wanted nothing to do with him." He stopped, hands on hips, mind reaching back. "Come to think of it, we had that conversation on the eleventh, just before I found out what happened." He paused again. "As the first plane was flying into the World Trade Center building, Jack Franks was expounding on the beauty of Arab women and grilling me about my wife. There's a meaning in that somewhere, don't you think?"

Salwa watched her husband, surprised by his reaction. "I find his bluntness refreshing."

"Do you want to invite him to dinner now?"

"No, but I thought I'd see if he'd like to go swimming with you every morning."

"That would give him a chance to tell me more about your beautiful eyes."

"Jassim!"

"Subject closed?"

"Fine, subject closed."

Jack Franks became a gray thought in their house. Nothing more.

—ᘉ ᘉ—

Hassan's heart sent blood around his body at super-speed, made him dizzy as he pulled up Salwa's name and phone number on his cellular. For more than a week he had rehearsed what he would say, but how different it was in real life!

It was now or never, he decided, and pressed the call button.

The phone rang. And rang. By the third ring his thoughts were a jumble. What if he had entered her number incorrectly? What if Jassim answered? What if she didn't want to talk to him?

After the fifth ring he heard a click and *"Hello. This is Salwa Haddad. Your call is important to me. Please leave a message after the tone and I will get back to you as soon as possible. Thank you and have a great day."* And a beep.

Hassan was shocked. He stared at the phone a moment before he hung up. Salwa Haddad. She had taken Jassim's name! Even if a lot of women did take their husbands' names, he never thought Salwa would be one of them. She had erased Palestine from her very name. He couldn't believe it. *Your call is important to me.* Really? What did that mean? Was that something she had to say to the people who wanted to buy houses from her? Hassan found nothing familiar in her voice. Would have thought this was another Salwa Haddad. Did this voice really belong to the woman he had once loved more than life itself? Still loved? He looked at his watch. It would be ten in the morning her time. Did she not answer because she saw who was calling? No, international calls did not come through with the caller's name or phone number. Perhaps at work she could not answer her phone. This was difficult. If he were to call her at four in the afternoon her time, that would be one in the morning his time. Or two; he always confused time differences. If he called her on a weekend, Jassim might answer. Early in the morning. He would try her then. Before work. Sometime before eight her time.

Funny how a person can go on for years and years as though he is doing fine, as though the loss of his beloved is nothing more than a blip. And then something happens, another loss, a change, something happens to resurrect that love, as though it were just lying dormant all this time. As Hassan stood, poised to change his life, it all came back: the day he first saw Jassim's name, the day he knew Salwa would leave him. Still his heart skipped at the thought, at the humiliation of all those years in love with Salwa, who had run off with a stiff, well-to-do scientist who promised her America. Hassan paced in his room, trying to imagine how she had changed in the past nine years, trying to imagine who she was now.

The irony, Hassan had realized long ago, was that if it had not been for Dr. Jassim Haddad whisking his fiancée (unofficial) away to America, then he would not have gone to Romania. Would not have had the chance to become what he had become. He would have stayed and would have focused too much energy on Salwa. Many times he thought of the incongruity of this, that in fact he had Dr. Haddad to thank for making his situation possible. By doing graduate work in Romania, by coming back, and by having nothing to lose, he had stretched himself further than he would have thought himself capable of. No, he had not won back his country, nor the woman he loved, but he helped to produce a high-quality television program, current and honest, and send it all around the globe.

Hassan tried one more time. Again the phone rang, and again the ludicrous message. And though he desperately wanted to say something, he couldn't make their first communication in nine years a recorded message.

Chapter Three

Jassim slid into the water at the end of lane #2, the tension of the past two weeks detaching itself in clumps, the wreckage of four planes cluttering the space around him, ash filling his lungs. He pulled his goggles to his eyes, pushed his feet against the wall behind him, and began his strokes, tossing away wings and smoldering engines, smoke and the powdery residue of incinerated bodies. Stroke and stroke, smooth and straight, his mind forcing the debris into neighboring lanes as he pulled a picture of his office (of Corey and the secretaries) from between his shoulder blades and tossed it into the water so he could stare at it clearly even as it filled him with disquiet.

As he swam steadily, Jassim's thoughts tiptoed away from this picture and down a dusty path leading to his youth, to an early summer afternoon spent with his uncle Abu Jalal, who owned land both east and west of the Jordan and who had determined Jassim's career and life by fear and accident. On the afternoon of this memory, he and his mother, his father, and his two sisters had taken the half-hour drive to reach the farm where they had been invited for lunch. As they turned off from the main road, their car bounced up the unpaved drive to the house. Jalal and Tihani, Abu Jalal's two oldest children, were waiting for them on the porch.

After Jassim and his family climbed out and greeted everyone, the children walked off together, shoes crunching in the pebbly dirt, toward a small grove of trees near the house. His memory folded after that, a secretive wrinkle, and even though the grown Jassim tugged at it, he could not recall how they had spent that day, as their children's play was overshadowed by the adult thought that was later introduced to him.

The wrinkle unfolded at lunch, over lamb that had been roasted with garlic in the outdoor stove. For years to come Jassim could taste it, the garlic having left a pleasing taste in the recesses of his mouth and, later, in his years of being away, a taste of home. Afterward everyone drifted out to the porch, a small stone area facing east, looking over his uncle's dunums and dunums of land. Um Jalal brought watermelon and sour cheese and they ate and drank coffee and talked about Palestine, a subject Jassim's father couldn't get enough of. He tended to go on and on, as did everyone in those days. Jassim never liked such discussions, ones overtaken by passion. The conviction behind them fell flat for him, the argument lost in the rage expressed.

For Jassim's father, what happened to Palestine was a question both of pride and of humanity. Abu Jassim was a lawyer whose nickname was Mr. Idea, because so often he would start his conversations by saying, "I had an idea . . ." His sympathy for the Palestinians was both intellectual and emotional; his ire was immense and came from the injustice not just on a human level but also on an organizational level: something so wrong should not have been allowed to happen among civilized people. He raged and he ranted, providing an endless list of wrongdoers, an infinite set of consequential scenarios.

Behind his father's discourse was afternoon quiet, and Jassim tuned his father out and took pleasure in being in the company of his uncle, a man of little formal education but a very strong and powerful presence. They sat next to each other, leaning against the short stone wall and looking out over the quiet land. Jassim's thoughts wandered off, as did everyone else on the porch except Abu Jalal, leaving them with a silence that Jassim welcomed after his father's theorizing. Abu Jalal's voice was deep, not yet serrated from cigarette smoke, when he finally spoke, and he put his hand on Jassim's knee. "All these fools, so worked up over land and rights and they don't see the greater picture. Water is what will decide things, not just for us but for every citizen of the world as well. If we humans were smart, if we were truly as evolved as they say we are, we would all work together to figure out how to turn saltwater into drinkable water, how to use water wisely, preserve the water that falls each year. With all of our advancements, we have become stupid, relying on the government to pump water to our houses. Even a generation ago they were smarter, with everyone storing their own water, conserving it. Mark my words: shortage of water is what will doom the occupants of this earth, and they are fools not to know that."

Jassim wondered who "they" were. Politicians? The king and the royal family? People in general? It seemed more likely that Abu Jalal was talking about Jassim's father and people like him. On the one hand, Jassim was pleased that Abu Jalal had included him in his unstated category of nonfools, but he also felt hurt and embarrassed for his father. He turned and saw that Abu Jalal had closed his eyes, ended the conversation, leaving Jassim to wrap himself around this new topic. Water? Imagine, in the face of Palestine being destroyed, of more people being made refugees, of their culture being stolen, of Jordan being placed on the brink of civil unrest as a result—imagine talking about water as the more important issue!

Whether by God or destiny or chance, Abu Jalal's words of that summer afternoon seeped into Jassim's subconscious, dripped into his daily thoughts. They doubled in size and power, became a tsunami that possessed him at times, drove him to scream at his sisters if they let the water run while they were scrubbing the dishes, or at his mother, who tended to overwater the garden.

"Jassim, habibi, the garden needs water to grow. This is the proper use of water. This is why we need water. If not for growing plants, then for what?"

"Food, yes, but to waste it on flowers, that is not the proper use."

"Shame on you, to tell your mother not to grow flowers. Flowers bring joy to a house. Joy in a family is as important as water."

In those first few years of water awareness, his righteousness had no boundaries and was molded more by fear than by understanding. He had visions of shriveling up into an old dried fig along with the rest of his family, all because of flowers and clean dishes. Or of walking with his desiccated family over parched earth, refugees, because all the water had been squandered by foolish humans.

His obsession with water ebbed and flowed and seemed to be on the wane when two very important events changed the course of his life, or perhaps just paved the road rather than leaving it dry and dusty.

The first event was the discovery of water on Abu Jalal's farm and the subsequent transformation of Abu Jalal—like the oil sheikhs in the Gulf not so many years earlier—from a sun-dried farmer tilling his land year after year to a businessman who hired people to till the land for him.

Jassim heard his parents talking about it: how Abu Jalal had borrowed money to pay a diviner, a man with a sixth sense, to come with sticks and walk his land in search of water. He was so sure of the presence of water that he was willing *to bet the farm* (Jassim smiled at this thought) and then some. Jassim's father had talked about it with a salty edge to his voice, the one that said he didn't approve and that he himself would never do such an irresponsible thing, jeopardizing the family's security like that, would never borrow money from everyone he knew to have two wells dug on the basis of what a diviner told him.

Jassim was intrigued, and he begged his father to let him go and watch on the day the diviner came. He wanted to see firsthand the foolish thing, the enormous gamble that Abu Jalal had taken. Jassim and his father arrived early. The tension in the air kept both Jassim and Jalal silent, picking up pebbles and throwing them rather than battling or playing soccer while they waited. The diviner was late, and Abu Jalal's tension crept into his voice. "Go play—stop waiting around here like women."

That was enough, as Abu Jalal well knew, to send both boys around the side of the house with a soccer ball.

Jassim liked Jalal as an idea, but in person he found him arrogant and overly competitive. Nonetheless, they shared blood and they were close in age, so they often did end up playing together, as on that particular morning.

Jassim's goal was the tiny drop-off before the fence, and Jalal's goal was the well of the lemon tree. It was already warm, and Jassim felt at a disadvantage from the start.

"Let's play to nine."

"Seven."

"I'll let you get six and then get my seven straight in a row."

"Why would you do that? Just play regular." Jassim's call for logic in the face of Jalal's arrogance invariably caused problems.

"Fine." Before Jassim realized what was happening, Jalal kicked the ball into the lemon tree.

"No fair, we haven't started yet."

"Have so. One–nothing."

The next twenty minutes circled a dusty game littered by foul after foul, which compiled themselves into a list in Jassim's head. With each addition he grew more irritable. Finally, when Jalal pushed him out of his way, making him fall down with his arm bent under him, and kicked another goal into the well of the lemon tree, Jassim's frustration spilled out of his mouth.

"My father says that your father is crazy to risk everything he owns on a diviner's word. He says that there's probably no water anyway." These statements came out on their own, a collection of words he had not wanted to put together, and the minute they were out he regretted them.

"It doesn't matter what your father says, does it? When they find water, my father will be rich and your father will be wrong."

For years to come Jassim would replay his cousin's words in his mind, amazed at how clever they were, and how indicative of Jalal they were, someone with the presence of mind to say the clever thing at the required moment.

Jassim's memory folded again, but shortly afterward a pickup truck huffed up the dirt drive and they all stopped what they were doing. Like bits of iron on a magnet, everyone in the household came to the porch and watched as Abu Jalal went out to greet the man, who looked tattered and crazy, dark like a bean and dressed in the clothing of workmen. Jassim's first thought was that the diviner couldn't come and had sent this man to tell them so.

Abu Jalal welcomed him as the family watched from the porch, watched Abu Jalal with his back to them, his arm around the man who had come to make him a fortune. He gestured to the right, the left, and straight ahead, and then he released the man from his grip and said nothing more.

He watched as the diviner walked with two oleander sticks held out in front of him, a process that did not go quickly. One by one everyone went inside, except Jassim, who was riveted. He and his uncle sat side by side, watching as the man walked slowly, as if in a trance, up and back. When he headed down the hill, Jassim and his uncle followed at a distance, walking with hands held behind them, eyes fixed on the divining sticks.

And then, in the thickness of the afternoon, the diviner slowed. Abu Jalal and Jassim both saw it and stopped, transfixed. Abu Jalal put a hand on Jassim's shoulder and the two of them stood immobile, frozen in time by the great event unfolding in front of them. The sticks began to tremble in the man's hands, quivering of their own accord (Jassim clearly saw that it was the sticks vibrating and not the diviner making them quiver). One more step and it looked as though they would pulsate out of his hands entirely. "Here," the diviner said. "You should dig here."

"How far down?"

Jassim could not recall the diviner's reply, nor the rest of the afternoon (how, or if, Abu Jalal marked the spot so that he would remember it, for example), except for Jalal's face looking at him later, carrying in it the proof of his earlier words: *My father will be rich and yours will be wrong.*

Over the next six months, men and machines dug through layer after layer of ground to the secret culled spot where the earth had tried to hide its stash of water. During that time Jassim listened to the adults in his world talk about Abu Jalal's foolishness at hurling all their money into the depths of the earth for nothing. In his heart he knew that it was not for nothing, and he was proved right: Abu Jalal's dunums and dunums of land sat atop an immense reservoir of water.

The second very important event occurred a short time later: he taught himself how to hold his breath. Jassim's feelings toward water, at least toward being immersed in water, were not positive ones. The idea terrified him. Though rationally he understood that holding his breath would keep water from going into his lungs, emotionally the thought of being underwater was like that of being buried alive.

The first time he went to the bright blue pool owned by rich friends of the family who lived in the fertile valley area, he thought he would suffocate, even with just his legs wet.

Abu Fareed had spent many years in the United States and had developed a passion for swimming. When he came home to settle, he built a pool, the first one of its kind, he claimed. Jassim's sisters were in the shallow end, splashing around happily, but Jassim couldn't. He sat and stared and imagined dying. Then Abu Fareed sat next to him. "The thing about swimming is that you just have to do it, have to go right in and tackle it. Let me show you." In less than a blink, Abu Fareed picked him up and dropped him in the water.

Terror cannot be smoothed away by rational thinking. Jassim kicked frantically toward the surface, inhaling water as he went. Hatred and rage and terror combined as his lungs tasted the liquid in which his body was submerged. After what felt like many minutes but was surely only a few seconds, the strong hands of Abu Fareed lifted him up out of the water and banged on his back. Jassim leaned over his shoulder, coughing and gasping as Abu Fareed laughed. "That's the only way to do it."

Jassim felt quite sure that that was not the only way to do it, and he was determined that such a thing would never happen again. He got out of the pool, swore that he would never go in one again, but prepared himself just in case by practicing holding his breath. Sometimes when he was in the car, or walking, or reading, or at school, he would take a deep breath and hold it and count to himself: 1, 2, 3 . . . In the beginning he could get to 12, then 15. By the end of the week he got to 30 and told his father, "I can hold my breath for half a minute."

His father looked at him, tipped his head this way and that as though he were a bird sizing him up.

"Well, why don't you try for a whole one now?"

And so he had. He realized that if he sat quietly and relaxed, his need for air was not so great. To prepare himself, he would take two deep breaths, inhaled through his nose, held for a couple of seconds, and released through his mouth. He imagined that this prepared his lungs, a kind of stretching routine to increase their capacity for oxygen. Then he would slowly inhale through his nose. As he did so, shoving oxygen into the corners of his lungs, he felt his shoulders rise, his posture straighten, his head lift closer to the sky. In those moments of captured breath, Jassim's thoughts cleared, as though there were not room for both this clear substance and worldly clutter. As he held those oxygen molecules hostage, he felt himself to be one with the earth, with nature.

Years passed, and his lung capacity increased as his belief in God dwindled. He began to create challenges for himself, physical ones at first, like learning to swim. Like going underwater to the end of the pool and back. Like lifting weights. Or staying awake all night. Or sitting completely still for hours at a stretch. As he taught his body to fight instinct, so his mind rejected the notion of God.

"Baba, why do you believe in God?" he asked his father one evening when they were sitting quietly reading.

His father looked at him. "I believe in God because I always have believed in God. Because the world is too large and complex to have just happened on its own. Because mankind would not survive without God."

"Why?"

"Because without God there would be no hope."

Jassim didn't argue, just turned these thoughts over and over for a few days. *I don't believe in God, and I hope,* he thought. And at that moment several of the threads that tied him to land and home were severed. But of course he didn't know that, nor would he have believed it if he did.

—∽—

Amal. Jassim rolled it around in his mind as he finished his last strokes. *Hope* meant you could see tomorrow. Hope. He squatted in the pool after his last lap, submerged to his neck, and thought that if he and Salwa were ever to have a daughter, perhaps they could name her Amal.

—∽ ∽—

Wrapped in silk between sleep and morning, Salwa flipped and flopped, and not for the first time got twisted in the extra material. She had twice been cursed early on in her life: by place of birth and by a fortuitous gift of silk pajamas.

As the only child in her family who happened to be born in America, Salwa had already been the subject of teasing, irresistible pointing and poking and giggling: *Made in USA. Miss America. Oh, don't make Salwa do it; she won't know how—she was born in the U.S.* And then, to formally cement her difference from the rest of the family, when Salwa was six years old, her aunt visited Thailand and returned with a set of silk pajamas for each of her four nieces. The pair she gave Salwa was royal blue.

"What kind of life does my sister-in-law think we lead here, to give the girls pajamas like that?" Salwa's mother had asked. "They're useless. Not warm in the winter, not cool in the summer —springtime pajamas?—and they'd probably catch fire if anyone even thought about smoking a cigarette near them."

In what became a famous family comment, Salwa argued, "Oh no, Mama. These pajamas are beautiful, because in them you can be a queen."

Her mother had stared at her as if she had fallen from the sky. "We already have one queen, and that is quite enough."

From then on the occasional nicknames became constant: from the more affectionate My Pajama to the mocking Queen of Pajamas (or simply Queen), Silky Salwa, Owner of the Pajama Bazaar.

Salwa ignored them. She loved the silk pajamas, loved how they made her feel beautiful and almost naked, both at the same time. The lightness on her skin was like the touch of a butterfly, or kohl spilling. Her sisters wore their gifts a couple of times each, but wearing them made it difficult to play, so one by one, tops first, then bottoms, silk pajamas of all different sizes came her way (in lavender, jade, and champagne). Sometimes Salwa piled all the pairs together and threw them in the air so they would fall on her in a cascade of softness.

It wasn't just the feeling of the pajamas that she liked, it was the act of wearing pajamas such as these and what it symbolized to her: leisure. Women who wore these pajamas were rich, either in their own right or in someone else's. Women who wore this kind of pajamas did not have the wide fingers and thickened wrists that raising children and cooking and cleaning every day produced. As Salwa grew into the larger pairs, she imagined lean and lovely magazine ladies sitting by bright blue pools and servants bringing them exotic drinks. As she outgrew the pajamas, her fairy-tale visions involved adoring rich and handsome men who offered exquisite jewels to match the pajamas. Sometimes on weekends, if she had nowhere to go, she would stay in the pajamas the entire day, changing out of them only to do housework.

For the first few years after she returned with her new husband to the country of her birth, her pajama purchases were in much the same style as the original pajamas she had worn as a child, with long pants and a long-sleeved shirt with tiny buttons. As she became more accustomed to American life, however, her pajamas narrowed to fit her body more precisely. She still favored the sets with long pants, but on top she wore a lacy camisole and a flimsy robe that tied over it. As her years away from home lengthened and her susceptibility to American marketing increased, her pajamas transformed, morphed from elegant and flowing to tight, more revealing, more alluring. During most trips to malls and shops, with or without her husband, if there were pajamas to be bought, she was there, at least to investigate, if not to purchase. If Jassim was with her, had been asked to *wait for just a few minutes while I go see,* he could not resist commenting.

"You must have twenty pairs, Salwa. Two entire drawers of just pajama bottoms. Half a closet for the tops. Why do you need more than two or three?"

"Jassim, two or three? That would be impossible. Look, I wear one each night, so that is seven if I do the laundry only once a week. Then I need a couple of extras just in case. Then there are the special-occasion ones."

"No, don't get rid of those for my sake."

"Then there are some that I don't wear much anymore but that I don't want to get rid of. That's it, really."

"It's fine, Salwa. It just seems that two entire drawers filled to bursting with pajamas is a lot. That's not including another drawer for panties and bras and another one for socks and stockings. You have filled a whole dresser with undergarments. You could probably clothe an entire village in underwear."

"Jassim, do you have an objection, or did you just want to talk about my undergarments?"

"I think I just wanted to talk about it. I love your underwear! My sweet Salwa, Princess of All Undergarments."

What Jassim didn't know and what Salwa hadn't fully realized yet was that in breathing her first breath on American soil, she had been cursed. Because while place of birth does not alter genetic material, it does stitch itself under the skin and stay attached by virtue of invisible threads, so that if a person leaves that place for somewhere else (whether because she's been kicked out and forcibly sent away or because she is simply returning to the home of her parents), there is always an uncomfortable tugging as the silken (in her case) threads are pulled taut. And if the person returns to her place of birth, especially after a great deal of time has elapsed, quite often the threads have knotted or tangled somewhere between here and there, there and here, causing the person countless awkward moments. Sometimes the knot of crossed threads becomes so thick that it creates a painful and constant yanking no matter where the person finds herself. At that point the best thing to do may be to snip off the threads completely, but that is a last resort, as it is painful and traumatic.

There are many people who find the spot where the threads were originally stitched and have them severed by choice, regardless of tangling. There are other people, acrobats generally, who manage their threads quite well, stitching patterns behind them so as not to be pulled and yanked and tripped by them.

Unfortunately, Salwa was neither acrobat nor pals with a clever surgeon, and as a result, America pulled and yanked on her from a very young age, forever trying to reel her in. Only the America that pulled at her was not the America of her birth, it was the exported America of Disneyland and hamburgers, Hollywood and the Marlboro man, and therefore impossible to find. Once in America, Salwa still searched and tripped and bought smaller and sexier pajamas in the hope that she would one day wake up in that Promised Land.

—ↄ Chapter Four ↄ—

Once upon a time, under a bright and sunny sky, a bright and sunny young man saw himself too clearly: each flaw floated to the surface, each criticism was a thickened wrinkle in the unforgiving sun. As the last of three children, he felt he had upset the existing balance and symmetry in his family. Sweet boy just wanted to pave his own way, do his own thing. When so many things have been done before, and done well, it's hard to reach the goalposts or the top of the mountain, easier just to forge a new path, even if it's a path going southwest. He didn't want to be the richest or the smartest or the fastest, which was why he veered away from winter and Ivy League, why he chose a state school in Arizona, and why he turned his back on his accounting studies and worked part-time for almost a year as a valet parking attendant at Flash, a topless bar on one of the ugliest streets in the city.

On clear desert nights, summer through spring, he took keys and dollars from the sweaty palms of lonely men, parked their cars a few feet away while they were left with the illusion of crossing the threshold into a grander place, not one where enhanced tits and asses and high-heeled shoes and empty pockets and loneliness filled the rank air. He made the job tolerable with the help of the occasional pill, an odd line of cocaine; stayed awake with nicotine and speed.

His friends thought his job sounded cool, mostly because he didn't tell them the whole story: that almost all the girls got high or drunk to perform, that it was not just dancing they did for a fee, and that some of the men who went there and worked there were real-life scary. One night he went to work straight and sober and saw all those people through the filter of a clean eye. It scratched at his heart to see the dancers—not the touched-up kind from television and not the temporary girls who worked for a few months or a year to make extra money before they went back to their respectable lives; the women who pulled at him were the regulars, degraded women with pink skin and stretch marks and buckteeth and nasty boyfriends, the women who tried to hide their flaws in the dark club by shaking themselves here and stretching themselves there, by saving up their tips to pay rent and support their children. In a credit to his parents, he realized he could do better for himself, became anxious that his experiences there would damage him, thought perhaps he wouldn't be able to have normal sex because he had seen so much, was already bored by the college girls he met in his classes.

He dawdled over the decision to leave even as he came to dread going to work those three nights a week, dreaded being exposed to other people's sicknesses. Then one night two men argued in the parking lot. One pulled out a gun and aimed to shoot a tire on the other's car, but missed and grazed the young man's leg. The young man would have called home and begged his parents for help if it had not been for the health insurance policy his father had insisted he have so that he could take care of himself.

"My parents were diplomats," the young man told the counselor one of the nurses at the hospital suggested that he see. "They did all these great and exciting things and expect us to do the same. My sister is this superstar athlete in tennis and skiing, as if one sport isn't enough. My brother naturally makes money, steals money, however you want to look at it. A gift is what my parents call it. I have done nothing outstanding except get in trouble."

"So you are seeing yourself in relation to the accomplishments of your parents, your brother, and your sister?" asked the counselor, a novice who was making an effort to employ reflective listening within his motivational interviewing.

This is crap, the young man thought to himself. But he promised he would try and he sincerely wanted to make his life better, so he answered. "Nothing I do will ever be good enough for them."

"What about for you? What about your own standards?"

"What about them?"

"Try to close out the image of your family for just a moment and tell me how you see yourself."

He said the first word that came to his mind. "Alone."

"So what I am hearing is that you are alone without them but
don't measure up with them."

"Yeah. I suppose."

"What is it that you want from life?"

"I don't know. I guess to enjoy it."

"And what do you enjoy?"

He wished he could offer a lofty, worthy answer. What ran
through his mind was: Sex. Feeling good. Being high, being happy.
He knew this was shallow, so he found something else to say.
"Making other people happy." Which was not untrue.

"Do you ever use drugs?" the earnest counselor asked, though
it was not necessarily part of his protocol.

"I do not," he replied, wondering if the counselor could see his
lie, wondering if people employed as counselors and psychologists
had especially good abilities to see through deceits.

Talking with the counselor allowed him to see his situation
with more clarity, and so he aspired to pull the loose strings of his
life together and get a real job, one he could tell his parents about
and that would also give him the opportunity to meet women outside of college who weren't strung out or bogged down by other
kinds of troubles.

And when the fall semester was upon them (why did fall
semester start in August?), on a whim he signed up for an Arabic
class, mostly because he thought the script was pretty and he could
learn the language of opium (and since he told no one his reason for
taking the class, no one could correct him and tell him that Arabic
was quite definitely not the language of opium). He also thought it
might seem exotic if he spoke a distant foreign language. His parents had been stationed in the Far East and both spoke Japanese;
they had no connection to the Middle East. He had not yet realized
that the short foreign lady who worked at the bank where he
landed a part-time job spoke Arabic. Nor did he have any idea that
Arabic would soon become one of the hottest language classes at
the university. Just one of those odd strokes of luck.

Take control. Make it stop. Salwa gritted her teeth and tightened her stomach muscles, hoping to freeze the tension in her body, convince the angered contents of her stomach to stay put. It was no use; gluing top molars to bottom molars did nothing to erase the need to throw up. Jassim lay deep, deep asleep, and even as she fought the vomit rising up, she marveled at his internal clock, which woke him up before his alarm on the days he swam and allowed him to sleep on his nonswimming days. Out of bed with no creaks and squeaks, jaws still slammed shut, she dizzily raced on tiptoes to the back bathroom, closed the door, turned on the fan and the water, and vomited into the shiny, white, citrus-scented toilet. Hunched over in silent prayer, squeezing the wetness from her eyes, she waited, then flushed and washed her face and mouth of all evidence of food returned and rejected.

Please let that be it for today, she pleaded silently over the thud of her heart. *No more.*

In silence and semidarkness she carried her soundless entreaties back through the house and slid into bed. Jassim had not moved from his confident pose, stretched on his back with an arm draped over his forehead. Her movements produced no ripples as she curled on her left side and listened to the thumping of her heart.

Salwa stared at a thought that had scratched at the back of her brain a few weeks ago: perhaps she was pregnant. Given the urgency and desperation of the past several weeks, even months, her heightened desire for her husband, and the complete and total exhaustion she felt now, it seemed at least a possibility.

She forced her eyes shut, forced her mind to reject that possibility and cover more acceptable thoughts for the next thirty-six minutes, before she had to get up.

—⁂—

Later, when she was seated at a desk in the real estate office, tension knotted itself at the back of her neck and shoulders, tangled her thoughts. Keeping to herself all morning, she filled in documents detailing the most minute aspects of home ownership: property taxes, schools, municipalities, saving for last the description of the home to be listed, 450 characters to sing the praises of one piece of property. Each time she walked out to get papers from the printer, to get something to drink, her ears stretched to other people's conversations, all repeated, all said yesterday, last week, last year, but coming to Salwa as if for the first time. Out of nowhere, a thought louder than any of the voices popped into her head, a thought she had not had before: *We cannot live here anymore.*

All those years of schizophrenic reaction to American culture, disdain for the superficial, which she had buried with each new purchase and promotion, a spray of loathing she had denied in order to justify her current arrangement—it all burst forward as if she were seeing it for the first time, as though she had not spent the past nine years living this very life.

It is different now, she thought. *If I am pregnant, I cannot raise my child here, away from everything I know. If I am pregnant.* In the brightness of the day, such an idea seemed impossible, and again she forced it away, tried to drink her soda and read through list after list. Thoughts crept in: pictures of her bank coworkers, Petra in particular.

"I am gay," Petra had told Salwa the second day they worked together. "Just so you know."

"Okay," Salwa had told her, not knowing what she was supposed to say and struck by how readily people shared intimate secrets with others but how emotionally distant they seemed, how they didn't connect the way people at home did. At first she had thought it was a result of language, or of her being from a different culture, but now, all these years later, she was beginning to think it was simply the culture of America to show everything but to remain an island, a closed-up individual. In the past month that distance had been stronger, an aftereffect of what had happened in New York and Washington, like the cars sprouting American flags from their windows, antennas to God, electric fences willing her to leave.

Joan came in and put one of her wrinkled manicured hands on Salwa's shoulder. "You're not working too hard, are you, honey?"

Salwa started. "Oh no, Joan. I just want to make sure I have all this information correct before I submit it."

"That's why you're good at this—you're so thorough." Joan

stood with her hands behind her back. "Honey, I wanted to give you these." She held out her hands; each contained an American flag decal. "You should put one on your car, on the back window. You never know what people are thinking, and having this will let them know where you stand."

Salwa stared at the decals, at the stripes pushing the stars into a corner, and tried to remember what each stood for, wondering why it would matter where on her car she placed it.

"I bought one for your husband too." Joan smiled at her, and Salwa stared at the cracks in her thick and too-dark foundation. Joan always referred to Jassim as "your husband," as though the six letters that filled his name in English were too scary, as though in trying to say them she might trip, or show some secret, private part of herself. And then to imagine placing a seventy-five-cent decal on his $50,000 car—well, that was amusing too.

"Thank you," Salwa replied.

"Is everything all right?" Joan's voice came poking through these thoughts and Salwa started. "Are you okay, Salwa?"

"Oh yes, I'm fine. Thank you, Joan. I think my body is tired of the heat. I've been feeling so tired and nauseated lately."

Joan settled herself on the arm of the leather chair while her thumb and forefinger fiddled with the top of her blouse. "I hope you don't have some yucky flu."

Salwa shook her head. "If it were the flu, I would have had it and finished it by now. I really think it's just the heat. You know how you reach a point where you just can't stand it anymore?"

Joan stared at her. "Salwa, honey, are you pregnant?"

"Oh, no."

Joan's face fell a bit. "Oh well, I hope you feel better, whatever it is. Perhaps it's hormonal. I remember having panic attacks when I was in my mid-twenties, before I had children. I never knew if it was because in my mind I wanted to settle down and have a family or because my body was ready to have babies. I really do believe that that happens, that your body tells you things. Maybe if you are deaf, like me, it has to tell you with something more dramatic, like those panic attacks."

Salwa and Joan smiled at each other, the warm smile of women who connect as women rather than over ideas or common issues in their lives. Joan got up and put her arm around Salwa's shoulders. "You feel better, honey, you hear me?" She left the room with a trace of her fruity perfume.

Salwa folded herself up in the heavily air-conditioned office, which at 74 degrees denied the 93-degree reality of the desert in mid-October. Thoughts bustled through her brain, scrutinizing the life she was living. *Denying reality. That's what I've been doing. Killing time, not living.* Legs crossed, arms wrapped around herself, she sat, rattled, staring at decals given to her in kindness and in themselves loaded with hatred.

She tried to imagine Jassim's reaction: "It's a compliment, really. She thinks you're one of her kind, and that you need the protection of a four-by-two-inch sticker to prove it." He would see no harm in it. He would think it perfectly acceptable. Inoffensive. Natural. This made her angrier than the stickers themselves. How could he be so complacent?

Later, as she was driving home, Salwa stopped at a red light with her windows closed against the unbearable heat, which seemed as though it would never, ever end. She pressed the forward scan button on the radio, searching for the station with soft rock and no commercials. A man's voice blared out: "Is anyone fed up yet? Is anyone sick of nothing being done about all those Arab terrorists? In the name of Jesus Christ! They live with us. Among us! Mahzlims who are just waiting to attack us. They just want..."

Salwa's heart sped. For a moment she didn't register where the voice was coming from and stared at the dashboard. A car's honking startled her, and a glance in the mirror gave her the driver of the car behind her with his hands in the air. Looking up, she saw that the light had turned green and lurched forward, not able to wave an apology. Unsettled, she pulled into the parking lot of a strip mall just on the other side of the intersection and sat, collecting herself behind tinted windows, staring at the buttons of her radio, which was now dancing from station to station. She turned the radio off and looked up. Her eyes counted four American flags, three in stores and one flying from a car.

Shaken, shaky, disgusted, Salwa pulled her car back onto the street and wound her way home in silence. She turned off the main road earlier than usual so that she could drive slowly up the looping streets in their neighborhood, only to be jarred by a flag on a pole that she'd not seen before, five on mailboxes, and one in the corner of a picture window. Seven flags in less than a mile of houses. After pulling into her driveway, automatically opening and closing the garage door, sealing out the red, white, and blue, she entered her house to find her husband in the corner of the living room that looked out at the mountains beyond the flags, reading and drinking tea.

"Hi, habibti! How'd it go?"

"Hi, Jassim. Fine." She could not talk about the radio broadcast. Or the honking. Or the flags. Or work. Or anything.

"Are you okay?"

"I'm fine. Just hot. I'm going to go get changed."

Down the tile hall to the carpeted bedroom. Feet slipped out of sweaty shoes and washed in the bathtub. Soap and cool water between her toes to wash away the raging man's voice in plops of dirty suds. *Living among us. Arab terrorists. Babies.* Each into a soapy pile washed away by clear, pure water. Thick brushed Egyptian cotton dried away the last traces, absorbed the pointy ends and corners of stars and stripes. Salwa regained her balance as she washed face and hands, soaked her skin in lotion bought duty-free, and changed into an older pair of cotton pajamas. A glance in the mirror at a shiny face and clean feet in sparkling slippers before she wandered back out into the living room.

"Everything okay with you?"

"Mostly."

"Mostly is not entirely. What happened to the rest of you?"

"It was knocked in the head by American patriotism."

"Oh God, Salwa. Did somebody say something to you?" Jassim put his article on the table next to him. Closed the lid of the pen and placed it parallel to the paper.

"No, not to me. Joan gave us both American flag decals for our cars, so that we can announce to every stranger we drive by that we do not intend to blow anything up."

"Do you think people who might intend to blow things up are putting those same decals on their cars for disguise?"

"Jassim!" Salwa couldn't tolerate his analysis at this moment, as though in looking at the details he had missed the entire point. "Who do you think wants to blow things up? This is all made up, *hocus pocus*. It's a big fat excuse to cause more problems back home." Salwa was standing but found she couldn't be still, needed purpose to her movements.

"Did something beside the decals happen?"

Salwa reviewed her day, her life, and the word *happen*, and in fact nothing had happened. It just *was*. "I accidentally landed on a radio station that was rooting out Arab terrorists. *'They're living among us,'* you know." The words that sat under her tongue were wrapped in fear and anger and so she kept them there, because she was scared that Jassim would counter her outrage with calm and reason.

"This is new for Americans. They don't know what to do, and they are unexposed to the rest of the world. The real world, as you would say. Just be patient, habibti. This will pass."

Salwa wanted to shake him, to scream that for God's sake, somebody could report him, have them both deported because his eyebrows were too thick, his accent was not welcome, especially in his line of work. Perhaps closing reality out allowed him the luxury of focusing completely, without distraction, on his work.

Jassim's voice broke into her thoughts. "The Japanese are incredible. Did you know that they have thirty-four different categories of recyclables? Only twenty percent of their trash goes to landfill, whereas eighty percent of American waste does."

—◈—

Amal. Alia. Widad. Sima. Names of relatives, movie stars, and singers scrolled through her mind as she stared at the merchant lists on her desk. Her mind wandered, tripped over *Amal* and *Sima* and the sweet feelings those names produced as they ran under her skin and inside her veins. Chipping away at this daydream was the feeling that someone was watching her. Across the carpeted floor from her partially glass-encased cubicle, standing at the information desk, waiting to direct people making transactions in cash, stood Jake, a part-time teller, part-time college student with whom she had exchanged a few empty conversations. Her impression of him was one she had had of many young American men she had met: no purpose, and that lack of purpose had translated into lack of manliness. When she looked up, when their eyes locked, his mouth opened into a broad smile, an intimate smile, as though they shared a secret, a joke. It was not the first time their gazes had collided, but never before had his smile seemed so brazen, as if they were old friends. She half smiled back, but she did so only out of courtesy. To leave a smile like that unanswered seemed rude. When Jake's smile broadened and he winked, Salwa felt as though she had been pinched, and she looked back at her papers, forced her eyes to glue themselves to her work. Breathing a professional breath, she folded up *Amal* and *Sima,* tucked them in her briefcase, and turned her attention back to the merchant reports in front of her.

Confidence like razors—where did this boy get such a thing?

Suddenly she felt a snarl in her stomach that was pushing its way up. *Oh God, please let me make it to the bathroom.* She ran behind the banks of tellers, customers and coworkers glancing her way. Into the bathroom, into the stall. Thank God.

—m—

As she could no longer deny the possibility, Salwa made an appointment to see her doctor, sneaking off before work to wait in a pink room stuffed with expectant people, where she saw pregnancy in each face. Forms filled out, updating this and answering that, not one with the most important question: *Does your husband/lover/ father of the child know you are pregnant?* Perhaps if she could have checked a box announcing her big Lie, she wouldn't have felt as though she were waiting for a lover to come meet her. Salwa still doubted, hoped a little that she was wrong.

When her name was called, Salwa walked through the door that led to the exam rooms, submitted to checks of blood pressure, temperature, and weight, all proof that she was alive and not transformed by the contents of her womb. She turned in a urine sample and had an official pregnancy test, which the nurse informed her was positive in the same flat voice she had used to call her from the waiting room. Salwa took this information with her as she settled into another pink room, a tiny exam room with accessories to make a woman feel at home (a mirror, two hangers, an assortment of tampons and pads, magazines). Each year when she came to this office, she waited for the doctor on the pink stool and read one of the magazines provided. Each year she spread her legs apart and stared at the pink flowers on the wall, thinking that it was nice they made an effort to remove the ugliness from a medical check.

Salwa sat in a crisp cloth gown that opened in the back. She was otherwise naked. Exposed. Her Lie, tucked deep between her legs, had been found out. This visit would be different, but even as she looked at *Healthy Pregnancy* magazine, skimmed through articles on gas, exercise, sex during pregnancy, and "Husband Feeling Left Out?" the official news had not registered completely.

Her doctor came into the room, and Salwa applied her Made in America face for the rest of the visit, dug into her memory to answer the questions about diabetes and cerebral palsy and cancer, high blood pressure, heart attacks, and obscure illnesses she had never heard of before. She nodded and shook and answered appropriately and then said goodbye to Dr. Bauer, took her prescription for prenatal pills, and walked out of the office, chin up, eyes quivering.

In the safety of her car, hidden in the medical center's parking garage, she allowed the tears to come. Sat there for many minutes sobbing and moaning, wishing Jassim were next to her, wishing Jassim wanted this, and more than anything wishing that things between her and Jassim were as they used to be, not as they had become. The tears she released had been blocking tiny crevices that held bubbles of anger and resentment, packed tight so as not to surface, but now it all spilled out into her car. They had been married for nine years; what was wrong with her husband that he did not want to have children? That he had forced her to lie about this most important event?

The official knowledge that she was pregnant came like a sentence, for now things would change. Things over which she had no control. She swallowed it like a rock, gulped the realization that she had crossed a line, leaped over a concrete barricade that grew beanstalk height and wouldn't let her back, wouldn't even let her see what it was she had left behind.

─◦ Chapter Five ◦─

Each day that Jassim had gone swimming since that fateful Tuesday when the planes hit, his mind had not cleared on entering the water but rather captured memories, mostly of home, and rolled them around for the duration of his swim. The memories were neither pleasant nor unpleasant; it was as though he had a stack of DVDs to review that could be seen only while he swam. (It was the events of the past weeks that had sent him back. Tragedy has a way of making a person examine his past, he reasoned, and he allowed his memory to continue, to replay as he swam.)

His laps were not coming easily, and he got out of the water to get a kickboard. A couple of laps of easy swimming sometimes helped to jump-start him. He swam with the kickboard extended in front of him and his face in the water. But it was not to work that his mind went; instead his thoughts rewound back to before his American beginning, when he had flipped thousands of somersaults over sea and land, all the way from the deserts of Jordan to study water in arid lands with Iranians and Jordanians and Bahrainis and Kuwaitis in the deserts of Arizona. He fine-tuned his English, spun idioms, split words apart, and floated along in his master's-degree coursework, happy even as he thought it all temporary. Or perhaps because he thought it all temporary.

From the first moment that Jassim set foot on American desert soil for his graduate education, he had been ready, willing, and able to return to Jordan upon completion of his studies, to implement all that he would learn. America's ease and comfort was not so much greater than Jordan's that he considered staying.

At the end of two years he received his master's and went home puffed up to work at the Ministry of Water Resources. In spite of his degree and swelling ideas, in the ministry he dangled from the lowest rung, with less education than most, so not only was he passed over for the interesting projects, but his ideas for improvement of existing projects were largely ignored. Meanwhile, America was calling him daily, with her Anytime Minutes whispering stainless steel promises of a shiny lab and possibility. Jassim re-thought his life, decided that more education was crucial to his success, and squeezed out the justification to return for a Ph.D.

"You will be the first Ph.D. doctor in the family," his father said when he explained his decision. "You make yourself the best, strongest candidate for a successful job that you can. And then come back and fix things."

Jassim went to America a second time, still filled with dreams of saving Jordan from drought and dependency. His focus narrowed to rainwater harvesting. With him in his doctoral program was Cornelia, a South African who awoke in Jassim something new. (Even now the thought of Cornelia poked at him a bit through the water.) If he had believed in romantic love, she would have been his first. Instead he viewed their relationship as a perfect connection. Cornelia was bright, open, ambitious, independent, and sexually confident, easily welcoming him to entwine his life and body with hers.

Two years rolled by. He was still at least a couple years away from finishing, and Cornelia was ready to return home to South Africa. As Jassim looked down the road toward his future, he could not imagine his life without her. She was the perfect partner in all matters. They could open a consulting firm, Carter and Haddad. So he asked her to marry him.

"I have to go home, Jassim. You have to go home. We are both of us too wedded to our countries to change."

His body fought and screamed with his mind, pounded at him to commit irrational acts, to follow her, to stop her at the airport, to make love to her in public places. Horribly illogical thoughts. Thoughts that scared him with their passion and irrationality. Thoughts he forced out of his system by swimming, drowning them in the over-chlorinated water of the university pool.

And then Cornelia left and he closed out the real world and studied and wrote and swam. For months that turned into years he did nothing else. From morning until night his world was obsessive and predictable, from the time he got up in the morning, went swimming, and worked to the time he ate virtually the same dinner alone each night. He didn't mind so much the repetitiveness, found the routine and predictability comforting.

Things moved along as they were supposed to. He defended his dissertation successfully. His parents and sisters came for his graduation. Just days before Jassim was going to pack up and go home, Marcus, a former classmate, called.

"I'm now a partner in a consulting firm," he said, "and I would like it if you would work with us. I know you have plans to go home, but I think the experience would help you in the long run. We have one client who is obsessed with rainwater harvesting, has loads of money to experiment with, and I would put you in charge of his account."

Jassim said he would have to think about it.

"Really, Jassim, you could give it a year and then go home. I can arrange for you to stay. And it may not matter to you, but I can offer you a substantially higher salary than what you'd get in Jordan. Plus, it's experience."

To the disappointment of his family, he stayed. *Just for another year.* The work was all that Marcus had promised, and Jassim was happy, truly happy. After almost two years, he again wrestled with the decision of staying or going home.

"Why don't you take a few weeks, go home, and see what the situation is like?" Marcus suggested. "See if you can find a place that works for you. If not, you stay with us."

Jassim made calls and sent e-mails to old friends, relatives, and ex-professors, promising himself that he would do his best to find the right place for himself in Amman and this time would not get disheartened so quickly. (Yes, even then he was determined to be home.) And so he went with plans packed in his suitcase, each one detailing how he would solve the water crisis. Cisterns for individual home use, and for greedy agriculture he proposed a special dam to capture the rain. Pride carried him into the ministry and disillusionment carried him out. His Ph.D. and experience were very impressive, but America, once tasted, is hard to spit out, with its shiny tools and machinery. Jordan pumps through the blood, but America stays in the mouth. Even with all the American and

European support, the ministry was nothing in comparison to Marcus's firm.

The second day back in Amman, a city now bursting with traffic and recently displaced Iraqis, Palestinians, and returned Jordanians, Jassim accepted an invitation from an old friend, now a professor, to give a lecture for the friend's class about his dissertation and the need for self-sufficiency in countries in the region, the need to look at the wisdom of the past in sustaining life in a region that was subject to large and unpredictable shifts in population and did not offer much water.

The day of his talk was sunny and sharp as he made his way to the designated classroom and passed clusters of students standing by the black-and-yellow-striped curbs that lined the hilly internal streets of the university. Jassim felt as though he were invisible. While barely ten years had elapsed since he had been a student, it could have been five times that. It seemed as though there were many more students on campus, more women wearing hijab, more intensity in the bustling than when he had been there.

"Jassim!"

"Hello, Nabeel. Good to see you."

He and his friend shook hands and kissed each other twice on each cheek. Reviewed the years lost between them, walking arm in arm toward the lecture hall.

"Thank you again for agreeing to do this, Jassim. I know the students will love you. Perhaps it will convince you to stay." Nabeel patted Jassim's hand and headed to the dais while Jassim remained standing in the corner, impressed by the orderliness of the students.

"I'd like to introduce to you a very dear friend of mine, who is one of Jordan's great minds, with so much to offer," Nabeel began. "He has been temporarily wooed by the seductive swish of America's broad hips, but he promises that he will return to us one day soon to fix our water problems. Professor Jassim Haddad is a purist and has come to talk to us today about his first love: water."

Jassim stood before the students and spoke easily about what was closest to his heart. When he had finished his talk and answered students' questions, he said goodbye to Nabeel, promising to go to his house to meet his wife and three children before he left for America. He then left the lecture hall and wandered out into the courtyard, admiring the brightness of the sky.

"Excuse me, Dr. Haddad."

He turned around and saw a petite young woman with thick hair and clear eyes. She had been sitting in the front row of the lecture hall.

"Dr. Haddad, I wanted to thank you for your lecture. It was very interesting."

"You're welcome, Miss..."

"Salwa. Salwa Khalil."

"Miss Salwa. Are you in hydrology?"

"No. I'm in economics, but I saw the flier for your talk and I thought it sounded interesting. And it was, very interesting, especially the part about what the Israelis have done with our water. Jordanian water and Palestinian water."

"It is quite shocking." He chuckled. "I'm glad you enjoyed the lecture." He smiled at Miss Salwa Khalil and then, having nothing more to say, wished her well and headed out of the university.

And that had been that. Only, Salwa's face had floated pleasantly in and out of Jassim's thoughts.

He called Nabeel that night. "Do you know the young woman who was sitting in the front row during my lecture?" He didn't want to say her name first thing, didn't want his friend to think that he was chasing after a student.

"I didn't notice. Which one? Describe her."

Jassim wanted to describe her, to savor the thought of her large clear eyes and delicate face a bit longer. Instead he pretended to strain at remembering her name. "I think she was Palestinian, from Nablus, or Hebron. Khalili. Or Khalil. Salwa. That's it. Salwa Khalil."

"She's not one of mine. Sorry. What about her?"

"Nothing. I was just wondering."

"Jassim...?"

He felt so embarrassed that he changed the subject and hoped Nabeel would forget he had ever brought it up.

Out of an odd thumping need, one that encompassed the pretty face of Miss Salwa Khalil, Jassim created one excuse after another to visit the university in the hope of running into her. Two afternoons after the lecture he went to a restaurant near the university. Whether by fate or luck or coincidence, Miss Salwa Khalil was also there, sitting with an eager-faced young man.

Jassim approached their table. "Excuse me. Hello. How are you both? Miss Salwa. I am Jassim Haddad. I gave a talk ..."

"Of course I remember you. Nice to see you again, Dr. Haddad. This is ..."

(Here Jassim's memory failed. He could not remember the boy's name or the boy's face, just the general eagerness he emitted and the fact that he left the table just after Jassim greeted them.)

Jassim remained standing. Salwa remained sitting. Both watched the boy walk away.

"Please," Salwa said, gesturing to the empty seat across from her.

Jassim sat down.

"How are you changing things, then? You have these ideas, but how are you using them?"

Jassim was startled by her interest, not because she was a woman but because of the intensity of her questions, as though it really did matter to her. He talked a lot about his job and watched her watching him and felt extremely comfortable. He asked her if she would meet him the next day and she agreed. For Jassim, the twenty-two hours until the next afternoon were excruciating, and he thought of little else. He arrived half an hour early, and his palms were sweaty. (Yes, she had made him nervous, excited.) Salwa arrived (late, as he remembered), and they settled into conversation effortlessly and chatted through sodas and shawarma.

(Here his memory closed around a gray cloud. Somehow the subject of Palestine had come up, and he had dismissed something, though he could not remember what, and she had become quite upset, had told him he was arrogant. He remembered worrying that she would never want to talk to him again. So many years in the States had hardened his memory to the rawness of the subject.)

The next day, just in case, he returned to the restaurant. He stayed there for an hour and a half, pretending to read the newspaper. The following day he went back and this time lingered for two hours. There was no sign of Salwa. Then came the weekend. When the new week began, Jassim promised himself that it would be his last attempt to try to talk to Salwa. If she wasn't there, he would give up and not try to find her. But she was there, alone and with her back to the door.

"Miss Salwa?"

"Hello, Jassim," she said. A good sign, he thought. "You can sit down if you'd like."

"Thank you." He sat. And against all rational behavior, his words spilled on the table. "I am sorry for what I said last week. It was insensitive and thoughtless and I am sorry to have offended you. Truly."

"I'm also sorry, for getting so angry. I realized that your perspective is a different one and I cannot fault you for having it."

(Jassim forgot the rest of the conversation, was left with the impression that they recognized in each other a different approach to life and were willing to leave it at that.)

Salwa talked about her family, Jassim thought, though he was not listening so much as he was succumbing to the pressure of his impending return to the States and to his job, which was squeezing his throat, forcing unplanned words off his tongue. "Salwa, I know this may seem a bit unexpected, but I wonder what sort of plans you have for your future."

"What do you mean, Jassim? What are you asking me?"

"I would like to ask you to marry me. If you agree, I will come with my family to ask officially."

(Yes, he had entertained the idea of asking her to marry him before that, but not so soon. And he had lied when he had apologized. That he remembered clearly. He had not been sorry for what he had said, nor did he think he had been insensitive or thoughtless.)

"I would like that very much. I would like to go to America too."

(Yes, she had said that; he remembered her words clearly. At the time he had been shocked, not expecting her to agree so quickly without asking more questions.)

Two days later he and his mother and father arrived at the less than fancy home of Salwa Khalil.

"Welcome, welcome, Professor Jassim," Salwa's father said. He was a small man, stocky, with the look of the earth in him and the hands of someone who had made his living by them.

When the formalities had been exchanged and the coffee served, Jassim offered the words he had come with: "I am returning now to the States. I have a good job, the means to buy a home. I would like to stay for at least another year to work and then come back here to Jordan for good, to apply the technology I have learned to improve the state of things here. I would like to ask you for your daughter's hand in marriage."

"Salwa has told us some of your theories, about your passion for proper water usage. Did she tell you that she is the worst culprit of water waste in our family?"

"Abu Siham!" her mother said, reprimanding her husband.

"It's all right. He must know the good and the bad. The good he can see—the bad comes later."

"She had not mentioned that," said Jassim, glancing at Salwa.

"Perhaps it is enough for you to know that Salwa's water use threatens the water supply of the entire country, perhaps the entire region. It has always been like this. When she was a baby, she could have stayed in the bath for the entire day. When she was a child, she liked to run the hose and splash and make rivers in the mud. Now she likes flowers that are not native to our climate, and her poor mother has to choose between Salwa's flowers and the rest of the family eating. I think it is God's will that she change her ways." Abu Siham's face was serious even as his wife and daughter were giggling. "Salwa, habibti, my youngest daughter, would you like to answer this proposal now, or would you like to think about it?"

Salwa was sitting back in her chair, watching her father, Jassim thought, with the same expression she might have if she were watching a movie. "I would like to accept."

Amid tears, ululations, and coffee, the details were discussed.

"I will go back and arrange for Salwa's visa," said Jassim.

"There is no need for that."

"Excuse me?"

"Salwa didn't tell you?" said Abu Siham, smiling for the first time. "No, it seems she did not." Here he looked at Salwa and smiled broadly, as though they shared a joke. "Salwa is an American citizen."

Jassim raised his eyebrows and looked from Salwa to her father.

"No, she probably didn't tell you, because, as I am sure you can imagine, American citizenship is a big draw in marriage proposals. Perhaps she thought, rightly, that if you did not know, it would be better for everyone. You see, many years ago we went to the United States. I had a brother in Chicago who had a restaurant, and he arranged for me to go. We thought of staying there, but it was too hard on Um Siham. She had three small girls, was pregnant with Salwa, and I was constantly working. My father was ill, as was Um Siham's mother. After Salwa was born, we decided that it was not worth losing our souls so we could have nice things. Our lives in Jordan were not so bad, and our life in America was miserable." Abu Siham stopped to drink a coffee in one gulp.

"Your life is different, I can see, because you have an education and you are dealing with the good of America. I was working like a dog in a restaurant and dealing with people who resented foreigners who were willing to work harder than they did. I am pleased that Salwa will return to America, the country of her birth, and be offered what is good." He stopped for a moment and gazed at his daughter.

"Salwa is Palestinian by blood, Jordanian by residence, and American by citizenship. That is why she uses so much water and has a taste for luxury. We tease her that she is really first world. A colonizer. You see, she even studies money!" Abu Siham's eyes twinkled as he said these things, his love for his daughter welling up in his face.

At the very back of Jassim's mind, in only the faintest lettering, was the idea that Salwa's American citizenship would enable them both to stay. Forever, if he chose.

Jassim swam his final strokes and stopped where he had started, exhausted. It seemed as though hours had passed since he had gotten into the pool ... Odd to relive all those moments, and odd that they came now. Or now that everything Arab was newsworthy, perhaps it was only natural to go home in his thoughts. And it would always be home, but here, nine years after he and Salwa had wed, he had no desire to return to Jordan. What would he do there? He couldn't imagine living in that bureaucracy again, had become comfortable in this easy, predictable life.

Jassim squatted, so that only his head was above water, and looked at these memories frame by frame: one European woman (Cornelia could hardly be considered African) and one Arab woman, both educated, worldly, understanding women. Neither of whom he really understood.

Never a fan of turkey, mashed potatoes, or apple pie, the boy, sixteen, worked his way to apartment 1216, a small wad of money shoved deep and damp in his pocket. It was not the first time he had bought drugs, but it felt like a big deal because it was the first time he had bought drugs from a stranger. An early Christmas present to himself. That he was buying an eighth of a gram of meth on his own from a real dealer filled him with pride. Used sparingly, it was enough to make the long Thanksgiving weekend tolerable. And then some. He was buying early, before the holiday crowds.

Saturday afternoon, crisp and clear and trying to be cold, the boy got off the bus and skated toward the apartment building. He had thought twice about bringing his skateboard, because it made him nervous that if something went wrong, maybe someone would try to take it from him. What the something going wrong might be he couldn't imagine.

Something in the brightness of the day made him feel sad, droopy, as if he could lie down anywhere and stay. His dad had been such a jerk. Why did he still fall for it? All the promises of *we'll do this* and *we'll go there* that his father never delivered on.

Should have known that his father would forget that he had promised to take him to the Auto Mall to look at cars.

The boy walked past two gardeners and wondered why all the gardeners he saw were Mexican. Didn't white people want to garden? It didn't seem like such a bad job. He followed the signs, walked up the stairs, and stood in front of #1216 for a moment before he rang the bell.

What would he say? "Hi. I'm here to buy meth. We spoke on the phone."

The door opened, and the boy thought he must have mistaken the apartment number. In front of him was a college boy dressed in khaki pants and a button-down shirt. No shoes.

"I'm so . . . sorry," he stuttered.

"For what? You called, right? Brant?"

This confused him for a moment. On the phone, he had used the name Brant, which was the name of his mother's last boyfriend. "Yeah. Brant."

"Come on in."

The boy walked into the apartment, still unsure of himself. The place was neat, grown-up, not what he expected from someone selling drugs.

"Have a seat."

The boy sat down and felt a little angry as he watched this drug dealer who looked like he had just stepped off a golf course.

"You wanted an eighth of Tina, right?"

"Right." The boy touched the wad of money in his pants, money collected in part from the wallets of his mother and sister.

"How'd you find out about me?"

"Brad, in my school, he said to call you."

"I guess that's how it is these days. Word of mouth."

"I guess."

Golf Club, as the boy decided to think of him, went to his kitchen and reappeared with a small plastic bag, the corner of a plastic bag actually, stuffed with pinkish flecks and closed with a green garbage tie. The boy felt he should ask something about the quality of the product he was buying or where it came from, but he couldn't think of anything.

"Sixty."

"I only brought fifty. That's what they told me."

"Shit, this is the problem with word of mouth—prices change over time. Price is sixty."

The boy felt like an idiot. He pulled the wad of cash from his jeans and counted it in front of Golf Club so that he could see that was all he had, also so that if a ten was hidden among the fives and other tens and ones, it could take this opportunity to reveal itself. "Fifty. That's it. That's all I have." Wished he had left his board at home. Glad he kept his bus money in another pocket.

Golf Club looked at him. There were no more than a few years between them, but the boy felt there was a concrete wall that reached to God blocking them from each other's world.

"It's okay. This time fifty. Next time sixty."

"Thanks for giving me a break. Seems like no one else has lately."

"I hear ya, man," said Golf Club.

The boy looked around the apartment. There were books and a couple of paintings on the wall, including one of something Japanese in a thick silver frame.

"You like that?" Golf Club asked, following his gaze.

"It's different."

"Japanese. It's part of a series. Myths about happiness and truth."

The boy was only half listening, the rest of him noticing the thickness of the frame and how it looked expensive, very expensive.

"Don't you worry someone will try and steal it?"

"Can't imagine who would want it. We done? Anything else I can help you out with?"

"Nah. Thanks."

"Later."

The boy left the apartment, walked out the door and didn't turn around to say goodbye. His heart pounded more when he left the apartment than it had when he got there. Exhilarating and terrifying all at once to walk out into the possibility of being arrested. He thought about Golf Club; he wasn't what he had expected or what he wanted. The boy would have been more comfortable with a normal-looking person, someone like himself, who didn't have it so easy. This was like buying smack from Walgreen's. He bet that Golf Club had a rich mother and father somewhere who would save him from his life as a drug dealer when the time came. If no one shot him first. *And what kind of retard let people buying drugs into his house?*

He decided that he would take the bus going toward the Auto Mall, decided to go by himself to check out cars. Blue sunglasses on, he sat at the bus stop looking at the world in filtered azure. An older black man was also waiting. The boy rarely saw black people in the city except when he took the bus. He sat on the top of the bench with his skateboard leaning between his legs, while the man leaned against the pole that supported the awning over the bus stop.

"You know when it's supposed to come?"

"No idea."

"Which one you taking?"

"The one that goes to the Auto Mall."

The man looked at him and laughed. "You buying a car today, son?"

There was something in the man's laugh that felt like a hug, something that forced out unplanned words.

"My dad promised he'd take me, but he's a blowhard, so he didn't. I was in the neighborhood, so I thought I'd go myself."

"What kind of car were you planning on buying, you and your father?"

"Not buying. Just looking."

"What kind of car were you planning on looking at?"

"I don't know. Something big. Chevy Tahoe, maybe."

"Now that'll put you back a penny or two. If it was me, I think I'd go for one of those Japanese luxury cars, like a Lexus or Infiniti."

The boy thought it odd that Lexus and Infiniti were Japanese. "You going car shopping too?"

"Nah. Going to buy me some shoes. And a tuxedo."

"What are you buying a tuxedo for?"

"My funeral." The man grinned. "I figure if you're looking at a Chevy Tahoe, I might as well go tuxedo shopping."

They both smiled and stared in the direction the bus would be coming from.

An overweight woman sidled up to the bench from the opposite direction. She was enormous, with rolls of flesh drooping off her arms and her belly and her legs. She had shoulder-length brown hair that hung dry like straw, and she held a half-gallon-sized plastic container that said *Thirst Buster* on the side.

"That's sure a lot of thirst you're going to be busting," the black man said as she sat down, filling half the bench.

The woman looked at him through glasses. Only one of her eyes focused on him. "Did it come already?"

From his perch on the bench the boy decided she was crazy and was irritated that she had intruded on their conversation.

"Did what come?"

"The bus. Did the bus come already?"

The man stared at her, his eyes twinkling as he looked a bit indignant. "Now what would we be doing here if the bus had already come?"

The woman thought for a minute. "Maybe you two are the reception committee." She looked at the boy and then at the man again and broke into a smile followed by a guffaw.

The pulsing of loud, exposed engines approached, and they watched as four enormous Harley-Davidson motorcycles drove past them single file in the center lane, each one shined and groomed, each one occupied by two riders, a man in front and a woman in back. The boy didn't pay much attention to the riders, was stuck on the chrome and the shine and the grace, especially the one that had the tall handlebars. He watched them as they passed.

"Ex-hippies," said the black man. "Used to be that outlaws rode those things. Now it's doctors and lawyers and people who work for tech companies. They're the only ones who can afford them. Then they go and buy the get-up. The leather chaps, those suitcase things with the silver studs you put on back to put your important things in. And the do-rags. Those boys aren't finding any old thing and tying up their balding heads. Nah, they're going to department stores and paying premium to look tough and rugged. In fact, that one in front looked a lot like my doctor."

The woman was nodding and smiling. "The lady with him looked like my psychiatrist."

The two of them laughed easily, but the boy did not. He was still thinking of Golf Club, thinking that it was people like Golf Club who made money off people like him and the black man and the crazy fat lady. He swore to himself that he would never go back to him. Ever. After he had used up the meth in his pocket, he was done.

"Nice board," said the black man.

"Thanks."

The woman looked at it and nodded her head.

"What you got a hunting license on a skateboard for?" the black man asked.

The boy didn't answer, held it up for him to take a closer look.

He read it out loud: "Terrorist Hunting License." He stared at it some more and looked up at the boy. "So this gives you the right to go hunt you up some terrorists?"

"Sure does."

"How are you going to know one when you see one?"

"I'll know."

The man shook his head. "Tell me, son, what would you do if you found one?"

"Kick his ass."

The man smiled, not unkindly, but said nothing.

The boy felt there were words behind his silence, laughing words, and this feeling made him want to argue. "What would you do?" he asked.

"What would I do about what?"

"What would you do if you saw a terrorist?"

The man looked at him and thought. "Son, there's so much more to it than that." He laughed, his shoulders shaking. "Isn't it crazy what's happening to this world?"

The boy didn't know what the man meant by this, felt that his laughter was directed at him.

"There it is!" said the woman, and slid off the bench with a kind of jump.

The man turned away from his conversation for a moment to reach into his pocket.

The bus pulled up to the curb, but the boy didn't feel like going to the Auto Mall anymore, so he got up and turned in the other direction. "Later," he said to the man and woman, but they didn't notice as he skated away.

—◌◌—

"What have I done, what have I done?" muttered Salwa in English as she chopped onions, onions, more onions. It would not be out of place to cry, but she didn't want to cry. Instead she wanted to explode, or implode, or just vanish. "How could I have done this?" More onions and more onions for delicious *musakhan* to please her husband's palate, to distract him from her yellow face and her nauseated being. In the afternoon she didn't feel nauseated, but smells could be overwhelming. Incredible how a tiny baby inside could change your whole physical perspective.

Shit, shit, shit, shit, shit. What have I done? An anger rose in her and knotted her throat, made her want to vomit, anger vomit, not baby vomit. *This is not petty deception. I have undermined everything. Our marriage will mean nothing now.*

She had to lie down again, didn't care that onions lay partially chopped on the counter, their smell wafting about the room, clinging to any fabric. Jassim would be gone awhile on his Saturday morning errands, and Salwa, her news clattering inside her, needed to talk to Randa.

"'Allo, Randa."

"Hi, Salwa. How are you, habibti?" Salwa loved Randa's accent, loved how her Arabic was like a song.

"Randa, I have to tell you something."

"Of course, habibti, go ahead."

"I'm pregnant."

"Congratulations, my love! This is lovely. God willing, you will have an easy pregnancy and easy delivery. Praise God."

Salwa stared at the phone and said nothing.

"What's the matter?"

"Randa, you know Jassim doesn't want a baby yet."

"Oh, Salwa. He thinks he doesn't want a baby, but that doesn't mean anything. Men often think they don't want something, but they just haven't realized that they do want it. He'll come around to it. You'll convince him of it in a way that he will think he came to it on his own."

Salwa forced Randa's confident words into her brain, swallowed them whole and let them soothe her gnawing guilt, allowed herself to swing away from what she knew to be true toward what she wanted to be true. After all, Randa's advice was often right on the mark; perhaps this too would be, must be. Randa's women's words pushed away what Salwa knew: that Jassim's objections weren't likely to change anytime soon.

—⁓—

During the evenings she was overcome with fatigue, which absorbed her in gigantic waves, sudden exhaustion knocking her over. Her eyes would seal and she would sleep, just like that. Jassim tried to wake her up, but it was as though she had been drugged. She could hear his voice but couldn't make her body respond, could barely pry her eyes open.

"Salwa, what's going on with you?" asked Jassim.

"I don't know. I must be fighting something." She tried to smile, barely opened her eyes to see his concerned face peering over her.

"Your face is yellow. I hope you feel better."

"I'll be fine."

In her sleepy haze, stretched awake/asleep/drugged in his arms as he carried her to their bed, other words drummed in her head: *How long can I continue this?* How long could she possibly continue tiptoeing down the hall at breakneck speed to vomit in the back bathroom? Salwa couldn't think how to tell him, could never seem to come up with the right collection of words.

—⁓—

One Sunday afternoon in late November, Salwa drove herself to the mall to think. It had taken her all day to get up and get showered, every movement a strain. She was feeling very thankful she didn't have to show any houses today.

Tiredness still dragged at her swollen feet stuffed into her youthful half-platform sneakers. She drifted into the holiday hoopla of Dillard's, eyes touching racks of suggested gifts, holiday clothes, clearance clothes, latest fashions, the latest in intimate apparel. She found her eyes gravitating toward the more revealing camisoles and lacy panties rather than the more traditional nighties and top-and-bottom sets. Her eyes landed on a pale pink camisole with matching panties and diaphanous robe. Without looking at the price tag, she picked up a size small and continued browsing, her mind gently rocking the thoughts of the baby in her stomach.

"I think this would look fabulous on you," said a man's voice.

Salwa looked up to see in front of her a man in his sixties, his dyed orange hair combed back meticulously. He stood in front of the sale rack and held up a transparent leopard-spotted camisole.

Salwa grabbed the laugh that started to escape and looked toward the woman he was addressing. She could not have been younger than seventy, petite, with a full head of blond hair. "Oh, that is nice. See if they have it in a medium."

"This is a large. The only other one is extra-large."

"Hold on to it and I'll try it on." She continued browsing on the far side of the rack, her head barely visible above the top.

"Will do."

Salwa couldn't help herself; she stared at the man, at his pleated grayish blue polyester trousers, at the windbreaker he wore, and at his face. And then he turned toward her. His eyes fell to the outfit she held and he looked back at her face. And winked.

Salwa felt her face burn. She had been caught staring at someone's most private moment.

She continued browsing, but the embarrassment of being in the middle of their conversation nagged at her. She wandered by racks of undergarments. Bras, panties, camisoles, matching sets. Without a rational thought to explain it, she picked up a wine-colored lace bra and the thong that matched it. She had never purchased this kind of undergarment, and she could not say what it was that motivated her to do so now. She walked to the register, having forgotten about her pregnancy.

A woman was ahead of her in line. She was too thin and wore brown pants and a pale blue blouse that swallowed her femininity. She was buying eight pairs of plain cotton thong underwear. Standing in line, Salwa found herself thinking, *What on earth does she need eight pairs of thong underwear for?* and smiling as she heard Jassim's voice asking her the same question about pajamas.

Suddenly she felt an intense urge to urinate and wished the woman would hurry up.

After Salwa paid and thanked the cashier, she headed toward the bathroom. She found herself walking in a shuffling kind of way, with her thighs smashed together, as if that would hold in her urine if it tried to escape. With relief she rushed into the stall, not even bothering to hang her purse and bag on the hook behind the door. She sat down on the toilet and felt a huge relief. She glanced at her underwear. On the perfectly white panel of her no-seam panties was a brownish red oval. She leaned closer. Blood.

She wiped herself and looked at the toilet paper. More blood, though this was pinker, fainter.

"It's nothing," she said aloud, her voice forcing away the thoughts that came out from under rocks, behind doors, the thoughts that wanted to remind her of what she had done, that this was no easy place in which she had put herself. The thoughts that shopping had almost covered up.

She washed her hands and glanced in the mirror. She was not glowing, as the magazines suggested she should be. Instead she was yellow. Perhaps glowing didn't come until later. *It will come,* she tried to promise herself. *A little blood is normal.*

She forced these thoughts on top of the ones that she had just considered. Stapled them. Sealed. Laminated. Deep breath.

She walked back out of the bathroom and into the store. It was changed somehow, now garish and loud and unpleasant. Even the bag she held at her side felt unnecessary. The darkness shadowing these thoughts made Salwa nervous, though perhaps it was inevitable—to become pregnant against your husband's wishes was asking for trouble. These things happen, getting pregnant while taking the pill. It's possible.

He will believe me.

She drifted into the mall again and went to the food court, vaguely hungry. She stood in front of a French-style bakery and stared at the rolls and pastries, suddenly undone by the need to vomit.

"Oh God," she muttered aloud, and turned and ran to the cavernous bathroom in the heart of the food court. *Please let me make it. Please, please, please.* She went into a stall, lifted up the seat, and leaned over the toilet. Nothing. Deep breathing. Her eyes and nose burned. And then she vomited.

She would have to tell Jassim soon. Maybe tonight.

But tonight came and went, as did the next night, and still she did not tell Jassim.

Leaving his job at the topless bar and that whole environment had signified to him a step up, a few inches out of the hole he had started digging for himself. He had lolled around jobless for a few weeks, until Sweeney, an ex-girlfriend (not really ex, not really girlfriend), told him that the bank she worked for was hiring, and didn't he used to work in a bank? He spruced himself up and played sophisticated college boy, pointed out his knack for numbers, and was hired (helped along by the ex-girlfriend's kind words) by First Fidelity. Didn't take him long to work his way into a nice routine. Would have been just fine if his grades hadn't been so low, if his parents hadn't gotten involved and informed him that until his grades improved they were not providing him with spending money. Tough love, his mother had said.

Sweeney saved the day again. "I got good drugs from you a couple of times," she told him. "That's a good way to earn extra income. Not dealing, just helping people who are looking for it. Meth is hot these days," she said.

He stopped going to see the counselor. Cringed from the face in the mirror and from his failures, academic and lifestyle, real and perceived (perceived having become real), and ran from everything he knew to be right, turned instead to the powdery promise of euphoria. He learned to change the mundane into cheery action, giving each detail his full attention, each customer his fullest charm. The straight and narrow curved and widened. Caution thudded by the wayside. Parental guidance traipsed away down a different path. He was left with his job, his apartment, and his newfound excitement for life, a scrubbed-behind-the-ears white boy who liked to have a good time and live a life of his choosing. For the first time in ages, he felt good about himself, had no difficulty getting through the drone of the day, even managed to make his part-time job as a bank teller interesting. Hope still speckled his horizon as he teetered between highs and lows, softened the crash with chain smoking, even though it parched his throat so severely that eating was painful. All alone, without the help of any one person, he had made his life good, and he bumped along with tolerable grades, happy customers, and a sense of well-being.

No way to know when your heart is racing and you are feeling so fine, sped up for days, that your body is being gobbled up by the greedy promise of perfection, that it is only a matter of time before the bottom drops out, along with your teeth. *Plink plink.*

Chapter Six

"Hello. Salwa Haddad speaking." No trace of an Arabic accent in her English (or so it sounded to Hassan). No trace of the Palestinian city where her family originated.

Hassan moved the phone from his mouth and took a deep breath. "Salwa, hello, how are you?"

"I'm well, thank God, and you?"

"Thank God, I am well."

Pause. He could not make his words come.

"Who is this?" Formal. Simple. As though a phone call on her cellular from a man speaking Arabic were not so extraordinary.

"Salwa, it is I, Hassan."

"Hassan? Hassan Shaheed?" There it was, the lilt of hope that always appeared in the second syllable of his last name.

"Yes. Hassan. How are you, Salwa?"

"Hassan? It's been so long. I'm fine. How are you?" How could *how are you* feel so intimate? As though she had been waiting nine years to ask him.

"I'm well, thank you."

"Are you all right? Is everything okay at home?" He remembered this, the panic of an unexpected phone call when you are far away.

"Yes. Everything is fine, Salwa. Don't worry, please. I am not calling to tell you about troubles."

Silence.

"Congratulations. My mother tells me you got engaged." Her voice was hard and reserved. She would not ask the reason for this call, and so she turned to formal conversation.

"I got engaged."

"Congratulations. God willing, you will have a long, happy life together. Who is the girl?"

"Her name is Intizar Hamdan."

"How do you know her?"

"She works with me at the studio."

"Congratulations, Hassan. Siham tells me you are doing very well, that your talk show especially is getting attention, worldwide attention."

"The show is getting a lot of attention, and it is very exciting to be working there." He didn't want to talk about the show. "Salwa, I..." *I what? What is it that you are going to say, you fool, Hassan? Are you going to say you still love her? After nine years? While she has been married and a million miles away? Impossible, It-Is-I-Hassan. You fool. What were you thinking?*

"Hassan, I am so happy for you that you have your dream." *My dream is in America, married to a stiff Jordanian with a giant's name.* "Thank God, it is good. It is all good. How is Jassim?"

"He is well, thank God. He says hello."

Hassan smiled at these formalities. When he had first lived in Romania and translated his Arabic thoughts rather than thinking in Romanian, he had said this to someone who asked after his mother. The man had laughed. "How can she say hello if she doesn't know I exist?" *Yes, sweet Salwa, how can he say hello when he does not know I am calling you? That I still exist?* "God protect him. And your work? Your mother tells me that you have a new job."

"I am still at the bank and I am also helping people buy and sell houses."

"Do you like that kind of work?"

"It's all right. It pays very well, and it can be interesting."

"How is Ramadan?"

"Praise God. How is Ramadan with you?"

He told her about his mother, about how only half the people at his work actually fasted. As his tongue poured out speakable words, others hovered just behind them: *I love you, Salwa, and I heard you are not happy. I will wait for you.* Words that got stuck in his throat and made him feel foolish as he stood alone in his room in the middle of the night with the phone resting against his face.

"Hassan, thank you for calling. I've taken up too much of your time. Please say hello to your mother and your sisters and brothers."

But I'm just getting warmed up! I've not said anything yet, Miss Salwa. I've not asked if you still love pajamas (yes, I know all about your love affair with silky materials). I've not asked if the Americans are cruel to you because you are a Palestinian and a Muslim. And, more important than all that, I have not asked you if you are miserable with your husband and will be returning to me.

"Not at all, Salwa. It is so good to talk to you. To hear your voice."

"It fills my heart to hear from you, Hassan."

"May I call you again?"

"God willing. Goodbye, Hassan."

"Goodbye, Queen of Pajamas. Goodbye, Salwa."

A childish conversation in which nothing was answered. Nothing. A small fortune to answer nothing.

Hassan paced. Walked the perimeter of his room as he imagined Salwa. Was she now as she used to be? Why had she cut off their conversation? Was she in a hurry to be done with him? Perhaps someone else was in the room. He had not asked her if it was a good time to talk. No, there was an echo. He imagined she was driving her white SUV—a Nissan, he had been told. Someone else must have been in the car. Jassim, perhaps. No, if it was Jassim she would have been different.

No way for poor Hassan to know that Salwa was not driving, as he imagined her, but instead had answered the phone while sitting on the toilet in her bathroom at home. That she had thought it might be Randa calling her back. That she would never have picked up if she had known it was Hassan. Not because she didn't want to talk to him, but because she was in such an indecent and miserable state.

Randa moved around the kitchen and family room with the telephone wedged between her shoulder and her ear. She put away stacks of dishes, wiped counters, and picked up miscellaneous items (a handheld electronic game, two magazines, a bowl of beads and some wire, an empty bowl of ice cream) with smoothness and grace. Her ability to tidy a room in just a few minutes impressed her husband, though he never told her so.

She hung up the phone and placed it in its cradle on the counter. "Habibi, I am going to Salwa's. She's not feeling well."

"If she's not feeling well, then why are you going there? She has a husband."

Randa looked at her husband. "Habibi, Salwa is having a miscarriage."

"Her health. I didn't know she was pregnant."

"Nor does her husband."

"How can her husband not know?"

"Because she didn't tell him."

"But why not? He's her husband."

"Do you really want the whole story?"

Munir thought for a minute. "Probably not."

"Okay, then. I don't know when I'll be back."

Munir searched his mind for the precise words he wanted to use. What he really thought was that he did not approve of Salwa Haddad. What he said was, "Salwa has problems." But not wanting to argue, he walked over to his wife. "Randa, you are a good friend to her. Maybe you can solve every last one of them. I'll finish up here." He held her shoulders and looked at her face. She was so easygoing, so giving. How blessed he was not to have married a woman who thought only of herself.

Amazing how blood can be so red, how the body can drain so much and still be alive. Amazing how tiny a person starts out, a delicate muting, a wild secret fusion that blossoms into a someone, a lovely or brutal or perfect or, God forbid, deformed Someone. Amazing as the deep, velvety red pours out in buckets, how in the mass of DNA and tissue and membrane goes Hope.

"I'm bleeding so much—is that okay?" Salwa hissed into the phone.

The emergency room doctor's voice boomed through the receiver. "As long as you're feeling okay, not dizzy, not fainting, not filling more than four pads an hour, and as long as it slows down, say, within the next two hours, then it's okay. If not, just come into the ER."

Just come into the ER, he said, as though it were like stopping by a neighbor's house for tea. Salwa muffled the "off" beep with her hand, though Jassim was nowhere near, and shuffled back to the bathroom, holding her thighs as tightly together as she could, willing the spoiled contents of her uterus to stay put.

Pajamas off in a silky heap, she sat on the toilet to change another pad—the fifth? The sixth? Thankful for that day before the Lie, so many months ago in the supermarket, when she had stared at the blue and yellow and green and pink boxes and packages of pads, designed for heavy flow, medium flow, light flow, overnight, overnight with wings, overnight with flash-flood warnings. After reading box after box and studying picture after picture (thin maxi, regular maxi, extra-long thins), she had taken two boxes of ultra-thin maxis with wings for overnight use for the price of one. It turned out that these pads reached from the middle of her bottom, between her legs, and up practically to her belly button, like diapers.

The first time she used one, she couldn't help laughing. As she unfolded the tidily packaged thin pink envelope, a pad so large that she could barely fit it onto her underwear materialized.

"Were you telling yourself jokes?" Jassim asked when she came out of the bathroom. So she went back and brought a folded pink plastic package and handed it to him.

Jassim turned it over between his fingers. "Lightweight materials," he said, weighing it with his hand. He slipped his finger between the plastic and the adhesive seal and began to unfold it in segments. "What is this? A poster? A magic carpet? An aeronautically engineered washcloth?" He held it up to the light, turned it over and around, while Salwa laughed to the point of tears. He unpeeled the strip and stuck the pad to his hand, wrapped the wings around on either side. "Note the fine adhesive layer, perfect for affixing to any surface. Difficulty holding on to your dustcloth? Well, we have the answer: Super Adhesive Winged Dusters." He took the pad back to the bathroom and poured half a glass of water onto it. Then another. He felt it. He checked for leaks. "They should market these for flood control."

Salwa saw this memory as she stared at the pad that, like the several others before it, was soaked through to its adhesive in bright red. Carefully, so no blood would get on her, she peeled it off and wrapped it in toilet paper and then in a plastic bag before putting it in the trashcan, erasing what evidence she could of the massacre that was taking place within her. Up and into the warm water of the shower, refuge from reality, soothing as she moved her feet apart and let the blood fall out of her in streams and chunks and clumps. Time passed in blood loss, a rivulet, a stream, a torrent, with an occasional mass in between. Salwa stood transfixed, felt like she used to feel when she waited for Jassim at the airport and watched passenger after passenger go by and suddenly, in the middle of a flood of people, there he'd be, a full-grown collection of DNA and tissue and blood, nattily dressed in a suit.

Only this time it wasn't Jassim she was looking for, it was whatever Jassim's sperm had created. Part of her expected a miniature baby to slide by on its way to the drain, to look up at her and wave goodbye with its tiny perfect hand. Five minutes, ten minutes—she had no idea how long she had been standing under the water, over the blood, but she was starting to feel dizzy again, and even though the water was warm—she knew because the arrow pointed to the letter *H*—she couldn't shake the chill from her, as though there were icicles under her skin.

Jassim's voice appeared in a distant fog. "Salwa, habibti, are you okay in there?"

"I'm fine," she called back, pushing cheerfulness into her voice, but she couldn't make it loud enough for him to hear.

"What?"

"I'm fine. I'm just having a really bad period."

Silence.

"Are you in pain?"

"Some pain, but too much bleeding."

Another silence.

"Do you need anything?"

"No thanks. I thought a shower would help." He must have heard the water being wasted, humming through the pipes as he twisted in discomfort, came running to save a few precious droplets as he scolded her in his mind: "Salwa, for God's sake, we live in a desert. We have to be responsible!" He would have to live with it. This was the cleanest way of washing away whatever it was that still remained inside her. "Sorry about using so much water."

"Don't worry about the water. Just don't pass out from the steam."

"Okay. Thanks, habibi."

She heard the door click as Jassim turned away from her and from the corrupted fetus that was sailing down the drain in parts.

I need to lie down, she thought with a panicked urgency.

Even after she turned the water off, the blood still dripped and dropped, splattered on the shiny white porcelain in abstract streaks and dots. Unrolling thick wads of toilet paper, she wiped the diluted mixture of water and blood from the inside of her legs, then dried herself with a thick white towel, careful to keep it clean. She was so lightheaded that she had to sit down on the toilet to paste a super-absorbent pad to her still pristine white underpants, could barely stand up to pull them on as the smell of her blood and insides filled the bathroom, as if she had turned herself inside out. Salwa fought the giddiness in the name of Clean and turned on the vent, squirted antibacterial spray on the bathtub and the walls of the shower, and then rinsed it all away with water. The *ocean-breeze* smell and the noise from the vent and the shower overwhelmed her with an intense heaviness and she struggled to put on her pajamas before staggering back to bed, cell phone in hand.

"There is no god but God. Maybe it will stop if I lie down." She propped herself against pillows and lay still. Nonetheless, she could feel the blood racing out, as if there were a fire in her uterus and all the blood cells were stampeding to escape, could feel the wave of its flow inside her. She picked up the phone and called Randa.

"Habibti, I'm having a miscarriage. Can you come?"

"I'm coming, Salwa. Does Jassim know?"

She clicked her tongue. "He just thinks I'm having a really bad period."

"I'll be there in ten minutes."

Twenty minutes later Randa appeared at her bedroom door.

"Your health, habibti. Are you okay?"

"God protect you, Randa."

"You are so pale. Do you feel okay?"

"Weak. There's so much blood, and it won't stop. It just comes and comes, and I don't know how there can be any left in my body. It's like five periods, and you know my periods are heavy."

"How long now?" Randa sat next to Salwa on the bed and stroked her hair.

"I don't know. Hours. A couple hours maybe." The touch of her friend helped her to relax.

"Heavy the whole time?"

"Chunks of blood. How can blood fall out of you in pieces like that?"

"It's okay. The body is incredible—it's getting rid of corrupted tissue all on its own. Did you try sitting in the tub with the shower on?"

"I stood in the shower, but it made me too dizzy."

"It's better if you sit. Did you call the doctor?"

"I was on hold with the triage nurse for a long time, so I called the emergency room, and the doctor there said if I'm not bleeding too much and if I'm not dizzy and fainting and if it starts to slow down within an hour or two, then it's fine."

"Has it?"

"I don't know. It doesn't seem like it, and I'm still changing pads constantly." As if it were an injury that needed covering and treating. The tears and exhausted sadness that Salwa had been fighting were starting to show through. Randa's fingers loosened the tension in her scalp and were releasing all the wishes that had been stuffed inside.

"Are you okay, sweetie?"

"What can you do? God's will, as they say."

With Randa's help, Salwa got up to sit in the tub and then change her pad again, and then she went back to bed. It was like being home, almost, having Randa there to stroke her hair and help her to the bathroom and with her clothes and hold her up and talk to her. And then she drifted. She was floating on an inflatable bed in a pool of diluted blood. From time to time the bed would bump into a buoyed mass, a baby, a wrecked car, her family. Jassim stood by the side of the pool at a podium and lectured an invisible audience on how wasteful private pools were and how he was proposing a law to make them illegal, proposing to forcibly drain all existing pools. Oblivious of his wife. His fetus. The lost blood.

Randa stayed with her into the night. Out of loyalty, she folded her words of judgment and tucked them under the mattress for later. For now she stroked her friend's hair and took her to the bathroom and helped clean her up. She talked to Salwa's doctor, who was on call.

"I'm in my office by nine-thirty tomorrow. If the bleeding hasn't increased, you can wait and bring her in then. Otherwise take her to emergency."

Randa's fingers rubbed Salwa's head, her back, her hands, reminded her of home and thickened her sadness. Fingers stuffed with centuries of wisdom, knots of history and meaning, somehow accidentally transported to this desert world where life comes in Large, Extra Large, and Enormous, where it is served on plastic trays now, now, now, where synthetic pads can absorb the blood of one lifetime. Those fingers kneaded out what Salwa had been avoiding for close to three years now: that she was not happy in her life. Randa's fingers pushed and prodded, held on tight when the cramping was painful, and wiped away the tears with gentleness. Salwa lay still, a blanket of truth draped over her: this was the life she had chosen, but it was not the life she wanted.

Randa's fingers and hands continued prodding and mopping as Salwa drifted in and out of a soaked sleep, half conscious as the thoughts came up and out of her body. In the redness of her blood she saw the crevice between her and her husband, saw how his life ran right while hers was veering left. She had not realized until now that they were no longer driving in the same vehicle and that his had an eight-cylinder engine to roar him off and up and away while she lay. In bed. In blood.

Sometimes her thoughts came at her too fast, and she closed them out by talking to Randa or whispering prayers. Other times she read them with perfect clarity, saw that when this was all over, if she did not bleed to death, she needed to change the direction of her life. That if Jassim was not ready to have a family, a whole entire complete family, maybe she would turn this into an American story and leave.

And Hassan. She could not bring herself to think of Hassan just now. To wonder why he had called.

Thinking these thoughts under the drunken influence of massive blood loss, Salwa breathed deeper, allowed the sadness out in sobs, and let Randa swish them away. Somewhere in the night, Randa traded places with Jassim, who rubbed her back and spoke to her.

By morning the bleeding had let up quite a bit, but she felt too dizzy to get up.

"I'm not going to work today," she told Jassim as he came and went from the room during his morning routine. And he should not think this odd, as she sometimes had very difficult periods.

"Salwa, do you need to see the doctor?"

There it was, a straight pathway to the real story. But she couldn't make herself say *yes,* couldn't force the words off her tongue. "I think I'm fine. I'll take some medicine and sleep."

The thought of Jassim escorting her to the gynecologist's office as he had for all her routine visits in her first few years in the States was so appealing, so safe, but the Lie had come to life, or come to death, and was bloated between them, preventing her true words from coming out. "If it gets worse during the day, then I'll go. For now I think I'm fine."

"Call me if you change your mind, Salwa." He kissed her on the forehead and left for work.

—ɯ—

Salwa drifted in and out of sleep. Slept and remembered. Remembered her grandmother telling stories while she and her sisters sat bunched up together, huddled with anticipation entwining them. *Kan ya ma kan fee qadeem az-zamaan . . . There was or there wasn't in olden times . . .* a woman who could not get pregnant. Years passed, and her yearning for a baby grew and grew. One day as she was working in her house, she heard a merchant's cry through her window: "Pregnancy apples from the mountain! Pregnancy apples from the mountain!"

She said to herself, *Could there really be an apple for getting pregnant?* and ran outside to see what sort of apples he was selling.

"If you eat one apple, you will become pregnant," the merchant told her, so she bought a large red apple and took it home. Instead of eating it right away, she left it on the counter and went outside to finish her work. While she was gone, her husband came in from the fields and, seeing the apple on the counter, bit into it once, twice, then three times, giant bites that consumed half the apple. He decided to save the other half for his wife.

When she came in and found the apple half eaten, she screamed, "What have you done?"

"What are you talking about?"

"You ate half the apple."

"I saved you half the apple!"

The woman picked up the fruit and finished it off, down to the seeds, but because she had eaten only half, the boy she gave birth to was very tiny, so tiny that people called him Nus Nsays (which in Arabic means *half of a halving*). In spite of his size, his mother was overjoyed. Nus Nsays grew (children in tales always grow quickly), but he remained the size of a very young boy. His hands were tiny, his legs were short, but his voice was loud and strong like the voices of all the other children.

One day one of his friends, the Neighbor's Son, said to him, "Tomorrow I am going hunting on the horse my father bought me."

Nus Nsays said, "I would also like to go hunting."

The Neighbor's Son laughed at him and said, "You? You, Nus

Nsays, are very small. You can't go, because you have no horse
to ride."

Nus Nsays went to his mother and said, "I want a big horse so
I can go hunting."

"But you can't ride a horse, my son. What would you think if I
bought you a goat?"

Nus Nsays was overjoyed when his mother bought him a sweet
small black goat.

The next morning all the townspeople came together to see
Nus Nsays and his big friend leave for their hunting trip. When
they saw Nus Nsays riding a goat and not a horse, they laughed,
but Nus Nsays didn't pay them any attention.

"Good luck hunting, but be careful of the ghula!" the townspeople cautioned the boys.

The Neighbor's Son set forth on his horse and Nus Nsays rode
his goat. When he was out of sight of the villagers, he said,

Fly like an eagle, fly.
Fly, my little goat, fly.

The goat flew in the sky as an eagle would.

When they reached the fields, Nus Nsays chased after three
gazelles and caught them with his rope. As for the Neighbor's Son,
he didn't catch anything. When they returned to the village, they
draped the gazelles over the Neighbor's Son's horse and the people
said, laughing, "Nus Nsays, where are your gazelles?" but he paid
them no mind as he didn't want them to know his secret.

The next morning the two boys set off again, and again when
Nus Nsays was out of sight of the villagers, he said to his goat,

Fly like an eagle, fly.
Fly, my little goat, fly.

The goat flew and the horse ran, on and on to a very distant
place. But this time they lost their way. Just as they were about to
lose hope, an old woman appeared and said, "Welcome. Welcome,

my nephews. I am so glad your fathers sent you to stay with your auntie."

The Neighbor's Son was very happy to have found a relative in such a faraway place, but Nus Nsays whispered a warning in his ear: "That is not your aunt. She is a ghula. Look at the fire coming out of her feet."

The Neighbor's Son refused to listen, so Nus Nsays got off his goat, because he couldn't leave his friend in this time of danger.

The ghula said to the Neighbor's Son, "What does your horse eat and drink?"

"Hay and water with sugar."

The ghula gave the horse some hay and sugar water.

Then she said to Nus Nsays, "What does your little goat eat?"

"The barley residue that's left in a sieve."

"What does she drink?"

"Water. Water in a sieve."

The ghula separated the barley and went to the well to get water for the goat. She scooped the water from the well and poured it into the sieve, and the water went all over the ground. She scooped and poured and scooped and poured, but the water would not stay in the sieve. The ghula became very angry. Sweat was pouring down both sides of her face from all her scooping and pouring, scooping and pouring, from dawn until dusk. She realized that Nus Nsays had played a trick on her.

By the time she got home she was furious, but she tried not to show it and said to the Neighbor's Son. "What does my brother's son eat?"

"Roast chicken."

"And where does he sleep?"

"On the bed."

"And you, you little monkey, what do you eat?"

"Fava beans."

"And where do you sleep?"

"In a hanging basket."

The Neighbor's Son ate roast chicken and slept in the bed. As for Nus Nsays, he munched on fava beans one by one in a basket hanging from the ceiling. When the sound of crunching stopped, the ghula began to sharpen her teeth and said in an ugly voice, "Oh my teeth, oh my teeth. I want to eat these boys."

Just as she was about to eat the Neighbor's Son, Nus Nsays took the last fava bean and broke it between his teeth. The ghula heard the sound and went back to her place on the floor because she knew Nus Nsays was still awake.

She said, "Sleep, Nus Nsays. Sleep, my love. What's wrong that you aren't sleeping?"

He answered her: "How can I sleep? How can I sleep when my tummy is empty?"

The ghula gave him another bowl of fava beans and waited for him to eat them and fall asleep. When she thought that he was finally asleep, she said in her ugly voice, "Oh my teeth, oh my teeth. I want to eat these boys." Just as she stretched out her hand toward the Neighbor's Son, Nus Nsays broke the last fava bean between his teeth.

"Sleep, my eye, sleep, my love. Why don't you sleep?" asked the ghula. "After a bit it will be morning. Sleep, my love."

He said to her, "How can I sleep? How can I sleep? When my tummy is empty?"

She gave him another bowl of fava beans and lay down, pretending to sleep, but she was so tired from all her efforts that she slept as soon as her head rested on the mat.

When the sun came out, the ghula decided that she would eat the boys that night. "I will go get your breakfast ready," she said.

While she was gone, Nus Nsays told his friend what had happened during the night. "Come on, let's go before she comes back," he added. The two boys escaped.

When the ghula returned, the boys had already left. She chased after them, fire coming out of her feet. "If only the hay your horse ate didn't have thorns," she shouted after them. "If only the sugar water I gave him to drink wasn't poisoned!"

The hay thickened into thorns in the horse's stomach and the sugar water knotted in its blood; the horse fell to the ground and couldn't get up. As for Nus Nsays's goat, because she hadn't eaten any barley or drunk any water, she was fine. Nus Nsays said to the Neighbor's Son, "Come on, get on behind me."

Fly, little barley, fly.
Fly, my little goat, fly.

And the goat flew like the wind and left the ghula far behind. When they arrived at their village, the Neighbor's Son told the people what had happened and they understood that Nus Nsays was the one who had saved the Neighbor's Son and that he was the one who had caught the three gazelles. The villagers were pleased by his cunning and bravery.

He said to them, "What would you think if I brought you the ghula?"

"No, no, no. Don't go there again."

"I will bring her. I will catch her for you."

Nus Nsays got a huge box and filled it with sweets. He strapped it to the back of his goat after he painted her white. He arrived at the place where the ghula was and called, "Sweets, sweets..."

The ghula heard his voice and came out. When she saw him, she couldn't believe it, and she said to him, "I know those eyes. Aren't those the eyes of Nus Nsays?"

He said to her, "Who? Nus Nsays? Who is this Nus Nsays? I've never heard of him."

"Isn't this also Nus Nsays's goat?"

And he said to her, "This is not a goat. This is a white sheep." Then he gave her a sweet and said to her, "Taste it, auntie."

She ate it and said, "Give me a little more."

"Go on," he encouraged her. "Eat what's in the box."

She went inside the box to sample the goodies. Nus Nsays closed the lid and returned with her to the village.

"Open up, Nus Nsays. Open up and I'll give you all my gold and silver and money," the ghula screamed.

"I don't want gold or silver or money. I want peace for my village," Nus Nsays replied.

When the villagers saw that Nus Nsays had captured the ghula, they looked at him with surprise. He was standing across from them, and the sun shone on him with his shadow behind him. Even though he was so tiny, his shadow was tall, tall, taller than all of their shadows.

He got on his goat and rode back to his mother.

———

When Salwa was a child, she always asked her grandmother for the meaning behind the stories.

It is just a story.

But what is the point of him being so small?

To show that with determination and a clever wit, small characters can defeat larger evils. Every Palestinian has a bit of Nus Nsays within him. Or her.

Why does the husband eat half the apple?

Her grandmother had two answers for this. When she was feeling kindly toward her own husband, she would say, *Because he's hungry. He's kind too, so he saves some for his wife.* However, if she was irritated, she would tell Salwa and her sisters that it was because he was greedy and couldn't leave well enough alone.

And the ghula? Who is the ghula supposed to be?

This was one question her grandmother never answered.

Now Salwa wondered if her grandmother was somehow warning her. With these confused thoughts filling her head, Salwa slept a sad and washed-out sleep in which yesterday mixed with today. There with here. Here with there. *(But Salwa wasn't anywhere.)*

Maybe this was the fork in the road, a last chance to go right. Or left. A chance to remember the meaning in her grandmother's rustic tales. Too bad that forgetting is so easy, especially for fickle girls in fairy tales.

Chapter Seven

Eyes closed in feigned sleep, Salwa lay under fresh sheets, her mind racing.

More than one week had heaved itself by since blood and baby had escaped from her negligent grasp. More than one week, and sadness ate her from the inside out, a ghula munching and gnawing around an achy skeleton, gobbling all fleshy parts, all except her eyes, which saw everything in hyperdetail. She trudged through these days with a huge damp lump of sadness at the base of her throat, which threatened to explode when she spoke. Now, folded up and breathing unevenly, she rested under the ache as though it were the warmest blanket, as though it could keep her safe forever.

Raw thoughts poked out: exposed toes in winter. *What now?* and *How can I go back to work?* and *What does it matter?* Each one lifting off the safe warmth and letting in cruel gusts. She would tell Jassim; now that the story had a tragic ending, it was much easier to explain.

Dreams packed in a hard-shelled suitcase, dragged to America and shaken carelessly out, no tidy folding or hanging up to prevent wrinkles, no separate plastic sheet to keep them fresh: simply scattered randomly in small heaps across thick carpeting. Each one had been worn, lived in. Lived out. So what was left? This life was the one she had custom-ordered according to her specifications, each bullet point checked off. It was all there, exactly. Almost exactly. Having a baby was a recent addition; it had not been on her original checklist.

She had not thought to fine-tune her wishes, had just assumed that *fulfilling* would come along automatically with *American freedom.* Tucked in the word *freedom,* somewhere near the double *e,* was the code that for a husband to offer his wife the freedom to do as she pleased, his attention would have to be drawn elsewhere. Therein lay the problem—that in Jassim's enthusiasm for his work and in his offer of the life she wanted, he had somehow neglected her.

Or did this have nothing to do with Jassim? Was this all her fault for not marrying the man she loved (had she truly loved Hassan?) and instead marrying the man who had offered her the best opportunity? Or had there been something wrong inside her from the beginning?

The answer clanged through her head with her mother's voice: *The problem is clear: you need to have babies. Women are made to have children. A relationship is strengthened by having children, and a couple who does not have children is unnatural.*

For the past several months it had seemed to Salwa as though she had no other meaning in her life. It was all so difficult to sort out. Her used-up dreams left her empty, wanting for something. Home, perhaps. Familiarity and warmth. Something pure, like the white of milk. Children.

On Monday she had forced herself out of the house, planning to go to work even though she just wanted to lie down all day. As she got closer, the thought made her queasy, and she ended up pulling into the parking lot of a nearby school and sitting in her car. She watched a line of seven children follow a teacher, dutifully traipsing behind her, dirty sneakers and excited sandals slapping tiles as they went, arranged from large to small, fat to thin, loved to unloved. Did love show in shoes? she wondered Could you tell from the scuff marks on a child's shoes how loved or unloved she was? That tiny one at the end, the one with thin blond hair pulled tight into rubber bands, gray bags hanging under her eyes to catch and hide whatever fell—not tears, but maybe a glance, a peek of envy—her boots were too large and too high for a tiny child to wear to school. Didn't they have rules about that? Her walk compensated for their size, so that from the knees up it looked as though she were skiing. Everything could be told through those boots, Salwa felt sure. And if she and Jassim had a baby, how would he or she have fit into that tattered line? There was a raggedness about these American children that unsettled her.

She forced herself away, back to the pristine grocery store near her house where tidily arranged aisles offered fifty choices for every product. Standing in the tea aisle, looking for something soothing, she saw it all clearly, saw how all those orderly cellophaned boxes in pinks and yellows and turquoises were distractions, attempts to shift her focus from any emptiness in her soul. If lived correctly, this American life was deceptively full: a giant house filled with desired items, cars too large to fit in their owners' garages, fine designer clothes to decorate the manicured body and all to cover the shell.

Here she was, Tuesday, stretched out in the dark and staring at the clock: 5:26. And it was all too much. The hopelessness poured out of her eyes and into her pillow; the ache in her stomach and throat was huge and cruel. Green Arabic numerals reminded her that she had at least another twenty minutes to cry before preparing for her husband's return.

Everything in Jassim's day was awry, off-balance, verging on helter-skelter. The unraveling began before dawn: his morning ablutions complete, he coasted down the desert roads from the well-to-do hills to the Fitness Bar, walked quickly past the dreaded Diane, through the building to the pool, and found it circled with yellow tape, as though it were an accident scene and flimsy plastic tape would prevent people from picking up evidence or dropping fibers. Panic crept up Jassim's back, a prickly discomfort settling into his bowels. He walked around the safely protected yellow-taped pool and back into the building.

"Hi, Jassim. I tried to stop you. The pool is closed this morning until nine."

"Why is that?" asked Jassim, his voice tilted while his thoughts rejected the possibility of a police issue, as there were no police. Probably chemical.

Diane looked around like a teenager on the brink of telling a mean secret and then took a step toward Jassim. "Someone pooped in the pool," she spat in a whisper.

Jassim couldn't help himself. He gasped. Wrinkled his forehead. Clicked his tongue as though she would understand his meaning. "An adult?" Because a child pooping in the pool was not so sickening, not so shocking, but an adult...and it must have been an adult, because it had happened in the early hours of the morning. His mind stretched for reasons.

"An adult," replied Diane, her thickly made-up face smooth and smug.

Jassim could see her revulsion, her superiority to such a vile thing, as though the person had done it on purpose.

"Poor person. He must have been very ill to lose control like that."

Diane's lips pushed themselves out slightly, an edge of disgust lining her face. Disgust at the act? Disgust at his sympathy? Hard to tell. "She. And I don't know if she was sick or drunk. Anyhow, they have to blast the pool and let it sit for four hours. Sorry about that." She smiled, no edge, no disgust, just an open smile that to Jassim said nothing.

"Oh well, these things happen," Jassim said, not wanting to go home without achieving balance in the day, vaguely wondering who had to clean up the feces and whether it had floated or sunk.

"They'll be done by a little after nine, or you could come back later in the day."

"I just may do that. Thanks, Diane, and have a good day."

"You too, Jassim." She paused before she spoke, a pause a second or two too long. "If I didn't have to stand at this desk, I would say we could go for a cup of coffee."

But Jassim had already started walking off, had closed the conversation, and decided to pretend he did not hear her. Left her words on the floor behind him, hoping he wouldn't slip on them the next time he came.

Walking out to the parking lot, Jassim weighed his options. He could go back to the gym and exercise, though this wasn't really a possibility, because he hated exercising with other people. He could go for a run or walk along the wash by the gym, but this was not appealing, as the area wasn't very safe and he hadn't brought running shoes. He could go home and take a walk or run. That sounded tolerable. So he drove back up the hills in twelve minutes and pulled into his driveway. Moving on silent feet, he flicked on the hall light in front of their bedroom door, and then an unfamiliar sound, a sobbing sound, startled him. He opened the door completely and found Salwa curled in a ball and sobbing so hard that she didn't even notice the brightness from the hallway or his unscheduled arrival. Prickles crept up his back, and he stood for another second before going to her.

"Salwa, habibti. What's wrong? Did something happen back home?" That was the only logical reason for her to be crying at this time of day. Someone must have called.

Salwa started visibly. Jassim put his hand on her head and smoothed her hair back.

"No, it's nothing like that, Jassim. It's nothing. I thought you went swimming."

"I did plan to go swimming, but when I got there the pool was closed. You won't be able to imagine why."

"Why?"

"Someone defecated in it."

Salwa's face twitched. "Who would do that?"

"I think it was someone who was sick. So I thought I would come home and go running instead, and I came to get my shoes and I found you here crying. What's the matter?" And why do people say "nothing" when it is clearly something? Is it so you won't ask and will just believe them, or is it so you'll ask more because you really don't believe them? Human beings were baffling creatures, and Jassim was unsettled, now feeling very off-balance. And he wanted to turn off the light in the hall. Salwa was not a woman who cried, and certainly not this kind of crying, crying unattached to someone's death or illness. Jassim didn't know what to do with it, how to wash it away.

"Oh Jassim, I'm so sorry." Salwa turned her face into the pillow.

"Sorry? For what? Has something happened?"

She sobbed a bit more and then turned over. "Jassim. I feel awful, and I wasn't going to tell you why because it will probably upset you very much, but it's worse saying nothing."

"What is it, habibti?"

Salwa sat up, repositioned the pillows, safe and sniffling in the soft darkness. Silence. Deep breath for Salwa. Two silent swimming breaths for Jassim. A mangled Kleenex knotted itself between her delicate hands, and while Jassim tried to stare at them, at her, the light from the hall was seeping into his consciousness, adding to his unease. "Jassim, I was pregnant. I miscarried. I didn't have a really bad period, I had a miscarriage. I am sorry that I lied to you. I think the pills made me sick, so I stopped taking them. I didn't want to upset you at first about being pregnant, and then all of a sudden I was miscarrying."

Jassim's mind stretched. That was two weeks ago? Last week? "Salwa, habibti. Are you okay, your health?"

"I'm fine. Now I'm fine, thank God. I'm fine."

Jassim leaned forward and embraced his wife, held her deeply, for he had no words to offer her and he recognized that the crisis was over. Her lie, her pregnancy, her miscarriage, had all worked themselves out without his having to say anything, decide anything, so it was not so hard to give himself to her. He would think about it later, process what it meant that she had gotten pregnant (on purpose or by accident?) and not told him (to protect him or because she was scared he would get mad because she had done it on purpose?), but for now he could console her. He felt warmth in holding her, in being able to offer her comfort. After all, he was not a man given to irrational loss of control or anger. It was not anger that he felt, either. It was . . . nothing that he felt. That would come, when he had time to think about it more, but for now he would hold his wife, as that seemed the right thing to do.

Walking across the parking lot, Italian leather against American asphalt, Salwa felt as if her skin had been peeled back, so she had no safe layer between her most private self and this alien public world in which she lived.

Stepping inside the building, she shortened the conversations of her coworkers with only the most necessary of words.

"You feeling better?" Because they all thought she had been out with a stomach virus.

"Yes, thank you."

"Nice to have you back." Because what else could they say?

"Thank you."

Her self had gone down the drain with her blood and the invisible fetus. What she felt now was beyond sadness, was closer to numbness. The interest she had in this job, this life, had evaporated, floated off, leaving her lodged in an American bank to pay for her sins.

"Welcome back," said a man's voice, fresher than the others, thought Salwa with her back to him. That thought was so slim that it vanished as quickly as it came.

"Thank you," she said, putting down her bag and turning.

Jake, the part-time teller, part-time college student, stood watching her, a more subdued version of his usual smile decorating his face. Close up, he was shorter than he seemed from a distance.

"How are you, Jake?"

"Oh, I'm fine. I missed you, though."

"You did?" she asked, an automatic question for an out-of-place answer.

"Mm-hmm." He leaned against the doorframe that separated her from the rest of the tellers.

"That's always nice to hear."

"Salwa, could I tell you something?" He turned his lips in to moisten them.

"Sure, Jake, what is it?" *Say it and go,* she willed him.

He looked behind him and then down at his thick hands. "I don't want you to take this in a bad way, because I don't mean it in a bad way."

Salwa felt a twist inside her. "Go ahead, say it."

"Okay, promise you won't get mad?"

"Ooof, what could you possibly have to say that would make me mad?" She didn't like the way her voice sounded, almost as if she were speaking to a small child. "Just say what you have to say." She smiled, hoping that would take the edge from her voice.

Still leaning against the doorframe, he looked directly into her eyes. "I just wanted to say that I think you are beautiful. I mean, on the outside you are beautiful, but as a person especially. I like how you are with people, even when you disagree with them. You show a lot of integrity, and I've learned from watching you. I wanted to tell you that before, and then you were gone and there was a hole somehow. I just wanted to tell you that." He turned up his palms, as if in the midst of prayer. "That's all."

She stood looking at him, at a loss for just a moment.

"And you thought I'd be mad to hear that? That's very sweet of you, Jake. Really. It's a nice way to come back. Thank you." Public face. Public thank-you for such intimate words.

"Okay, back to work then. Have a good day."

"You too."

Jake pushed himself off the doorframe and walked away.

Salwa stared at the back of him, at the way he almost swaggered when he walked, the way athletes did when their bodies were forced to slow down and assume day-to-day life. Nine years in America, and such words had never been for her before. And for the tiniest sliver of a second, she forgot what had kept her home for more than one American workweek. What she had finally told her husband. Now it came back in a torrent, the part of herself that she had lost, that was gone forever.

Once a day has shifted off-kilter as badly as this one had, there is almost no way to get it back, not even by retracing exactly the steps taken, unraveling and reraveling (was *raveling* a word? or was *respun unraveling*'s opposite?) the knotted yarn. Turning off the lights left on. By early afternoon Jassim's unease was physically uncomfortable, and while work was going well, intrusive office activity was adding to his discomfort. He was on track with his own projects, ahead of schedule in fact, and had settled down at his desk, attempting to create a graph that would represent the success of their reclaimed-water irrigation project, when Corey came in.

"Did you change the toner cartridge in the printer?"

"Hi, Corey." Jassim had been printing off and on all day. Yes. Now he remembered. "I had to print and it came out half printed and half not. It seemed it was a matter of shaking the toner, so no, I didn't change it, but I did take the toner cartridge out and shake it. Why? Is it broken?"

"No, it's fine, but Lisa would prefer that you go to her or to Bella if you have a problem. It's their job to deal with those machines, and we have to let them do it."

"Sorry, Corey. I'll go apologize directly." Jassim said this half-jokingly. He could not believe that Corey wouldn't see the humor in not allowing the engineers to touch the office equipment and instead leaving it to the secretaries with high school diplomas. And when had Corey become their spokesperson?

"That's all right. I'll take care of it. Just let them know if there's a problem in the future."

"Certainly," Jassim said.

Corey walked out as Marcus stepped into his office. "Are you pissing off the conservative right again, Jassim?"

"Apparently. I overstepped my boundaries and shook the toner."

"He came in to talk to you because you shook the toner?"

"It would seem so. What do you think he would do if he knew I opened the copy machine and cleaned it instead of having the repairman come?"

"Report you to the FBI for tampering with government equipment." Marcus laughed. "Sorry. That was in poor taste." He pushed his hands deep into his pockets. "So we're squared away for today. Report's in. Meeting's postponed. Toner's shaken. I say we take off for the day."

"That would be good. I didn't get my morning swim today."

"Take off early, why don't you, and swim."

"I want to finish this graph. Maybe when I'm done."

"Well, I'm taking off. Picking the kids up from school for a change and going for a hike." Marcus stood grinning with his hands in his pockets and looked to Jassim like a large boy.

"Take care, Marcus. Have a nice hike."

Jassim had hiked a bit when he had first come to Tucson. Cornelia had been crazy about hiking. Once he had tried to take Salwa, but she had already softened, become more sensitive to the outdoors, preferred the mall. On this bright cool day, hiking sounded appealing. Jassim decided to ask Salwa, to see if maybe she would want to go for a hike on the weekend. Salwa, whom he had last seen this morning. It came back now, her miscarriage, and Jassim was unsettled all over again.

At two-thirty he decided that he *would* take off early, as his boss had suggested, and go swimming. The thought had rolled around his mind in the morning, when Salwa had been sobbing, when he had realized that there was no way he could leave in the middle of it to go running, though if he had been able to do that, everyone would have been better off. No, instead he had thrown his already packed and prepared gym bag in the car, just in case. Just-in-case was here, and he left the office with a goodbye (*No, I don't have a meeting*) to Bella and headed toward the Fitness Bar to retrieve some equilibrium in his life.

The Fitness Bar was a different place in the afternoon than it was in the morning. The most noticeable difference was the sheer number of people, many of them teenagers, who were milling around. Where normally Diane sat alone at the front desk, now there were three just-past-teenagers (Generation X? Y?), who took his membership card with a much too friendly hello. The pro/gift/snack shop (and who ever heard of a gift shop in a gym?) was open, and a whisper-thought suggested that he go and see if it had something nice for Salwa. A shouting thought told him to keep walking. He stored the whisper-thought away for later, decided he would stop in before he left.

In the dressing room, out of his work clothes, which he hung in an unlocked locker and hoped no one would take, and into his Speedo, he took his gym bag with him to walk to the pool (no way would he leave wallet and car keys in an unlocked locker). Going out into the afternoon, he was shocked to see that two lanes had been opened for a free swim and that they were teeming with people, mostly children. In December. His feet moved slowly. All the lanes but one were occupied, and that one was on the east side, the faster side. He didn't care. The beauty about swimming, a physical activity in a defined space, was that the mind could wander over any topic and didn't interfere with the body's movement; it didn't work that way in a shared lane.

Jassim stretched and slid into the pool, which was kept at a brisk 79 degrees, and felt himself calming, let the prickles fall away and drown in the chlorinated water. His first lap was rushed by the cold, but his mind relaxed as the tension crept from his pores and floated off to be chlorinated into oblivion. His thoughts wrapped around Salwa. Clear thoughts held her in firm tentacles and analyzed the situation. Salwa pregnant. Yes, she had mentioned wanting to have a baby numerous times, and he had told her his feelings about it, and he hadn't really thought that she was serious. Once recently she had asked him directly if he wanted to have children soon, and he had refused to discuss it. But it was not so much an adamant refusal on his part as that on that particular day he didn't want to talk for the sake of talking. Hypothetical conversations were ridiculous, accomplished nothing, consumed thought and emotion. Yes, that had been the day when he had overheard Corey at work talking about "crazy Mahzlims."

Stroke, stroke, stroke...It was all clear in his head, a tiny DVD player putting him in that moment when he had been on the brink of telling Salwa about Corey and she had come up with her prattle about having a baby. And that is what he had wanted to tell her, but somehow he had gotten lost in her chattering and then irritated, and then reminded of his coworker and then distracted to the point where he couldn't talk about anything.

Stroke, stroke, stroke...The tension was going; his breath was hard to come by, and he slowed himself.

So that must have been it—she must have brought up the conversation because she was pregnant and was looking for a way to tell him, only he had not waxed and polished the doorway for her to come in smoothly and tell him the truth. She had not lied about being pregnant, then, had just not told him about it at all, which was really the same. And then she had lied about having a really bad period. And that was why Randa had come and stayed with her most of the night. That was why she had stayed home from the weekend outings that they usually took together, why she had looked as though she were getting sick. Amazing how having one tiny bit of information was the key to the whole puzzle. How it suddenly gave you the ability to put all those other misplaced pieces in their appropriate spots.

A miscarriage. Jassim could not fathom having a helpless baby in the house. Humans were so odd, to give birth to creatures that were totally powerless and dependent for so many years. Evolutionarily speaking, it was amazing anyone survived. At this point, there was no way their lives could accommodate a child, since they had no family around to help. Had Salwa really wanted a child, or had this been an accident? He knew she was taking birth control pills, both for contraception and to help regulate her periods. If the birth control pill was 99 percent effective, that would mean that one out of one hundred women would get pregnant. Possible. Possible, but unlikely. But she said that she had stopped, that the pills had made her sick. When had she stopped? He mulled this over for several laps and was out of breath enough to have to stop, take a *good hard look* at the story in front of him. He had made it seem that he was opposed to having children, but in fact he was opposed to women having children simply because they got married. Over time, perhaps he had hardened this stance. Had gotten used to their lives together, to her loving him exclusively. Perhaps he needed to *come clean,* tell her that he just wanted her to have all the opportunity she wished for so that she would not look back on her life with regret.

He stood in the pool for a couple of minutes before getting out.

Out of the pool, he was aware of his bathing suit and aware that this was America, where men did not wear Speedos unless they were serious swimmers, which he did not consider himself to be. Drying himself, he also became aware that his tiny hand towel wouldn't cover him as he took the long trek to the men's shower room.

Voices and steam filled the bright shower room, along with the smell of mildew and feet. This place was not for the fastidious, Jassim thought as he looked at the wet floor and soggy benches. Water on, shower curtain closed, Speedo off and rinsed out. Jassim stood with his eyes shut, allowing the water to hammer out his tension, wondering if this is what Salwa had done that day when she was in the shower for what seemed like hours. Even with the water pouring over him and steam floating off, he felt unsettled, as though he'd not yet discovered the secret of her sobbing. She seemed so sad, so out of control. He would have to find out the whole story, because he knew somewhere beneath his skin that there was more to it than what he was seeing.

The locker room surrounded him with voices and hums and buzzes of chatter and banging lockers. Jassim felt invisible as he dressed, deposited his wet Speedo and hand towel into a plastic bag. It was just before four o'clock; he would have time at home to read.

"Hello there," bellowed a voice from behind him.

Jassim turned around, remembered the face, and felt his stomach flip.

"I wondered if I'd run into you again—I don't usually swim in the morning, and it seems you don't normally swim in the afternoon. Jack Franks, remember?"

"Hi, Jack. Jassim Haddad. Of course I remember." He held out his hand, and their handshake was firm, a deal made, agreed upon, and closed.

"How have things been for you? You and your family okay?"

Jassim nodded. "Fine, thanks."

"You know, I talked to that lady at my bank about you. Salwa. She said it sounded like I was talking about her husband."

Jassim looked at him with what he hoped would be a blank, uncomprehending expression. He remembered their conversation verbatim. Remembered his own denial that he knew the woman at the bank. Did not like to see his wife's name in the mouth of another man, especially one as tactless as Jack Franks.

"Remember? I told you about a lady I knew at my bank who was from Jordan and asked if you knew her?"

"Sorry. I remember you asking if my wife was veiled. I don't remember you asking about a woman at your bank." Jassim lied what seemed like a safe, social lie.

"Well, the showers were on—maybe you didn't hear me."

What does it matter? Jassim wanted to say. *I have a right to my private life as much as anyone.* But he didn't say these things. "I guess not," he replied. "How have you been?"

"Very well, thanks. Tucson is a small town. Salwa Haddad is my banker and your wife."

My banker and your wife. "Nice to see you again, Jack."

"Likewise."

Jassim shook Jack's hand again and walked out of the dressing room, all of the relaxation of his swim gone, replaced by the awkwardness of being caught in a lie that he had not meant to tell, by a man who unsettled him with his boldness.

—⟡ ⟡—

Salwa walked through the bank lobby and felt the eyes on her, felt the stares gluing themselves to her bottom, her hair, wished she could unpeel them, flick them back at their owners with a smack. She had walked through this lobby a thousand times, but being gone and coming back, she was too aware of herself, couldn't figure out what people were thinking.

She spent her afternoon counting out hundreds of dollars in small bills.

"Excuse me."

Salwa looked up. Standing in front of her was a woman in her mid-forties with short frosted blond hair. Her large head rested directly on her shoulders—she looked as though her neck had been removed. She wore a matching oversized maroon shirt with a sailboat on the chest and stretchy knit pants, both virtually identical in color to the carpeting on the bank's floor.

"Hello. May I help you with something?" asked Salwa over the safely locked barrier that divided merchant telling from civilian telling.

"I want to make some deposits?"

"Sure. A business account?"

"Oh no, it's a personal account."

Salwa looked at the short line of customers waiting for an available teller and then toward the customer service desk. Jake was talking to someone and must not have realized that she handled only merchant accounts and the personal accounts of a few old clients. If they got extra-busy, she would come out to work at a different desk, but he should never send a personal client into the merchant section. Deciding that she would discuss it with him later, Salwa buzzed the woman in and extended her hand. "Certainly. My name is Salwa. Have a seat." She gestured.

The woman sat down, her eyes fixed on Salwa's face.

Salwa sat back down behind the desk and cleared her computer screen.

"What are we doing for you today?"

"I have a question about my savings account." The woman continued to stare at her as though Salwa's face were interrupting her thoughts.

"Ma'am, is everything all right?"

"Oh yes. I'm fine. Sorry. Could I ask you a question first?"

"Sure. Go ahead."

"Where are you from?" asked the woman.

"I am Palestinian from Jordan."

The woman continued to look at her. Chewed it over. Spat it back out. "What does that mean?" she asked, her thin lips pursed.

Salwa's perfect eyebrows lifted. "What does what mean?"

"What do you mean that you are Palestinian from Jordan?" *Does it mean you will steal my money and blow up my world?*

"It means that my parents are Palestinian but that I was born and raised in Jordan, because my parents were refugees. They were kicked out of their homes in 1948 when the state of Israel was established. Where are you from?" Salwa smiled her sweetest smile, the one that would force her to believe that this woman was only asking out of curiosity, would force her racing heart to speak with professionalism instead of anger.

"Here, born and raised. I'm a native Tucsonan, American born and raised."

The women stared at each other.

"What is the name on the account, ma'am?" Salwa asked with a professional smile, all emotions hidden.

The unnamed woman still looked at her with a stony face and thinking eyes. "I think I'd like to work with someone else."

Salwa's heart thudded in anger, and she willed her blood to stay calm, to keep away from her face. Her perfect English puddled on the floor, her manners and kindness all scattered and soggy.

"And is there any particular reason for that, ma'am?"

"I think I'd feel more comfortable working with someone I can understand better."

"Of course. Would you like to work with a Mexican man or an American lesbian?" The words that slid out were angry and unprofessional, words that were meant to stay silent.

The woman's angry eyes hooked onto her. Salwa stared back, pushing the woman away. The woman stood up and huffed, "You're out of line, lady."

"No, you're out of line. But you are welcome to speak with our manager," said Salwa, honey sweet and gesturing toward Bill, who had caught her eye earlier and now stood at the door.

The woman's gaze followed her gesture, tripped over Bill's face. Salwa couldn't help but smile. Both Bill's parents were Chinese.

The woman turned back. "I don't want anything to do with you people," she stuttered, and walked out. Bill followed, and Salwa's body caught up with her thoughts, her heart pounding out too much blood, making her dizzy with all its racket.

"Salwa? What in the world was that all about?" Petra poked her head in the door.

"It was nothing."

"No. Really. What happened?"

When it was clear that Petra was not leaving, Salwa told her. "She asked where I was from. I said Palestinian from Jordan. She asked what that meant. I explained. She said she was American born and raised and that she wanted to work with someone else, someone she could 'understand better.' I asked her if she'd prefer a Mexican man or an American lesbian, or if she wanted to talk to our manager."

"Bill. Who's Chinese. You really said that?"

"Mm-hmm. It seemed that if she was picking her banker by background, then she should know what she was getting up front."

"You go, girl. That took guts."

"I hope you don't mind." Smile folding to one side, eyes looking away, fighting the tickle inside.

"Mind? Not at all. Besides, this isn't about me, and I'm really sorry that happened to you." Petra came in and put her hand on Salwa's back. "That kind of person has problems, and it has nothing to do with you, even though she makes it seem like it has everything to do with you. Salwa, are you okay?"

"I'm fine."

Jake stepped in. "Why did Bill take that woman to his office?"

"Because she was rude and inappropriate to Salwa and Bill is such a peacemaker it's gross and now he's going to make everything better at the expense of what's right." Anger edged Petra's voice.

"But what did she do?"

Salwa repeated the story, wishing that Jassim were there and remembering the recently liberated Lie that sat between them. She squeezed her fingers.

"Why did you have her anyway?" asked Petra. "You only do merchants." Petra looked at Jake. "You didn't know that she only does merchants at this window?"

"Oh my God. I am so sorry. I forgot. Everyone else was busy, and I was trying to be efficient."

"It's okay. No harm done. Excuse me," Salwa said in the middle of her own words. She got up, walked past her coworkers, past the stares and the words, let them all fall gently onto the lush maroon carpeting, disconnected and unimportant.

—◌ ◌—

The surge Jassim felt when he put his foot on the accelerator dupli-
cated itself internally; he and the car were One, a complex, powerful machine capable of racing on the autobahn, of speeding to
the scene of any disaster, of escaping the mundane. *Slow down,
slow down,* whispered a voice. Eyes on the speedometer, and a distant whisper willing the needle to move down instead of up. As he
drove, the pleading continued, an interloper trying to separate man
and car. As the speedometer crept down, the car slowed to the slug-
gish driving standards demanded by the city: roads made for 45
miles an hour or more were given a 35-mile-an-hour speed limit at
best, sometimes even 30 in the center of the city.

Jassim could see up the gently curved road for a distance, and
registered two figures on skateboards.

His stomach clenched. Jack Franks had unsettled him. Again.
The unease pulled his right foot up from the accelerator, pulled the
needle down to 33, under the speed limit by 2 miles an hour. The
nagging persisted, a greedy squid yanking at his brain and stomach.
Perhaps it's not Jack Franks. Jassim reviewed his day, searching for
the lost item, the missing clue. *Have I forgotten something?* This
thought swung back and forth through his mind as he approached
the two skateboarders...*An appointment?*...Both were tall, both
wore dark clothes...*A birthday?*...The one in front had black
hair, and the one in back had no hair at all...*A phone call?* Skin
went cold with panic. *Salwa had a miscarriage.* For the briefest moment he had forgotten, completely forgotten.

The distance between him and the figures ahead closed in short
seconds. His chest tightened with dread, forcing his foot to ease off
the accelerator even more, moving it over to pump the brake instead. The needle hovered at just under 30.

The boys rode along the side of the road, but not smoothly.
The one in front swerved erratically. His head drooped forward as
he glanced behind him, once, twice, and again, zigzagged, moved
crookedly, swerving from the edge to a third of the way into the
road, stretching and contracting the distance from his friend. The
second boy pushed off and rode tall, his arms by his sides.

Jassim approached, sweat occupying the space between his

hands and the polished steering wheel, the first sign that he and the car were not really One. Registered in Jassim's brain were a car quite a distance away, coming toward him in the opposite lane, and a car some distance behind him, allowing him the room to pull left, which would give the boys the full five feet suggested for bike riders.

Closer, and he could see them more clearly: the droopy one in front had his black hair in spikes and wore baggy black pants with what looked like thousands of safety pins along the legs. The other boy smiled as he rode. He also wore a black T-shirt and pants. *Salwa had a miscarriage.* Jassim's conscious and semiconscious thoughts were colliding, creating a heady, almost blinding panic. Deep breath. Hold it. Exhale. One more time. Two breaths.

Two breaths: the length of time it took for Jassim's life to swerve off the autobahn and onto an American frontage road.

Both boys moved faster than Jassim would have thought possible. Almost even with him, the stooped boy in front looked up at Jassim through reflecting blue sunglasses.

For some time to come Jassim would remember that face, the blue lenses becoming larger and larger in his memory. In the breath of a butterfly, the boy turned his head away again, not facing forward but drooping, as though his neck were made of rubber. He then pushed off and jumped, propelling himself straight into the front of Jassim's car. Jassim swerved left, felt a sickening *thunk,* and watched as the boy flipped over the hood. The oncoming car in the other lane was suddenly in front of him and he had to swerve to avoid it. Movements he would review for a lifetime to come.

For three or four seconds sound stopped, only to return at full volume, filling Jassim's ears and stomach as he pulled the car to the shoulder, aware even at this awful moment of the smoothness and silence in the handling of his car. Turning around in his seat to look, he felt his heart slamming against the shell of his body. The boy lay in a motionless heap; his friend was running toward him. A shaky hand reached for the door; the other took the keys, dropped them into a loose, roomy pocket, and removed the cell phone that sat on his left hip. Trembling fingers, too large for the tiny keypad, pressed

911 as his body took lightning steps to the boy. Traffic stopped, people ran and shouted, and Jassim's world spun and banged as he squatted next to the boy, dropped on his knees to put his head to the boy's chest, fingers to his neck. The boy's eyes flickered at him for a second (when did his sunglasses fall off?), pasting Jassim's face on his pupils to take with him wherever he was going.

"Nine-one-one operator. Your location, please."

"I'm on River just east of Swan." East of Swan. Or west? "West of Swan. I've just hit a boy with my car and it seems that he is unconscious." He was not sure still whether they were east or west of Swan.

"An emergency team will be right there. Is he breathing?"

The boy's chest was not moving, but his eyes had just been open, so he must be breathing.

"Barely. Should I move him or do CPR?"

"No. Don't touch him. Don't move him. Ambulance is on its way. Just hold on, sir."

Jassim stroked the boy's head, knowing deep in his self, all the way down to his toes, that it was useless. "Hold on, young man. The paramedics are coming. Hold on. Try to breathe," he said to the slumped figure, more for his own comfort than for the boy's. Even before he slid his hand to the boy's neck again and felt nothing, he knew that the boy was gone, had left this world for good, and behind that thought was the knowledge that the boy had done it on purpose and used him.

It was then that Jassim registered the boy's friend and the other people and the chattering.

A woman's voice called, "Is he all right? Someone call nine-one-one!"

And a man's answered, "No. I already called them."

Circles of helplessness.

And the other boy's voice: "Shit. Oh, shit. Evan. Come on. Wake up. Shit. Shit." He squatted on the other side of him.

"Don't move him at all," Jassim said, trying to be calm, trying to be reassuring.

The friend looked at him, absorbing his words, touching the

boy's side. "Shit. Come on, Evan. Don't die, Evan." The boy had no hair except for a tiny tuft at the base of his neck, which Jassim thought looked obscene.

"It's going to be all right," Jassim said, saying words he did not believe, trying to make that ultimate jump into American life, the one that promises a happy ending for everyone if you just believe it hard enough. The friend slumped on the other side of Evan, shaking and crying. More people, more noise, the world's banging escalated as Jassim kept talking to Evan, still patting his head, holding his hand, the way he would for his own son if he had one. "Be strong for your friend." Deep breaths, swimming breaths. Force calm, calm, calm. Let none of this be happening. *Dear God, let this be a nightmare.*

Jassim was aware of people and noise and sirens as he crouched next to the figure, the shell. The boy was in his late teens at most. He lay on his side, but his neck was at an impossible angle.

"Paramedics!" Jassim moved, or was moved by the rushing people who came to clean up this American disaster scene. A woman touched his back as she took his place.

"He's not breathing," Jassim offered.

"Step back, sir." She spoke firmly, commanding him away. The paramedic put her hand under the boy's head very gently. At her side were two men, both dressed in blue, both with *Tucson Fire* stenciled in white on the back of their shirts. They moved around him in a blur of blue shirts and rubber gloves, finally sliding him onto a stretcher, holding tight so his bones would not shift.

"Excuse me, sir," a voice next to him said. Jassim turned and found a police officer at his side. "Are you all right?"

"I think so. He's dead, isn't he?"

"Too early to determine. We'll let those folks work their magic."

"He's a child." Jassim was aware that these sentences belonged to a young person, had been uttered in the hope that some kind cartoon genie would hear them and come to change their order, change the events, undo what was done. The panic Jassim had felt just before the accident was back, and he felt his neck stiffen, his head throb, as though all the blood that had stopped was now pumping in super-time. Police were everywhere, and Jassim began to sway.

"Sir, I need to get a statement from you. Are you up to that, or would you like to have the paramedics check you out first?" Jassim stared at the police officer, filtering his words and trying to make sense of them.

"Sir, let's go this way and I'll get your statement." The officer gently but firmly placed his hand under Jassim's elbow, the way you would help an old person who might lose his balance. He guided Jassim through a maze of mayhem to a police car, opened the passenger door, and had him sit down. "Sir, my name is Officer Barkley. I need to see your license and registration."

Jassim leaned right to pull his wallet from his left pocket. Slid his license out and handed it to Officer Barkley. "The registration is in the glove box."

The officer spoke into the microphone that came off his shoulder, read Jassim's license number into, it and then spoke directly to him. "Sir, are you on any kind of medication?"

"No. I don't use medicine."

"Anything that would make it difficult for you to drive a car?"

"No."

"Okay, Mr. Haddad—did I say that right?"

"You did."

"Okay, Mr. Haddad, I need for you to tell me what happened."

Jassim leaned his head forward and took two deep breaths, swimming breaths, before he recounted the details that promised to alter his life for good.

"I was driving east, as you can see, and slowed with the speed limit. I remember that, remember thinking that this is a thirty-five-mile-an-hour zone. As I was driving I kept thinking that I had forgotten something, and that made me drive slower. I saw the two boys up ahead." For all the years his tongue had been using English to communicate, he now found it difficult to work through, standing at the end of each sentence and translating it back to make sure he said what he had wanted to say. "Really, how stupid—I mean, that's what I thought. The one was doing loops, zigzags out into the road, as though this were a schoolyard and not a narrow two-lane road with curves and blind spots. When I got close to them, they were back by the edge and I pulled out at least five feet—you know how they say you should give a bike five feet? Well, that's what I tried to do, only as I was doing it, the one boy just came out, but he looked at me first, like he planned to do it, or like he thought he would do something else, like jump over the car, only he ended up going right into it. And then there was a thud and I tried to swerve and I swerved back because there was a car coming and I pulled over and he was lying there and I called nine-one-one." Jassim gasped a bit.

"So you were into the other lane when you hit the boy?"

"I was halfway in the other lane when he jumped out toward me. I saw the car coming from in front, so I swerved back. I hit him when I was in the other lane. He came out far, diagonally toward my car."

"So you hit him before you swerved back?"

"Yes. Here, let me show you." Jassim leaned over the dirt and with his finger traced two curvy parallel lines for the road. "These two curves are the hills." He placed two small pebbles at one end of his diagram. "These are the boys. This is what they were doing before I was close to them." Here Jassim held one pebble in each hand. The pebble in the back moved straight, but the one in the front looped into the road and back. "This is my car," he said, picking up a small rock and making a faint line to show the divide between the lanes. "I drove like this. When I got about here I began to pull out." The car rock was eight inches from the first pebble. He placed two other rocks at either end of the road. "These were the other cars that I saw. Neither was close to me. I pulled out, and when I was almost parallel with the first boy"—here the rock and first pebble were on a slight diagonal—"he looked straight at me." Jassim drove the rock with his left hand and the front pebble with his right. "And he shot out like this." The front pebble veered toward the rock, which Jassim pulled further to the left. "What I don't understand is how the car in front was suddenly here. That is when I swerved back." Jassim pulled the rock over. "I wonder if maybe another car came from somewhere else." Here Jassim did not trip over his words. It was simple, *a piece of cake,* to explain a physical event with the help of visual aids to keep from getting lost in the words.

He sat up, but felt dizzy and leaned so his right side rested against the seat.

Officer Barkley had a notepad and his license. "Your name is just as it is on your license: first name J-A-S-S-I-M, last name H-A-D-D-A-D?"

"Yes, Jassim Haddad."

"Mr. Haddad, where were you coming from just now?"

"I go to the Fitness Bar to work out—to swim, actually—and I was coming back. This is not my normal time to swim. Usually I go in the early hours of the morning, but the pool was closed" —something kept him from explaining to Officer Barkley why the pool was closed—"and my day was not going too well, so I thought going for a swim might help. You know, the body gets used to being treated a certain way, doing certain things, and then when you stop it is unsettled, off-balance."

"Why was your day not going well?"

Jassim rewound to the beginning of the day, wishing he could record over the events. A moment of caution kept him from going into detail, kept him from giving Officer Barkley details of his wife's miscarriage. "I think it was just that unsettled feeling, that I needed to exercise."

"Have you had a drink of alcohol today?"

"No, sir."

"But you were upset when you were driving?"

"Just now? No. When I say my day was not going well, there were no disasters or major problems. My boss suggested we leave early, so I thought I would go swimming."

"Would you stand up for me, sir, with your arms out, and stand on one foot."

"You're joking."

"No, sir. It's standard procedure."

Jassim stood, stretched his arms out, and lifted one foot.

"Good. You can sit down again. Mr. Haddad, have you used any recreational drugs in the past forty-eight hours?"

"I don't use recreational drugs. Am I going to be arrested?"

"Mr. Haddad, I need to check with the other officers who are processing the scene." Officer Barkley gestured at the huddle of police. "For now, sit tight. Do you want to call anyone to come and be with you or to drive you home?"

Jassim was aware that these two statements contradicted each other. Or in the one the mystery of the second was dissolved. No, he would not be arrested.

"No. I'm fine, thank you," Jassim answered, as though Officer Barkley had asked him if he wanted an iced tea or soda.

"I'm going to have a paramedic come and check you out now, and then I'll come back. Why don't you sit tight for a few more minutes?"

Jassim wrapped himself around the phrase *sit tight*, trying to attach a literal meaning to its figurative connotation. He settled himself, but he was not *sitting tight*, he was slouched and trying to breathe. Instead of facing the dirt and the desert, he turned himself to face forward, sank back in the passenger seat of Officer Barkley's patrol car as though he were watching a film of emergency vehicles clustered together and busy figures bustling among them. The street had been closed off: more yellow tape to prevent contamination. Jassim counted six police officers, five firefighters, and three people who were somehow involved. He also saw several people standing, watching, who seemed to have nothing to do with the accident. Perhaps they were friends or acquaintances or passengers of the other drivers the police were talking to. What other reason could they have for being there? Jassim tried to pick out Officer Barkley. He was taller than the other officers, bulkier. As he sat, a moviegoer, viewer, minus popcorn and a soda, one of the firefighters, a woman, walked toward the police car in which he sat, already another person.

"Are you okay, sir?" she asked in a large, safe voice. "I need to check you out, okay? You can stay sitting, but could you turn this way a bit?"

Jassim shifted and she lifted his arm, placed her thumb against his wrist. He tried to smile. "I think I'm okay. Probably not." He felt fuddled again, as though his ability to speak had gone along with the boy to the hospital. "I've never really been at the scene of an accident before, and you are very quick and professional." These were words he did not need to say, and they disguised other ones, pleading-for-help words like *How do I undo this situation?* and *Will my life be the same after this?* How to ask a stranger such things? He decided to say nothing more.

"Thank you, sir, for taking the time to say that." He saw that her eyes were greenish and in them were questions. "I'm going to feel for anything broken, listen to your heart, check your eyes. It's all standard, and it's just to make sure that you're not hurt. Sometimes shock overrides pain." She did as she said she would, in the order she said she would.

"Your vitals are fine, but are you sure you're okay? Have you called someone to be with you?"

"No, I think I'm okay. The officer told me to sit tight for a few minutes, before I leave. I don't want to tell my wife, don't want to worry her."

The paramedic placed objects in her bag and smiled at him as she worked. "Sir, if you don't mind my saying, that's what wives are for, for times like this. Trust me, it's better to let them worry a little. It will make it easier for both of you in the long run if you tell her. This is no small thing, what happened today."

Jassim was intrigued by this woman who was so open, so *cut to the chase.* Here they had been talking for less than five minutes and she was already discussing intimate aspects of life. He had never talked to an American woman, this type of American woman, like this, not *up close and personal.* But she had misunderstood what he had said. Of course he planned to tell Salwa; he just didn't need to call her to take him home. Did he say *tell* or *call?* And *worry* was the wrong word too. *Bother* perhaps would have been better. No. What he should have said was, "We have a complicated schedule, and she will be on the other side of town at the real estate office, because she has a second job, and by the time she gets here she'll be overcome with worry, and it would just be easier for me to tell her when she comes home at her normal time." That's what he should have said, because as with many American conversations, the words he spoke had not conveyed what he had intended by them. He could never decide if it was his English, his actual use of language, or if it was because people didn't really listen and instead put into the words they heard the words they expected to hear.

"Well, thank you again," Jassim told the woman, hoping she would feel his gratitude.

"You're welcome. Take it easy, sir."

"Okay, will do," replied Jassim, trying to keep up with her jargon, when really he felt like he was drowning. The very sensation that he had fought his entire life to control was now swallowing him, only it was not water that was taking his breath away, filling his lungs; instead it was air.

She walked away and he leaned forward, rested his head in his hands, and stared at the pebbles between his legs on the ground. He found himself looking at patterns, connecting the dots with the tiniest grains of dirt as he forced deep breaths.

"Mr. Haddad." Officer Barkley was standing in front of him again, and Jassim wondered why he hadn't sensed him coming, hadn't felt his shadow or heard his footsteps. Found himself thinking that Officer Barkley must be a very good police officer. "Mr. Haddad, we have had statements from four other witnesses: the other boy, a woman who was driving from the other direction, a man who was some ways behind you, and the driver of the car that pulled out of that street." Here Officer Barkley gestured north. "You were right about the car you swerved to avoid—it had just pulled out. All the witnesses have corroborated your statement as to the events and the speed you were going. I will need to get some personal information from you, and a detective will come to talk to you."

A detective? He associated detectives with television, not real life.

"Would you like to call someone to come and be with you, or to drive you home once the detective is through? Your wife?"

Jassim wondered how he knew he was married. "I live very close," he finally said. "My wife is on the other side of town."

"Honestly, Mr. Haddad, you are in shock now. It's important to have people around, to talk about it with someone. Trust me."

Jassim looked into Officer Barkley's face and was surprised at how young and soft he looked. His voice had presence and weight, and while he was bulky, his hands looked soft the way a schoolboy's would. "Has this ever happened to you?" Jassim asked, though it seemed a stupid question once it was spoken.

"Let's put it this way, I know what you are going through, and I know what's to come."

—ৎ ৎ—

By late afternoon Salwa felt the weight of the day in her feet, which were ready to burst out of her shoes, and was thankful for this new job, where she spent less time standing and where the day went by more quickly than it had when she was a regular teller. Exhausted, she sat waiting for the energy to get up and go, to drive to the real estate office before returning to her husband and home. No baby. She sat, not in pain but numb, closed her eyes for just a minute, but opened them as she felt someone watching her.

"Are you coming, Salwa?" Petra and Jake were staring at her. "You all right?" asked Petra.

"I guess I'm ready to go." Money counted and accounted for. Standing up, she avoided Jake's gaze, his open face.

Out in the cold parking lot she headed to her always clean, shiny white SUV. "See you tomorrow." Briefcase in hand as she clicked the button to unlock the door. Thoughts colliding, scattering on the ground around her swollen feet. Swollen for nothing. At least there was no more Lie between her and Jassim.

"Salwa?"

She started. Jake was again standing a few feet in front of her.

"Salwa, I want to apologize. First for bringing that lady to you and also for what I said this morning. I didn't mean to make you uncomfortable. I've been thinking about it and I thought maybe it was inappropriate to say at work. I'm sorry."

"Jake, it was sweet of you to say what you did, and it didn't make me uncomfortable."

"You sure?"

"Yes, I'm sure. What is on my mind has nothing to do with you."

"I can imagine that you have a lot to think about. I don't think it would be easy to be an Arab these days. I mean, with what's going on and investigations and all that."

"Right," said Salwa, caught off-guard. Unsettled.

"Okay, I'll see you tomorrow. *Ma'a salaama.*"

"What did you say?"

"*Ma'a salaama.* Did I say that right?"

"You did. Where did you learn it?"

"In my Arabic class."

"You are taking an Arabic class?"

"Mm-hmm. I can say *marhaba, ana talibun.*"

"*'Azzeem.* Very nice. Can I ask you why you are taking Arabic?"

"Everyone is talking Arab this and Arab that, and I thought I'd try to see it from the inside."

"Nice, Jake. *Ma'a salaama.*"

"*Allah yisellmik.*"

"Bravo."

As she drove to the real estate office, before her mind arrived at serious thoughts it floated over Jake, and for the smallest flake of a second it occurred to her that he was flirting with her—a boy several years younger than she—flirting, just the tiniest bit. And then it was gone and her thoughts thickened, hardened.

Detective Sorenson came and went. Asked the same questions Officer Barkley had but seemed much less interested in Jassim's answers. When they were done, he told Jassim that Officer Barkley would come back and give him some phone numbers. Jassim watched Detective Sorenson spray pink paint on the street.

"What are they doing?" he asked Officer Barkley when he returned.

"They paint the road where the cars and pedestrians were, then they plug the coordinates into a GPS system and recreate the accident. Before GPS they used rulers and math. This makes it much easier for everyone." He paused. "About the boy..."

"Is he dead?" Jassim asked, once again in control of his words.

"I don't have that information, Mr. Haddad."

"How will I know? Can I call the hospital?"

"That's not a good idea, Mr. Haddad. The detectives should call you once they know. If not, you can call the station and ask for Detective Sorenson."

"Could I talk to you instead?"

"That would be fine. Mr. Haddad, I'm just about done here, so why don't I follow you home, since you live so close? I'll also give you the phone number for the community resources office. I'm going to let the other officers know that I am following you home. Why don't you give me the keys, and I'll pull your car over here for you."

Jassim handed him the keys and Officer Barkley walked away once again while Jassim remained where he was, a changed man. He watched as Officer Barkley stepped toward a group of three officers and a detective and then to his vehicle. He watched his car pull off the shoulder and in front of the police car in which he was seated. The design of the car's frame impressed him. He and the officer exchanged cars and Jassim sat in the driver's seat again, drove slowly home, conscious of the police car behind him.

He pulled into his driveway and parked in front of the house, under the acacia tree.

Officer Barkley wrote down some numbers on a card. "Here is your license and the two numbers I told you about. I would encourage you to call." Jassim took the paper and his license and walked toward the door, not sure whether he should invite Officer Barkley inside.

"Did you want your briefcase?"

"Of course." Jassim walked back to his car, fumbled with the door.

"Let me help you." Officer Barkley got out his bag and briefcase and walked toward the door.

Jassim said nothing and entered the house. He walked into the kitchen. Officer Barkley followed, put the bags down, and looked around.

"This is a very nice house you have, Mr. Haddad."

Jassim looked up. "Thank you. It is my wife who makes it that way."

"Women. They do that for a home. Did you know that in some villages in India women put flowers on the doorstep of their home so that when their husbands come from work, they see something lovely? Even among the poor. I could live in India."

"Too many people in India," replied Jassim, wondering how Officer Barkley came to know such an obscure folkloric fact about villages in India.

Officer Barkley smiled. "I'm sorry for what happened to you today, Mr. Haddad. Take care of yourself."

"Thank you. You do the same."

After Officer Barkley left, Jassim stood still for some minutes. He put his license and the card with the phone numbers in his wallet and stood, staring absently. He traipsed through the tidiness of his house and deposited the contents of the guilty duffel bag in their appropriate spots (wet hand towel draped over the white wicker hamper in the bathroom, Speedo rinsed and hung on the shower rod). He went to the closet and got a clean folded hand towel and his second Speedo and dropped them into the bag, which he returned to its corner in the walk-in closet of their bedroom—all movements that came automatically, and yet they produced in him the feeling that he was treading through molasses, that his legs had been opened and the bones infused with lead. How to get on with the day when you've just killed a boy? Jassim knew with certainty the boy was dead. He longed desperately for Salwa to come home so he could tell her and she could push away all the tension and fogginess that sat in his head with her clear, clear thinking.

That was his plan: to tell Salwa everything that had happened as soon as she walked in the door. No telling how it is that such a good plan can slit itself apart, bleed across the tiles, through many layers of glaze, and leave stain after stain to remember, always to remember.

Jassim had not started blaming himself for what had happened, had not yet become obsessed with who the boy was, had not yet even remembered that the boy's name was Evan; all that would come later. For now he was stuck in the moment. Could not get to thinking about what it all meant because he had not told anyone yet. Still it was not completely real, maybe just a cruel trick played by his overworked brain. Perhaps he would *snap out of it* and it would all have been a dream. A nightmare. For now, his thoughts did not go beyond his wife's arrival home, beyond the act of telling her. Once that was complete, once she had worked her magic on the situation, then he would figure out how to deal with the whole mess.

Odd indeed, with all the energy devoted to thinking about the moment in which he would tell Salwa what had happened, that he had been driving *well below the speed limit,* and had hit a boy and killed him but that the boy *had clearly had a death wish.* Odd how those words would take so long to get uttered.

Things should never be addressed out of order; a day should follow its logical steps. When order is disturbed, so too is the natural balance of things, and Jassim did not know what was supposed to happen next. It took him fifty-three minutes of pacing before he remembered that Salwa had gone to the real estate office and would come home late; Tuesday was also the day on which he was responsible for dinner. This realization was too overwhelming. Somehow having to come up with food was more than Jassim could bear, so he sat down in the thick brown chair to watch television, to let his mind be bothered by someone else's problems. The chair had been a gift from Joan. It was enormous and had buttons that made it recline or apply heat to one's lower back. It had hidden cup holders and places for magazines. Joan had bought it for her husband but then rearranged her house and found it didn't fit, so she had insisted that Salwa have it. They put it in front of the television in the family room, with the couch adjacent.

"This is American technology at its finest," he had said when it entered their house and he inspected it extensively. At the end of the right armrest was a sliding tray for the remote, so that it would always be at your fingertips. On the left side was a tray that folded up and contained a cup holder and an indented section for food. Further down, a box for magazines and newspapers pulled out. The chair reclined, massaged, and comforted, and now Jassim sat in it and stared in front of him, unable to summon the energy to slide out the tray for the remote or even to press the button that would make the whole chair recline. The afternoon began to replay, back to his driving, his slowing, his registering the boys up ahead, beyond the curve, his awareness of their stupidity for skateboarding on such a narrow, curving road—all of it came back in slow motion, right up to the impact of the boy's body on his car. Jassim's palms were sweaty as the filmreel stopped and then started over again. He desperately wanted to lie back but could not find the strength to do anything about it, so he sat.

"Perhaps making dinner will help," he muttered to himself, offering a voice to combat the accusatory silence. He pulled himself up and went to the gleaming kitchen, opened the tidy white refrigerator. No leftovers. Then to the freezer. No leftovers. One package of frozen chicken. He stood thinking about the possibilities contained in this frozen chicken and decided that he could not cook, could not bring himself to prepare food, that this would be a good time for ordering out. Thankful for the luxury of living in a country where any kind of food was minutes away, he got the pile of menus from a drawer beneath the counter and began picking through. Ethiopian—too far away. Italian—no. Pizza—no. Thai . . . yes, Thai food would be perfect. As he studied the flier he found his eyes drawn to the words on the bottom: *We Deliver. Live rewed. Devil were. Liver weed. Led review. We reviled.*

"Hi, habibi," greeted Salwa as she walked into the kitchen.

"We reviled."

"What?"

"Have you ever noticed that *we deliver* can be changed into *we reviled*?"

"How about *we relived*?" asked Salwa.

"Oh yes, of course. Good."

How to introduce a killing into this moment?

"How was your day, habibi?" A question asked from habit but with no interest, but Jassim couldn't see it, was just thankful for the opportunity to answer.

"Not so good, Salwa. Not so good."

But instead of asking why, Salwa walked out of the room.

Searching for the functional aspects of the day that would make life seem normal again, Jassim raised his voice. "I was going to order Thai food for dinner. Is that okay with you?"

No answer. He pressed the intercom button next to him, so that his voice would extend to each room in their house. "Salwa, is Thai food okay with you? Over."

He smiled, hoping she would too.

Static. "That's fine." Click. He guessed she was in their bedroom.

He picked up the telephone and dialed the number on the flier. He placed his order, and then the woman's voice asked him, "Pickup or delivery?"

"Pickup," answered Jassim automatically, but his brain slid back to his car and the boy. "No, delivery—delivery, please."

"We'll be there in forty-five minutes."

"Yes, thank you."

He placed the phone in its cradle and made his way back to the chair. "Salwa?"

"Yes, habibi, what's the matter?" Velvet slippers shuffled across the floor.

"I had a car accident today."

Already wearing pajamas, the white cotton ones he thought were sexy, she stopped and stared. "Thank God for your safety. Are you all right? What happened?" She came over and sat on the sofa.

Jassim was pleased that she was listening, that she seemed interested and worried. He began to recount the story, about leaving work early to go swimming because he had felt unbalanced and thought that would help. Then about driving. He didn't tell her about slowing down, just about driving slowly. Then the two boys. And then hitting the one boy.

"Oh, God. Is he going to be okay?"

"Oh yes, I'm sure he will be," replied Jassim, another Jassim, one who desperately wanted to believe the story he'd just recounted. The American version, the one with no crooked neck, no teenage boy with a death wish.

"I'm so glad you're all right, Jassim." She sat for another moment looking at him, got up and kissed his forehead, and then walked out of the room. Somehow she did not know what Jassim knew: that the boy was already dead. Somehow he had not conveyed the severity of the situation: that he had hit and killed a boy. Was that on purpose? It was hard to tell. He sat staring at the menu, which he had left on the coffee table, thinking that he needed to return it to its spot in the drawer. He thought of the pool and remembered the gift shop being open and thinking he should get Salwa something, which he had absolutely planned to do but had then forgotten because of the unpleasant Jack Franks. And finally his mind reached the center of the labyrinth, the key to everything, the memory that just this morning Salwa had told him she had had a miscarriage and here he was, hours later, the miscarriage totally forgotten.

He stopped. Blame and hypothetical thinking offended him, wasted time and committed emotions to nonexistent problems, and he was imagining that the reason for his accident was that she had disrupted his schedule. Which was not true. Yes, her telling him had thrown off his schedule, but he had chosen to leave work early. He had chosen to go swimming when he did and drive home when he did. And she was upset because a miscarriage is a serious thing...So *why didn't she tell me before?* Thoughts rewound to where he had left them when he was swimming. Had she planned this pregnancy, or had it been accidental? Surely if it had been accidental, she would have told him. Would he have been upset if she had told him that she was pregnant? Oddly, the thought did not displease him as much as he had expected.

Salwa pregnant. The thought was an attractive one. He imagined them lying together in bed, he with his hand on her giant belly, their child underneath absorbing this love. And to have a child? Well, that might be all right too. Salwa could quit her job at the bank and they could make do on his salary, though they might not be able to stay in this house, might need something more manageable, maybe something closer to his work, but they would be okay. It was not perfect, but it did not offend him as much as he had anticipated. Perhaps he was ready to have a child. He would have to tell Salwa.

Jassim stood up, relief flooding him, as though he'd just lost a burden, sold it, knocked a monkey off his back. And then his eyes landed on the takeout menu for the Thai restaurant and he remembered calling it, why he had called it, and finally the accident. His heart pushed out a mass of blood that made his legs go weak, and he sat down again. Officer Barkley had said that Detective Sorenson would let him know how the boy was doing. If he didn't call by tomorrow morning, Jassim would call the hospital. But which hospital? And what was the boy's name? He had no idea. He knew nothing about him. How would he find out where they had taken him? He would have to call the police station.

Salwa walked back into the room. He wondered if she knew how lovely she was, how irresistible those pajamas made her.

"Salwa, how are you feeling?" Jassim asked, though it sounded like the wrong thing to say once the words were in the air.

"I'm fine."

"Are you sure? You seem sad."

She sat down on the couch and rearranged magazines. "I am sad, Jassim. It felt like we had a baby that died."

Jassim was not prepared for this. Should he sit next to her and hold her? She was still straightening piles of magazines. He should say something. For some reason he was not reacting to her, was looking at her through a window but could not quite get to her. "Salwa," he called out, hoping his voice would reach her.

She looked at him, so sad and vulnerable that he managed to get up and sit next to her, to hold her and let her cry on his shirt, sobbing and shuddering. As he held her, the aftermath of the accident bubbled up in tears and he held her tightly, soothing himself as he did, promising himself that he would not let the accident upset her further, would focus on her instead, would help her get through this somehow and in so doing would get through it himself.

Part Three

—⌁ Chapter Eight ⌁—

Behind (and sometimes in front of) every story there is another (and sometimes another and another). At thirty-eight, Penny, the waitress with the warm eyes and deep cleavage, looked older, mid-forties perhaps. Watching her child die ages a woman faster than anything else. In the snapshot of today, the grief around her eyes seeped into her skin, the edges of her mouth folded calmly and pleasantly, as if she were on the brink of happiness. A nice disguise for a shell containing an enlarged and very sad heart.

She had gotten pregnant with Josie when she was just seventeen, but she had raised her right, loved her as much as anyone could love a child. When she turned twenty-one she met Sky, a thick man with twinkly blue eyes and a taste for drinking. His love for her was deep and intense, allowed her to loosen up on the tight rein with which she held on to life. As a child he had been beaten by his mother, and Penny loved him to make up for it. Never crossed her mind that some sins cannot be atoned for by anyone. She had not yet read articles in *Time* and *Newsweek* about the children of abusive parents. All she knew was that Sky was a man she could love and feel safe with. They had two more babies, a boy and a girl, Bryson and Bentley.

Years passed, some good, some bad, but none awful, not until Josie turned thirteen and Penny turned thirty. Sky woke up one morning, unemployed for his second long stretch during their marriage, and realized that his stepdaughter was edging on womanhood. His love for her turned fierce, and he fenced her in with rules and regulations, usually delivered with shouts. Everything she did was crooked in his angry eyes, and he even turned the babies against her, said she was a selfish whore. Josie (short for Josephine, a name Penny still thought was beautiful) loved her mother but couldn't help her see through Sky's anger, since most of it was delivered when she was at work, and so the girl spent as much time out of the house as she could. Penny worried as Josie distanced herself and Sky humphed and sulked and scowled, neither one realizing they were in competition for Penny's love. For the sake of her daughter she thought she should leave Sky, but what about Bryson and Bentley? She had been pushed into a corner, told her husband that he needed to leave, take some time to get his shit together. She loved him and he could come back, but not while he was hell on earth to live with.

Sky swirled and moaned with mythical anger. He apologized and promised he would go easy on Josie, only cared about her, worried about her, loved Penny more than life itself. She let him back, and the next day he beat her black and blue, sent her to the hospital, was arrested and released. Their family was forever changed, dropped into a cycle that never seemed to complete itself. He never beat his own children, only Josie and her mother. Penny's hope was to leave her husband but to keep all three children. She saw that this would not be easy, that things needed to be done in stages, starting with a restraining order. And then she gave a whispered prayer of thanks when he was arrested for disorderly conduct and assaulting a police officer, giving her a breather to get things together. A week before his release, she could see the writing on the wall, so she begged Sky's father and stepmother to take the little ones for a while, and she and Josie left to settle somewhere else, which is how it came to be that she moved to Tucson. There was no way for her to know then that pulling up on the thick adhesive that bound mother to children allowed in doubt and insecurity, that the gum would never really stick again.

But for now she was on a mother-daughter adventure with her firstborn—only by that time Josie was trying to get away from the hell of her life, even though she loved her mother. Too much time alone, too much violence, and too much anger had taught her to use cigarettes for calm, then pot for serenity, then speed to get through the day, during school and afterward, when her mother was at work. Then one day she tried heroin, shooting it into her veins, and died. Overdosed on her first try.

Penny was stuck in Tucson, her sweet daughter dead and her other two children under the watchful eye of their grandparents. She rented a room from a woman she worked with, because after Josie died she couldn't bear to be alone. She cut down on her expenses as much as possible so she could save her money, get stable, and bring the children to live with her. No way for her to know that Sky would come back into their lives and turn them against her, telling them that she had run away, that she had abandoned her babies because she didn't love them enough. He yanked off the giant BandAid that was her love for them and tossed it in the trash, didn't care that he pulled up skin as he went, infected the wound with his dirty fingers. He had taken up with a woman who had found God at just about the time Penny was entering hell.

_cʒ ᴖʒ_

Jassim woke up at 4:30, though it was not a swimming day, and blinked at the darkness. Turning on his side, he stared at the green numerals illuminated on the clock: 4:31. Wednesday. Go back to sleep. Eyes closed. No swimming. Swam yesterday. In the afternoon. Eyes opened.

Reality crept in and tied knots in his muscles while Salwa slept, oblivious. The words sat at the back of his throat, promising to choke him if they were not released soon. He so wished that he had finished recounting the story, but the disappointment on her face and his forgetting about her miscarriage made it somehow impossible. How could he possibly say, "That car accident I had—well, the boy died"? Those words were held down beneath the surface for well over six minutes instead floating up in his ridiculously simplistic lie: "I had an accident. It's okay. A couple of teenagers." Careful to walk around the truth, leave it safely protected by a white picket fence.

Following his version, Salwa could never have guessed that there had been flesh to peel off the front of his car. (Had there been?) That he had held the boy's hand as he breathed for the last time. The version she heard was a simple accident with a couple of kids and a happy American ending.

How was it that he knew for sure the boy was dead? Every part of his body knew, but Jassim's brain demanded proof. Was it too early to call Officer Barkley?

Jassim didn't know what to do with himself, so he decided to go for a swim, even though it was very early and he didn't normally swim on Wednesdays and bending his schedule made him feel off-balance. He got up, washed his face, and followed the routine, automatic movements that now dragged about, begging to be revised.

He forced himself to follow his normal route to the gym, driving down the winding road, hyperconscious of every living thing his headlights picked up, every rabbit, every person walking, every extra thing beeping madly on his radar screen. When he finally turned into the parking lot, he felt as if he'd been driving for hours, and looking at his cell phone clock, he realized four fifty-two was too early to call Officer Barkley. Four fifty-two also meant that he had to sit in his car and wait eight minutes for the building to open.

Weren't police stations always open? He got out his wallet and pulled out the card that Officer Barkley had given him. Other cars were pulling into the parking lot, many of their occupants getting out and waiting by the front door, jiggling away the cold. Others remained safely sealed in their metal bubbles. He pressed the seven numbers and waited. Waited as the phone rang. Waited as he was connected and then put on hold, excruciating seconds while he waited to hear the result of his accident.

"Sir?"

"Yes, I'm here," said Jassim, who was leaning against the seat with his eyes closed.

"The boy in that accident died as a result of his injuries. Is there anyone else you would like to talk to or leave a message for?"

"No, thank you." Jassim hung up and stared. *The boy died as a result of his injuries.* Injuries inflicted by the car in which he sat. Injuries inflicted by his own hands. This knowledge sucked the breath out of him, and he had to force himself to pull air into his lungs, force himself to breathe steadily, smoothly.

So now he knew. His instinct had been correct. But what to do with this information?

As if in answer, the light in front of the Fitness Bar's door went on and the small flock of people waiting vanished. Jassim got out of his car, walked to the building, his feet leaden. Instead of running his card through the scanner, he handed it to Diane and stood there for a minute, wondering how old the boy had been.

"How are you today, Jassim?"

"Fine, thanks."

"Here you go. Here's your card. And don't worry. No one has pooped in the pool today."

Jassim stood at the counter, his brain scrambling to make sense of her words.

"May I help you with something?" Diane stood in front of Jassim. He could see clumps of mascara on her eyelashes and red veins in her eyes. He wondered if she was tired. Close up, her face was thick with makeup, even though it was early in the morning.

"Oh, no. Sorry. I'm a little tired today," answered Jassim, his mind stretching and snapping back: it was only yesterday that his day had been knocked off balance, that he had found out about Salwa's miscarriage. Only yesterday that he had had the accident, and Diane had been there to push it along, hadn't she?

The boy in that accident died as a result of his injuries.

"Really? Hard night?"

Jassim stared at her, wondering what a hard night meant for Diane and feeling sure that her version would not match his. Heavy drinking? Dancing? Sex? "No, just tired."

Diane didn't move, just glued her bug eyes on him, and Jassim felt unsettled.

"Well, have a nice swim." She said these words quietly, as though they possessed another meaning. Jassim took his card from her powdery hands. Their fingers touched, and he was startled at how cold hers were. He fumbled the card into his pocket.

"Thank you."

"Anytime, honey. Anytime."

Jassim walked away, feeling as though she'd just said a word in code, only he didn't have the key to break it. Why did she stare at him like that? What was she thinking? Was she remembering that he had ignored her when she invited him to have coffee? Surely she wouldn't remember that. Surely she said things like that to other people.

Heavy, murderous feet carried him the not so many steps out
to the pool, and there was no one, a blessed no one. Jassim did his
stretches, jumping jacks, warm-ups, forced focus into his brain,
squeezed out the nervousness and the Dianes and the memory of
the past twenty-four hours, scattered them around on the dark
concrete. Stripped down, goggles on, feet wet, he slipped into the
water and swam, bitter cold at first—did they not start heating the
pool until morning? Surely it was something that had to be done
continuously. It was supposed to be set at 79 degrees, though perhaps the chemicals from yesterday affected the way the heating
system worked. Heart beating a frantic pace inside him, he swam,
eyes closed in the cold darkness, body following a routine of many
years, mind playing tricks, suggested by Diane the Sneaky. First lap
and he was in his Mercedes driving, second lap and he was driving
in the middle of the afternoon after swimming. Two boys up ahead
and cars and *thud* and the boy was dead. Third lap and the police
and fire department were there and interviewing him and he was
explaining what happened. Fourth lap, reviewing the accident, into
the fifth lap. And then the whole scene replayed itself, the boys, the
swerving, the last glance through blue sunglasses. How unsettling
to have your face be the last sight someone saw before dying. Jassim's thoughts did not stretch beyond that to an afterlife or a next
life, as he believed that death was the end.

After the sixth lap Jassim stopped to catch his breath and look
around. The pool was still empty, and his heart was trying to escape its imprisonment. He swam a couple more laps, more slowly
this time, and again replayed the crash. Stop. Breathe. Swimming
again, and this time Officer Barkley appeared to talk with him.
Again he wondered about Officer Barkley, the man. Was he strong?
Honest? Was he a good police officer? As he thought about him, it
was not his face he was seeing but his uniform and the soft boyish
hands as they wrote down what Jassim said; how baffling it was
that he could capture the entire story of the accident in a few pages
of such a tiny notebook.

Back to where he started, and Jassim squatted, so that he was
covered in water up to his neck. Again he forced another lap, and

again the pictures came back, obliging him to speed up and lose his breath too quickly.

Usually he counted the laps as he went, not in the forefront of his brain but somewhere in the back, a quiet little clicker tallying each length of the pool. Today he had not the foggiest idea how many laps he'd swum, sure that it was not even half what he normally did, though it was 5:20. For a minute he stared at the clock. How could it be only 5:20? He had woken up early. Had he turned off his alarm? He couldn't remember. He hoped so, because Salwa wouldn't appreciate having to wake up so early. He pushed off for another lap, forcing his brain to concentrate on his job, usually the thing he forced out of his brain so that he could relax. Within one lap the accident came back to him, began to replay from when he was driving, only this time he considered what he could have done to avoid hitting the boy. Short of being somewhere else or stopping the car and pulling over, he had not had any other options that he could see. It was almost as though the boy chose him, chose to jump in front of his car.

By 5:25 he had run the boy over several times. Terrified to discover that his one way of meditation, of being at peace, no longer worked. Terrified to realize that he'd met something bigger than he could handle. A voice of reason popped into his head and told him to be patient, that these things took time. *Think of Cornelia.* He had agonized over her for months and months and eventually recovered, but at least then swimming had helped to quell the intensity of his emotions.

Out of the pool and into the shower room, and Jassim carried these thoughts with him, spilling a couple onto the smooth tile floor as he went. Under the shower, he decided that life was like chess and you really did have control if you knew how to play properly. Perhaps if he went back through his day, he could figure out his mistake. Once again he replayed his day under water, starting with the pool and the feces and Salwa and the miscarriage. His other thoughts stepped back, allowed this one center stage. Salwa and the miscarriage. Could that be the key? Could he have missed all her cues about wanting a child? No, he had picked up on them and dismissed them. Was that his wrong move? But he hadn't been denying her children, he had simply been postponing the event.

Water pounded into his face as he thought about this, about children, about wanting children, about not wanting children. But how could this have caused an accident? Ridiculous. It didn't cause the accident. An accident, by definition, is something that happens without intention, a combination of poor timing and bad luck.

Jassim could not, at that moment, fully accept the idea that his lack of balance with Salwa had in some way tipped over and affected another's life. Taken another's life. It was too huge at the moment.

And while his shower lasted easily twice the time it normally did, Jassim didn't notice, allowed his mind to stretch a bit further until a new thought came to him: *I will turn this around, help the boy's family. I cannot undo what I have done, but I can offer to help with the damage.*

Out of the shower, dressed, out the door of the locker room, out the door of the gym.

"What, now you don't say goodbye?"

Jassim turned to see Diane standing at the desk with her hands on her hips and her head tipped a bit to one side.

"Sorry, Diane. I was just thinking."

"Those must be some pretty serious thoughts you're thinking right now, honey." She winked.

Jassim let the door go and continued out to the parking lot. And in the early morning darkness it truly came to him what he had done, that he had taken a life, and he knew that it would always, always be with him. He drove home along the same route he had driven yesterday, less than twenty-four hours ago, his palms moist with sweat (just as they had been yesterday, as if part of his body knew) as he neared the incline where the boy had chosen to fly into his vehicle. In the dark it was hard to see the exact spot, but he slowed down where he thought it was, looking for some sort of evidence. But there was none. Quietly, he promised the boy—Evan? Was that his name?—that he would shift the balance back, that he would find a way to help him. And then he drove on.

For the rest of the day Jassim moved in a fog, not so much thinking about the accident as being deafened by its echoes. Several times on that Wednesday his mind reached back to that moment when he had lost control. He had walked far outside himself and couldn't find the way back in, could only watch through a gleaming window as the Jassim he knew went about his day, doing his job, chatting with coworkers.

On Thursday he drove to the Fitness Bar and swam, but his enthusiasm stayed in the car, or made it only as far as the edge of the pool. An ever-weakening force dragged each lap out of him, the battery running closer to zero. The exhilaration he used to feel at the end of a swim had drowned and lay at the bottom of the pool, not even bothering to float to the surface.

Slowly Salwa regained strength. Her thoughts managed to stretch beyond the lost baby, to drape themselves over the beautiful things in her life: her home, the ease of her existence, her jobs. Somehow, in the few days since she'd told Jassim the enormous story that sat within her, she had been purged of guilt and was ready to resume the guise of her checklist life.

In the parking lot, stepping out of her car, she found Jake pulling up and parking next to her. She didn't stop to think that in the time they had been working together, they had never before arrived simultaneously. At no time before it was too late did it occur to her that she did not control her day. All she thought was that it was nice to see him and that he had a rather magnetic aspect to his personality.

"*Sabah al-khayr,*" he said as he got out of his black and shiny sedan.

"*Sabah al-noor,*" replied Salwa with a smile that made creases around her eyes.

"*Kayf al-haal?*" Jake opened his mouth so wide when he said this that someone who read lips might think he was shouting.

"*Mneeha, alhamdilillah.*"

"Uh-oh. What does that mean?" He smiled and stood in front of her.

"It means 'Fine, thanks God.' "

"*Mneeha, alhamdilillah.* Is that right?"

"Yes, except if someone is asking you how you are, you need to say *mneeh,* because you are a man."

"Of course. *Mneeh. Ana mneeh.*" He said the last *h* in this word as though he were having a breathing test that required him to expel the last vestiges of air from his lungs. Salwa laughed.

"Are you laughing at me?" He smiled again, and Salwa had the feeling that it was just the two of them in the world, that his intensity and energy were focused just on her.

They walked side by side toward the designated entrance to the building, and Salwa floated an inch or two off the ground. Twice during the short walk from their cars to the secured doors of First Fidelity their arms touched. Clock turned back, and Salwa was minus one marriage, nine years of exile. So long ago, and yet just a few breaths and she was there, walking along the streets that lined the university in Amman, with clumps of students discussing politics, or waiting, or chatting and watching. The edge of possibility in the air.

Salwa had loved being a student, actually being a student and all that implied: the books, the staying up late, the excited discussions with friends and classmates, with Hassan; the coffee, the hurriedness of the morning, the lack of responsibility outside of schoolwork. Her university days had been her happiest, and she longed to go back to that easier time. Salwa left behind the wife, the mature banker, the real estate agent, and found instead the interested student, the one who loved numbers, who played with them for the sake of stretching her mind.

"Hey, Salwa," said Jake as they stopped in front of the building.

"Yes, Jake?" And why did her heart skip when he said her name? As if she had just woken up from the purest sleep.

"I wanted to ask you about Ramadan."

"Sure."

"We're almost at the end of it right now, right?"

"Right. This weekend is the Eid."

"Our teacher talked about it a little bit. What do you and your husband do for Eid celebration?"

"This year we have been invited to some friends'. The man is a Palestinian from Syria and the woman is an American, but she lived in the Middle East quite a bit and she cooks really well and makes a big deal for Eid."

"Is it different from how you celebrated when you lived in Jordan?"

"Oh God, what a difference! Back home we would be cleaning for Eid for days before. Fasting and cooking and cleaning and fasting and cooking and cleaning more."

"That doesn't sound too fun."

"It's a lot of work, but it's all worth it. Almost the whole country celebrates Ramadan, so I guess it's sort of like Christmas here, where you feel the anticipation for it. You know that all that cooking and cleaning is going to be very nice at the end. Businesses close for a few days. Schools are closed."

"Do you get presents?"

"Kids do. It depends on the family. Usually kids get new clothes and some money. The best thing is the visiting. For a few days relatives come over or we go to them and we take sweets and talk, and it's so relaxed and no one does anything." Lost in the memory. "We have one friend, Hassan." *Who was to be my husband. Who called me not long ago even though we have not spoken in years.* "He would come to our house first and bring flowers. These were flowers he started from seeds months before, that he grew on his own for the very special occasion of giving them to us on Eid. Because we follow a lunar calendar, the date changes, so the kind of flowers he grew would be different depending on the time of year. Then on Eid he would bring them to us, a beautiful pot of flowers for our family." *For me, because he loved me and knew I liked beautiful things.*

"Gosh. It sounds so magical," said Jake, reminding her of a child in his excitement and curiosity. "I love to listen to you talk about your home. Do you miss it?" Jake stood in front of her, arms crossed. It was the ease of his smile, she decided, that transported her. It was as though time just stopped when he was with her. She shook away her memories.

How to explain the missing? How to tell this innocent boy that lately all she could think about was going home, being surrounded by her family, by her sisters? How could he understand what it meant to be in a place that didn't want her? To have lost a baby and not really mourned it? This sadness gripped her, shook her, squeezed something in her throat that made her eyes water.

"Salwa, are you okay? I'm sorry if I said something..."

"Oh no, Jake. It's not you. It's me." She put her hand on his arm, surprised at how natural it felt to touch him. "I always feel a bit homesick during Ramadan and Eid. Especially this year, with everything that's going on."

_____ᕤ ᕥ_____

Jassim's alarm beeped, piercing the morning's darkness, jangling the quiet into razor-edged pieces. He reached to turn it off, his hand the only part of his body with energy, a snake attached to a dead elephant. He was the dead elephant, a giant pinned to his bed by heavy thoughts.

Jassim crept into consciousness to find reality worse than any dream, any nightmare, and he turned away from Salwa.

The thinnest voice prodded at him, nudged him toward the edge of the bed. *Swimming is what keeps you even, gives you control,* the voice said.

I have no control, Jassim answered back. *No control. It's gone. My life is no longer in my hands.* This thought overpowered a quieter wish for God, for belief, for an answer, or at the very least Balance. He lay at the edge of the bed, his thoughts a crowded pile of characters competing for space on the marquee: *Salwa Shops for Pajamas, Jassim's Child, Water, Swimming, Officer Barkley...*

"I will not let this eat me alive," he muttered silently, in English, sitting up and swinging out of bed in such an abrupt move that he had to stop and steady himself.

His everyday, automatic preparations were now slow and conscious: washing his face, looking in the mirror at the same face, the same eyebrows, the same self who had killed a boy. Jassim's head throbbed, and he opened the medicine cabinet.

"Jassim, are you all right?"

"I'm fine, Salwa. Sorry to wake you."

"Have a good swim."

Dressed now, his duffel bag by the door, Jassim moved silently. In the glow of the bathroom light his eyes caressed Salwa's face, her porcelain skin, and her shapely fingers resting long and delicate on the pillow. Usually this sight moved him, filled him with desire. Today it was like looking at a painting whose mechanics were brilliant but which did not reach inside, did not tug his blood into mobility.

Jassim toyed with the idea of waking Salwa and telling her everything in the hope of reknotting their severed connection, but the imagined conversation was sharp and impossible: "Salwa, you know that accident I had a few days ago? Well, I killed a boy."

He saw the horror on her face, a gasp, her clear eyes filling up with sympathy that over time would slide into anger and blame. She knew he drove too fast. She knew he cherished the time he spent alone in the car, and he knew that if he told her what had happened, he would also have to tell her that he had been speeding beforehand, and that she would blame him. (And would she be right?)

He flicked off the bathroom light and walked through the hall, through the kitchen, and out into the cold morning.

As a teenager he had strengthened his legs by wearing ankle weights. He would walk around with cans or tools secured to his legs by a kaffiyeh. As he increased the weight it got harder and harder to walk normally, mostly because the items themselves were so cumbersome. This is how he felt now, as though two heavy hands were clenching his legs, preventing him from taking normal steps. He sat in his silent Mercedes, his murderous vehicle, turned the radio off, and closed his eyes.

"In the name of God," he said aloud, and inserted the key in the ignition. The engine turned over, quiet and powerful, and the car crunched over the driveway and moved down the darkened road. Automatic windows rolled down and welcomed a cold, quiet morning.

The crowded marquee of his brain morphed into an electronics store with hundreds of television sets programmed to different stations, soundless video clips of the older woman in the luxury SUV who had witnessed the accident. Thin, sexless, competent. And the boy's friend, both before and after the accident, straight, strong, and confident on his board, and then later shaking and filled with curses.

Guilt sat on Jassim's chest like an angry woman, pressing and squeezing and threatening his breath. The pounding inside his chest and head was unbearable, and he steered his Mercedes to the side of the road, stopped, closed his eyes, and breathed slow, deep swimming breaths, the kind he used to focus, to narrow his thoughts into his body and his strokes and to close out his problems and distractions.

The engine idled quietly against the morning and he opened his eyes. Better. Instead of going to the Fitness Bar, he found himself retracing his route to the scene of the accident, arguing in silence that it would give him peace and that he would then go for a short swim. It seemed right to confront his demon in the safety of the dark morning, when he had control, rather than during the naked glare that filled the city once the sun came up.

As he got closer, even from the opposite direction, his heart raced and his palms were clammy. When he came to the spot, he pulled over to the side and got out of the car but did not turn off the headlights.

Someone—the boy's parents? friends?—had put up a small white wooden cross. He had seen many similar crosses along the highway and had never given them a second thought, but now he wondered if they were sold somewhere. Surely there wasn't a store that sold white wooden crosses. Along the horizontal part of the cross, someone had written a name in thick black pen: Evan Ezekiel Parker. Around the base of the cross were three candles, a stuffed bear, and a small succulent plant. The face with the blue lenses that lived in Jassim's mind did not evoke any of these items. He stared at the bear; it was the kind you would give to a three- or four-year-old child, not something a teenager would have. Jassim squatted in front of the marker, illuminated by the headlights of the machine that had killed the boy. A school photo had been pasted to the center of the cross. The face in the picture bore no resemblance to the face Jassim had seen days earlier. It was dizzying, and the awfulness hit his stomach in a wave of nausea. He staggered out of the light and vomited next to a creosote bush, then wondered if he should cover the vomit with dirt.

Shaky, sweaty, dizzy. *Focus. Breathe. Push it away.* Horrid thoughts. *Salwa, think of Salwa.* Salwa and her miscarriage. Salwa and her sadness. Salwa, his anchor, who seemed to be drifting now.

He walked back to his car and sat with the door closed and the lights of his car illuminating the small shrine. *Come on, leave— you've come, you've seen, now it's time to go.* Pulling away, he couldn't shake the unsettled feeling that sat in his bowels, couldn't push it away. Something within him fought wildly, pounded at the walls of his chest, needing to run and scream and wail. Yes, wail. His face remained smooth as he thought about funerals at home and the women wailing and the men crying.

He glanced at his watch. Five twenty-five. With no energy or desire to swim, he pulled off the road's dirt shoulder and headed west, no purpose in his mind other than to avoid his thoughts. It was still dark as he drove down the comforting, looping street and approached the always busy Oracle Road, where he found there was an entire world awake. He drove slowly, watching. A short dark man carrying a plastic bag (filled with his breakfast? lunch?) reminded Jassim so much of home it confused him for a moment. A bus had just deposited its human contents by the side of the road and they drifted north and south, some west into the parking lot of an electronics store. One, a young girl with a backpack, sat down on the bus-stop bench. Jassim felt as though he were watching a movie. While many times he had driven into the city early, especially years ago, when his work times had not been so regular, he had never noticed these people. He passed a Denny's and saw many heads in the warm plastic glow. It seemed to call to him, and Jassim turned into the parking lot. Yes, there was something appealing about being in that restaurant with other strangers. Five forty-five. He would not go today, but maybe some other time.

He left the parking lot and headed south on Oracle, noting the activity that was teeming along the well-lit streets. He passed parking lots being sprayed clean with water (he was too overwhelmed to react to this waste), marquee after marquee announcing discounts and deals on tires, oil changes, and twelve-packs; free layaway or no interest for six months; *No credit? We will cash your paychecks.* The announcements were not just on businesses, either. Every car that passed seemed to have at least one, but in many cases several, bumper stickers affixed to it: *One Day at a Time, With Jesus, These Colors Don't Run,* and *United We Stand.*

While Evan's presence sat somewhere inside Jassim, he was lost to this world that lived only minutes from his house. It was not until he drove past the gigantic cemetery and saw through the darkness that a FedEx truck was parked along one of the tiny roads that wrapped around the grass and graves that he laughed aloud at the idea of a rushed delivery, and then that his entire body remembered why it was he was driving around in the early morning hours instead of swimming, and what it was he was trying to forget.

—⁓ Chapter Nine ⁓—

Tuesday, a week after, found Jassim staring in the darkness before his alarm pounded him out of bed. He opened and closed his eyes to see which was darker, all his energy concentrated in his eyelids, every other part of his body paralyzed.

Duty won and he pulled himself up and to the bathroom, forced himself to follow the routine, forced the day to be normal. Salwa was completely still, not even the flutter of her breathing audible, which meant she was awake and pretending to be asleep. Another heavy stone in his pocket.

He walked through the quiet darkness of the morning like a ghost who might vanish at any time without being noticed. That thought stretched his skin tight, pulled at his scalp: Jassim, the visitor. A visitor to this country, to this woman, to this life.

Finally, after what seemed like impossible hours of preparation, he was in the car, his death machine. Flirting in the back of his mind was the idea not to go swimming, to allow his body a day of rest, but not at home. Maybe go for a drive instead. A picture of the warm glow of Denny's percolated in his brain, tickled and tickled closer to the surface of consciousness. Coffee. He could go have coffee and read the newspaper. This thought appealed to Jassim. Maybe his routine was drowning him, maybe he needed to do something new to take control again.

Which is how it came to be that one Tuesday in mid-December, with the world still in darkness, Jassim and his silver Mercedes pulled into the parking lot of Denny's, a lifetime's distance from the Fitness Bar. He bought *USA Today* from a box outside (no *Wall Street Journal* or *New York Times*), pulled open the door to be assailed by the smell of coffee, and waited to be seated at the counter.

"Hey, buddy, pick your spot," called a waitress, and Jassim settled himself on a short swivel stool at the farthest end of the counter.

"What can I get you?" asked the waitress.

"Just a coffee, thanks."

He read without reading, and if anyone had asked him about the articles he looked at, he wouldn't have recalled a word. Several other men were sitting by themselves, sometimes in twos. No one looked at anyone else; they all just zeroed in on their newspapers or out the window or on a distant spot on the other side of the restaurant. Jassim felt loneliness creep up and grab him around the throat, pressing and squeezing until the world moved and he felt he would vomit. Fear pushed him out of his seat and back by the restaurant entrance to the bathroom, inside, to a stall, where he stood over the toilet bowl, heart thudding and a cold sweat creeping over his scalp.

Heart attack—I'm having a heart attack. He forced himself to breathe, the closed-down kind of breathing he had done when he was training his body to defy instinct so many years ago. It took a minute, but finally he could feel his heart shifting gears and gliding back to its normal pattern. The nausea passed. He stood up, took a deep breath, and went to the basin, where he washed his hands and face, which, according to the mirror in front of him, was pale, with a yellow tinge. Eyes closed, deep breaths. Jassim washed his face one more time and then returned to the restaurant, to his newspaper.

"You okay, buddy?" asked the waitress behind the counter.

"Yes, thanks, I'm fine."

"You looked kind of queasy, like you were going to be sick."

"It felt like that, but then it passed." Jassim did not feel like talking, just wanted to lose himself in the paper that he wasn't actually reading.

The waitress stood watching him, her face open and her skin smooth. "Sounds like a panic attack to me."

Jassim rubbed his sweaty palms against his pants. "What exactly is a panic attack?"

"How I see it, it's where you have too much crap loaded in your head and sometimes you just get this electric shock that bangs everything together and for a minute you think you're going to die, or puke, or pass out, but then it passes." She stared into his eyes as she spoke to him.

"How could you know that?" Jassim asked. "It's never happened to me before."

"I used to get them when my husband was stalking me. Sometimes, like at work where it felt safe, I would let some part of me relax, and then all my senses would start sizzling. It's like you've been nervous and on guard so much your brain doesn't know what to do when you relax for once."

"That sounds like it," said Jassim.

"Eating protein helps a lot. Lots of small meals, you know. Want me to get you some breakfast sausages or eggs or something?"

And while Jassim was not remotely hungry, he told her that he would eat, even though he never ate breakfast out, especially after he had been swimming. But he hadn't been swimming. Even worse. He glanced at the clock on the wall. Twenty-five more minutes before he needed to leave and still be on his schedule.

The waitress went to the kitchen and he pretended to read, having long since learned that this was not a staring culture and that it was best to have something to keep your eyes busy. In spite of the nausea, this experience was pleasant, like going traveling and knowing no one, being completely anonymous and therefore free.

The waitress, whose name tag read *Penny,* came back with a plate of food. "Here you go. Feeling better?"

"That was quick."

"I kind of switched the order. Thought you needed something ASAP."

Jassim folded the newspaper next to him and took a bite of scrambled eggs, wondering why some phrases became acronyms, like ASAP and RSVP, but others didn't. He bit into a biscuit and was startled by how tasty it was. Not heavy or filling, though, and he found himself eating quickly, propelled by each bite to have another one. (Was this how fast food came to be named?)

A few minutes later the waitress came by again. "How is that?"

"It's delicious, thanks. You were right—I am feeling much better."

"So, where are you from?"

"I'm from Jordan."

Penny, relaxed and tall, looked at him as if she were an old friend of a friend who had been waiting for years to meet him. "Do people give you a hard time these days?"

Jassim's mind became a jumble. He wished to answer that question honestly, to tell her about the man who had stared at him and mouthed "Go home" when he was having lunch with Marcus, to tell her about Corey, about the triumvirate of small-minded office girls. More than anything, he wanted to tell her about Salwa, about the woman he loved more than life itself, who had walked so far away. But how could he? How could he say these words to a woman he'd known for less than fifteen minutes? "No, not so much."

Penny smiled. "Then you must be hanging out with some good people. A lot of the people I know and see would give you a hard time."

"But you wouldn't?" The question slipped out, the corner of a thought not meant to be given a voice.

"Naw, I wouldn't. I know what it's like to be blamed for someone else's actions, to be put in a category and left there. I will never do that to anyone, no matter his color or his ethnicity. Not even because of his sexual preference."

Her smile was broad and her teeth were large and he guessed that she was in her early forties. As he sat there with his newspaper uselessly in front of him, Jassim felt a mounting desire to be with Penny. Jassim, who had never been unfaithful to his wife, Jassim, who looked at women and recognized their sex appeal intellectually, now lusted for a waitress named Penny.

Stacks of thoughts piled themselves higher and higher, to where he couldn't pull at a single sheet, a single idea, in any stack. His desire was not connected with thoughts, really; it was tidal and giant and had a greater intensity than he had experienced with Salwa, even with Cornelia. His senses were awake, and Denny's overflowed with noise and movement.

"When do you finish working?" Jassim asked.

"Three. No, two today. Two o'clock. Why?"

"Could I see you?"

"After work? I don't know about that." She smiled with creases that told him she would, she could, she did, and she wanted to.

The control that had been tugged out of his hands in the form of Evan and Salwa was being replaced and returned in the form of Penny and pure desire.

"I'll pick you up at two," Jassim said to her, not caring who heard him.

"Oh, no. I don't know you—you think I'm going to get in a car with a total stranger? No way. I'll meet you somewhere public if you want."

Disappointment filled Jassim's shoes. He didn't want *somewhere public*. He wanted *somewhere private*, though he hadn't thought where that might be. Where could they go? Where to go at two in the afternoon with a woman who is not your wife?

"As you wish," said Jassim, smiling but feeling irritated.

"How about the mall? We could get coffee or something."

Jassim did not want to *get coffee or something*. He forced himself not to look at her full breasts pushing against the thin olive-green material of her shirt. "That's fine."

"Call if you change your mind. Otherwise, I'll meet you in the food court," she said, writing a number on the back of a blank bill and handing it to him. "I have rules. Never get in a car with a strange man the first time you meet him, regardless how handsome he is. It's my life and I'd like to keep it, thank you very much—you just never know these days."

Jassim took the piece of paper, pulled out a ten-dollar bill, and left, his heart thudding. Back in the safety of his car in the still darkness of the morning, the reality of his actions came seeping in. The quiet, familiar hum of the engine did not soothe him, did not offer comfort for his guilty soul. "What in God's name, on God's earth, am I doing?" he asked himself out loud in English. "What have I done?" His head throbbed, and he wished deeply and dearly that he had gone swimming instead. His mind cruelly returned to

Salwa. Was he trying to hurt her for lying about the miscarriage? No, not so complicated as that. Penny had done nothing more than to awaken a coiled desire in him. He had no interest in a relationship. He just wanted to be with Penny and her large breasts and her soothing easy smile and her lack of connection to his life.

The further away he drove from Denny's, however, the more impossible this scenario seemed. At a stoplight, he pulled out the piece of paper on which she had written the phone number. "I can't do this," he said aloud in Arabic. "I could have then. Could have taken her away, somewhere private, and had American sex with her, fulfilled this need, but this takes too much thought." He got out his cell phone and dialed the number.

"Good morning. This is Denny's on Oracle. How may I help you?"

"Yes. Penny, please."

"Pardon me?"

"Yes, could I please speak with Penny?" Jassim enunciated as he drove.

"Just a minute."

Jassim turned onto River Road, too distracted to enjoy the fluid movements of the car as it followed the gentle curves of the road.

"This is Penny."

"Hi, Penny. I'm sorry. I can't meet you today."

"That was fast."

"I didn't want you to wait. I realized afterward that I have a meeting."

"Mm-hmm."

"No, really. I forgot then. I'm sorry."

"It's okay. Thanks for calling."

"You're welcome. Maybe some other time."

"Maybe."

The phone clicked. Relief covered him, the way he would have felt if he had veered more when Evan was zooming along on his skateboard. And for safe measure, Jassim called Salwa to say that he would be late, that he needed to eat something. He needed to think about what he had almost done. And the food court in the mall, of all places!

Desire was a funny thing, so unpredictable, so sneaky in form and timing and power. Jassim the predictable, Jassim the faithful, had morphed into Jassim the lusting. Sitting in his car, headed toward home, he stared at the mountains and thought about what he had almost done. Even the thought of Penny brought it back, that tidal craving, and it terrified him.

—⌒⌒—

The morning she turned the corner, her thoughts edged on the idea that her life was just fine and it was time to move on, to accept how things were with Jassim and stop trying to force everything to fit into an American tale. He had already left, she realized, gone off to swim, and for the first time, the very first time since all of this had happened, she felt a deep, sad yearning to hold him, a realization that he too must be suffering and need her, and that in her selfishness and determination to hide her pregnancy, she had failed him as a wife, as a woman.

Timing or the stars or God's will had Jassim calling her, saying that he had stayed longer at the Fitness Bar than he had intended, felt a little lightheaded, and was going to go get something to eat before he came home, that he might not be home before she left for work. And although he had done this only once or twice before, Salwa was not suspicious, did not worry.

"Jassim, are you all right?"

"I'm fine, habibti. It's you I'm worried about. Are you sure you're okay?"

"Thank God, I think I am back to normal."

Connected to her husband with just this cellular wisp of a conversation, Salwa went to work, feeling hopeful, her blood clean and no longer trying to escape.

At lunchtime she walked into the break room to find Bill and Sweeney, one of the tellers, chatting. She thought about turning around, walking outside. No, she was hungry and tired and she

was going to sit down and look at her magazine and snack on the
fruits that she had packed. Out of the fridge came a tiny airtight tub
of cut melon and strawberries (*in December!*), and she took it over
to the empty table by the window.

"Hey, Salwa. I was just telling Sweeney that the woman Jake
sent to you last week was crazy," Bill said. "Bona fide. She sat in my
office for another half an hour, going on and on about foreigners
taking away jobs and 9/11. It was pretty awful."

Her stomach lurched slightly at the thought, because she had
pushed it into a corner of her brain, tuned it out.

Absently eating, she stared out the one-way tinted window at
the passersby, broke them into categories: business people, older
people, mothers with small children, and random people. She
found herself attracted by the mothers, looking for herself in that
puffy overweight woman with curled hair, pimples, and three small
children running to catch up. And that thin woman in lean jeans,
shiny mules, and a made-for-TV haircut, stopping to offer a pacifier
to a tiny baby lodged in its stroller.

As she searched for something familiar, she was impressed that
no one around her asked her how she was feeling, that no one
had the slightest inkling that she had lost a baby. Or that Ramadan
had just ended and she had spent the weekend talking to her sisters,
her parents. It didn't matter. All of what she was, who she was
(Palestinian, Muslim, recent mother of buckets of blood), hid in her
shoes, in the padding of her bra, stitched into labels that no one
would see or even look for. All of it tucked away, so she could sit
here on wood chairs with coworkers.

"Salwa, do you want coffee?" Bill offered. "I'm going down
the street."

Salwa nodded. "Espresso, please. Three sugars."

"Sweeney?"

"Nothing, thanks," said Sweeney, and Salwa heard her get up,
clear her things off the table.

Salwa's mind wandered between walkers and people and cars
and she stared in a daze, wondering what Jassim was doing,
vaguely wanting to go outside for a walk. It was sunny now, so it

wouldn't be too cold. She turned to find Jake standing by the table and gazing at her, smiling. The moment seemed too intimate to share with a stranger, but what choice was there? She smiled back.

"I like to watch you eat those," he said, gesturing toward the strawberries. "Your mouth is full. Very sensual."

Before Salwa could be shocked, or even truly register what he had said, he sat down.

"How did your Eid celebration go?"

"It was nice, thanks." Tidy answer to cover up the sadness and tears after she had talked with her family, when they had spent the evening with Bassam, Jassim's friend from his university years, and his American wife, Pat.

"Really?"

"Well, frankly, it was sad. I really miss my family back home."

"When's the last time you went for a visit?"

"It's been a few years now. When I came to the States, I always thought we'd go in the summers, or I'd go, or they'd come, but somehow it doesn't happen that way."

Jake leaned his elbow on the table, rested his head in his hand, and watched her as she talked, the space between them growing narrower and narrower until they touched each other, until fingers reached inside to the recesses of thoughts and their intimate selves.

Suddenly Jake sat up. "Sorry, I forgot something. I'll be right back." She watched him walk out the door, again impressed by the energy his body exuded when he walked. In a blink he was back, with one hand behind his back. "This is silly, I know, but I got you a tiny something. Close your eyes."

Salwa closed her eyes. She heard the crinkle of a bag, the tiniest scrape on the table.

"Okay, open them."

In front of her was a small silver pot designed to look like an old-fashioned bucket, and in it was a tiny plant covered with miniature yellow rosebuds.

Jake sat in front of her, smiling. "*Eid mubarak,*" he whispered.

Salwa felt the pressure in her eyes, though the last thing she wanted to do was cry here, in this bank.

"One espresso. Three sugars." Bill set the cup in front of her. "Aren't you on desk, Jake?"

"Oh gosh. Sorry, Bill. Time slipped away."

In a blink Jake was gone and Bill sat down in his place. "Nice flowers."

Salwa stood up. "Thanks, Bill. Let me give you some money for the coffee."

"It was a dollar forty-nine."

"My purse is in my locker." She returned the tub of fruit to the fridge and carried her roses and aching homesickness into the tiny employee room, which had lockers and a bench. Once there she couldn't bring herself to walk back, to give Bill $1.50 (would he give her a penny back?), and so she sat and stared at the flowers.

Jake came in, holding her coffee. "You forgot this."

"I know. I came to get money to pay Bill, but somehow I just didn't feel like walking back. Jake, it was so sweet of you to bring flowers. They're beautiful."

"Like in the story of your neighbor, though I'm sorry to say, I didn't grow them. Still, I hope you like them. And don't worry about Bill. Coffee's on me." He placed the purple cup on the bench between them. Just as his hand let go it bumped the cup, which started to tip. Both he and Salwa reached to steady it, the result being that his hand grabbed hers.

"Close call," he said.

She felt it, the spark that comes from unprotected flesh touching unprotected flesh. All those innocuous conversations had softened them both, had worn away the protective coating human beings come wrapped in, and Salwa's heart sped. Still trained in formality, she grabbed her hand back. "Sorry," she said without looking at him, amazed and shocked by her reaction.

"Don't be," he said as he sat smiling next to her, leaning forward, his face too close to hers. Their gazes filled the employee room and she forced herself to turn away, willed him to leave, forced her professional self to come gasping back to the surface as he got up and walked out to the front. How could this unacceptable thing be happening? Underneath were other thoughts, ones she barely acknowledged, ones that pointed to the way he looked at her, the way the world vanished when they spent time together. Salwa did not study these thoughts, however, did not pull them out and try to unravel them; to do so would mean to accept that she was attracted to Jake, that some part of her wanted to be closer to him. Those were unacceptable thoughts, ones that needed to stay packed away.

Nine years in America, and never had she been faced with something like this, so shaky and uncertain, something that tugged at her from all angles, left her scrambling to arrange herself properly. She got up and lifted the flowerpot, carried it out to the front, and placed it on a low wall behind the entrance to her secured cubicle. In moving her hand away, she felt a scrape. Then she saw that the seam on the bucket had not been completely folded over at the top, had a sharp metal edge that stuck up and had snared the tiniest bit of flesh from her finger.

Once, more than a quarter of a century earlier, there had been a drunk. Not a pass-out-every-day drunk. He saved passing out for special occasions. He was a coat-his-unfulfilled-tongue-with-drink-and-fill-his-unfulfilled-belly-in-front-of-the-television-until-he-could-tolerate-the-world drunk. If his teenage children were lucky, he would be a fall-asleep-in-his-chair drunk. Static and controlled. This man, an ex-Marine (he hated the *ex*), had been robbed of the possibility of glory by a genetic mutation that surfaced in his thirties. For this, he resented everyone and drank to create for himself a world in which he could leave his mark.

His wife, who worked at the local community college, was having an affair. He knew this because she had been fat and frumpy and suddenly, in what she claimed to be a continuous act of self-control, she became thin and self-conscious. To announce her weight loss to the world, she wore tight clothes that clung to every private moment he had ever shared with her.

The man's daughter hated him, hated her own life, and made

her feelings known by outlining her eyes in thick black pencil (or crayons, as his son liked to say). That fall, the fall when everything changed, his wife signed up to host a student from Jordan, who would not live with them but would come to their house every weekend for a hearty dinner cooked by his wife, who now ate vegetables to the exclusion of everything else. The man did his best to have nothing to do with any of it. Slouched around everyone, snarling here and there to keep them at a distance. His daughter, eighteen and a senior in high school, was suspended for fighting and had to stay home for three weekdays, three weekdays that happened to coincide with her mother's work and his "trail meeting" with two of his Marine buddies. Something happened in those three days, chased her into the arms of the Jordanian student, and within two weeks they had both vanished.

The man's world turned incomprehensibly upside down. Inside out. His wife ate a pie in its entirety. He searched all over the city, asked all his old Marine connections for help. *Semper fi.* More than a year passed before his daughter finally called to say that she and the exchange student had gotten married and were living in his village in Jordan. With only the name of the village, the man went to find her, to bring her back. Expected her to be smoking dope in some sort of primitive harem.

The last thing in the world he expected was for her to be cooking meals with her extended family, helping to tend the crops and animals, and teaching schoolchildren English. His daughter, who had bristled at every breath either he or his wife had ever taken, looked relaxed and contented and happy. The black eyeliner was gone, and her face was smooth and clear.

"It's time you came home with me," he told her.

"No, Daddy, I'm happy here. You are welcome to stay with us for as long as you like, but this is my home now."

"You might like it now, tomorrow, even next month, but there's going to come a time when you won't, when you'll want to leave here and come home. Don't think you can snub me now and then call a few years down the line when you can't stand it anymore." He had not meant to sound so harsh, but once the words had been spoken, he couldn't take them back.

The man returned alone to his country, drank himself into a state of unconsciousness, and woke from it without a wife or son. *This drinking thing is controlling me,* he realized. *I've got to stop.* In an effort to close the chapter in which he was married and had children, he moved himself to a new city, whose winters were not so severe. He stopped drinking, began exercising, returning himself to the shape he had once been in, determined to start over and come to grips with his demons. Just as when he had tried to close the chapter on his military career, when he had realized he could not be an FBI agent or even a police officer, rejection scraped at the center of his soul, only this time he ignored it, kept busy by putting his handiness to work: he bought houses, fixed them up, and sold them, usually for more than twice what he had paid for them. Eventually he got tired of moving every year, so he rented an apartment and lived alone until he was adopted by a cat. Somehow the cat brought life back into his heart, gave him purpose. He began to buy food for it, let it sleep inside sometimes. Even tried to teach it to poop in the toilet, rigged up a device in the spare bathroom. One day when he was watching the news in the living room, he heard the sound of a flush. This simple act filled him with inexplicable satisfaction.

Not two weeks later, the Twin Towers were flattened. In those few hours and the days that followed, everything he had run from, every weakness he had disguised, came bubbling to the surface. All that was really wrong in his life came back to haunt him, to erase the man he had become.

Jassim went through his days in America bulldozer style, an Arab in a Mercedes, oblivious of the sizzling around him, the words tossed his way, the puddles of fear and loathing he skirted and stepped through. After the accident, his diorama sufficiently shaken, he began to see, slowed down, and looked at those looking back. And for the first time he felt unsettled in his beloved America, vaguely longed for home, where he could nestle in the safe, predictable bosom of other Arabs.

In a fog of unknowing, of trying to wedge himself into this easy world and suddenly finding no space, not an inch to spare, Jassim lost his grounding. His purist thought and intense technological dedication went only so far in the real American world. He could hinge himself to nothing earthly. No thing. No person. Penny's face popped into his mind. Her openness, understanding, uncomplicated frankness. All of this attracted him, as a man, he thought, but also on a much more basic level. She promised a safe refuge, a hideout while his real life careened off track after track.

For days he fought Penny's image, her open face and deep cleavage. In the back of his mind he promised himself at least a week—he would wait until after Christmas before defying his routine and going to see her again. His mind could wrap around her all it wished, he promised, as long as he was not unfaithful to his true life. For eight days he held strong, going to swim by rote, replaying Evan's death over and over and over, exhausted rather than exhilarated at the end of each swim. At work he was focused and productive, though not as accurate as usual. At home, Salwa kept her distance and he didn't push her, did not desire her.

Thursday, two weeks and two days after he killed Evan, he looped down the hills and went west instead of turning, wound his way to the American promise of a hearty breakfast. When he pulled up to the restaurant, Jassim's palms were moist. Car off and two final swimming breaths and a whisper. ("There is no harm in talking, in imagining.")

A man of habit, Jassim did not think about where to sit, simply returned to the seat he had occupied on his previous visit. On the wall above the coffee station, a gold-foil garland hung in uneven loops.

"You came back." It was a statement, and it carried no irritation.

"I did."

"You really did have a meeting."

"I really did have a meeting," he lied.

"Okay, what can I get you this morning?"

"Coffee will be fine. Black."

"Do you want to eat something?"

"No, thank you," he lied again, though he could still taste last week's eggs and sausages and biscuits. "On second thought, I would like to have breakfast, maybe some pancakes and sausages this time."

"You got it," she said, and wrote something down on her pad. "Had any more panic attacks?"

"No. Hopefully that was the first and the last. You remember."

She stood in front of him, eyes locked on his and her mouth wide in a grin, hiding nothing. "Some people are easier to remember than others."

"I see," said Jassim, and he thought he might have a heart attack, his rational mind trying to break this apart, to dissect meaning from his frantic desire and inability to stop his words. "I thought of you this past week. Every day. I had to come back."

And he didn't care that he said these things, couldn't care less who might hear them or what they might think. There was no question in his mind; these words needed to be spoken.

"Good you come when I don't have too many customers," she said, pouring his coffee without taking her eyes from his.

"When do you start work?" he asked.

"Five sometimes. Six others. Tuesday is a five. And what do you do this early in the morning?"

"I get up early to go swimming."

"You come in here before or after?"

"I came in here instead. Two weeks ago I killed a teenage boy. I mean, I was driving and he jumped in front of my car and he died and I can't do anything without thinking about him." Jassim felt the tears coming, surprised and overwhelmed by his confession, that he had waited over two weeks to utter it and that he had chosen a waitress he didn't know.

"Oh my God, how awful." Her eyes scooted to the left. "Shit. Spoke too soon. Hang on just a sec, honey. I completely forgot about this customer. Hang tight, I'll be right back."

Hang tight. Jassim wondered where such expressions came from. Days of public executions? Circus days?

"I'm so sorry," he heard Penny say behind him. "My friend over there is having a really hard day. I'm so sorry for the delay. What can I get you?"

Jassim's face burned at the word *friend* and he breathed deeply, forcing away the tears that had appeared so unexpectedly. *Take control. Do not let it swallow you.*

A hand rested on his shoulder. "Okay, I'm back. Jesus, buddy, you must be a mess."

"I've not told anyone about it."

"Not even the police?"

"No, no. I told the police. They came. It was in the middle of the day. No, I just haven't told anyone outside of the police. Until now. How do you bring up something like that?"

"Yeah. Too bad you're not married. That would sure help at a time like this."

Jassim had never been one to lie, and here he'd lied twice since he'd been sitting there, once actively and once by silence. But saying it, telling Penny, had been such a relief.

"Did you talk to the kid's parents?"

"No." This was something that had not occurred to Jassim. He had thought about sending money to help them, but it had not crossed his mind to talk to them.

"Maybe if you talk to them, that would help you come to terms with it. They say that in AA, that you should make peace with those you've hurt."

Jassim watched Penny as she spoke, absorbed her movements and her warmth, couldn't understand what it was that made him feel so close to her. "How could I do that? I mean, how could I find them?"

"You could start with the phone book. Do you know their names?"

"No. I know his name, but not theirs."

"Look for his obituary. It should have everyone's name in the family in it, and then you can see if they're listed in the phone book."

"You are amazing." Jassim couldn't help himself. Walking through the doors of this American institution had transformed him into someone else. History and true self were erased and he became a creation of the past couple of weeks of his life: a man who had killed a teenage boy and was trying to come to terms with it, a man whose wife was not only distant but had recently deceived him. Here the primal man emerged, the one he'd spent a lifetime layering with degrees and ideas and plans. Here he was simply a man with a load of problems turned on by a large-breasted woman he knew nothing about.

She brought his food to him. "I can't talk any more right now."

Jassim glanced around; the restaurant had filled up. He forced himself to eat slowly, again surprised by the tastiness of the food, by the warmth of the environment. He finished and glanced at his watch. Five-fifty. How could the time have been eaten so quickly? Lately when he swam forty-five minutes lasted an eternity, but here it was as though time was taken when he wasn't looking.

Jassim got up and went to the register to pay. He walked back to his seat and had a last sip of coffee, determined not to leave until he had spoken with Penny again.

"Are you going to come back?" asked Penny with a look on her face that Jassim did his best to paste in his brain. Her question was plain, edged with hope but not with some other meaning.

"Yes, I hope so."

"I hope so too." She stood back a little, but the tension pulled at her too; he could see it clearly.

He left a five-dollar bill on the counter and walked out of the restaurant to his car. On his way out he passed two men in their early twenties, both heavily built, both staring at him.

"Good morning," he said automatically, forgetting for just the tiniest moment the world in which he lived. They did not respond, and Jassim looked ahead, walking through the doors and leaving within the building the man he had become.

Into his bubble and back up, unwinding his detoured route to home, trying to push Penny out of his mind and instead think about Evan's parents.

It was several months since acquaintances had taken over a nearby apartment in his complex in order to create their own pharmaceutical company. He was hired as sales representative. At first he had had scruples, sold only to friends and to friends of friends. And then to occasional strangers. Before he knew it, people he had never heard of were appearing at his doorstep, calling his cell phone at all hours of the day and night. It was too close to home, and the part of him that had not yet been overtaken by his own increasing fascination with the product recognized that, recognized that he was without protective gear and heading down a steep grade into traffic. Sometimes he thought he needed to stop right then and there. Twice he even entertained the idea of going to his parents and asking for help, though ultimately he chose not to, never managing to pull himself together enough to make the call.

When he had worked at the topless bar, he had been introduced to methamphetamine, crystal meth, Tina. Finding a drug that made him always feel as though he were in the throes of an orgasm was a delight, a gift, even as his conscience told him to stop. It was as though he were two people: one who went through the day doing what was expected of him, going to class, going to work, and one who was entirely focused on maintaining his high and having sex.

Which brought him to the gorgeous Arab. In a blink she had transformed from being a turn-on to being an obsession. He liked her, liked the cadence of her words when she spoke, but overriding all his thinking about her was a gigantic need to be with her physically. Behind each conversation sat that need, that wanting, to the point where it was almost unbearable. Maybe because she was older. Maybe because she was foreign. Maybe because he felt good in her presence, felt he could be himself. And that she liked him. He couldn't help himself: looking at her across the room, he imagined his mouth on hers, his hand on her breasts or between her legs, and it was all he could do to focus on the customer in front of him.

No way to know how obsessions get their start, which little kernel of one person creeps into the soul of another to make the brain sputter frantically, unable to concentrate on anything else.

What baffled him was that he had never really noticed her until late in the fall, when she had glided onto his radar screen one morning, a golden apple dropped into his lap. She was lovely, with thick hair and light brown eyes that looked as if they held tears. She was shapely and tiny and at least eight years older than he. At least. She was mature without seeming old. This mixed with her foreignness made her sophisticated. Exotic. And married. The challenge of this combination turned him on, and he wondered if all Arab women had this allure (the physical one and the shadow of a man behind them) and if that was why they veiled themselves. He couldn't ask his Egyptian teacher this question, though it had occurred to him.

One day a television reporter came to his Arabic class to interview the students, to see why they were learning Arabic, and he had thought to say initially it had been to learn the language of opium, but now it was because he desperately wanted to make love to an Arab woman and he thought this was the best way to get to her. But of course he hadn't said a word. In fact the whole idea of being on camera had made him so nervous that he had left the room when they began filming.

"Hi, beautiful. How are you today?" Jack asked as he handed Diane his membership card.

"I'm fine, Jack. You?"

"I'm doing just great." He looked behind him, cleared his throat.

Diane looked left and right as well, not at all worried about what Jack was preparing himself to say.

"Diane, I was wondering if you know a Jordanian fellow who comes here in the mornings. Early mornings. He's a swimmer."

"What do you want to know about him?" She smiled, leaning on the counter and resting her chin on her closed fist.

"Anything you can tell me."

"You're talking about Jassim, I guess."

"I guess."

"He's such a sweetheart. Did he do something to get on your bad side, Jack? Don't tell me Mr. FBI is surfacing again."

"Oh no, not at all. I work with his wife and I was just curious, just wondered what he is like."

"Wife? That's too bad. He's very polite and nice. He always comes in at the same time, swims for thirty to forty-five minutes. Takes a shower. Leaves. Wears the same clothes when he comes, always wears a Speedo when he swims. Drives a nice-looking Mercedes. What more do you want to know?"

"He does that every day? Comes in every day to swim?'

"Yes, well, until recently. I usually just work weekdays and he used to come in every day but Wednesday. In the past few weeks he hasn't come in as frequently, and when he does come, he seems preoccupied, like sometimes instead of swiping his card, he'll hand it to me and just stand there, like he doesn't know what to do. It's weird, like something heavy is on his mind. In the past I've tried to talk to him, but he doesn't say much about his personal life." Or anything. She smiled. "I didn't think he was married. He doesn't wear a ring or anything. Wishful thinking."

"Do you think you could try to talk to him some more? I mean, could you try to find out what changed? Or anything." Jack stood back so a couple could scan their membership cards. They nodded at Diane.

"It would help if I knew what this was about, what it was you wanted to know."

"If I knew, I'd tell you, Diane. I just have a funny feeling about him, feel like he's not on the up and up. These days it's important to know, if you get what I mean."

Diane opened her eyes wider but did not seem surprised. "I get it, Jack—you *are* back in FBI mode, aren't you? Talking to your buddies and tipping them off, hoping they'll include you in their work. And you're thinking Jassim is a terrorist or something."

Jack said nothing. This is why he came to Diane; she was quick on the draw and had a good sense of people, especially if she was pointed in the right direction.

"Jack, let me tell you, that's absurd. Jassim is a swimmer, not some religious freak. He wears a Speedo! He's been swimming here for years."

Jack looked at her, narrowed his eyes so that she would feel the importance of his words. "You're probably right, Diane. You're probably right. Let me know if you find out otherwise." He walked into the club, knowing that she would not be able to resist.

The more Jack thought about it, the more he was sure that Jassim was not the man he portrayed himself to be, though he was not necessarily sold on his being a terrorist. He had already talked to his FBI friend Samuel about him. Twice. Would continue to keep him posted, as Samuel had suggested. He harbored no ill will toward either Salwa or Jassim, just felt that not everything was in its place, was as it should be. *These are some scary times we live in,* he reasoned to himself. *My number-one duty is to help protect my country. The president said that specifically, that it is our job to be on the alert for suspicious behavior, to help the police, to be the eyes and ears of the community. Besides, if it turns out to be nothing, then no harm done to anyone. Dammit, if you're going to live in this country, you're going to have to abide by the rules here.*

Jack had no need to see beyond the act of what he was doing. For the first time in years he felt armed with a righteous and vital responsibility and therefore important, selfless.

She was almost herself again, with only an occasional thought of the baby. Late Friday afternoon tinged in gray; the sun keeping to itself, leaving a bite to the air, one that Salwa loved, that reminded her of home.

All of the other tellers had already left, most of them going to meet at a bar for happy hour, encouraged by Bill as part of team-building, an American concept she found pointless. She decided not to go, partly because she didn't like to spend time with them socially, but more because she wanted to get home, wanted to enjoy this evening when she didn't have to meet with a client wanting to buy or sell a house, didn't have to do any comparative market analyses for anyone, didn't have detailed paperwork to fill out. Having secured all the balanced drawers in the vault, she and Bill walked out of the building with the security guard.

"Are you coming to happy hour, Salwa?" asked Bill.

"Not this time. Have fun, though, and please give my regrets. I'm too tired."

"How about you, Bob?"

Bob shook his head and Bill said goodnight, hurried to his car.

"Big plans for the weekend, Salwa?" asked Bob in his tobacco-stained voice.

"No. Just house things. Relaxing things. You?"

"We've got a barbecue for my son tomorrow. I'm hoping the weather will be on our side."

"That sounds nice, Bob. I'll keep my fingers crossed for you. Have a good evening."

"You too, Salwa. Looks like we're in for a cold night."

"Finally! See you Monday."

Bill drove off and waved; Bob walked off the lot to the street, where he always parked his car. She always wondered about this, why he didn't park in the bank's parking lot. He drove an old Toyota station wagon, and she wondered if he was embarrassed by it. Only a few steps to the safety of her car; she was almost home free. If only she had not stopped to talk to Bob. If only she had not paused to look at the giant mesquite tree at the back of the parking lot, at the gray clouds above it, and actually taken a minute to think of God and the beauty of life. In those extra two minutes, Jake appeared, pulling back into the parking lot, swerving his car in next to hers. She watched as he got out, his back straight, his eyes fixed on hers. Closer, closer, until he was in front of her, gazing into her, pouring his own self in.

These things don't come planned, don't come with a rule book.

"Am I too late?" he asked. "Did everyone already go?"

Salwa nodded, aware that he was standing too close to her.

"Do you want—" he started to say, but she put her finger on his lips. In a breath he opened his mouth, tasted the delicate finger, moved closer, and cradled her head with his hands. Her hand dropped to his chest, and he pushed his face lower and closer until his lips touched hers, gently at first, quiet like a butterfly's wings. He stopped, pulled his face away from hers, and held her close to him, folded her with his arms against his chest, his body.

Salwa's conscience fought within her, shouted the impossibility of what she was doing, allowing an American boy to envelop her married self. While her body was embraced and adored, her brain and soul fought hard to get away, shouted for him to let go of her. Instead he kissed her again, this time not so gently, not so innocently. This time it was full of wanting and passion, a long kiss Salwa had not tasted before, a minty, indiscreet kiss that silenced the shouting and exiled her from her life.

She stopped and pulled away.

Jake's voice came. "I—"

Again Salwa covered his mouth gently with her fingers, this time pulling herself away. "I have to go."

Jake opened her car door, closed it when she was settled, kissed her through the window she opened for him, and watched her pull away, force herself back into her real life.

Salwa's body fought itself, aching with delight and gnawed through with guilt. No voice of reason calmed her, only guilt, and finally tears in floods and shouts. "What have I done? What have I done?" Salwa demanded of herself in English, this being an American problem, an American situation. She promised herself to think about it only in English, even as her brain shouted at her in Arabic, cursed her with her mother's words.

It had been so easy. A few smiles, a few innocent conversations, a touch here and there, and suddenly they were kissing in the parking lot. That kiss was so unconnected to any part of her reality, her family, her job, her anything, as though it could just happen in the moment and be what it was and stay there, a breath in history that could harm no one.

"This is crazy," she said aloud. "It will never happen again. Finish. No need to dwell."

Self-talk ironed her smooth so that by the time she reached home some twenty minutes later, she was her usual cheery self.

Jassim wasn't there, which was odd, since he came home early on Fridays.

At this moment, walking into the house that she had helped design, that she had decorated, that was totally hers and totally empty, Salwa felt lost, which is how it came to be that she began thinking again about going home. Back to Jordan, with her family and her language and her predicable world. The shock came when she realized that in this fantasy she had not included Jassim, had left him in Tucson.

—◦ Chapter Ten ◦—

At work Jassim entered Evan's name in the search box of the local paper's obituary page. Not even a blink and Evan Parker's face appeared on his computer screen, a small black-and-white rectangle, the same posed portrait that was glued to the cross marking the spot where Evan had died. There was nothing particularly striking about him, and as before, when Jassim had knelt before the tiny cross, he could not connect the boy's face to the one that had stared at him through blue lenses before he jumped. For some reason it was that image and not the one of him lying unconscious on the street that lingered in Jassim's mind.

EVAN EZEKIEL PARKER (1985–2001)
In loving memory of our son, who left this world to be in a better one. Evan was full of life and will be missed by friends and family. He is survived by his mother, Mary, his sister, Bethany, of Tucson, his father, Todd Parker, of Tucson, and his grandparents...

Jassim read it several times. He wondered why Todd Parker was not listed next to Mary, why Bethany had been placed between them—a buffer, perhaps. Maybe that was why donations were requested to help pay for the funeral. Perhaps the parents were divorced and the father was not working. Jassim turned the possible scenarios over and over in his mind and felt a wave of dizziness. Nauseated dizziness.

He clicked off the obituary page and closed his eyes. A life spun out of control. A tie to the world so tenuous, so shaky. Wedged there at the front of his brain was the knowledge that he needed Salwa to get through this and that without her things could only get worse.

Thinking of Salwa was a tangled pile of knots, however, so if Jassim could not turn to her, then he would turn to his first love: water. Lining the eastern wall of his office were two narrow bookshelves filled with books and binders and stacks of unread articles that waited for moments such as these, for times when he needed to be reminded of his life's mission, needed to be distracted from today by its importance. One bookshelf contained *problems* and the other contained *solutions*.

The *problems* shelves contained books and articles about water crises in various countries, the result of any number of factors, including natural depletion in supply, population shifts, contamination, and industry misuse.

The *solutions* shelves included a much larger collection of unread documents, stacks dealing with rainwater harvesting, desalination, and innovative technologies that focused on self-sufficiency and commonsense approaches. A final group of articles stacked next to his technical reference books fit into neither of his two general headings, miscellaneous articles that were broad in their scope: recycling efforts around the world, various articles related to health and literacy rates.

He turned to the *problems* shelves, took the top article in the unread pile, which related to historical issues in the Middle East. "The Stealing of the Banyas" sent Jassim's thoughts thousands of miles away, to one of his last conversations with Abu Jalal. "The Golan Heights had nothing to do with it," he had argued. "It was control of the Banyas River they wanted. They want the headwaters of the Jordan. This fight is not about land or God, it is much more primitive than that: it is about water. Without it they die. Whoever has control of the water wins. It is as simple as that."

Rather than being swallowed by the complexities of the problem, of what had already been done, Jassim had decided to focus his energy on the solution, on an idea that had nothing to do with the Israelis but rather concerned self-sufficiency in the face of injustice. "If we can be self-sufficient, we can determine our future."

Abu Jalal had looked at him as though he were six years old. "Baba, we cannot be self-sufficient if the supplies are horded from the beginning. When they stake a claim to God and water, we have nothing."

Jassim had disagreed but had not said so, and now, sitting in his office in the middle of an American desert, he let this picture evaporate. How far removed this chair, this reading of articles was from his life, or rather from the life he had planned for himself. Where had he put his ideals, his dreams? Here in America, what was he doing? He'd killed a boy. The reminder sent a sickening feeling throughout his body.

This was an American problem; perhaps it needed an American solution. Perhaps Penny was right—perhaps if he made amends to the family, then he could move on with his life. Penny and her face blipped inside him. What had she done to make him feel so close to her? And so far from Salwa?

Jassim got up and pulled the phone book, the white pages, off a top shelf. He looked at its thickness, estimated where he thought *Parker* would fall, and opened the book. Three pages from the correct page. He found *M Parker,* followed by an address and a phone number. This was something he needed to do in person, but how could he know for sure it was she? He could call, but what would he say? ("Hello. I am calling to find out if you are the Mary Parker whose son, Evan, just died. I am the man who killed him, and I want to come to your house and apologize.") Perhaps if he drove by her house he would know if this was the right M. Parker; perhaps Evan's friend would just happen to come by at that exact moment.

Jassim closed the phone book and put it back on the shelf. Sat down again at his desk to read about the stolen headwaters but saw nothing; no words marched before him. Instead his mind tugged at the idea of going to Mary Parker's house.

All weekend her thoughts wrapped around what she had done, what she had allowed to happen. It was the kiss itself, the fact that she had let her lips, which had never before touched the skin of a man outside her family (somehow Hassan didn't count), be kissed by those of a man several years her junior. But what shocked her more was that she wanted to do it again. She thought this during dinner on Saturday with Jassim. She thought it on Sunday as they walked side by side in the mall, saying only the most necessary things to each other, pushed apart by some unseen force, by a family of lies that walked rudely between them. She thought it as she walked away from Jassim on the pretext of looking at pajamas and then walked past Dillard's and instead went into the much racier Victoria's Secret. It occurred to her as she crossed the silky threshold that she and her husband had not been intimate since before her miscarriage, and she wondered what had dampened Jassim's predictable need for her.

She let these thoughts go, too wispy and light to hold her attention as she perused pajamas in flannel, silk, and satin. A few more steps, however, found her facing tables and racks of bras in red and black and pink and white. They were beautiful, titillating, and very expensive. Each one held different promises (enhancement, push-up, maximum nipple coverage, smooth fabric). She fingered one lovely lacy bra after another and was daunted by the options.

"I'll get a dressing room started for you, ma'am," said a salesgirl, lifting two bras out of her hand.

And while Salwa never tried on intimate apparel in stores, she made an exception.

"Are you looking for anything in particular?"

"No, just something pretty."

"Lacy pretty or sexy pretty?"

"Sexy pretty."

After more than a half an hour, she walked out of the store, bag in hand, containing one silver-blue plunge bra and one black cleavage-enhancing, unlined push-up bra. And matching panties for each. And a feeling that she had done something she shouldn't have, so much so that as she passed by Dillard's on her way out, she stopped in and asked for a bag.

No one needs to see what is in the heart. It can be disguised, covered up, left for dead. That is what must happen. Desire is cheap and easy and like a drug can overpower even the strongest person, Salwa thought as she headed back to the food court with her tissue-wrapped spills of silk and lace.

Here in America, no one said anything, no one intruded in other people's business or stopped things like this from occurring. No one tiptoed into the dark rooms of other people's homes with their buckets of judgment and said what they really thought. There were no intrusive neighbors or blunt aunties to announce what they knew and say, *You'd better not, or else.* Here people sat on the front lawn waiting for the aftermath, the hideous carnage of advantage taken.

There was no doubt in her mind that the kiss had been allowed to happen, permitted, even encouraged; desired desire. Salwa should have been smarter, should have seen it coming and should have been able to stop it (should have wanted to stop it). For a brief moment, walking back to find her husband in this crowded and noisy mall, she stepped outside her guilty self and saw American marketing and embedded reporting written all over her situation: *Innocent College Student Taken by Exotic Arab Banker.* It was a ploy, a Fox News setup.

And then those thoughts slipped away and she stood in the middle of the food court with more than $100 worth of promising underwear carefully packaged and wrapped, having forgotten who she was looking for, lost in the delightful memory of her illicit kiss.

"Hey, Madame Pajama, where are you going?" called Jassim.

Salwa looked around. He was still in the same spot where she had left him, unabashedly staring at passersby.

"You bought another pair of pajamas, didn't you?" asked Jassim. "That's it. I will have to move out. There simply is not room in our house for all of me and another pair of pajamas."

"Very funny." She saw that he said these words out of habit and not out of enjoyment, saw that his mind was elsewhere. "Are you okay, Jassim?"

Jassim put his hand on hers, and while his touch was sincere, she could feel a barrier between them, as though she wore thick gloves. She looked at his lean, dark hand covering her own and felt an ache that brought with it dizziness. A few seconds later she pulled her hand away.

Those two days filled by domestic activities did not lift the desire out of her bones even as she soaked herself in loathing.

And now to have to go back to work, not to be able to change what happened or at least run away from it. Driving isolated from all those other human beings in their own bubbles with their own agonies and desires and disgust, Salwa practiced a stiff face even as her insides rumpled, rolled up in a tiny jittery ball. In all her nervousness, she had not managed to pry herself from the house on time and was a few minutes behind schedule—something she had done maybe five times in all her years working in America. This increased her self-loathing and she hoped that she would arrive after Jake had already settled in, prayed that she could lose herself in her work. At the same time, she glanced in the rearview mirror and adjusted the wisps of bangs that softened her forehead.

Turning off the street and into the paved parking lot, she scanned around but did not see Jake's car. A last glance of assurance in the mirror, a last tiny adjustment to her lipstick, a last whiff of disgust before she stepped out onto the black American pavement, ready to deal out hard American cash.

Insides giddy like a teenager's, like a prospective bride's, like a guilty wife's, she stepped in, a being split in two, a good half and a bad half, wondering who would win today.

"Morning, Petra, how are you?"

"Hi, Salwa. Good weekend?"

"Very nice, thank you. Yours?"

"Shitty."

Salwa stopped. Petra defied all rules, including small talk.

"That doesn't sound good. What happened?" Salwa asked, even though she didn't want to know.

"Just everything. Molly's moving out. We're breaking up."

"Oh Petra, I'm so sorry."

"That's not the worst of it. She's moving in with a man. Molly, who hates men, who makes fun of men, who thinks they're all stupid, has supposedly fallen in love with one and is leaving me for him."

Not knowing what to say, Salwa put down her briefcase and hugged her coworker, and to offer proof that she had been living in

America for many, many years, she gave her best answer: "You're going to be okay, Petra."

"I know. I knew this was coming. It just feels pretty rotten."

"It must be awful." Really, how awful, and how odd to feel such sympathy and disgust all in one moment. Salwa burned to walk away, not just from this conversation but from this culture, where men and women could choose between men and women, where there were no limits, no taboos.

"Have you seen Lover Boy today?" asked Petra with a sudden edge to her voice.

"Who's Lover Boy?"

"Jake. He must have struck gold, because he's strutting around here like he owns the place, like he spent the weekend fucking some college girl into oblivion."

"Petra! That is such an ugly way to speak about someone."

"Sorry. Since when do you defend him?"

"I'm not defending him," replied Salwa, a flush of heat working its way up her face. "But that kind of talk about anyone is just ugly and unnecessary."

"Sorry for offending. I forget you come from a conservative culture. Really, sorry. Thanks for listening, Salwa."

Salwa left her things in her locker and settled at her desk.

"*Marhaba ya jameela.*"

Salwa had been so absorbed in thinking about Petra that for a few impossible minutes she had forgotten Jake, had forgotten her own treachery. His voice, his accented Arabic, slid into her veins, spread throughout her body, made her unsteady on her two feet. Deep breath, deep breath, invisible deep breath. Be calm, professional.

"*Sabah al-khayr.* How was your weekend, Jake?"

"Horrible."

"Why horrible?"

"Because I missed you every second of it. Every minute was like a month without you. I thought I would die. And now that I see you again, I will probably die at your feet." He took a step toward her, his right hand over his heart, and feigned a slight stagger.

Her formal façade was gone, her self-hatred withered. Forgotten were thoughts about what was right, and she could not keep herself from laughing, a deep, intimate, delighted laugh, the kind she used to laugh with Jassim.

"Talk to you later?"

"Okay, talk to you later."

He lingered, close enough for her to smell his cologne (strong), smiling his intimate smile, the one that pulled her to him and away from all that she knew, the one that opened her soul to the possibility of sin.

She saw in his eyes, in his body language, why Petra had called him Lover Boy.

"Do you want to have lunch today?" he asked, and under his words she heard these: *Could I make love to you?* Salwa shuddered with fear and enchantment and a distancing from God and from all that she knew to be right in the world.

Against her will and a thousand and one cautionary tales, she said yes to both questions. He turned away to cope with his day while she remained in her cubicle, excited and terrified.

Can't unpeel memory, can't make things unhappen. Salwa had stepped out of her real life, knew in the depths of herself that this was disaster in the making, and yet couldn't help but enjoy the anticipation.

She pushed Jake out of her mind, shoved him away from her thinking and dragged Jassim back. At 10:30 she called him on his cell phone and got his voice mail.

"Hi, Jassim. Do you want to have lunch today? Call me. Bye."

At 11:00 Jassim had not called. Jassim always called her back. He must be in a meeting.

—⁂—

If wishes came true, she would wish that things were now as they once had been, but Salwa knew in the marrow of her bones that wishes don't come true for Arabs in America, recognized that the shift had come just months before, on the very day when she had tried with all her soul to drown her deception. It was not just her Lie that had brought distance between her and her husband and surrounded them with tension, it was the patriotic breathing of those around them. American flags waving, pale hands willing them to go home or agree. Jassim didn't seem to be bothered, but Salwa could not tolerate it, those red, white, and blue fingers flapping at her, flicking her away.

Again the idea of being home settled itself into her, offered her peace for the rest of the morning.

—⁂—

Almost noon, and she checked the messages on her cell phone.

"Salwa? Hi, it's Joan. I have some great news for you—the house you showed to that couple for the Tomkinses sold. For $650,000. That means almost $20,000 commission, for one house. All your hard work is really paying off."

Salwa listened to Joan's breathy words, her voice spilling in genuine excitement, no pinpricks of jealousy.

"They are so pleased with you, Salwa. They told me they will recommend you to everyone they know. I knew you had real career potential! Maybe you'll quit your other job now. I gotta go, honey. Call me if you want, or I'll see you when you come in today."

Salwa pressed star-one and replayed the message, looking at $20,000 extra in her mind. Thought about home. The two thoughts met, merged in a terrible union. Twenty thousand dollars would mean financial leeway for her if she decided to leave, would offer her freedom to go home, though she would be unable to continue to help Siham pay for her daughter's school.

In the middle of these thoughts stood Jake. "Are we having lunch together?" His snake-sweet words stained his face, pulling at the corners of his mouth, *together* a knot on his tongue. "You look happy."

"One of the houses I was showing just sold."

"That's nice. So how much are we talking here? Five thousand? Six thousand?"

A hair of caution crossed her thoughts, and she said nothing. "So are we on for lunch?"

No, no, no, bellowed Salwa across mountaintops, but not quite loud enough to reach Jake's ears, and her simple self, still miffed that Jassim had not called back and pleased with the commission on the house, answered instead, "Okay. Where do you want to go?"

"It's up to you." As if it were, as if Salwa's choice in this tiniest of matters would make a difference to the outcome, as if she didn't know that the destination would be the same whether her path was narrow and dusty or paved smooth.

They walked out together, a couple of people, not yet a couple, not yet coupled, the decision about lunch still not made, still on Salwa's shoulders. She let it fall behind her, dragged it along by the dainty heel of her shoe as they crossed the parking lot.

"How about I drive?" said Jake, erasing the possibility of a question, of choice, instead paving the road, adjusting the arrival time in his favor. She settled into his car (through the door he held open for her and shut behind her), which was shiny black on the outside and spotless tan on the inside. (Scratching at the back of her mind was the thought that maybe he had planned this down to the shiny clean interior.)

Jake slid into his seat, closed his door, and sealed them together sharing the same air. "Are you okay, Salwa?"

"I'm fine, Jake." She turned to look at him, at the fineness of his hair (was it as soft as it looked?), at the smoothness of his skin (like a child's).

Instead of facing forward and starting the car and heading toward a restaurant, he turned to look at her, to allow his eyes one giant greedy gulp. "You are so beautiful. I don't think I've ever seen anyone as beautiful as you, not close up, not true beauty."

She felt his words seep through the pores of her skin, spread their way across her body. His simple sentences worked their way into tissue and organs and muscle and bone and spread, weakening her as they went. At the core of those words was desire, now lodged in every one of her body's cells. The real words, for they translated internally, were *You turn me on and I want you and I intend to have you*. (Heady plans for such a young man, but this is America and everything is possible.)

Their faces were inches apart, but the air in the car had become thick and he turned the key, started them on their freshly paved way. "I have an idea. Let's take advantage of the beautiful day and get takeout food and go to a park and eat there."

"That sounds nice."

Mexican takeout food, midtown park. The silence between them was now intimate as they walked with unhurried steps through the browning grass toward the most distant picnic table. At first they sat across from each other, but the expanse of the table seemed unnaturally large and Jake moved next to her. Not touching her, just closer.

He finished his food and fingered her hair, his touch reaching deep, deep inside her, forcing an end to her eating, even as she told herself *No, no, no.* Knowing what was next, savoring the anticipation, she wrapped up her half-eaten lunch, sipped her soda, wiped her mouth, and turned her eyes to his.

"Salwa, may I kiss you?" he asked with the face of a boy.

She did not answer, just moved toward him, allowed him to envelop her entirely, consume her in one indiscreet gulp in the middle of an American park. Salwa lost herself for minutes while the rest of the world shut down.

Relieved that they were in a park, that this could go no further, she stopped, leaned into him.

"My God, but you are incredible," he said, and Salwa blushed, though her brain had come back and scolded her bilingually: *Really? What is so incredible? Do you really think you are the first woman he has kissed? Come on. Who is he trying to impress?*

They each sat in their own fantasy of what this really meant. Salwa's eyes wandered across the way and snagged on a toddler in overalls climbing on the orange-and-blue jungle gym as his pregnant young mother watched him, smiling and giggling.

The earth beneath Salwa rocked violently and she held on to Jake, tears falling from her eyes.

"Salwa, what's wrong?" Jake's arm was around her, gentle and soothing, and she leaned against him as her sobbing convulsed her. He said nothing, just held her, rocking her ever so slightly.

"Oh God, I am sorry, Jake. I don't know where that came from." But she couldn't stop.

"Salwa, is this because of us, because of this?"

And that question knocked it out of her, because her sadness was so much greater than *this*, than *us*. It was everything, culminating in the loss of a child that never was. It was plans lived and meaning nothing, hatred simmering around her, real life, not a staged TV kiss. Her grief did not explain itself properly and came out as a confession instead.

"I had a miscarriage. My husband did not want a baby and I did. I stopped taking my birth control pills in spite of his wishes. When I got pregnant, I couldn't tell him, and then all of a sudden I was miscarrying and I couldn't tell him. I guess seeing that mother and her child playing over there undid me. I'm sorry, Jake." *Sorry for telling you, for burdening you, not for what I did.* She hated her voice as she spoke, felt it came from somewhere else, some other body.

"So you never told him?" asked Jake, latching on to the least important of her words.

"Not at the time. One day I was crying and he came home early, so I told him then, but not the exact details."

"It doesn't sound to me like you have a very open relationship."

Salwa pulled away from this man who could be her lover to defend the man who was her husband. "We do, actually. But there is also respect. In not telling him about being pregnant, by getting pregnant in the first place, in a way I lied to him. I chose what I wanted to do over what we together agreed to do. I couldn't tell him because I feared his disappointment and because I hated myself for doing it." These words were right, correct, true, and it was a relief to release them.

Jake stared at her, his eyes deflecting her honesty. "I guess. It just seems that when you're married, you should be able to tell your partner anything and everything."

"Perhaps anything and everything are not always necessary. Over time you realize that things are not so simple. You are younger, too. More idealistic, perhaps."

Salwa's heart was beating fast, her feelings of just a few minutes ago drowned by his simplistic themes, his romantic notion of husband and wife, his judgment.

"Salwa, do you love your husband?"

"I do love him. He is a good man, an honest man."

Jake thought, his arm still draped over Salwa but his heart not as involved. She felt it, sensed the change in his touch. They sipped their sodas in silence with a haze around them. Salwa's anger at herself was enormous, and she tried to focus on what she knew to be true, what gave her peace. Silent words invoking God rolled around her mind, shielding her from Jake, protecting her.

"I'm sorry, Salwa. I didn't have the right to say that," Jake said finally, more automatically than honest. "I guess I am young and I am idealistic and I do think that a man and a woman should be able to tell each other everything if they are married."

"And there is nothing wrong with that, nor is there anything wrong with accepting that not everything needs to be said. I chose not to tell him to protect him. Often when you do that, the damage comes to you instead."

Jake was staring at her again, but this time she deflected him with the confidence of hundreds of years of civilization. "I think we should go now, Jake."

Back in her cubicle, fed full and cried empty, Salwa tried to focus, to put her entire being into her work. That was the American way, after all, wasn't it? Let your soul get sucked out but work hard in the meantime.

—◊—

White and wet and impossible. The promise of American romance was a lovely box filled with teeth that devoured you with gigantic gnashing and crunching. Before, Salwa would not have believed that life could be transformed in a day by one event so tiny as a kiss in the parking lot. Two sets of lips, wet on wet. But it had. The kiss had lifted from her eyes the last threads of the remaining tidy veil of name brands and small talk, the cellophane promise, the two-ply vow that anything you wanted could be yours. Anything. From a Mercedes to a house in the foothills to sex with your coworker. It was all, down to the last breath, a neatly packaged lie to disguise real life. In that kiss, Salwa had torn it all to shreds, let the tatters blow away, and now she stood at the top of Mount Ararat and viewed the world for what it was: rocky and impossible. She stood there, windblown in her bright yellow self-hatred, wispy slivers of her self caught on the crags below.

All the wanting inside her pooled just under the surface, trained in containment but yearning to break free. The miscarriage had released this new thing into her bloodstream, a horrid kind of craving that excluded Jassim and his cerebral steps.

Desire ate at her, carved notches in her veins, pockets to store more, to allow buildup. Whatever this new thing was, it pushed Jassim away even more than the Lie had, a wild winding river overflowing its manmade banks. Not intentionally. There was no bone in Salwa that intended to deceive or to hurt. Maybe it grew out of distance.

That was another lie to the self, she realized. The distance grew from her Lie, the one that had spilled out from between her legs and been carried away by his precious water.

Somehow, in giving birth to a dead baby (*No, Salwa, it's not a baby, it would never have been a baby,* murmured Randa's voice), Salwa had entered another plane of existence. In this one, time moved slowly and quickly at once. Smells were all-powerful and tears were just below the surface. Just as Jassim had walked through an invisible door, stood behind an impenetrable wall, so she now had separated herself.

No rules here, no rules telling a twenty-something college student not to pursue a married woman. At home that wouldn't happen. Tongues would have wagged from the first glance, and nothing would have gone beyond.

Fly across the sky upside down and beg forgiveness from God.

A kiss is not an affair, Salwa repeated to herself. Several kisses and an embrace or two. Nothing. She pleaded with herself to believe this largest of lies, the Lie that smothered all the previous napkin-sized lies. The one that denied life. That hid from the world a whole story. Surely that Lie was far more monstrous than a kiss.

In the mornings she could believe it, could believe that everything was fine, that she had only kissed her young coworker and miscarried a mangled wad of flesh. Mornings were when she found hope.

Night was different. It was at night, during those hours she lay awake, that she was trapped by her thoughts, pinned down by the ugliness of what she had done while her clean husband lay next to her.

—◌ ◌—

Penny liked it that Jassim came in at least three mornings a week and occasionally at lunchtime. She liked it that he so enjoyed the meals she served him, and it didn't hurt that his tips were usually larger than the price of the meal. She was no fool and recognized over the several weeks since the first time he had seated himself at the counter that he came to her in part because he ached so much for what had happened to that boy. It didn't matter that it wasn't his fault, she well understood; it felt like it was, which is why she hadn't objected when he had asked for her help. When he explained that he wanted to go visit the family and apologize in person but he wasn't sure about the address in the phone book, Penny agreed to call and find out if it was the same woman who had lost a son. Evan. Jassim gave her his business card, and Penny said that she would call when she found out, that she would do it in the next day or two.

Penny sat in her room and steeled herself for the phone call. At first she thought it would be simple, just a made-up story to get her information. *Hi, is Evan there? Oh, sorry.* But she couldn't bring herself to do it. *How can I make this easier on his mother?* she asked herself. *How can this be positive rather than negative?*

"Hello, is this Mary Parker?"

"It is."

"Mary, my name is Penny and I am sorry to bother you." She paused, not sure if she could continue. "I heard about what happened to Evan—my daughter—and I want you to know I am so, so sorry."

"Thank you. It's kind of you to call. Was your daughter friends with Evan?"

"I don't know how close, but she is so sensitive to sadness in others, would have been looking out for him."

"That's nice to hear. Funny how it takes him dying to hear these things from people."

"I know just what you mean," said Penny, her eyes filling with tears, her mind racing back a couple of years. "Mary, it's always going to hurt, thinking about your son."

The phone was silent, and Penny knew the woman was crying, knew that every part of Mary's insides ached in a way she would never have thought possible.

"I'll say a prayer for him, for Evan. And my daughter."

More silence.

"He's in a better place now. You have to believe that." Still nothing, only the faintest noise to tell her Mary was still on the other end. "Goodbye, Mary."

Penny hung up the phone, lay across her bed, and sobbed. Almost two years, and it felt like she had lost her baby yesterday, that her world had begun to chip apart yesterday. The chips had started falling off earlier, she saw now, but somehow she had not noticed until it was too late. Even in her anguished state she saw that, saw how hard it was to get it right while you still had the chance.

Chapter Eleven

For several weeks in the early part of the new year, Jassim drove past 4165 E. Fifteenth Street looking for clues, hoping someone would emerge to let him know for sure that it was the right house. Sitting in his office, he pulled out his wallet, and in the back, slipped down in the skinniest of spots, was the piece of paper he was looking for. He dialed the numbers and asked for Penny.

"Hi. It's Jassim."

"The M. Parker in the phone book is Mary Parker, mother of Evan."

"How did you find...?"

"Don't worry; I have my ways. Are you going?"

"I have to think about it."

"Don't think. *Just do it,* like the commercial says."

"Okay, Penny."

"Okay." A seed in her voice propelled itself through him, took root in his body. "Hey, good luck. I hope it helps."

"Me too."

Jassim hung up and looked again at the silent stacks covering the surfaces of his bookcases. Managing water properly was the single most important issue that faced mankind, of this he was absolutely sure, and yet at this moment in American time he didn't care, could not climb out of today.

Perhaps if he went to see Mary Parker, if he took her flowers and apologized in person, his life could go back to normal. Back to Salwa, to his routine, to his swimming. No more visits to Penny.

Jassim closed up his desk, turned off the computer, turned off the lamp, got up, and walked out of his office, past the reception desk.

"Goodbye, Bella."

"Oh, do you have a meeting today?"

Jassim stopped in front of her desk and let his eyes rest on her large face. "No. Why do you ask?"

"Oh, no reason. Just in case Marcus wanted to know." Bella

looked at her computer and stammered, "I...uh...I don't have anything scheduled for you today."

Her words grated in their pointed nosiness. He looked at her as severely as he could. "I will see you tomorrow," he said, and walked out the door. Had she not asked him to account for himself, he might have asked her what kind of flowers to buy for a woman who is grieving over the death of her son.

—⁓—

Jassim stepped up to the concrete stoop, which, like the neighborhood, and really like the whole city, had too much sun on it: an exposed wound with skin seared back, clean, white bone and fresh tissue open to all the world's germs. Jassim, child of Jordan, whose feet learned to walk on holy soil, was a beautiful cancerous growth in his pressed dress pants, Armani tie, olive skin, holding a bouquet of lilies to mourn the dead, penance for his enormous sin.

Heart thudding against the walls of his body forced a shudder. Too late to run away, doorbell already rung, nothing to do but wait.

The screen door was not flush with the frame, poked out a bit at the bottom, a little bent and not closed all the way. Had Evan Parker kicked it once in a rage? Had someone tried to break in? Jassim rang the bell again and heard a raspy "Coming!" from inside.

No evidence littering the front yard suggested that a teenage boy had lived there, nor that one had died recently. Was he standing in front of the wrong house?

The inside door swung open and a whiff of stale cigarette smoke greeted him.

"Yes?"

For a moment Jassim couldn't speak.

"Yes, may I help you?" The woman stood close to the screen, her face almost touching it, and stared at him.

Jassim had expected her to be in her late thirties or early forties, but through the screen he saw an older, more tired woman than he had expected, one with a thick hank of hair collected in a band and swung around her neck to rest on her left side, reaching all the way down to cover her breast. Jassim had spent a lifetime around long hair, mostly thick, and often lustrous. In America, long hair seemed to be cut off by the time a woman reached thirty, at least among the women with whom he dealt. Among poorer women, women he came across at the grocery store or saw crossing the street while he was sitting at a red light in his car, hair was maintained, a dowry not to be disposed of easily.

"You're Mary Parker?"

"Yes."

"I . . . I . . . I'm sorry. I brought you these, for your son." He lifted the flowers. "I am so sorry about what happened to him." Jassim did not like the way his voice sounded. Though his words came from a deep straggling sadness, they came out professionally packaged in a tidy little box.

"Thank you. That's kind of you. Do I know you?"

"My name is Jassim Haddad."

"Jassim? That sounds. . . . Oh my God . . . you're the one who . . ." She stood behind the screen door, frozen for a second as her brain leaped over the name and what that name had brought her. Her body shifted, muscles woke up, head nodded ever so slightly.

"I did not come to upset you. I came to tell you in person that I am sorry. That it was an accident and that I am sorry, so very, very sorry. I cannot imagine what on God's earth you must be going through. I wanted you to know that. I thought it might help."

Her heavy words came out jagged. "Did you? Did you think I would feel better seeing the face of the rich prick who ran over my son?"

Jassim had prepared himself for this and held her gaze through the filter of the screen. "Yes, I did. I know that I would rather have a complete picture than an imaginary one. I know that I would rather know it was an accident than something else, and I would want to know that from the person who did it, no matter how angry I was. I assumed you might feel the same. Forgive me if I am mistaken."

Mary Parker did not look away. Her head was still nodding, as though she were searching for some answer and if she stared deep enough, she would find it.

Jassim forced his professional face, his controlled feelings. He pushed aside the gnawing feeling that it was his fault a boy had not had the chance to become a man, turned away from the awareness that the woman behind the screen had probably aged ten years because of him.

"I am full of hate right now. I need to hate you." She stared at him, her head still quivering slightly. "It sure took balls to come over here."

The sun and the situation were forcing sweat out of Jassim's scalp. He lifted the flowers a bit, hoping she would open the door to take them so that he could be done with this most difficult situation.

"Life deals you some wild shit, excuse my language." Mary Parker pushed the screen door open and Jassim held out his bouquet. For just a second, their eyes met in plain, unfiltered space. Jassim felt it, almost an electric shock, and he could see Mary jerk slightly, ever so slightly. Instead of taking the flowers, she stood back. "You might as well come in and have some coffee. I just made a fresh pot."

Jassim had not plotted this as a possible scenario. "I couldn't do that. I don't want to upset you more. Please, take these."

"Hey, buddy, I'm in suspension right now. I'm floating. You couldn't upset me more right now—you've done that already. Now it's just a matter of getting through the day."

Jassim hesitated before he walked in and stood just inside the door, still holding the heavy, fragrant bouquet as she closed the door behind him, sealed out the sunshine. The living room was dark and thickly carpeted. Shadows of furniture punctuated the room, but it was so dark he couldn't see much beyond that.

Mary Parker's voice was soft, with no stitch of anger now. "For a long time my brother was living with us, and he slept here. I hung blackout curtains so the sun wouldn't wake him, but I never got around to taking them down. I don't see any point in letting sun in now anyway. Come into the kitchen."

Jassim followed her, with his head slightly bowed, as she took the few steps from the front door to the kitchen. She took the flowers from his hands and put them on the counter while he let his eyes adjust to the change. The kitchen was bright and cheerful, with shiny cupboards, gleaming countertops, and country knick-knacks decorating the shelves. In the center was a small multicolored Formica table.

"Have a seat. How do you like your coffee?"

"Black, please."

"Black it is." She gave him a red mug that did not match her own green mug and sat down across from him, looking at the pack of cigarettes on the table. "I used to smoke a long time ago, and I thought it would help now. It doesn't. Just makes me dizzy and cough. Do you think you could throw them away for me? If I have them around, I'll smoke them, and then God knows how many years I'll have to spend quitting again, on top of everything else." She pushed the pack of cigarettes toward him. "D'you mind?"

"Not at all." Jassim kept the other words he wanted to say inside his mouth, the words that said *May I save your life to make up for your son's life?* and pulled the cigarettes closer to him.

"I used to drink too. Not so much, but pretty regularly and to the point where it got in the way of things. So I stopped that. Stopped smoking pot. All to be a good example for my kids." She stopped and looked at him, her eyes blinking away the glassiness.

"You have other children?"

"Mm-hmm. I have a daughter. She's having a hard time with this. Sleeps with me and cries a lot. Says she feels alone and scared, and I feel pretty shitty for not being able to soothe her, to get out of my own grief enough to help her."

"How old is she?"

"Fourteen. They're sixteen months apart. I remember when they were little thinking I would go crazy having two babies to take care of. At the same time it was the happiest period in my life, though I didn't realize it then. It seems like yesterday. Don't all parents say that, how quickly it goes? I just can't believe he's not here. Sometimes I wake up and forget—that's when it's the worst, in the mornings. Some days I can't make it out of bed, can't get past that."

Jassim said nothing, just sat with his legs uncrossed at the too-small table and watched the mother of the boy whose life he had taken, and behind his listening sat a thought: this was the first time since he had married Salwa that he had been alone in a house with a woman to whom he was not related by blood or by marriage.

"What was Evan like?"

Mary Parker sat back in her chair, pushed away from the table and folded into herself, as if she were trying to stay in a tiny space with no arms or fingers poking out. Hands wrapped around her coffee cup. She wore no rings. Her skin was unblemished, and in spite of the tiredness and sadness scribbled all over her face, Jassim enjoyed looking at it, saw in it a warmth.

"Well, God keep him, he was an odd kid—good, but odd. He never liked to do what everyone else did, which I guess is how he came to hang out with all the punk kids—though all the punk kids act like each other, so how different is that?"

"Kids are kids."

"Yeah, kids are kids. He liked games and imaginary things— whatever took him out of this world. I think the divorce really affected him. He needed his dad, not so much to keep him in line but to teach him to be strong, not to be scared of the world."

She leaned forward and pulled the pack of cigarettes back toward her. "One last one." She offered one to Jassim, who put up his hand, watched her light the cigarette, drag the polluted air into her lungs, and fight the cough. Her relief was perceptible, coating her face, pinning her together.

"Evan never really liked sports. At least not the kind you do in groups. He liked riding his bike, skateboarding, listening to that god-awful music of his. Bang, bang, bang. What do kids get out of that music? I was a kid once and I remember needing to get away from my parents and listening to rock and roll, but that music—it's horrid, it's just noise."

"Did he like school?"

"Sometimes. It depended on the class, not the subject so much as the kids in the class and the way the teacher interacted with them. He enjoyed his geometry class. He wasn't school-smart so much as he was people-smart. He could really see people for what they were, good or bad. I think that's why he had so many problems with his dad. He could see the loser side of him and he didn't like that—it scared him."

Jassim's brain fought the pictures of the accident, the heap on the asphalt. They sat in smoky silence. He drank his coffee and looked at her with all the waiting in the world in his eyes as she smoked her cigarette and rocked gently in her chair.

"I keep thinking about when he was little and how things were so hard for him. Each new school year he would cry for the first month or so. In the early grades he would even have temper tantrums—six or seven years old and he was lying on the school lawn, kicking and screaming. I didn't know how to help him, and I never seemed to have enough time with him. I keep thinking that's why, that's why he liked that music, that's why he couldn't fit in. The worst is that I think I pushed him away and that maybe at the end he felt alone and that's why he left, 'cause he didn't feel enough love or attachment to this world." She inhaled deeply on her cigarette and sat staring at the memory.

Jassim's voice came out low and safe. "That's the worst part of parenthood—that we've no one else to blame, so anything that goes wrong, any sadness they have, it may not be our fault they feel it, but it comes to be our fault for not being able to stop it." Jassim realized that he was giving the impression that he had children, that he could identify with her.

She stared at him through the smoke. "It's true. I feel like I missed the boat with him. Somehow I should have done something different, but I didn't know what, and there was never time to think about it because I was always working."

"You don't think it's possible that he was who he was, that no matter what you did, he was bound to come out the way he did?"

"No. I feel like I failed him. That's the worst part. I look back on so many situations where I failed him. It's my fault he was out with that boy that day, because somehow I didn't teach him enough responsibility or safety skills or common sense. What happened shouldn't have happened, and it can't be undone and it will haunt me for the rest of my life."

"Me too." Jassim had not meant to say these words out loud and felt exposed. He had not come here with the intention of baring his own soul, but simply to offer an apology.

"They told me, the police told me, that the guy who did it—you—did what he could to help him, that it was an accident. Even that asshole friend of his he was with said Evan just jumped out into the street, like he was trying to jump over your car. Still, I want to blame you, and I do."

"That's okay, Mary. Blame me. Like you, I keep looking back at what I could have done differently." But he did not go on. Could not say, not even in his mind, that he had been speeding just a few minutes earlier, that if he hadn't been, he would not have reached Evan when he did, and that indeed he was guilty. Instead he said, "I will never forget that day, and again, I am so very sorry. Please know that. I also want to offer help, any help I can give you, financial or otherwise."

"That's kind of you. We're good. I think I can manage okay, but who knows, might take you up on that someday. Where are you from? India or something?"

The question caught him off guard, but his answer came out smooth and ready. "I'm from Jordan."

"Jordan—where's that, exactly?"

"Between Israel, Iraq, and Saudi Arabia."

Silence. She looked at her coffee and nodded her head in a rocking sort of rhythm.

"You're Arabic?"

"Yes, I am an Arab."

Silence. She continued staring into her coffee, rocking gently. "God is one twisted motherfucker."

"Excuse me?"

She was laughing, almost guffawing. "I'm sorry, but that is so fucked up. See, when 9/11 happened, Evan was freaked out, totally freaked out. It was weird, because once he was a teenager, he didn't lose it very often. But he did then, ranted and raved about how Arabic people should all be kicked out of this country, rounded up, herded up, and thrown out. I ignored it for a while, thought he was just scared. We were all scared those people were going to blow us all up. Then he started talking about how he wished he could kill an Arab—my own son talking about killing someone! I sat him down and told him two wrongs don't make a right, that most Arabic people don't have anything to do with this. He wouldn't listen—refused to. Talked like a bigot, and I was so mad at him. I think he got it from his dad, who is a racist prick. That's why I say that God is one fucked-up bastard, to have Evan die under the wheels of an Arabic person's car."

She started rocking a little more, but now he could see shaking in her shoulders and he knew she was going to cry.

"I should be going. I am sorry I have upset you more."

"No, really, I'm always upset. I won't say I'm glad you came, but maybe to know you are suffering too does help, and to have a face to put with it. You can show yourself out."

"I'm leaving you my phone number in case you need anything, in case I can help you. Please, don't hesitate to call." Jassim took the envelope he had prepared earlier, with the business card and the $500, from his shirt pocket and put it on the table, then stood up and put his hand on her shoulder. "Be strong. Your daughter needs you."

She held herself and nodded. "Leave the cigarettes, okay?"

"If you wish."

And Jassim left her with her grief, her cigarettes, and her empty, dark house, walked into the brilliant, obscene last day of January and back to his car. A man stood in the front yard of the house across the street and stared at him. Jassim stared back, numb. Neither stare was friendly. Finally the man turned to busy himself with the house and Jassim turned away from the flags and the stickers; his blood sat heavy in his veins.

The nervousness that had given him the energy to come had all sifted out of him. What remained were heavy dark globs of sadness that made him deeply tired, the kind of tired that could make him fall asleep in the street or in his car. He forced himself to turn the key, to drive out of this unwelcoming American neighborhood, which clearly blamed him personally for recent suffering, and back through the more liberal streets where fear and hatred were disguised.

_C> <2_

Something in Salwa had changed from blue to purple, woke up with a sharper, more daring hue, a louder color that shook up the particulars of her day, the daily details, forced monochromatic people she had been watching for years to come through in rainbow shades. Like that crooked man edged in green who came into the bank every Friday and signed his check and wrote up his deposit slip. No direct deposit, no ATM. Baggy trousers draped over his sneakers, and his button-down plaid shirts were usually wrinkled. Today, not a Friday, he was talking to a short woman he seemed to know, a neighbor or coworker perhaps, and he was gesturing toward the ceiling. He was not ugly, but he disguised it well by parting his greasy hair too far to one side. In America this gray-tinged man was lost. Invisible. In Jordan he would have had his place, his history, an explanation to go along with him, a family to connect him. The color green to announce him.

This thought dragged her back, *thunk, thunk, thunk,* over American roads and highways, through the clouds close to the heavens, and plopped her into her scrubbed-clean house, white and yellow, with her parents and sisters. Her longing for them was a surprise, a kick in the gut, followed by looking back from there to here and seeing that these years in America could be erased to nothing. She saw herself no better than before, only older.

On her ergonomically correct vinyl chair, which swiveled, adjusted, and contoured to fit her body type, Salwa sat atop a carpet of memories several years long that amounted to nothing, not a dung heap of disasters (thank God) nor a mountain of treasure. It was more like a speed bump with a real estate license and some fine home accessories. Her American freedom had given her exactly that: American freedom.

Emptiness is a dangerous substance, allows its possessor to believe in taking rash measures as a way to fill up the tank cheaply. (Like going abroad in search of water or oil.) Salwa desperately wanted to fill it, but having nothing to barter with, no weapons, and no maps with which to find a well, she was left with nothing more than her own flimsy silk-pajama fantasies of *potential*. Today, this translated into welcoming what came her way, in the form of a job in a real estate office that netted tens of thousands of extra dollars, and in the form of a young college student with a tongue that tried to dance in Arabic.

Salwa made no pretense of working, just sat and stared at past and present. She did not move when Jake strolled from the teller bank and leaned into her cubicle, though she felt a tingling in her palms, a vague shift in her bowels.

"Salwa." His voice spilled softly onto the floor, seeped across the memory carpet through her shoes and up her legs, settled just beneath her belly button, and melted away the residue of her irritation from the park.

"Jake." A statement. An invitation. It was a matter of time, minutes, hours, days, Salwa knew, before they were intimate; they were in a line at an amusement park ride, with an undefined wait time in anticipation of a few seconds of contained terror/pleasure and the probability of returning safely to earth minutes later. Alive but somehow changed. For one clear, thinking moment she could see that the words they shared or disagreed over did not matter, that her connection with Jake was primal and already decided.

"I had an idea. I thought maybe you could come to my house for dinner. I made an awesome spinach lasagna yesterday."

Hours.

"Sure. That would be nice." She smiled.

"Really? That'd be great."

When Jake left, she called Jassim's cell number and left a message, promising to be home by ten, saying that she was having dinner with coworkers. Only the tip of a lie, an accidental plural.

The afternoon puttered along with customers and phone calls and glimpses of something new. Salwa smiled and answered questions as though this were a day as normal as any other, as though she were not about to throw her faithfulness out of her customized American window.

At 5:30, Jake, messenger bag slung over his shoulder, came into her office. "I've balanced out and I'm going. You have to stay late tonight, right?"

"I'll probably be here until six."

"Here's the address." He walked up to her desk, looking into her eyes, and handed her a piece of paper with a street number and directions. "Do you want to just come by when you're done?" His easy smile and physical confidence danced in front of her.

"I've got to stop by the real estate office when I'm done here. I should be done by six-thirty or seven at the latest." The nervousness that had barely suggested itself before was growing inside her, squeezing sweat from her palms and twisting her intestines.

"Awesome. I'll see you around seven then." He stood with his legs spread slightly apart, hands on his hips and a smile at the corner of his mouth.

"*Inshallah.*"

"God willing?"

"Mm-hmm. *Inshallah.*"

Jake's pose shifted, his cockiness challenged by her answer.

"Okay." He left her office, and she forced herself not to watch him go, not to glance at the paper he had handed her. Instead she turned her attention to the work before her.

At 5:58 she collected her things and left the bank. Not much traffic to contend with, and she reached the small stucco building in minutes. The front door was still unlocked, and she walked toward Joan's office without seeking eye contact with other agents, without poking her head into other offices.

"Oh hi, honey. I'm so glad you're here." Joan got up from her desk and hugged Salwa.

"Thank you, Joan."

"Matthew and I were going to dinner tonight. Would you like to join us? You and your husband? Celebrate your success? Your fifth house."

"Thank you. That is sweet of you, but I can't tonight."

"That's okay. We can do it another day." Joan squinted at Salwa. "Is something bothering you?"

"No, why do you ask?"

"You seem preoccupied. I just want to make sure you are comfortable here. If you feel overwhelmed or need help selling the Moraleses' house, please just ask me."

"Oh no, Joan. It's nothing to do with that. It's nothing at all."
Joan looked at her. "Well, I don't believe that for a minute, but
it's not any of my business, either. I just want you to know that
you can come to me with anything. I think of you like a daughter,
Salwa. It's so important that we have people we can talk to. I mean
it, Salwa, you can come to me anytime with anything."

Not for the first time Salwa wondered why Joan, who was so
very American and patriotic, reminded her of someone from home.
Not anyone in particular, just a someone whose warm nosiness
forced its way into your heart, whether or not you liked the person
or agreed with her politics. Salwa thought of telling Joan about
her evening plans, to hear Joan's negative reaction, perhaps negative enough to keep her from going.

"Thank you, Joan. You've been so kind to me, and I really appreciate it."

"Well, here are some listings, and here is Mrs. Morales's wish
list, though you've talked to them, so I'm sure you have a good
sense of what they want. Basically, they want to live in a house that
looks old but has been completely remodeled. All of these homes
have been renovated in a style consistent with the original building.
Read through them, and I would say start with three or four to
show. You also might drive by each of them to get a gut feeling as
to which would work best. We can talk about them on Monday or
over the weekend, whichever you'd prefer." Joan handed Salwa a
thick manila envelope. "Happy reading."

"Thanks again, Joan." Salwa kissed Joan on the cheek and
hugged her.

It occurred to her as she sat in her car that she could just drive
home, could not do what she was about to do. No, Jake would
have prepared dinner and be waiting for her, and it was unlike her
to leave someone waiting; she would have to tell him she was not
coming, and she didn't have his phone number so she would have
to go to his house and apologize in person for changing her mind
and then go home.

Because she was just going to run in, apologize for not staying,
and then go home, she did not feel nervous as she pulled up to the

apartment building he had directed her to. The complex was enormous, a series of identical misshapen two-story cubes painted different shades of brown to blend in with the desert and set at odd angles to avoid the summer's afternoon sunlight. She drove the prescribed 10 miles per hour and followed the arrow and sign that said 1200–1240. Across from the cluster of buildings that contained #1216 was a tidy row of parking places with VISITOR PARKING painted on the curb. She tucked herself into a perfect slot, sat for a moment, and because she was just running in for a second, she left her bag in the car, half tucked under the passenger seat, locked the door, and stepped onto the sidewalk.

"Good evening."

Salwa turned her head toward the voice; a man stood next to a pickup truck filled with branches and with the logo of a landscaping company painted on the side.

She was disconcerted. "Hello."

"Sorry. I don't mean to surprise you. I just say good evening." The man was short, barely Salwa's height, and stocky. His skin was chocolate dark and his face was broad. "I sorry. I tell everyone this. Don't leave valuable things like purse and money in your car. There has been too many broken windows and robberies. Here is not a good idea."

"Thanks." A whisper in her thinking told her to get her bag. A louder voice said to just keep going, that she was only staying for a minute, was not going inside. Salwa continued on her way, *click-click* up thin slabs of concrete stairs in which rocks were drowned. She stood on the landing in front of the only door and placed her finger on the button that would bring Jake to her, though it hesitated, the level-headed Salwa trying desperately to reel it in, to turn her around and rush her back down the *click-click* stairs and back to her car tucked between two neat white lines and designated a visitor.

Too late. With the *pling* of the bell, the door opened and Jake stood with his easy open smile. "*Ahlan wa sahlan.*" He welcomed her barefoot and pushed her resolve down the stairs.

"Hi, Jake. I can't stay. I am sorry, but I can't."

Jake smiled. "I thought that might happen. Look, this whole thing is so weird. Come in for a few minutes, eat, and then go. Okay?" He stood aside, opening the door of his apartment so that she could come in.

She hesitated. Truthfully, the minute he opened the door her resolve had melted, slid through the gaps between the stairs, and landed dead on the concrete below. "Really, I should go."

"Salwa, look, I understand that this isn't right. But we enjoy each other's company and I make a killer lasagna. So come eat, we'll talk some, and then you can go home and we can do our best to return to normal. As friends."

Against all that she knew to be right in the world, and well aware that *as friends* was one of those lines Americans tossed back and forth without meaning, she entered his apartment and stood, awkward, out of place. Visitor Parking. She looked around. A black leather couch faced an enormous television.

"Both hand-me-downs," he said, following her gaze. "From my brother, the official adult in the family."

Jazz tingled quietly out of giant speakers. (What was it about Americans and speakers and music?) The tidy living room faced a massive pine tree outside. A dining area and a tiny kitchen clustered on one side, and on the other side a narrow hallway stretched, she guessed, to the bathroom and bedroom. The small dining table was set with candles and one pink rose, none of which Salwa had expected.

"Let me get us something to drink. Wine?"

"No. thank you. Soda or sparkling water is fine." Somehow in this small space, he seemed larger and more manly than he did at work. Not older, but stronger and more in control of things, of this situation.

"Salwa, relax. We are adults, and you aren't going to do anything you don't want to. We're eating lasagna and then you're going home to your husband and I am going to study Arabic, which, by the way, is a very difficult language."

"It is, but it is also logical."

"Our teacher showed us a passage from the Quran today, the

first one. He read it and it was so hypnotic. Someone in class brought up that in the Quran it says that when a man and a woman are alone, the Devil makes the third party. Do you believe that?" Jake filled a glass with crackling seltzer water and then added four ice cubes before she could say anything.

What was the American obsession with ice cubes? And why did people always latch onto the tiniest and least important phrases? "I believe that it is not difficult, especially in this country, to find yourself in a situation where it is too easy to do what you shouldn't do." *Like this one.*

"Eating a good lasagna dinner does not count as the Devil." He handed her the glass and gestured toward a chair.

"Could I help you with something?"

"Nope. It's all done and ready. Have a seat and prepare yourself." She sat down and observed the table again, the white table-cloth (he did not strike her as someone who would own such a thing), the basket of bread (did male American college students own baskets?), the colorful salad in a wooden bowl with wooden servers, the rose, deep pink and fresh in a tiny crystal vase. Jake went into the kitchen and returned after a moment with a thick white plate on which sat a dripping rectangle of layers of pasta and spinach and tomato. He placed it in front of her and then brought his own plate and sat down across from her.

"This looks very professional."

"Before college I worked in an Italian restaurant, which is where I learned to make lasagna. It's also where I got all this stuff."

The Devil's tension squeezed them both, sent their conversation up and down steep hills so that dinner was not so relaxing (interrupted five times by the telephone, which Jake answered in the bedroom), not so pleasant, and really not so delicious. Salwa wondered why he thought his lasagna was "killer." And she was relieved that now she had eaten, she could go home and resume her life.

"Coffee?"

"No thanks," she said.

"Here, have some of these." Jake held out a small plastic container with tiny seeds coated in pink and white and yellow.

"This is *shumur!* Sorry. I don't know how you say that in English."

"Is that what they are? I found them at the Arabic grocery store. It says 'candy-coated fennel.'"

"I love these. Actually, I've only had them like this in Indian restaurants, but we use *shumur*, fennel, in some foods, and the flavor is so distinct that one bite and I taste them." The crack of fennel in her mouth brought back desserts eaten only during Ramadan, brought back home in one tiny burst and then another, fireworks in her mouth that took away her breath.

The phone rang again, and Jake put the container and lid on the table. "Sorry. I'll just be a sec." He picked up his cell from the counter and trotted a few steps to the bedroom. "This is Jake." Pause. "Hey, how are you?" Formal voice. Pause. "Thank you. Listen, not now. You can come by tomorrow and pick it up." Long pause. "Absolutely. First thing tomorrow."

Salwa wandered around the tiny living room, munching on fennel, reading the spines of books, and promising herself that she would leave as soon as Jake was off the phone. A small picture in a heavy silver frame on the wall adjacent to the hallway caught her eye. It was Japanese, she guessed, and was a precise line drawing of a woman kneeling beside a crane, gazing at it with such sadness, such longing.

Jake's voice came over her shoulder. "This is from a Japanese myth about a young woman who searches for happiness, and each time she thinks she has found it, it escapes her. Happiness takes different forms, which are represented by different animals in different pictures. My brother has the picture of wealth, which is perfect because he's a greedy bastard." Jake stood just behind her, with his hands on his hips. "My sister has one and my parents have the rest of the series. This one has always been my favorite. The crane represents beauty. In her search for happiness, the woman loses her own beauty, which was one of the things that brought her happiness in the first place, but she didn't realize it until after she lost it. Of course, the point of the myth is that happiness is not something that is found, it is something that one has. Within." *Within.*

Perhaps if there had been more time to think, Salwa would have seen the irony this picture carried, would have applied it to her story, but in the flicker of an eye Jake's hands were on her shoulders, moving her hair to one side while his mouth kissed her neck, his body pressing into hers. He turned her to face him so he could place his kisses on her fennel-flavored mouth, fill her, as his hands and arms contained her.

Her brain was silent, transforming cautionary words into accusatory aftermath; that was wiser than trying to argue with a downhill skier in midride. His kisses slowed, but she clung to him, her mouth on his, so he continued, his hands pulling her closer to him. After a time he nudged her toward the bedroom and lowered her onto a stack of two futons, all the while kissing her.

Salwa's inner voice had grown weary, unwilling to battle, and so had turned off the light and gone to bed. Salwa, who at the moment of her birth was twice displaced from lands holier than this, allowed an American boy to push off her shoes with his toes, to unbutton her shirt and remove it, allowed him to unzip her skirt and place her clothes neatly on a chair next to the futons. To avoid wrinkles. Watched as he removed his own clothing in a heap, stood before her in underwear that reminded her of Jassim's bathing suit. He knelt on the floor and she allowed him between her legs while she sat on the edge of the futons, in her matching bra and panties, lacy and lovely, recently purchased from Victoria's Secret and worn, coincidentally, for the first time today. She allowed his hands to run along the edge of her waistband, his fingers to sneak beneath the elastic, to remove her bra, his mouth to kiss her breasts with gentle whisper kisses, to prepare them for what was to come.

"You are beautiful, Salwa, and I so want you," he said in a choked whisper, and he put his face against her stomach, pushed her gently back on the stack of futons with his mouth and tongue and hands so that she vanished and became a part of him, an adored, desired, and moving part of this young American man, barely more than a boy. These were moments Salwa had not experienced before; never had she allowed herself to vanish under the shadow of another person. The delight she felt spread over her body, as though every square inch had been given extra senses for the occasion.

"Wait." Jake, now completely naked, completely ready, reached between the futons and removed a tidy square. Salwa watched as he ripped it open and covered himself with the single finger of a glove, protecting her. He then lowered himself slowly and perfectly, with such skill that at the end of those many electric moments that rolled the evening into night, Salwa forgot where she was.

—⁓—

Nipples pointing accusatorily at God. For offering temptation? Avoidance wasn't even a possibility, for she had sought it, had invited temptation into her office, to swivel around with her on her black vinyl ergonomically correct chair, and it would be rude to run away from such a guest, improper to suggest that it leave immediately. No, she would make tea and cakes, and some fruits and, finally, coffee before she allowed it to be on its way. She had not lost all her manners. Hosting an invited guest was simple; it was the uninvited ones that required an artistic flair and an ability to lie.

Salwa lay on her back on the stacked futons, completely naked and absolutely lost. Just weeks earlier Jake had irritated her with his immaturity. And here she was, in his bedroom, naked. She sat up and looked at herself in the mirrors that covered the closet doors. Is this what Jake had seen and said was beautiful? She searched for herself in this reflection, pleading for familiarity with the thick legs, wide hips, round breasts, simple face, nothing like the bodies and faces shown on American television. She stood up and walked to the mirror so that she and the reflection were face to face, almost touching. They stared at each other, stranger at stranger. One loved silky pajamas and was outraged by injustice; the other had allowed a baby to die within her and in compensation had let herself be entered by a man who was not her husband.

Once your dream has been lived, what do you do?

She was standing in front of the mirror looking for her lost self when Jake came back from yet another telephone call, his skin smooth like a boy's, with a few hairs on his chest, none on his shoulders or back.

He stood behind her and wrapped his arms around her, looked at their reflection in the mirror. "Nice, don't you think?"

And she did. And she didn't. He held her, his left arm below her neck, his right hand playfully touching her right breast, taunting her nipple. And then both hands moved to her stomach, kneading. The palm of one hand rested against her abdomen while his fingers fiddled with the hair between her legs, stretched down beneath the hair, and still they both watched their reflection, as his hands and fingers moved on her body with familiarity and ownership.

"Do you see what happens to your body as you become excited? Look at it, how beautiful it is." His fingers toyed gently with the most private part of her, and she watched, intrigued by his openness, by her ability to let it happen. He stepped back and pulled her down to the futons again. "Watch." She did as she was told, curious to see. Never had it occurred to her to want to watch herself making love, being made love to. But here she was, watching a woman who looked vaguely familiar being licked and sucked and entered by a man she barely knew. She turned away to kiss him or look at him, but he urged her back: "Watch yourself."

"I can't. I don't want to. I want to forget myself."

He lay her flat on her back. "Then tell me when you like it." Again he kissed her breasts, teased them with his tongue and teeth and fingertips, and his mouth moved down her belly, his tongue dancing from her belly button to her hipbone to the top of her thigh. She knew what he was doing, could not seem to bring her voice to make him stop. And she didn't want him to stop. Not ever. With his body between her legs, his tongue dancing within her, Salwa became someone new. And when his tongue tired and he again reached between the futons, she thought she could live like this forever, floating in pleasure. She watched him as he worked within her, his body arching over hers, his face smiling and then contorting. Odd that the face of pleasure is not a happy one.

When he was done, he kissed her and lay next to her. "I am sorry, Salwa. This isn't what you wanted to do."

"It is and it isn't," she answered. "I think I have become something else." Something bad.

"Life is fluid and changes. Sometimes those changes are not easy."

Salwa leaned up on her elbow. "Once you have done something like this, you cannot undo it. Just as you cannot unsay something. You can only wish."

Jake put his face to her chest, kissed her breast gently, and while Salwa felt it all the way to her toes, she promised herself that she would not do this again, would not allow herself to be alone with Jake. Again. Ever. The Devil had come, and now the Devil must go.

—∾—

Nine-thirty and she had to leave, get out while she could.

"I need to shower before I go," she told him.

"I understand." But he didn't, and he tried to come in with her.

"My husband"—she couldn't say his name in this place—"has a very keen sense of smell." Which was not true. It was she who had the keen sense of smell, who would smell Jake on her the whole way home and be disgusted.

He kissed her again, but she didn't feel it. Cinderella's time was almost up.

She locked herself in the bathroom and looked around. Towels in the tiny cupboard. She picked one from the bottom and smelled it. Sour. Sour something. This she wrapped around her hair, careful to include the strands at her neck. Then she turned on the water, the cold water, and got in. Scrubbed herself with water and did not touch the soap. Cleaned between her legs with her hands and water, washing away all evidence, all memory of Jake.

"It still shows," Jake said when she reappeared, walked to the chair where her clothes were draped, and dressed as though it were the most natural thing.

"A little makeup, some lotion . . . Where did I put my bag?"

"You didn't have it when you came. I remember that."

Salwa remembered. Almost three hours ago, she had not planned to stay, had left her bag in the car. In plain view. Her heart thumped. "Shit."

"What's the matter?"

"I left my bag in the car. I wasn't going to stay."

"I'm sure it will be fine. Your car's locked, and the parking lot's too well lit for someone to break a window. I'll walk you down, just to be sure."

He picked up his crumpled jeans, slid into them naked. Put a T-shirt over his bare chest, and they left the apartment Together, down the clickety stairs to her car.

She knew before they got there what had happened, saw that the car window was broken, knew that her bag would be gone. But it wasn't. The car window was broken, but the bag was still on the seat.

"Did they take anything?" asked Jake, bouncing on his bare toes and seeming nervous.

Salwa opened her bag. Her phone and her wallet were still there. What was gone was the envelope of cash she had just withdrawn for the weekend: $200.

"Just some money. I had cash, but my credit cards are still here. Thank God. My wallet's still here."

"They must have gotten scared away."

"I should call the police."

"It'll just raise your insurance rates. Look, I know a guy who does glass. I'll get your window fixed tomorrow, and let's skip calling the cops."

"And for tonight?"

"We'll tape it up. I'm off work tomorrow. I'll come by the bank and take it over for you."

"Why don't I call the police? I have insurance."

"Salwa, if you and your husband share a policy and you file a report, he is going to know you didn't go to a restaurant for dinner."

They swept out the glass and put a piece of cardboard in its place, and Salwa drove home and into the garage, hoping that Jassim would not see it.

_꙳ ꙳_

Too much. Jack felt too much static in his head.

He knew that Jassim had not been going swimming in the mornings. He knew that on several occasions he had driven around aimlessly, had gone to Denny's. But why? How could that be important? Why did he drive up and down the streets of that midtown neighborhood? There was nothing strategic there as far as Jack could see, no office buildings, no municipalities. Jassim didn't meet anyone in Denny's. Talked briefly with the waitress, Jack noted through the window. Didn't make any phone calls. And then drove home, or in the direction Jack assumed to be home. Sometimes he went to work. Sometimes he would pull over by the side of the road and just sit.

Now, walking past tidily arranged lettuces and onions and radishes, Jack mulled over what little information he had. Jassim Haddad. Registered professional hydrologist. Professional geologist. Specialty in rainwater harvesting. Graduated with a B.S. in civil engineering from the University of Jordan in Amman and a master's and Ph.D. in hydrology from the University of Arizona. Married for nine years to a beautiful banker and part-time real estate agent. Home in the foothills. Avid swimmer.

There was nothing in this list that suggested sinister activity. Jack felt quivery as he thought this. Not because of it, but simultaneously. His heart thudded. His shoulder ached. He stood with his cart next to a heap of onions. He didn't need onions. He pushed on slowly toward the bananas and rested for a moment, sweat creeping along his scalp and forehead, pain settling in his chest. Surely this was not a heart attack, he told himself. He was healthy. He couldn't have a heart attack in the grocery store when there was still work to be done. He pulled off two bananas and placed them in his cart, next to a loaf of bread, a bag of apples, and a bag of butterscotch candy. It was difficult to breathe now. Other people were putting bags of fruits and vegetables in their carts; two employees were arranging waxed tomatoes and avocados in tiny mountains adjacent to each other. He could ask any one of these people to help him. No, he was fine, he convinced himself; if the pain continued, he would go see his doctor. With that he pulled a thin plastic bag from a roll beneath the peanuts. Kiwis. He would buy kiwis and try them for the first time. He reached forward to the little black wrought iron stand on which they were displayed and fell forward. Dead before he hit the floor.

GɔɔΩ

As he drove away from Mary Parker's house, Jassim's limbs felt weak, the adrenaline that had gotten him there having turned to lead. Before heading northeast, toward home, Jassim veered northwest, toward Denny's, to be debriefed by Penny, since if it were not for Penny, he would never have gone to see Mary Parker in the first place. His brain was a jumble of words and faces and roads and signals, and his efforts to focus on what was in front of him, to see the red lights and the pedestrians, sifted his thinking out. The fact that it was a weekday afternoon did not enter his conscious mind, just the fact that there seemed to be an extraordinary number of cars. There was no *why* behind it. Turning off Oracle, he drove his murderous car into the parking lot and pulled up within a designated white box, tidy rules laid down in paint. He sat and more than anything wanted to close his eyes, but instead he forced himself to get out of the car, go inside the restaurant, and head for what had become his usual spot.

"Hey, buddy, hang on and I'll see if we've got a seat over there. Will there just be one?"

Jassim nodded at the heavy voice of the waitress. "Is Penny here?"

"No, sir. She's gone for the day. She does the morning shift."

Jassim looked at the clock on the wall. "Sometimes two, sometimes three," she had said. "I see," he replied, turning around to go, feeling drunk and unstable.

Jassim left, walked out into the honest afternoon. What he longed for, straight down to his toes, was Salwa and his real life. Raindrop promises: *If she is home when I get there, I will tell her everything.* And yet he knew that only an accident or illness would bring her home from work this early. Jassim's being had filled up to the point where drips and drops of everything were spilling out onto floors. Puddles on which to slip, puddles in which to drown.

Jassim wound home past identical mailboxes large enough to accommodate a pair of boots, past houses of many styles—ranch, pueblo, bungalow, and even a Tudor—past American flags and paved driveways and Volvos and Land Rovers, and looped into the drive of his own Spanish colonial–style home, which he knew to be unoccupied.

Bleached white whispers. Gentle lavender touches. The invisible rhythm of American life pumped within him, but he could not seem to move with the beat. Jassim stood in front of his house and breathed deeply. No flowers decorated the front steps. *I have killed a boy and not told my wife about it. Instead, I have chosen to confide in a waitress whose ex-husband stalked her.*

It is important to be honest to the self, thought Jassim, *and that is my situation. Now, for the solution.* But here his mind was silent as his feet crunched over gravel to his front door, stepped across the threshold of his clean and empty home. This would all be different if they had children. There would be no silence. He would have hope.

Salwa had miscarried their baby. (Had it been a girl?) Maybe she was right. Maybe they were ready for children. He would talk to her about it, and he would apologize for not being more open. They would try again. He hated that expression, hated how Americans felt no shame in announcing that they were "trying to get pregnant," as though saying it did not imply two adults stripped naked and connected.

Death has a way of peeling the safety film from people's eyeballs, allowing in what is really there rather than the filtered view through the comfort of routine. What one wants to see goes out the window. The flat series of concocted frames running at superspeed through a rectangular eye is burned to a crisp. In killing a boy, Jassim had been released from that perfect prison, that made-to-order set, and stood now in his nicely decorated, quiet house, which was as empty as he had ever seen it. In a house like this, one did not have to fight for anything; one could simply go about one's day and work and say hello to the neighbors from time to time, and be absolutely disconnected from life.

How it had taken killing a boy for his soul to awaken, he couldn't say, but here, with leather shoes softly moving across Saltillo tiles toward the polarized window facing southwest, overlooking the city, he saw that the past nine years (and even more than that) had been a sabbatical from real life, a rich man's escape from the real world.

A dead boy and an incomplete fetus weigh the blood down with their unfulfilled promises. Jassim looked down over the hills and felt his misdeeds flood through him, a convulsion of sadness and guilt that brought him to his knees, facing southwest, a direction God could not receive.

Lying bent on the tiles, which had not before felt the softness of a face, Jassim gasped for air, for something to pull him up, for Abu Fareed's mighty hands to lift him out of the water. He waited, sobbing and gasping, but Abu Fareed did not come. No sounds, no signs, no change, except for a certain slickness on the tiles.

Jassim thought about going to bed, sleeping it all away. Perhaps if he slept long enough, it really would prove itself to be a nightmare and nothing more. Perhaps if he lay there long enough, he would cry himself into a puddle, transform into the substance he had spent his life revering and loving. And why were tears salty? Why was the American expression *a river of tears* when it should be an ocean, since the water was salty? Perhaps the Americans (did the British also use this expression?) were simply thinking of the long narrowness a river has, something akin to what a lot of tears streaming down the face looks like. The River Jordan on the earth's face. These thoughts stemmed Jassim's tears, rational thought drowning all self-indulgence.

The convulsions stopped, and Jassim wondered how Salwa would react if she came home and found him like this, pooled and puddled and facing southwest. Would she mop him up? Of course she would. She would make his life right. Had he told her this recently, that she was what got him through the day? (Even though he felt no desire to be with her? Even though he physically craved another woman?) That he still looked to her to make everything okay? Perhaps not—perhaps he had been stingy with his words. Words shouldn't be necessary. At this point in their relationship, he did not see the need to tell her what she must already know.

Sprawled on the floor, his sadness spreading along the grout lines, he began a short mental film of the women he knew: Penny, Mary, Diane, Salwa. He was now fully extended on his back, aware of a dull throb as he cradled his head in his hands, and also an ache in his stomach, just to the right of his navel. He shifted, but the pains stayed put, reminded him that he had walked away from the life he had planned. That he was currently doing nothing, in real, absolute terms, to solve the water crisis, or even to heighten awareness. He had gotten on an amusement park ride (not a plane), whose controls had been stolen, hijacked, sending him careening into buildings.

How long he lay there he couldn't say, only that it was dark when he sat up and his body ached from the hardness of the floor, from the hardness of his thoughts. And where was Salwa at this time of night? he wondered. Could the phone have rung without his hearing it? He checked the answering machine. Nothing. He checked his cell phone, which he had left on the counter. One missed call. One voice-mail message. "Hi, habibi. I'm going to have dinner with some people from work. Hope you don't mind. Don't know when I'll be home. Maybe ten. Don't wait up for me. There's some tandoori chicken in the fridge that just needs heating up. See you tonight."

Jassim pressed the number 4 to listen to the message again, to search Salwa's voice. Salwa didn't particularly like her coworkers. She always preferred coming home. She had been so different lately, since the miscarriage, but before that as well. *Have I done something? I don't see anything different.* He shook these thoughts up and looked at them again and still he saw nothing, no clue, no answer. Only hunger. He washed his face in the kitchen sink, put on the television to drown out Salwa's absence, and went about reheating Indian food for one.

Just as well that Penny worked the morning shift. As Jassim

ate, he thought of Penny. The oddest thing was that though he had
lied to her, he felt that with her he could be completely honest, allow his true self to sit at that counter in Denny's, as though the lies
he had told were erasing existing lies. Double negatives.

Part Four

—ꙮ Chapter Twelve ꙮ—

Jassim walked into his office and sat down, depleted. Would this feeling ever go away? Would he ever be able to shake the guilt?

His eyes fell on a business card placed in the center of his desk, equidistant from all corners. *Noelle James*. And in the center, in large letters: *FBI*. Underneath this was printed *Federal Bureau of Investigation*. A white Post-It note was stuck to his desk beneath the card, with looping writing in blue ink: *Would like to ask you some questions.*

Questions about what?

Marcus stood in the doorway. "Jassim, I have to talk to you."

"Sure, what's up?"

He looked at the card on Jassim's desk, symmetrically placed in the center of Jassim's world. He looked back at Jassim's face. "Let's go outside and get coffee. Do you have some time?"

Jassim checked his watch. "Sure." There was fresh coffee in the office. Outside to talk and get coffee meant going away from the ears of coworkers, which meant something was wrong.

They walked along in silence, each mulling over the words to come. Sleek loafers and scuffed tie-ups trod side by side down carpeted halls, turned right, and went single file through the fire door and down the echoing stairway. Out the automatic doors into the automatic brilliance of the day and automatically into Rosa's Rolls, the tiny shop that sold coffee, pastries, and sandwiches. Each paid for his own extra-strong black coffee and they walked back outside, motions mimicked by workers for generations past. They stood for a moment, surveying the courtyard, unaware of being under surveillance. Huddles of smokers, bunches of homeless people, and a few aimless wanderers. Marcus gestured to a lonely bench at the far end of the courtyard and they resumed their silent pace, arrived at uneasy sitting, uneasy sipping. No words, and Jassim's mind racing around Marcus and what he might have to say to him.

"Jassim, I don't know what's going on, but I am coming to you as your friend, not as your boss." Marcus looked at the ground as he spoke, holding his coffee cup with both hands. "The FBI came to our offices today. They asked about you, about what you do here, about your behavior. They asked me if you talk about your religion or any political issues."

"What did you say?"

"I told them that I have worked with you for some twelve years, that I have known you for almost fifteen, and that you are reliable and as apolitical and unreligious a person as I know. I said that you are someone who takes your job seriously. They asked me what your reaction was to September 11. They asked what sorts of Internet sites you look at." Silence. "They asked me about your reaction to the war in Afghanistan. What you thought about Jordan's leadership. I told them that you didn't discuss these things at work, that it was not something that came up in your professional world. They pressed me on that. Then they asked me if we had personal contact and if you discussed politics outside the workplace. I told them not particularly, that you really are not that interested in politics as far as I can see."

Jassim's head spun, his thoughts dashing ahead of Marcus's words. "Good God, Marcus. This is very serious."

"I know it is. There's one other thing. They said that they'd had complaints about you from one of our clients, though they wouldn't say which one. I actually laughed, because you have always been the most sought-after person here. I told them that too. I told them that you are never distracted by personal issues, that you are a purist when it comes to your job. I told them that if they had asked me whom I trusted most among my employees, I would have said you. Hands down."

Why *hands down?* Jassim had heard that one before, knew that it meant without competition, but he couldn't figure how it had come to mean that. His mind worked on *hands down* and almost missed the rest of what Marcus said.

"...emphasis on what a serious employee you are. They said that someone had been offended by your beliefs, which I just can't imagine. I think this is a witch hunt and I think you have to take it seriously, Jassim. Anyone who knows you knows that you aren't religious, knows you don't talk about religion. I got to thinking about who would say such a thing, and I bet you it's Corey. He's so right-wing, such an extreme Republican. He's eating up this terrorist crap that Bush dishes out. I've heard him a couple of times talking to his old cronies next door, and he's loaded with hate. Jassim, I don't know if I'm being paranoid, but if I were you, I would get a lawyer."

Jassim leaned back on the bench, arms stretched to either side, legs open, and stared into space. "A lawyer," he said, testing the sound of it in his mouth.

"The two agents cautioned me strongly not to discuss this conversation with you or anyone else. I am at a stage in my view of the world where I do not trust my government. I don't believe they have anything legitimate against you, but the atmosphere is such that anything could be misconstrued. Any misstep on your part could be used against you." Marcus paused, turning over some thought in his mind as he sipped his coffee. "Look, you do good work, and everyone knows that. All of our clients know it. Corey is the only one who concerns me. He is right-wing, he's active, and he hates everyone who has an education or an opinion. He is chums with Lisa and Bella, who are both unthinkingly flag-waving patriotic. They will stand up for a war and ignore human rights in the name of peace and freedom. What a load of crap. Peace and freedom for whom? What's more dangerous for you, though, is that they are all evangelical Christians. Anita is too, I think. Be careful what you say in front of them. Besides, you know how women are, just looking for something to churn up."

Churn up? Like butter? Butter is churned, not churned up, brought to the surface. As Jassim saw it, the women in his office were not looking for something to come to the surface, they were looking to invent a new reality, in which case *churned* might be more appropriate.

Marcus sat back and stared into the same empty space that Jassim was focusing on. "Jassim, please know that I am your friend. This is not an easy time for Middle Eastern people in this country. If you need anything, please come to me, to us. My family and I want you to know that. We would be happy to help you if you ever need anything."

An irrational desire to tell Marcus about Evan flooded through Jassim's body. A need, almost. The words were there, at the back of his throat, and he was about to let them free, to free himself, when Marcus said, "We should probably get back to work."

"Yes, we probably should," replied Jassim, getting up. He rolled around in his mind the possibility of telling Marcus what had happened, of righting his life by ridding himself of this awful burden. Because now it looked worse. If only he had told Salwa.

I am looking around, not knowing whom I can trust, as if I am guilty of something. All I am guilty of is not telling my wife and coworkers about an accident I had. Nothing more. I called the police immediately. I have done nothing wrong. Somewhere deeply embedded in this reflection was a sliver of culpability, which was poisoning every thought he had, every breath he took. Perhaps Marcus was right and he needed a lawyer.

No. Engaging a lawyer would imply that he had something to hide. Jassim's brain was bursting with competing arguments. His head throbbed, and he wished for easier times when he could do his job and dream of changing the world for the better through science.

"Hey, Jassim, do you ever listen to Amy Goodman?"

"No, who is that?"

"She has a radio program. She talks about what is really happening in this country, about the scores of Arabs and Pakistanis and other Muslims who have been arrested on baseless allegations, who are being held who knows where and are not allowed contact with their families, and how they may be deported because of visa violations. Jassim, she is the reason I'm telling you about the FBI. She has made me realize the extent our government will go to for the sake of justifying what they see as revenge. Look, my advice to you is to get a lawyer. That way, if you talk to the FBI, you do it with a lawyer and they won't be able to take anything out of context—you know, say you said something but give it a totally different meaning."

Jassim said nothing. Swallowed Marcus's words with his coffee. Walking back into the building with Marcus, he began to see that if he continued to do nothing, he would lose control entirely. His thoughts were muddled; he could not concentrate or see straight. The week ahead seemed impossibly long, and his fortitude had withered away.

Back in his office, he stared at the card that lay on his desk, equidistant from all corners. Noelle James. *I have nothing to hide,* he thought. *I might as well get this over with.* He dialed the number on the card, memorizing it as he went. (And noted that *FBI* could become *FIB* and *Noelle James* could be *lemon see jail.* No, there was no *i.*)

"This is Noelle James," said a woman's voice, a mix of steel and white wine.

"Ah, hello. My name is Jassim Haddad, and it seems you stopped by my workplace earlier this morning." He paused for a second. "You left a card and wrote that you wanted to speak with me."

He hoped she would say that it was all a mistake. That they no longer wanted to talk to him because his supervisor had cleared everything up and that it was a gigantic misunderstanding.

"Oh, of course, Mr. Haddad. I didn't understand you at first. Thank you for calling. Could you meet us today? At your convenience, of course."

Who was us? Jassim wondered, but he replied, "Of course."

"How about for lunch today?" she asked, more steel than wine.

Today? Why in such a hurry? Jassim wished that he had a lunch meeting so that he could say, *No I am sorry. I am busy today for lunch.* But he didn't and he had nothing to hide, so he said, "Sure, where?" made the arrangements, and then said goodbye.

He hung up and stared at her card. Noelle James. *Jello sea men.* In spite of her name, he imagined her to be a thin, blue-eyed woman with lank hair and a shapeless suit. It couldn't be too serious if she wanted to meet at a restaurant to have lunch.

They had agreed to meet at 12:15 at Mi Taquito, a small southside diner. Jassim parallel-parked across from the restaurant at 12:12, where he sat, with no trace of Evan on the grille of his car.

He did not see FBI agents enter; perhaps they were already there. He waited four minutes. Five minutes. Two swimming breaths and he got out of his car, crossed the street, and entered. The diner was packed and loud, and for a moment Jassim felt confused. How would he know who Noelle James was? He stood for another moment. Should he try to find a woman who looked like an FBI agent sitting by herself? But she had said *we*.

These thoughts were interrupted by a woman's voice. "Excuse me."

He turned around to find a very short woman with platinum hair that fell to her shoulders in tight ringlets. How had he not seen her approaching him?

"Are you Jassim Haddad?" she asked, though it was clear to Jassim that she knew who he was. How?

"I am. Pleased to meet you, Miss James." He extended his hand and shook hers, impressed by the tight grip, the coolness.

"Agent James. We've got a table already." She walked briskly into the dining area, which gave Jassim a chance to take her in completely. She looked to be in her thirties, wore very high heels, easily three and a half inches, with the tip of the heel tapering to the size of a nickel. Why would an FBI agent wear shoes that were so unstable? Gray tweed pants fell loosely over them but gripped her ample bottom. She wore a shiny maroon shirt that was tucked into her pants. On her left hip sat a pager and telephone, and on her right hip sat a gun. Surely it was protocol not to show her gun in a public place? When they got to the table, he saw that she had a jacket draped over the back of the chair. Perhaps she had gotten too hot and taken it off.

"This is my partner, Agent Adam Fletcher." She gestured to a man sitting at a square table and reading a menu.

"Howdy," said Agent Fletcher, standing up and extending his hand. Jassim shook it and wondered if hand-shaking was part of FBI training.

"Thank you for agreeing to meet us on such short notice," Noelle James was saying. "We really appreciate your cooperation in this matter."

Jassim felt like he was on a TV show. "And what exactly is 'this matter'?"

She smiled. "How about we order some food and then we get into it?"

"Sounds good to me," said Agent Fletcher. "I am so starving."

Jassim could not see straight. He held the menu in front of him, but it could have been in Chinese or upside down and he wouldn't have noticed. How could these people work for the FBI? They seemed so young and flip, which made him nervous. However, if this was something serious, they wouldn't be meeting at a restaurant and the FBI would have sent older, more experienced agents.

Once orders had been placed, questions would be asked. Jassim ate a chip, took a sip of water, and almost spat it out. He could taste the pipes, felt as though he had just wrapped his tongue around copper.

"How long have you worked at the consulting company, Mr. Haddad?" asked Agent Fletcher, oblivious of his discomfort.

Jassim wondered if maybe they had put this vile water in front of him to test his reaction. "Eleven years. Almost twelve."

"And what exactly are your duties there?"

"It depends who we're working with. Currently our biggest contract is with the city. I oversee the testing and quality control of the water supply, making sure the techs are conducting the regular tests and we're submitting the proper samples and paperwork. I am working on a few other contracts as well. One is a farm interested in implementing radical forms of rainwater harvesting, which is my specialty."

"What exactly is rainwater harvesting? Is it like putting chemicals in the air to make it rain?" Noelle James asked.

"No, that is seeding, which is something entirely different. Rainwater harvesting is finding ways to collect rainwater when if falls. Most rainwater is lost in evaporation. For places like Tucson, which is very dry, finding a way to capture and retain the rainwater, especially during the annual monsoons, and then recycle it could substantially change the way people farm, the way they use water. If all households installed something to capture the rainwater, whether on the roof or by the side of the house or underground, they could significantly cut their demands on the city's overall water supply."

"I see."

Jassim wondered what it was that she saw, felt that her attention was drifting.

"Could you please tell us about the accident?" asked Agent Fletcher.

For one brief, blessed moment, Jassim had no idea what he was talking about. "The accident?"

"The boy on the skateboard."

How did they know this? "What would you like to know?" *Why are you asking me about that?*

"Why don't you tell us what happened."

Jassim retold the story, without paraphrasing, using almost the identical wording that he had used with Officer Barkley, only instead of using pebbles to demonstrate, he pulled a pen from his breast pocket and drew on his paper placemat: two curved lines for the street, dots for the boys, tiny rectangles for the cars.

"And you were cleared of wrongdoing?"

"I was cleared at the scene of the accident. There were three or four witnesses."

Jassim didn't know where to look, was ready to move on to another topic.

"You've had contact with the family?"

Why did they ask these things as though they were questions when they obviously knew the answers? And why on earth was the FBI getting involved in a car accident? Jassim decided he didn't like Agent Fletcher; his questions did not seem thought out, as though he were asking the first thing to cross his mind.

"I have been there once."

"Have you given them gifts?"

"They asked for contributions for the funeral." Which was true, but Jassim's contribution came afterward.

"Are you familiar with this?" Agent Fletcher put in front of Jassim a photograph of a skateboard covered with stickers that were difficult to read.

"No."

"This was Evan's skateboard. Were you aware of his views?"

"His views about what?"

"About Arabs."

"His mother told me that since the attacks on the World Trade Center he had been very scared."

"Look closely."

Jassim looked closely without seeing, searching for letters that meant something. He found them typed in what looked like an official plaque of some sort. He moved his head back a bit and saw that the sticker read "Terrorist Hunting License."

He looked up and found both agents watching him.

"When did you first see this sticker?" asked Agent Fletcher.

"This moment."

"Mr. Haddad, are you saying that you never saw this sticker before?"

"Yes, that is what I am saying."

"And you are also saying that it is a coincidence that the boy you killed hated Arabs?"

"Having a 'terrorist hunting license' and hating Arabs are two very different things, Agent Fletcher. I think there is a good percentage of this country that feels the way Evan did, scared and at the same time tough against an unknown enemy. To answer your question, yes, it is a coincidence that the boy I killed hated Arabs." For God's sake, this was about Evan! But he had done all the right things. He had called the police. They had investigated. There were witnesses. What were they trying to do with these questions?

"What was your reaction to the events of September 11?"

For this question he was prepared. "I was shocked, saddened, unsettled. Probably much the same as most people in this country. It was so unexpected."

"Would your reaction have been different if it had been expected?" asked Agent Fletcher.

"My reaction was what it was. One cannot predict how one will react."

"How often do you pray in a mosque?"

"I have not prayed in a mosque since I was a young man."

"And why is that?"

Jassim thought for a moment. *Because I don't believe in God*, he wanted to say, but he felt this was not the forum for such a comment.

Noelle James interrupted, relieving him of having to express aloud his lack of belief. "Mr. Haddad, why don't you give us a sense of what a typical day for you is like."

Jassim decided that they were playing good cop/bad cop. "I swim, I work, I go home. Not unlike the rest of America, I suspect."

"That may be, but the rest of America does not have access to the entire city's water supply with the means to tamper with it," said Agent Fletcher.

Jassim couldn't help himself. "Means is one thing, motive is another. I am a scientist. I work to make water safe and available. I am a normal citizen who happens to be an Arab. Yes, I have access to the city's water supply, but I have no desire to abuse it. The mere fact that I am an Arab should not add suspicion to the matter." His stomach tightened. He knew he should keep quiet, but the words were bursting from his mouth. "I have spent my entire life trying to find ways to make water safe and accessible for everyone. Just because I am an Arab, because I was raised a Muslim, you want to believe that I am capable of doing evil. It is sometimes best to look within before casting such a broad net." The words got ahead of him, and he was not sure what he had just said. This righteousness was more in the style of his wife. He had never been prone to outrage.

The agents asked more questions, each more farfetched than the previous one. (*Did you ever meet any of the hijackers personally?*) He looked forward to telling Salwa about them. Salwa, whom he longed for right now. If Salwa were here, she would be able to make this right, would turn the investigators' questions around so they could see how ridiculous they were. That he was guilty of nothing.

The waitress came with large white plates of steaming food, and their eating slowed the questioning.

Noelle James looked at her pager, pushed buttons on it. She

looked up at Jassim, who was staring. "I am diabetic. This registers my blood sugar."

"So it's like a calculator?"

"Sort of. It's attached subcutaneously so it can add insulin as needed. I enter what I've eaten and it kicks out however much insulin I need based on that."

Jassim wanted to ask more questions about this device.

"What was your wife's reaction to September 11?"

"She was sad and outraged by it."

"Why did she send fourteen thousand dollars to Jordan on September twelfth?"

Salwa had never mentioned sending so much money home. To whom had she sent it? Her mother? What could he say? Should he lie and tell them she had sent it to her family? Was it her commission from the houses?

"To help her family," he decided to say, hoping they couldn't see his surprise.

"Are you aware of any personal relationship she has with any of her bank clients outside of work?"

"I don't follow you."

"Does she have any contact with clients outside of work, that you know of?"

"None." What were they insinuating?

"Your wife has received repeated calls from a Hassan Shaheed in Jordan. What was the nature of those calls?"

Although Jassim felt he had been kicked in the stomach, he replied smoothly. "Hassan Shaheed is an old friend of my wife's family." He glanced at his watch. He had been gone fifty minutes. The thought of the enchiladas on his plate made him nauseous. He stood up. "I'm sorry, but I have to leave now. Feel free to contact me if you have any other questions. I am happy to help." He shook Agent Fletcher's hand and then Noelle James's. It was clear from the looks on their faces that they had not been expecting this. He turned and walked toward the door before they had a chance to stop him. Not until he was outside on the sidewalk did he realize that he had not offered to pay.

Driving back, unaware of the sedan behind him that had also left from the restaurant, Jassim felt trapped, forced his breathing to slow. Why had Salwa sent so much money home? He knew she was helping with her niece's schooling, but with $1,000 a month at most. Why would she send $14,000 and not tell him? And why had Hassan called her? (Hassan Shaheed? That was the name of the boy she had been sitting with the day they had met in the café at the university. Had he been her boyfriend? Surely she had not sent the money to him! That was impossible.) And how many times was *repeated*? He noted that they did not say she had called him, which he thought was a good sign.

All this information was dizzying. Jassim took a couple of deep breaths and thought about the interview from the beginning. Odd that knowing about the stickers on Evan's skateboard and about Evan's hatred did not change his anguish at having killed him, or his sympathy for Mary. It made no difference to his feelings.

Jassim wondered vaguely if the distant attitude on the part of the city workers and the office girls was American racism. It seemed like a giant misunderstanding. Being hated outwardly would have been so much easier than this dancing around people's words and complaints and trying to figure out what they really meant. It made him shaky and unsettled. Unbalanced. An unfairly weighted scale. A globe tipped on its axis. An axis unable to rebalance. An axis of evil. He smiled to himself at this thought. Ludicrous.

Jassim had done nothing wrong and this was America and there should have to be proof of negligence on his part for his job to be affected. People, companies, the city, shouldn't be able to pull accounts on the basis of his being an Arab. Yes, finally he saw what had been sitting at the back of his consciousness for some time in a not-so-whispered voice: *with or against*. But was he not *with*? *I understand American society*, he wanted to scream. *I speak your language. I pay taxes to your government. I play your game. I have a right to be here*. How could this be happening?

Funny how nostalgia breathes heavily under pressure, how longing blossoms under the veil of hatred. Veiled by them. Hated by them. Hated for living. Hated for veiling. As he pulled into his parking spot and turned off the engine, Jassim allowed his eyelids to close gently, willed away the ridiculous wordplay that dwelling on any subject for too long always brought with it, focused on water meeting the horizon. A stable point. Proof that the world was balanced. His breathing slowed as he closed out everything but that which was more powerful. The sweet line that promised stability. The world that was far removed from the unpredictability of human interactions.

Interrupting this peace, jabbing at the evenness, was the very odd picture he wished he hadn't seen: Salwa sending $14,000 to Jordan on September 12. (Unfortunate timing.) And, worse, the even odder snap of Hassan Shaheed resurfacing, calling Salwa. Repeatedly. And the humiliation of hearing it first from FBI agents.

"I have the Christian right working for me," Marcus told his wife, Ella, as he put together one of his more complex pesto sauces and she poured them each a glass of white wine, her second, his first.

"Who? Anita?"

"And Bella, and Lisa, and Corey. How did you know?"

"Women talk. Women listen. It doesn't take a rocket scientist to guess that they are pretty right-wing. How did you find out? Make a poll of how many of your employees believe in the right to an abortion?"

"Bella's been keeping a notebook on Jassim."

"Why?"

"Because he's an Arab. I found that out after the FBI left."

"The FBI came to your office? Why?"

"Because Jassim's an Arab and he has access to the city's water and Bella's an idiot."

"Marcus, he needs a lawyer. Are you going to fire her?" asked Ella.

"What am I going to fire her for?"

"Spreading rumors. Slander."

"It's not that easy."

"I think it might be. You really need to find out."

"The FBI visit was scary. They seemed like such regular people, but then I remembered what they are doing." He told her about the conversation as he cut garlic, squeezed lemons and measured their juice.

"Marcus, do you know what is happening to Arabs and Muslims these days? Jassim could be arrested, maybe even deported."

"Yes, of course I know what's happening. That's why I told him they came. I told him he should get a lawyer."

"Poor man, imagine what he must be going through."

The words that were trapped in his head, the story that disturbed him more than anything, was that the FBI could start an investigation based on the allegations of one woman who probably couldn't find Jordan on a map. "This is why I hate religion. Religion makes people stupid." He pulled thick green leaves from their stalks, dropped them into a shiny silver colander. "Apparently since 9/11 Bella has been scheming."

"The FBI told you that?"

"Anita came to me after they left. She was guilt-ridden, realized that she had behaved in an un-Christian manner. Said that Bella's been keeping tabs on Jassim, called the FBI on him at least twice."

"He needs a lawyer."

"He does." Marcus worked in silence. Mincing. Sautéing.

Ella sat on a stool with her legs crossed while her husband filled a pot with filtered water and placed it on the burner. She sipped her wine and watched as he returned to the assembly of his sauce. "Do you think he could do something?"

Marcus had lost the thread of their conversation. "What do you mean?"

"I mean, do you think Jassim is capable of doing something bad to the water supply?"

Marcus turned around and stared at her. "Are you kidding, Ella? You know Jassim. Why would you suggest that?" Marcus didn't like having serious discussions with Ella when he was cooking; he worried that they would sour the taste of his food.

"I guess what I'm saying is that you need to know in your heart that he is the man you believe him to be, incapable of being bought, swayed, or moved toward evildoing."

"Of course I know who he is." He was glad his back was to his wife, since he felt that this statement lacked conviction. Something had been different in Jassim lately, something Jassim was not talking to him about. It could be anything, he had told himself over and over. It could be medical, or something in his marriage. Anything. Anything could be bothering him. (But why didn't Jassim come to him with it? Weren't they friends?) Not for the first time, his wife had brought to the surface the very thing that was nagging at him, harvested that vague doubt that had been lodged way back in his brain, undercutting the faith he had in others.

The water was boiling, menacing bubbles hissing from the top of the shiny stainless steel pot. Into it Marcus placed imported organic whole wheat fettuccine. He watched as the stiff, straight stalks of pasta succumbed to the heat and gradually slipped underwater.

How many hours did it take to unravel one person? Salwa wondered under the glaring sun of her American desert, sure that she was at least halfway through her own unraveling process. Or did it take days? Years? When she was a child, her finger often found its way to her belly button, sometimes for comfort, sometimes to pick out a piece of dirt or fuzz that was lodged in the folds. If her mother caught her engaged in this activity, she would scold her: "Be careful, habibti. If you pick too hard, you will loosen the end and unravel yourself." Salwa would imagine herself as a tiny skein of embroidery yarn, the tip of her thread held between the grubby thumb and forefinger of a naughty little refugee camp boy—Hassan, to be precise—being yanked along, flopping helplessly along a dusty road, trying to roll herself up but not being able to. Instead of a tidy wrap of color, she became a skinny, wiggly red river of cotton string, impossible to rewind.

Saturday, two days after Valentine's Day. And as Salwa traipsed through Victoria's Secret, her fingers drifting over nylon and silk and satin, her mind spun, twisted, rewound her back in time to the beginning of Jassim, to how it happened that she came to America and didn't marry Hassan. Poor sweet Hassan, a heap of tangled thread from the beginning. Gingerly, an elegant forefinger and thumb pinched the story by its very tip and lifted. Salwa peered underneath and was astounded by the radiance of its belly, the brilliant colors that could be seen by people thousands of miles away, the remains of her parents' dreams and Jassim's plans to return home. And Hassan. Mixed among the colors and scraps and lumps, stamped in the middle of its shiny synthetic tummy, were words that made her cringe: Made in USA.

It had been there all along.

—⁓—

One day when she was a junior at the University of Jordan, Salwa's eyes scanned the bulletin boards, landed on a tiny flier:

Water is the key to our survival. A lesson in self-sufficiency. Please join us this afternoon at 3 P.M. for a lecture by Dr. Jassim Haddad, hydrologist from America.

"This sounds interesting," Salwa said aloud to the other fliers rather than to Hassan, who was standing next to her.

"What does?"

"This talk on water." She pointed an already lovely index finger at the piece of paper.

Hassan pried his eyes from the finger and read aloud the words beneath it. He looked at the owner of the finger. "Please tell me what in that sounds interesting."

Salwa reread it quietly, finger tucked away. "I guess it's the 'self-sufficiency' part."

"You sure it's not the 'from America' part?"

Salwa looked at the flier again. Read it silently. *Water is the key to our survival. A lesson in self-sufficiency. Please join us this afternoon at 3 P.M. for a lecture by Dr. Jassim Haddad, hydrologist from*

America. She scanned the words slowly to see which ones pulsated the most. *Dr. Jassim Haddad.* No. That wouldn't do. She'd never heard of this man before. She tried again. *Water is the key.* Was this the phrase written just for her? Key to what?

Hassan pretended to move on and read fliers aloud, laughing. "*Meeting of the Communist Party. Four o'clock.* The communists should talk to your hydrologist, Dr. Haddad from America, for tips in making fliers. Come on, let's go have a soda." Hope filled his voice, pleaded with her.

"What time is it, Hassan?" Salwa asked, her mind stuck in the key of water, on her hydrologist, Dr. Haddad. *From America.*

"Two thirty-five."

"I'm going to hang around here for a bit."

"You're going to that lecture, aren't you?" Hassan turned and looked at her.

She spoke to the bulletin board. "I think so. I feel like I should, but I can't say why that is, exactly."

Hassan, who could say why that was, exactly, could sense this pull from the land of her birth and had been waiting for this moment all the years he had loved her but tried to be indifferent. "Take notes, okay? I'll see you tomorrow." He filled his eyes with Salwa's image, would have kissed her goodbye if it had been permitted, and turned away.

Salwa watched him go. She had no idea what he knew and instead enjoyed watching his jaunty walk as he left her; didn't see the pond that formed beneath the bulletin board, filled with every last one of Hassan's dreams.

Behind every story there is another (and sometimes another and another), and the story of Salwa and Hassan was this: they had known each other since they were young children, since Hassan's family moved into her neighborhood after his father died. Though he and Salwa were never particular friends, they acknowledged each other with a certain connection, a tie between the children of parents who have lost everything and are moving beyond that to become active members of their host society.

During their first year of university, they shared an English class, which Salwa excelled in and Hassan barely passed. Hassan's mother mentioned his difficulty to Siham, Salwa's oldest sister (best friends with Hassan's oldest sister), who promptly volunteered Salwa to help Hassan. And they'd been friends since. Salwa was appreciative of Hassan's handsome face, sense of humor, and political activism, saw him as a symbol of Palestine, and Hassan was smitten with Salwa, who in his eyes was the definition of perfection. Had been since he had first laid eyes on her at the age of six.

Their friendship tipped in Salwa's favor as she pushed one after another of Hassan's cousins and friends, most who still lived in Wihdat refugee camp, off the scale, filled it instead with her own, more established Palestinian and Jordanian friends. By their third year of university (the year in which Salwa felt the need to attend a lecture on water), Hassan had severed bonds with most of his disenfranchised pals in order to be with Salwa, to sit with her in the cafeteria, to go on picnics with her and her friends.

Salwa's family was divided in their feelings about Hassan. Siham thought he was good for Salwa, grounded her. "He reminds you who you are," she told Salwa more than once.

"Hassan is a good boy, but what is he going to do with his life?" her father asked one evening after Hassan had come and gone.

"He wants to work in television, to produce television shows."

"My dear daughter, I know that is what he wants to do, but is he going to? Is he working in that direction?"

"Well, he's trying in school. He is studying and making connections with people who could help him later on."

Her father nodded. Grumbled a bit in the way of fathers who don't really approve. "Is Hassan who you want in life?"

Salwa didn't answer as her brain filled with embarrassed thoughts. She liked Hassan—this much she knew. Beneath liking and the tiniest part of desire in which liking was wrapped, however, was her greed for a certain kind of life, and when she floated out those fantasies, Hassan was not a part of them.

Her father continued. "Salwa, let me say this. Hassan is a boy who is not ready to be a man. He likes to be the center of things. He is the kind who will spend his life spinning out dreams, swinging from one after another and getting nowhere. You are not that type, nor are you a person who could live with that type. Your tastes are far too expensive for the likes of Hassan."

After class the next day, Selim (her cousin, Hassan's friend) offered them both a ride home. Salwa sat in the back seat and Selim and Hassan in the front.

That morning Hassan had met with a television producer in the hope of finding an internship. "Today was beautiful," he said. "The guy I met will let me work on his set. There is so much to learn, and he says that I've a job when I'm ready." Hassan turned completely around in his seat to look at her. "They are so updated and modern, and I can learn so much."

Salwa watched him flaunt his joy and eagerness and sensed that under it was distress, something he disguised with joking and charm. It was a wisp of a feeling that she might not have registered if it were not for the conversation she had had with her father the night before. She pushed it aside, enjoying his attention and excitement. "I am really happy for you, Hassan. When do you start?"

"When I'm ready. That's what he said—that they had no spaces for internships but that when I was done with school I should go and see what was available."

Salwa didn't say anything, couldn't bring herself to flatten his enthusiasm by translating those words.

Selim pulled the car over on a shaded street and parked. "Guys, give me five minutes. I have to get some things for my mother." He got out of the car and ran back down the block.

"Here, Salwa, look at this." For the second time, Hassan handed her a brochure of the production company. "Look." He pointed, leaning from the front seat to the back. "Do you mind if I come sit there?"

"Of course not," she told him, though her stomach lurched.

Hassan got out of the front seat and opened the door of the back and got in. Sitting next to her, a hand's width too close, he went through the brochure page by page, pointing out each photo and telling her about this studio and that equipment. She could smell the coffee and cigarettes on his breath, and this, mixed with the enormity of his excitement, caused Salwa to shrink next to him. To keep her from vanishing, he put his hand, moist and warm, on hers. She stared at it and then looked up at his face, hard and handsome. He leaned forward, the smell of unfulfilled ambition packed in his mouth, and kissed her, not gently and tenderly, as she had expected; instead he shoved his tongue into her mouth as soon as their lips touched. Maybe it was the panic of kissing in the back of a car on a residential street, she reasoned. He loosened his grip, kissed her more gently, stopped shoving his dreams down her throat, one after another. It lasted a minute, maybe a minute and a half. Then she pushed him away, gently, politely. She felt a mix of fear (of being caught) and excitement.

Hassan didn't say anything and went back to the front seat. Salwa's heart thudded in her chest, seemed to shake the car and the street beneath it. She wiped her face when she thought Hassan couldn't see and stared out the window with the taste of another person in her mouth. Selim returned less than a minute later, and together the three drove home, as if nothing out of the ordinary had occurred.

The next day Salwa and Hassan's relationship had transformed, as though written on Hassan's tongue was a wordless agreement that she had signed and accepted by allowing it to enter her mouth. When he joined her and her friends that afternoon in the courtyard, he pulled his chair over by Salwa, even though it forced everyone else to move. Later, when they were leaving the university for the day, he took her books and carried them, as though she should not be burdened by the weight. His intensity, which he usually directed toward his future dreams or his lost country, was now focused entirely on her, cutting off her breath and turning her blue.

The day before they found themselves in front of the bulletin board, Hassan told her that he loved her, not for the first time but with a thickness she had not felt before.

"I love you too, Hassan," Salwa replied, though she was not sure whether she loved him enough, worried that his dreams were too big for him, fell slack around his waist.

—∞—

At just before three o'clock, Salwa arrived at the almost-full lecture hall. The man she assumed to be Dr. Haddad stood in a corner talking to Dr. Nabeel Zaytoun, the professor who led the seminar. The seats filled and the murmurs quieted. Dr. Zaytoun introduced his old friend.

Dr. Haddad walked toward the podium, and Salwa thought he looked awkward, unsure of himself. He was neither tall nor short, and his body was lean in an almost gawky way, emphasized by the expensive suit he wore. Odd that his name was Jassim, for if it were not for his face, with the large eyes and very thick eyebrows, he would have looked fragile, breakable. He stood for a few seconds shuffling note cards and not saying anything, and in that time Salwa worried that he was going to be one of those scientific types who couldn't present a coherent sentence to the general population. Why had she come here? This was ridiculous. She was sitting in the front row, and glancing behind her, she realized there was no way she could leave until the lecture was over. Very quietly, she slid a small notebook off her stack of books; she would doodle silently under the guise of taking notes. His voice interrupted her thoughts.

"I'm afraid it is true: water is my first love. Water in its natural form is beautiful, as it flows gently or wildly along its riverbanks or bangs into the sand and rocks in great waves. When you are thirsty and go to a well to drink, there is surely nothing more delightful than those drops of water falling on your tongue. And when you have been sick and you take your first sip of spring water after not eating for a day or two, is there anything tastier? Eighty percent of the earth is water. Depending on our age and gender, between fifty and seventy-five percent of our bodies is water. Pure water is odorless and tasteless. It is the major constituent of living matter. It is the only substance that occurs at ordinary temperatures in all three states of matter: solid, liquid, and vapor.

"Since the beginning of time, people have settled near sources of water and societies have grown on those spots. The first known permanent human settlement was on the west bank of the River Jordan. The earliest unearthed remains of dams date from about

3000 B.C. and belong to a complex water system that served the town of Jawa here in Jordan. The Quran specifically states that all living beings have a right to water.

"In America, where I live, native people settled along rivers and, like tribal people worldwide, accepted them for what they were: unpredictable, sometimes erratic, changeable beings. Instead of making a river their border, they viewed both banks as a natural territory. When the European settlers came, they diverted rivers and tried to harness them, with little regard for the people they might be affecting, which is similar to what the Israelis did when they hijacked the River Jordan in 1964; the 1967 war started because Israel was caught trying to divert the Jordan away from the West Bank and Jordan. The result of that war was that Israel controlled—controls still—most of the headwaters of the Jordan, much of the Jordan itself, and is in partial or total control of all the aquifers. By the way, both the Turkish and the Israeli prime ministers, Süleyman Demirel and Yitzhak Rabin, are former water engineers.

"There are estimates that some eighty countries, with forty percent of the world's population, are suffering from serious water shortages. In another twenty-five years, two thirds of the entire population of this globe will be living in water-stressed areas, most of these in our neighborhood: North Africa, the Middle East, and west Asia. We have deficits in water budgets, a decline in water tables, and prolonged droughts in many areas. I'm sure most of you have some firsthand knowledge of this; lack of water is a serious constraint for vital development here in Jordan. Aquifers are being depleted at a rapid rate, and some degree of water rationing is a fact of life for most of us.

"The World Health Organization recommends that all people have an absolute minimum of fifty liters of fresh water a day, five for drinking, ten for cooking, fifteen for bathing, and twenty for sanitation. In Haiti and Gambia and Mozambique, people live on less than ten liters of water per day. The average Palestinian has between fifty and seventy liters, though the Gaza Strip offers as low as nineteen, and will soon be the most water-starved place on the planet. In ten years, its approximately six hundred and fifty thousand residents will number 1.2 million—or roughly thirty-two hundred people per square kilometer."

He paused for a moment, let these statistics settle.

"Jordanians have less than ninety liters of water available to them each day. The average Israeli uses between three hundred and three hundred and fifty liters. Americans use about three hundred and eighty liters a day. Per capita fresh water in Jordan is less than a fourth what it is in the U.S."

Salwa's heart was pounding. The gawky man whom she had thought would embarrass himself had become an orator. His words fell like rocks, sure of themselves and indisputable.

"Don't believe it is just the Israelis who divert water though. It is the Chinese, the Americans, the Egyptians. It is everyone. Water is life, technology is power, and humans are thieves. Since the beginning of time, water has been of such fundamental importance that flaunting one's ownership of it in wasteful fountains became synonymous with wealth. This was as true in Phoenicia as it is now in Phoenix."

Salwa glanced around, wondering if she alone was being hypnotized. Her fellow students were silent, spellbound. She could not have said how long she listened to him, only that the lecture went by quickly and offered numbers and stories she had never heard before.

"Who has the rights to the rivers and oceans and seas? Is it the person who lives closest to them? Is it the person with the most technology? Here is my answer: no one. At the end of it, water is its own being and is far more powerful than man, a fact that man, with his enormous ego, cannot accept. As I've said, lakes and rivers are unpredictable beings. They overflow and flood and dry up. Man's foolishness lies in attempting to control and harness water's natural flow for his benefit rather than allowing it to follow its course, accommodating it. One of the greatest ironies I know is that some of the biggest aquifers are beneath deserts that get no recharge; many of the world's greatest rivers are in places no one wants to be. Whose water is that? Who has the rights to it?

"In Jordan, about ninety-two percent of annual precipitation is lost to evaporation. As I've explained, my specialty is rainwater harvesting, collecting the water that falls from the sky and using it both for agriculture and for individuals. The beauty in this is that it creates self-sufficiency, allows people not to be dependent on governments and companies, not to have to live on only eighty-three liters of water per day, as we do here. In India, whole villages have subscribed to some very simple steps in agriculture and for households. They have actually raised the water tables, so that not only are they not taking from the earth, they are giving back, because they are working as a collective. Here in the Middle East we have cisterns and intricate underground wells. When the government began pumping water into our homes a generation or two ago, we regarded these ancient methods of water preservation as primitive. The fact of the matter is, they carry the wisdom of the ages. Now, here in Amman, new houses are required to have cisterns to collect the rainwater. As we are parched with the new ways, we are looking back to ancient wisdom. We must do this if we are to survive.

"I will leave you with this thought. Suppose you are flying in a tiny plane and it crashes in the desert. You are reduced to your most basic existence. It doesn't matter if you have a nice car or suit or watch. You are alone in the desert, and there is only one thing that will keep you alive. Not land. Not oil. Water."

For a couple of seconds the class was silent. As Dr. Haddad collected his note cards, which he had not once glanced at during his lecture, the students popped out of their stupor and applauded him as though he were a politician accepting a nomination or an innovative scientist accepting an award. Or both. Several actually stood up.

He smiled and stood by the podium answering questions for another twenty minutes. Salwa remained transfixed until Dr. Zaytoun went to the podium and thanked everyone for attending. She took her time putting her notebook away (the blank page had remained blank) and picking up her bag, wishing that Dr. Haddad had talked longer. She filed out with the rest of the students but did not want to head home right away, so she sat down on a bench just outside the lecture hall and thought about what he had said. Even though her parents had been refugees, Salwa had never been conscientious about saving water—quite the opposite. While Dr. Haddad cited example after example of countries and governments and people who squandered their water, she felt ashamed as she thought about her own showers and her gardening. She didn't think twice about letting the water run unless one of her parents was at her side, scolding her. And to think that Nasser was not the hero she had always considered him to be! To think that Los Angeles stole its water from other states and no one stopped it! And the Israelis! Despite all her reading and discussions of their injustices, she had had no idea of the extent to which they had robbed the Palestinian people, even of their water. She was excited by these thoughts and couldn't sit still; the hydrologist had talked about so many things she had not known about.

She awoke from her musings to see the catalyst of her thoughts walk past her, alone. "Dr. Haddad, excuse me," Salwa called after him, fumbling to gather her things.

He turned around and waited for her.

"Dr. Haddad, I wanted to thank you for your presentation. It was quite informative and interesting. You seem to know so much about how the whole world uses and abuses water."

"I live for water," he replied.

"I was just thinking about the things you said, about the myths we believe about people."

"Your name is?"

"Salwa. Salwa Khalil."

"Nice to meet you."

Salwa held out her hand and shook his firmly. His palm was dry and cool.

"So what do you study, Miss Salwa?"

"Banking and economics."

"Do you like what you are studying?"

This struck Salwa as an odd question; usually professors just wanted to know what you were going to do with the degree.

"Some aspects are very interesting."

"What brought you to my lecture?"

Dr. Haddad seemed calm, and she thought she could see a sweet side to him as he talked to her so intently. His dark curly hair gave him a youthful look, and while he was not her idea of handsome, he was attractive. He wore no ring on either hand.

"I saw a flier for it." She couldn't tell him that it had called to her, that his name had throbbed on the bulletin board, yelled at her until she paid attention and promised in her mind that she would attend. "When do you return to the United States?"

"Well, it depends. In about two weeks, probably. Have you ever been there?"

"Only once, when I was very little, but I don't remember it at all."

They stood together, embraced by the spring day, by Hassan's absence, and by Jassim's impending return to the United States.

"It was a pleasure to meet you, Miss Salwa. I wish you luck in your studies."

"Thank you, Dr. Haddad. Goodbye."

At that moment Salwa had her first whiff of destiny, the same scent Hassan had picked up a couple of hours earlier in front of the bulletin board, the one that carried the name of her future husband. Somewhere it was written that Salwa would never marry Hassan; even Hassan knew this.

Hassan called Salwa that night, and she asked her mother to tell him that she was asleep.

"Why, habibti? Are you avoiding him?" her mother asked.

"No. I just don't feel like talking to him now. I'll talk to him tomorrow."

"As you wish."

Tomorrow came, and Salwa avoided Hassan. Did not go and sit with her friends in the cafeteria. Wished she could run into Dr. Jassim Haddad. A doctor. And not so old.

"So is water the key?" Hassan asked her when he finally found her at the end of the day.

"It turns out that it is. Really, the lecture was so interesting. I wish you had been there to hear what he had to say." Which was a lie. In the shadow of Dr. Haddad's talk, Hassan seemed like a little boy, and for the first time she wished he weren't so intense in his affection.

The next day she avoided Hassan again, more out of guilt than anything else. Each time her thoughts grazed the image of Dr. Jassim Haddad, which they did several times a day, she felt as though she were deceiving Hassan. In two weeks Dr. Haddad would go back to the United States, and she would never see him again and that would be that. Then she could say yes to Hassan's marriage proposal when it came.

At the end of the second day after Dr. Haddad's lecture, Hassan again found her at the gates of the university, waiting for a shared taxi. She wondered how long he had been sitting there waiting to ambush her. "Let's go have a soda before you go home," he said, and Salwa agreed, though she felt irritated.

Hassan came with ideas and proposals he planned to offer to Salwa, fancy words to will her his way even though they would have to wait to have the wedding ceremony until the following year, when they had both graduated and he had a job. This was his plan. To cement her to him as best he could. But each time his words formed to shift subjects, each time he prepared to ask for her hand and soul, Salwa introduced a new topic.

"Did you know that the U.S. sanctions in Iraq have directly resulted in malnutrition among children and the resurgence of diseases that were thought to be almost entirely eradicated? How ironic it is that the most advanced country in the world is sending everyone else back in time, so that they are ravaged by diseases that had been wiped out."

At that moment, Hassan didn't care. "Salwa, I have to talk to you about something serious." He had class in ten minutes. He opened his mouth to say, "I want to marry you; I am asking you officially." But just as the *I* slid out, Salwa interrupted him.

"That's him," she whispered.

"Who?"

"Dr. Haddad, the professor who talked about water."

Hassan turned, not expecting Dr. Haddad to be as thin or as average-looking as he was, nor dressed in an expensive-looking suit and shiny leather shoes. In her description of him and his lecture, Salwa had omitted his obvious wealth.

The man stooped a bit, though he was not tall, and came toward their table. "Excuse me, sorry to bother you both. I don't know if you remember me, Miss Salwa. I am Jass—I am Dr. Haddad."

Hassan watched Salwa look up at him and pinched himself on the inside of the left thigh so he wouldn't scream.

"Of course. Hello, Dr. Haddad, how are you? This is Hassan Shaheed. I told him all about your lecture."

Dr. Haddad extended his hand to Hassan, who shook it firmly, wishing that he could fling him back to America with his higher degree, his thousand-dollar watch, his save-the-world job and interesting comments. "Nice to meet you. Salwa is a newly converted water conservationist."

"I'm delighted to know I've made an impact."

Dr. Haddad stood. Hassan was not going to ask him to join them. He willed him to leave.

"Please, have a seat," said Salwa.

Hassan knew that if he were to stay, he would say something he would later regret, so he stood up, feeling as though he was an elegant finger's width away from bursting. He couldn't bring himself to shake Dr. Haddad's hand again and decided that instead of asking Salwa to marry him first, as he had planned to do, he would go over to her house with his family and ask her father for her hand, in the old-fashioned way.

Salwa knew none of this, of course, and her heart thumped as she and Dr. Haddad watched Hassan walk off and Dr. Haddad sat down.

"He's a pleasant chap."

"So what is it that you are doing exactly in America?"

"I work for companies and help them come up with ways to save water and to conserve rainwater. We as humans, especially in America, waste so much."

"Why do you think that is, Dr. Haddad?"

"Jassim. Please call me Jassim. As I am not your professor, I think that would be perfectly acceptable."

Salwa felt her face burn, but Jassim seemed oblivious.

"I think we misuse water because of the myth surrounding it in the first place. Because water is never destroyed, we believe we have an endless supply of the stuff. Water is a comfort, whether it is to feed our trees and plants, to swim in, or to drink. All of the ways in which water is used make us more comfortable in life. Especially in places where there seems to be plenty, like Los Angeles. Because that city is on the coast, it is difficult to comprehend that there is no natural water supply, that it is in a desert. Places like Los Angeles are deserts, which by definition are places not meant to be lived in. In English it is more obvious, as there is the desert, the place, and *desert*, the verb, which means to leave a place empty. The other reason we misuse water is that it is a force stronger than we as humans, and we don't like that, so we think we can control it, and so we try to harness it for our use. What people don't seem to understand is that while it sustains us, while we cannot live without it, we do not own it. Water is far stronger, both in will and in force, than man."

Salwa floated on his words, on the way they seemed to stream out of him effortlessly. The restaurant, the university, Amman all vanished as he spoke, and she felt that she was in the presence of the purest being she had ever met. Jassim Haddad and his words seeped into Salwa's joints and veins and soul, so that by the time she left him that day, it was clear to her that it was only a matter of time before he asked her to marry him.

—⁂—

Walking into the mall with a few hundred dollars' worth of intimate promises wrapped in tissue paper and tucked in a pink shopping bag, she saw that it had been Jassim's passion for water that had won her over, that had disguised the difference in their ages and nationalities and personalities. Thousands of miles and years and muddy puddles away from that reality, Salwa's threads were frayed and caked in dirt and loss. How to wash them? How to wind herself back?

—⁂—

By now, when Jassim turned off Swan into Evan's neighborhood, he knew his way around, recognized houses, like that white brick one facing south, with no awnings to protect the windows and doors from the glare of the afternoon sun. And how odd, he thought, that while the paint hung off the house in geometric slices, a massive SUV stood in the driveway. Gold in color and shiny and new.

Today, Sunday, Salwa was showing an outrageously expensive house, one whose selling price would be six or seven times that of the houses he was driving by now. Odd that this thought offended him, that he felt the need to protect a neighborhood he had not known existed a few months earlier. Jassim had not left the house with the intention of driving through Evan's neighborhood, but having gone to the Arabic grocery store and picked up some spices, olives, and a container of candy-coated fennel, for which Salwa had suddenly developed a craving, and being left with an entire Sunday afternoon, he could think of nothing better to do.

A cardboard box sat on a corner announcing a HUGE YARD SALE ALL DAY SUNDAY in uneven black letters. Jassim had not visited a yard sale since his college days, when students found their furniture and appliances in the backyards of strangers. He followed the arrow and pulled over in front of one of many identical black mailboxes perched at the top of a three-foot pole. He had not expected to be noticed, but as he got out of his car, a woman stared; her stare was neither friendly nor hostile.

"Good afternoon," said Jassim softly as he walked toward tables of items.

"Hi there," she said. Pink pants, tanned skin, and deep wrinkles on either side of her mouth. "Can I help you with something?"

"I saw your sign. I just thought I'd have a look around." Jassim tried to add an American swagger to his words, make it clear how long he'd been here.

"Knock yourself out. Prices are marked on the bottom of most items." The theme from the Lone Ranger began to play, and the woman with the creases and blond dye covering all but the black inch of hair closest to her scalp pulled a cellular phone from the waist of her pants, which Jassim saw were made of the same material as towels.

"Hey, it's Bob!" Though she was not shouting, her voice was enormous and sharp, pushing Jassim further away, bowing his head slightly. He kept his hands behind his back, mentally creating a picture of this woman through her rejected items.

The frame of a twin bed, metal, black, and not scratched. Guest bed, not child's bed, Jassim decided. Nothing indicated children, though he supposed she could have grown children. Jassim walked slowly from table to table, mentally tallying empty Coke bottles, porcelain figurines, tabletops and tabletops of decorative items. Military fatigues hung along the side fence, along with an American flag kite. Clothes were piled up on the back table, mostly women's in faded purples and pinks. His eyes whisked over dresses hanging from the tree. Tiny women's dresses in pinks and whites and oranges, some with lacy fronts, all with waists quite a bit narrower than that of the woman who was shouting into the phone from the other side of her front yard.

"Laredo? You're in Laredo. I think my parents got married in Laredo. Ma, didn't you get married in Laredo?" The woman did not move the phone from her mouth as she yelled to an older woman Jassim had not noticed before, who sat on an iron bench.

"It was Laredo," the woman answered. "Forty-six years ago."

"She says it was Laredo they were married in. Laredo. I can't believe you're in Laredo. She says it was forty-six years ago. Forty-six."

The house was well cared for: the paint was recent, the plants were watered, and there was an enormous shade tree in the center of the front yard that had been pruned to perfect symmetry.

Jassim's eye caught a flat, cheap, fake-leather briefcase. It was thin, brown, would hold a notebook or two. What struck him was how similar it was to one he had had in college at home. Made in China. He turned it over in his hands, his mind whizzing back through the years. Jassim lifted the cracked flap and saw the tiny fuchsia circle that held the price tag. One dollar.

"Laredo. My babe's in Laredo." The woman was off her phone

and seemed to be addressing the entire neighborhood, though she stood next to him now, her voice booming in his face. "You like that bag? I'll make you a deal on it if you want it."

"No, thank you. I was just looking at it. It reminded me of one I had years and years ago. I haven't seen one like it in a long time."

"That so?" She stared at him, her arms crossed, her face open. Dread crept up from Jassim's feet, waiting. He could feel the question in her, not quite ready to come out but percolating. He put the bag down, looked quickly around for something he could buy.

"How about perfume for your wife? These are Avon's latest." She grabbed one of the colored glass bottles in a way that made Jassim wonder if she had been drinking.

"Two of them have been used, two of them haven't," said her mother, who was putting some clothes in a plastic bag. "Your guess is as good as mine which is which."

"These look like perfume holders," he said.

"That's what they are. That's what I just said. Aren't you listening?" The woman laughed.

"Yes, I did hear you. What I mean is that these new bottles look like the antique kind of perfume holders that we have at home."

She ignored him. "Ma. Did you hear me? I don't think anyone's listening to me today. What's up with that? We're all having a trip down memory lane."

Emotional tie-ups, mixups, that's what the woman with the loud voice and the tight terry pants reminded him of. Problems. Unresolved life disasters. Unnecessary fixtures. Fads. Drugs. As much as he wanted to leave, to run at *breakneck speed* from this yard of unnecessary items, things to be purchased, unneeded, unwanted, disregarded, as much as Jassim wanted to hop into his Mercedes and be gone, he stood, he browsed, dancing with temptation, walking under the pruned tree of forbidden fruit.

"Buddy, you planning on buying anything? Maybe I could swap you some Avon bottles for that car of yours. What do you say?"

Jassim smiled because he could think of nothing to say, no brilliant comeback to *knock her socks off*. He worried that she would take him for an idiot (or worse, as a danger, though he would not allow himself to entertain this thought beyond the hint of its existence) and decided he would have to buy something. But for all the tables and piles littering her yard, there was exactly nothing that Jassim could imagine buying, and all he wanted to do was linger a bit, get a glimpse of Mary Parker's world. Perhaps there was something he could buy for her. Infused with this mission, he searched through Coke bottles, razors, pantyhose, doilies, potholders, table mats, glasses, mugs . . . an endless quantity of knickknacks, of unnecessary items in very good condition.

The woman was no longer watching him; instead she was prancing around the front yard with purpose and awareness that all particles were attracted to her, that she was the main event.

Jassim picked up four white mugs with pink lace painted on them and headed toward the older woman, two in each hand. The mugs were sturdy and matching and, he thought, would make a nice addition to Mary Parker's kitchen. Would match the pretty tidiness.

"I always liked those too. Good choice." The older woman's voice was slow and raspy, and her movements seemed painful.

Jassim opened his wallet. He had $360 in twenty-dollar bills. "Do you have change for a twenty?"

"I got change for everything today. We've probably sold over two hundred dollars' worth of things today. Crap, if you ask me, but don't tell her I said so." The woman gestured toward her daughter and counted out $18 in ones. "You need a bag for those?"

"Perhaps a small box?" They both looked around.

"All's we got is huge in boxes."

"This will be fine. Thank you very much, ma'am." He walked toward his car, mugs in hand. He put them on the front seat and looked at them when he got in. Thick white mugs with pink lace painted on them. Never had something so out of place found its way onto his leather seat, and Jassim laughed at the thought of what Salwa would say. He didn't care. As he drove off, up and down the grid of Evan's neighborhood, he began to envision himself giving the mugs to Mary Parker, and he wondered if she would be offended. Money and flowers were fine, but he thought she might find four mugs from a yard sale too insignificant. Coupled with $300 from his wallet, however, they would be fine, a kind gesture.

He turned onto her street, passed house after house hiding families, lives, tragedies that he had no access to nor reason to enter, and pulled up in front of Mary Parker's house, seeing that the curtains were pulled, just as they had been when he had gone there before. Inhaling with eyes closed and exhaling loudly, he picked up the mugs, felt his wallet, and got out of the car.

The day was bright and cool, and he didn't feel so out of place walking up the path toward the screen door (still bent out at the bottom). These past weeks he had acculturated himself, toured Mary Parker's America. He rang the doorbell and stood with all four mugs looped in his left hand. The door opened, and a girl's face looked out.

"Yes?"

It had not entered his mind that today was Sunday and that Mary's daughter might be home.

"Is Mary here?"

"No. She's at work."

Jassim didn't know what to do with himself, where to put himself.

"Okay, thank you. I'll stop by another time." He turned around before she could say anything else, before she could ask him who he was and if he wanted her to tell her mother anything for him. Simply dropped the mugs on the front seat and drove off. In his thoughts he lay the face of the sister next to the face that had stared blindly at him on the street that afternoon, but he could not find the resemblance.

_ᗧ ᗤ_

"Now, Salwa, make sure to get a name and address for everyone who comes in," hammered Mr. Torrey in free weekend minutes, his hot breath filling her ear.

"Certainly," she replied as she drove and listened and bit her lip to keep from talking back.

"We will be here in Phoenix until about three-thirty and then I'll call you when we head back."

"Okay, Mr. Torrey. Have a good time."

He hung up without a goodbye.

She pulled to the side of the road and let her car idle while she removed a sign from the trunk. OPEN HOUSE; MARVEL REALTY; SALWA HADDAD. She still liked to see her name printed like this, wished her mother and father could see it too. She drove on and placed the last of the six signs in front of the house, thankful at least that Mr. Torrey was not there to hang over her shoulder. She pulled her car up the steep drive and parked in one of two places designed for servants' cars, resigned to giving the next three and a half hours away, with the advantage of a comfortable house to spend it in.

She walked across the grass (she could hear Jassim's comments about the irresponsibility of having a lawn in the desert), plugged her code into the keypad, and retrieved the key. In setting the scene for the day, the Torreys had left flowers on the table in the entryway, on the dining room table, and in the kitchen. Each bathroom had a tiny vase with a gardenia filling the room with its deep scent. Each bedroom contained a vase of flowers that matched the decor of that room: a dozen red roses in the master bedroom, dramatic white lilies in the second bedroom, bright yellow daisies in the third bedroom, and naughty purple irises in the guest suite.

Salwa pushed the button for the preprogrammed satellite music stations on the tiny but costly entertainment system, searching for nonintrusive background music. Lowering the volume, she piped it into the entire house, unidentifiable tunes that blended into the walls, the carpets, the furniture.

She wandered through one more time, checking the kitchen for stray dishes; there were none. The bedrooms for forgotten articles of clothing; none. All seemed to be in order. She returned to the master bedroom for a moment to admire the mahogany dressers and nightstands that matched the sleigh bed, the quilt that matched the drapes and wallpaper. Salwa sat on the bed, and pictured herself starting each day from this spot. She didn't get farther than the bed: even if they could afford it, Jassim would never buy such a showy house, use land and money so arrogantly. His voice pushed her out of the bedroom, into the hallway and to the front door, which she unlocked to welcome three hours' worth of visitors.

—⁓—

Two brokers with clients and three groups of people off the street kept her busy enough. At 2:50 the door opened and a heavyset middle-aged man with round glasses and a white beard came in with his wife, who wore her dyed blond hair short and curly and her flowered dress just past her knees. Salwa glanced at her red suede rubber-soled sandals and winced.

"Hello, welcome," she greeted, getting up from the divan on which she had just sat down. "My name is Salwa Haddad."

"Good to know you. I'm Dave, and this is my wife, Mary." He shook her hand firmly, sincerely, she thought.

"Hi, Dave. Hi, Mary. If you wouldn't mind signing your names over there, and you can also pick up a sheet on the house. It is just under four thousand square feet, has a pool, Jacuzzi, and dual cooling system for both sections. There are four bedrooms, including both luxurious master and guest suites, three and three-quarter bathrooms with classic tiling in each, and a bright laundry room. The stereo system is connected to the entire house; the electricity is fully upgraded, and the kitchen has all stainless steel appliances, including a professional oven as well as a conventional one. The house was built in 1990 and has been lived in by the seller since then. Feel free to wander around, and let me know if you have any questions."

They thanked her and began a self-guided tour, looking at each room, at each detail of each room, from baseboards (need painting) to wallpaper (peeling at the edges in two rooms). Forty-five minutes later, Dave was still asking Salwa questions. "Even for this kind of square footage, they are asking an awful lot."

"Well, the market is changing, and the house is new and well built, with a lot of amenities. It's competitive compared to other homes in this area, and it's only been owned by the original buyer. All of these factors push the price up."

At this moment, while Dave droned on and his wife scouted the house (stealing the Torreys' most prized possessions, for all Salwa knew), Salwa was thinking that perhaps she was not destined to be a real estate broker; she could not see herself having this sort of conversation over and over again. And as that moment passed and a new one began, the door opened. Looking up with her agent smile, she absorbed the face and figure of the man who entered the house.

"Good afternoon," he said, a smile hanging at the edge of his mouth.

"Hello."

"I am new to Tucson and looking to buy in this neighborhood. Mind if I wander around a bit?"

"No, not at all. Would you mind signing in first?"

"Sure." He approached Salwa, his eyes fixed on her, his hand extended. "Name's Jake. Jake Peralta."

"Pleasure to meet you, Jake," Salwa replied, shaking his hand, flesh on flesh in a terrifying electric touch. Dave was still talking, but Salwa had tuned him out, didn't care what he had to say, what his wife stole, just wished they would leave.

"I'll just have a look around," said Jake with a wink, and walked off.

"So, you have a card you can give me?" Dave asked.

"Of course, right over here on the table." She had fanned out several of her business cards on the glass.

"Because we are looking, and we could use someone to help us. Now, do you take on new clients?"

"Absolutely. My information is on the card, and you can call me to set up an appointment." *Why had Jake come? What could he be doing?*

Dave's wife reappeared. "This is such a lovely house. It's out of our price range, but it is lovely."

"As I was telling your husband, why don't you call me and we can go over some listings together, maybe see what's out there that you might like that's in a range you will find affordable."

"Oh, that would be good. We've been going about this the wrong way," Mary said. "You know, driving around and hoping to see something that appeals to us."

"That's a hard way to do it, what with the market taking off. There's lots of competition, in some neighborhoods more than others. Also, we as brokers get listings as soon as a house is on the market, which means you'll get a much earlier start if you are working with someone." Salwa willed them to leave, to go away. She looked at each of them intently as she spoke, distracted and dazzled by the thought of Jake coming to see her.

An eternity later, Dave looked at his wife. "Shall we go, then? Salwa needs to help other clients and here we are going on and on."

"Don't worry yourself. That's my job, and I am happy to help."

"What time do you work tomorrow?"

"I could meet with you sometime in the afternoon, if you'd like."

"How about two o'clock?"

"I have another job, so it would have to be around lunchtime or after four."

Names, numbers, and lunchtime date recorded, Salwa said goodbye and followed the route Jake had taken. She would not have been surprised to find him in the family room, watching television. But the family room remained empty, silent but for the background music, as was the kitchen. She passed through these toward the guest suite, where she found the door closed. Odd.

"Jake, are you in there?" As she asked this question, she felt the vaguest gnawing that things were not as they should be.

"I am. Are you alone?"

"Yes, why?"

"Has everyone left?"

"Yes."

The door clicked but did not open. "Come here, habibti."

This word from his mouth made her flinch. She waited a moment before she walked in and found Jake lying on his back on the bed, undressed.

"Jake, *ya Allah,* what are you doing?"

"I want you, Salwa. I thought this would be fun."

"Are you crazy? What if someone comes? I'm showing a house —this is someone's house. You can't do this!"

"No one's going to come. I took all your signs down. They're in my car. No one will know to come."

"What if they read about it in the paper or a realtor brings them?"

"It's almost four. No one is going to come, but lock the door if you're so worried."

Instead of arguing, Salwa turned and walked as quickly as she could in her too-high shoes to the front of the house and locked the door. Bolted it against anyone coming and *click-clacked, click-clacked* back toward the bedroom where Jake lay. Her palms were sweating and her legs trembled. Part of her was raging, but another part of her felt exhilarated by the situation, so novel and odd and daring.

Another deep breath and she entered the room. Jake still lay on the bed, naked and leaning against the pillows. Salwa had to look away.

"Are you shy now? No, you can't be shy with me. I've seen how you are and what you like. I can see that this excites you. Come here. Come touch me."

His words were so ugly and bizarre, and yet she did as she was told, as though her brain had left her and a very tiny and potent spot deep within her was guiding her.

He moved to the edge of the bed and pulled her between his legs, placed her hands on his body, held her to him and unbuttoned her shirt. She let his fingers dance along her pink lacy bra, remove her left breast and suck on it, hard, unzip her skirt and let it fall to the floor in wrinkles, pull at her matching pink underwear, so she felt bound and ridiculous.

"Keep your shoes," he whispered into her neck. And she did, let him lean back and pull her on top of him and didn't care what awaited her. Didn't care that his mouth tasted sour, that he wore no condom, didn't care what she opened herself to, just let it happen.

—∞—

Reality crept in as she glanced at the clock. Four-fifteen. Jake lay on his back.

"I have to get up. We have to go."

"What's the rush?"

"The rush is there is a family who lives here and they are going to come home. The man has probably called me three times already wanting details." And as rushed as she was, she couldn't leave his smell on her. She went into the bathroom, locked the door, and quickly-quickly rinsed off in the shower. Sore and shaky, she washed between her legs, washed her feet, and rinsed off the rest of her body with clean cold water, and suddenly the reality of what she had just done seized her. That he had worn no condom. That traces of Jake would still be inside her and that no amount of washing would remove them. Names of diseases raced across her brain. Or worse, pregnancy. Her breathing became frantic and she began to tremble, naked in the Torreys' shower. This was not the time for it—she could not dwell now; she had to leave. She shook off as much water as she could in the shower and dried herself with one of the towels that was hanging for display. She thought about this for a moment, wondered how to deal with a used towel in a clearly unused room. She would come back to it, couldn't think straight enough to decide right now. Dressing hurriedly, she emerged from the bathroom looking much the way she had for Dave and Mary, though she was not the same person. This much she knew.

The room was empty. She looked at the rumpled bed, shook out the bedspread and fluffed the pillows. She ran her hand along the cover to make sure it was dry, and she leaned over and sniffed. Only the vaguest hint of what had taken place there. The room looked as it should. Smelled as it should, but she opened the French doors to air it out anyway. Jake must have gone back to the front of the house, she reasoned. Must be waiting for her there. Salwa walked back, but Jake was not there. She went to the front door, and it was no longer bolted. Her heart sped. Could he have left? Without saying anything? A wave of nausea passed over her again and she stopped for a moment to calm herself. What had she just done?

She went to her bag and pulled out her cell phone. Just as she had thought, three missed calls, one unlisted number and two from the Torreys. She called them back.

"Yes."

"Hi, Mr. Torrey. It's Salwa."

"I've been trying to call you, but you didn't answer."

"I don't like to answer my phone when there are people here."

"How many did you get?"

"Maybe ten separate groups. Two were with brokers. There was a couple here. They spent about an hour looking around and asking questions, but ultimately I think it's out of their price range."

"What did they waste your time for, then?"

"It's the nature of this business. And you never know."

"I see. Well, we left Phoenix early, so we'll be home in another fifteen, twenty minutes. You'll be gone by then, I would imagine."

"I'm on my way out right now, in fact."

"All right. We'll talk tomorrow." He hung up without saying goodbye, and Salwa cursed him, cursed herself, dizzy at the thought of what would have happened if they had come home earlier. What had she done? She bolted the front door again and walked through the house to make sure everything looked as it had when she had come. She saw without seeing. She walked back to the guest suite with paper towels to wipe down the shower, folded the used towel and turned it around so that the wet part faced the shower door. With the bathroom returned to its original state, she checked the bedroom, again ran her hand over the covers on the bed, closed the French doors, and left the room and all that it had seen.

Music off, business cards collected, Salwa walked out the door, locked it, and replaced the key in the lockbox. She walked to her car and saw her six signs piled against the left rear tire of her SUV. On top of the signs was a purple iris, and wedged in the stem was one of her business cards, on the back of which was written "Awesome."

Salwa loaded her signs in the back. Loaded herself in the front. And sat. She opened her bag and got out lotion for her hands. Her brush. Tidied herself to return home. Without warning, she started to cry, the feeling of panic and sadness choking her, a quick drop in altitude with no exit sign clearly marked, no oxygen mask dropping from the ceiling.

And when she had finally calmed herself enough to drive, as she backed out of her space and then turned down the driveway, the Torreys pulled in. She waved and continued driving, not having the strength to stop and talk with them. A minute later her telephone rang; no doubt the Torreys. She did not answer, did not even look to see who it was, just continued to drive away toward home.

Exhaustion was not the word to describe what he felt. Resignation, perhaps. In his heart he knew it was too late, but he couldn't help himself. All night when he should have been thinking about Intizar, Hassan was remembering Salwa, thinking about Salwa, breathing Salwa. *One last chance,* he told himself. *I will give her one last chance. I will call her and tell her everything.*

And so, in the quietest hours of the night and early morning, Hassan pressed the button to call Salwa. Without even a ring, her voice began, *"Hello, this is Salwa Haddad..."* but Hassan couldn't bring himself to leave a message. What would he say? *We have moved the wedding date up and are going to be married in a few days. This is your last chance.* But it wasn't really. Her last chance had already passed, had it not? At this point would he humiliate Intizar by breaking off their engagement? It all depended on Salwa. But her phone was turned off, so there was his answer.

Hassan lay on his bed, his heart pinched and sad. How could he feel such love for someone he'd not even seen in nine years? Was it real love or just nostalgia? He didn't know how long he lay there, drifting in and out of sleepy memories, before he felt a tug. He sat up and redialed. This time the phone rang several times before the message played. She was choosing not to answer. "Salwa, pick up, dammit!" Hassan said aloud, willing his voice to travel thousands of miles.

Chapter Thirteen

Head filled with loathing, Salwa readied herself for the morning, for the day, for the American workweek, with no energy, no interest, and no anxiety about Jassim's not having returned from swimming yet. Everything was spinning wildly away from her, and she didn't know how to grab it, to stop it. The thought of seeing Jake at work was sickening, all the wild excitement now dulled by revulsion.

Sitting in her cubicle later that morning, forcing herself to concentrate, she sensed Jake walking by, couldn't help herself, and lifted her head to stare at him, to will him to look in her direction. Maybe he didn't see her. Later, when he was working at the counter, she again tried to catch his eye, but he seemed purposefully to avoid looking at her. Instead he spent his spare moments laughing with Sweeney. Standing too close to her. Salwa mused over this, imagined them entwined as she had been with him just hours ago.

Petra walked into her thoughts. "You okay?'

"I'm fine. You?"

"I think they should fire Jake for sexual harassment."

Salwa's heart heaved. "Why do you say that?"

"He's disgusting. Do you see the way he is? Look, Salwa, I know you're friends, for whatever weird reason, but be careful. He's bad news."

"Why do you say that?" Salwa asked again, begging the concern to leave her voice.

"Salwa, he's not normal. There's something creepy about him. Sometimes he's okay, and maybe that's how he is with you, maybe with you he behaves, but around other people, especially Sweeney, he's just gross. It's like he leads his life with his dick. I mean, I know lots of men do that, but he seems to have a problem."

Salwa felt sick. Didn't want to hear more but at the same time couldn't make her words stay put. "Like what?"

"Like right now he was just telling Sweeney about how he met this much older woman and how he slept with her in a stranger's house, on a stranger's bed—how she kept her stiletto heels on and what a turn-on it was. If I were his manager, I would fire him."

Salwa's breath hid somewhere deep in her lungs, and she couldn't speak for a moment. Felt she might vomit.

"Salwa, are you okay?"

And then, grasping for words that would force Petra away from her, she asked, "Why don't you say something to Bill?"

"Because Bill will think I am saying something against Jake because I'm gay. It will go nowhere, or it will be a big horrible thing, and I don't want to deal with that. I just wish he'd stop. That kind of talk has no place at work."

"You're always telling me how conservative I am, and now you're bothered." Salwa tried to laugh, but it sounded to her ears more like a series of coughs.

"I guess we all have different things that offend us. The way he is talking right now is so degrading to that poor woman he screwed. If she really exists. I don't know why Sweeney listens to him, either. Sometimes I think he makes up these stories because he thinks it'll turn her on. They've always had something between them, and she's why he got this job to start with. I think to let someone, especially someone you've slept with, talk to you like that shows that you do not have a lot of self-esteem."

Salwa couldn't keep it inside any longer. "Excuse me, Petra." Didn't hear what Petra said as she brushed past her on her way to the bathroom, where once again she ejected all that was wrong within her into the city's sewage pipes.

—◊◊◊—

Later in the day, Petra's voice echoed in her ears: *an older woman.* He had told Sweeney everything. He was somehow involved with Sweeney. And to make it all uglier, he had referred to Salwa as an *older woman.* Her real voice, gagged and quivering for too long, stomped over Petra's and knocked her sickening self-pity on its side: *What does he know? He thought your shoes were stilettos!*

But this brought no solace or calm to her panic and queasiness.

And to have to talk to Dave and Mary today was impossible, would just drag her back to that god-awful house and what she had done.

"Hi, Dave. This is Salwa Haddad. We had scheduled a meeting for today, but I'm not going to be able to make it and would like to reschedule for sometime later in the week."

"That would be fine. I'm glad to hear your voice. My wife and I were a little worried about you."

"Worried about me? Why?"

"Well, after we left yesterday, we both couldn't help but think that the man who came in while we were there looked awfully young to be shopping for a big house. Mary kept saying that your job could actually be dangerous."

"Oh, I'm fine, thanks." *What was it that everyone was seeing but she had missed?*

"All the same, we did drive by later and saw that you had taken your signs down, so we figured you were fine. How about Thursday?"

Salwa numbly moved their names to Thursday as she again thought she might vomit, at the thought of this old couple driving by while she and Jake . . . No, she could not bear to think about it again.

—⁕—

By late morning Salwa was shaky inside and out and thought maybe it would be best if she left work, went home, and crawled under her covers. In the middle of these thoughts stood Jake, smiling.

"Hi, Salwa."

As much as she wanted to spit and scream, what could she do but reply? "Hi, Jake."

"You want to have lunch together?"

How she wished Petra hadn't said anything. Could she have made it up? No, she couldn't have made it up. *What she had said was true.*

"No, thank you."

"Salwa, is something wrong?" He looked at her, brow furrowed a bit, with what she would have taken for genuine concern if it not for what Petra had said.

"No, I'm fine."

"Salwa, I know when something is bothering you. Is it about yesterday? Is it because I left?"

She could not have this conversation at work. "No, it has nothing to do with that." She willed him to leave, terrified she would lose her outrage and resolve if he stood in front of her much longer. "Salwa, I left because I was scared about what would have happened if I had stayed."

She leaned back slightly in her chair. Crossed her arms. "Something has changed. I can see it in your face. Please, Salwa, tell me what's happened." He stepped in, squatted down next to her, and whispered. "Salwa, I left because I was scared I wouldn't be able to stop myself." He spoke as though he were testing out the words, as though he'd not used them before. "I love you and want you. You're all I think about." His skin looked clammy, but his eyes held a frantic sincerity.

Again his absurd remarks shook her real self back. "Jake, you don't love me. That much I know."

He pulled away from her. "Salwa, don't tell me what I feel and don't feel. I know what is in my heart. Something has happened. Petra said something, didn't she? She hates me. I know she said something to you. Salwa, whatever it was, please don't believe it. I want you in my life. I want to love you as you need." His desperation tugged at her. "I'm going to be completely honest with you, Salwa. I have made a lot of mistakes in my life, have done some ugly and stupid things. You are the best person, the one good thing I have right now."

Then why did you say what you said to Sweeney? The more serious his words were, the thicker her resolve became. "I have to think, Jake. Please, just let me think."

Marcus hung up the phone. Never in his life had he felt so torn. This was his third call from clients who no longer wanted Jassim working for them. This last phone call unsettled him more than the others had.

"Marcus, the FBI was just here asking questions about Jassim. What's he up to?"

"What do you mean, what is he up to?" asked Marcus.

"They say he sent money home to Jordan the day after the Twin Towers fell."

"I think he has family he helps. Maybe he sends them money on the twelfth of each month." Marcus tried to sound casual. The FBI had mentioned that money had been sent. Hadn't they said his wife sent the money? *Was it any different?*

"And he's had police trouble. An accident."

"People have accidents. He's probably been under a lot of pressure lately." Jassim had not mentioned an accident.

"He killed a boy. On a bike or skateboard or something."

Marcus said nothing, glad that Al was speaking with him over the phone and was not in front of him to see the shock on his face. Jassim had killed a boy and said nothing? "They must be wrong, Al. Jassim couldn't do that. There must be some misunderstanding."

"I saw the police report. Are you trying to tell me that you don't know what I'm talking about? It was in December. He killed someone, a child, who happened to have strong anti-Arab sentiments, and didn't mention it?"

"He didn't mention it," answered Marcus.

"Look, Marcus, Jassim has done great work for us in the past, but now I feel I need to scrutinize everything. I need to look at motive, at what he is getting from us. I simply don't have the time. I want to give you this contract, but as long as he is the senior hydrologist, I cannot."

"Al, the FBI is trying to get information on every Arab in the country right now. Our government is at a loss, so they're grasping at straws. Jassim is a straw."

"That may be, but I'm not willing to wait it out. It's too suspicious."

"I would be happy to pull him off and have someone else take his place. We don't want to lose your business, Al."

"I appreciate that, Marcus. Let me give it some thought. Something else I wanted to ask you about Jassim."

"What's that?"

"I've been hearing about his behavior changing. That he expressed some racist views. Is that true?"

"Where did you hear that?"

There was a pause on the other line. "Bella."

"Bella? Our receptionist?"

"Yes."

"What exactly did she tell you?"

"You know, as I think about it, it's not that she told me one thing specifically. It just somehow comes up. Does it matter, Marcus? Does it make any difference?"

"I think it does, Al. I absolutely understand your concerns and will pull Jassim off your contract if you like, but I have known him for fifteen years and I've never heard him utter anything that I would consider to be racist."

After he hung up, he thought he should call Bella into his office. But what would he say? That she had been slandering her superior and she would not be warned again? Marcus considered himself to be a good man who did the right thing, but he could not find the right thing in this situation. The right thing to do was not to let Bella's kind of thinking pollute the situation. He got up and went to Jassim's office. It did not look as though Jassim had been there recently. No light, no briefcase, no papers, computer off. Odd. He walked to the front. "Bella, has Jassim been in today?"

"Not yet."

And so he waited for his friend and colleague of fifteen years to return, while his thoughts battled one another.

—⟞⟐ ⟐⟝—

"Hey, Jassim." Marcus stuck his head into Jassim's office just before noon.

"Hi, Marcus. What's up?"

"You up for going to lunch right now?"

Jassim looked at his desk. "Yes. I've nothing pressing. Anywhere in mind?" Though he'd been in his office less than an hour and he had work to do.

"Yes. Let's go to Terrace."

"Isn't that kind of far?" asked Jassim, confused at Marcus's wanting to drive somewhere for lunch.

"It is, but it's supposed to be good. They have outside seating. I think the expected high today is eighty degrees, if you can believe that. Four days after Valentine's Day and it's eighty degrees."

"Sounds good." Jassim had forgotten about Valentine's Day and wondered if Salwa had as well. He felt unsettled by the tension around him. He wished so desperately to resume his normal life, his normal routine.

Simple conversation filled the car—no FBI, no Amy Goodman, just this and that, delightful small talk and work talk that had no further implications than the words themselves. Such sweet chatter lasted all the way through lunch. As Marcus drove back, the words that had been hanging invisibly in the air the whole time came. "Jassim, I have to talk to you about a couple of things. I need to get your perspective on this. The first is that Anita came to me with some information."

Jassim smiled politely, wishing with all his heart and soul that he were not sitting in a car with a complicated conspiratorial American but was instead having lunch with his simple, to-the-point wife.

"A lot has been going on that neither of us realized. A lot of things about you that shouldn't have happened. Apparently, according to Anita, after September 11, Bella and Lisa were both really angry. They wanted to get revenge and they wanted to be involved in that revenge. Bella especially."

"Revenge for September 11?" asked Jassim, not following.

"Mm-hmm. It didn't take long before they landed on you. Bella called the FBI on you a couple of days after it happened, told them you were a rich Arab with access to the city's water supply and you didn't seem very upset by what had happened. It seemed the FBI was not interested at first. Bella started to keep a notebook on you. She wrote down everything you said, what you wore, how you seemed. Then two months or so ago she said that she thought something was wrong, that your behavior changed. That you

seemed bothered and that she was going to call the FBI on you
again. Report you."

"Report me? For what? Are you serious?" asked Jassim, still
not believing.

"God knows, Jassim. Ironically, she tried to get Corey involved, thinking he would have a stronger voice since he has a
higher position, but he got very upset with her, defended you."

Jassim sat, reeling at the thought of an FBI investigation
launched by a receptionist whose main duties were answering the
telephone and making photocopies.

"So what I think you should consider," said Marcus, "is docu-
menting all of this and finding a lawyer. I don't have one, but I do
know of a couple, and I could give you their names if you'd like.
From my end, I will talk to Corey. I don't know if we can take
action against Bella for this, especially as we are in very strange
times." Marcus paused, as though he were trying to decide whether
or not to string together his next set of words. "I do have one other
thing I want to ask you about." He stared at the road.

Jassim felt trapped; he hated going with people in their cars,
hated when other people drove. He never quite knew what to do
with himself, where to put his hands, where to look.

"Jassim, this is so awkward." Here Marcus turned toward him
briefly. "Jassim, the FBI has gone to some of your clients and talked
to them about you, and they in turn have called me. In every case I
have told them what I have told you, what I believe, and that is that
the FBI is on a witch hunt and you, thanks to Bella, got on their
radar screen. Today Al Jess called me. He said that the FBI told him
about an accident you had in which a boy died." Marcus said nothing more. Glanced at Jassim and looked straight ahead.

"What is it that you'd like to know?" asked Jassim, almost relieved at having to come clean.

"Was there an accident?"

"On December eleventh I went to my gym to go swimming,
but the pool was closed. It seems that someone had been sick and
defecated in the pool and they had to treat it chemically. I went
home and found Salwa sobbing. She had been pregnant and had

miscarried a week or so earlier, but had not told me about it because she thought I'd be upset. Or disappointed. I'm really not sure what. I came to work and I felt tense all day, so I left early to go for a swim, thought that might realign my day. On my way home from the pool I was driving up River and there were two boys up ahead on those giant skateboards. One of them was swerving and doing all sorts of odd maneuvering in the street. I slowed down and slowed down. I pulled way out into the other lane, but just as I came even with him he sort of jumped into my car. I pulled over and called the authorities. They came—police, fire, ambulance, detectives. They took him to the hospital, but I knew he was dead when I saw him. I was probably there for a few hours. And then I went home." No visuals, no drawings, just straight narrative, and he'd gotten through it.

"My God, Jassim, how awful for you."

"It was awful. You don't really imagine how such a thing can affect you. There were plenty of witnesses, all of whom said I did all the right things, and yet there are very few minutes in the day that I don't think about it, that I don't think about this sixteen-year-old boy whose life I took." Even now, there was no relief in describing what happened. It had been too long left unspoken.

"I can't imagine what you must be going through, Jassim. Have you talked to anyone about it? A counselor?"

"Not really. I spoke with the boy's mother. I think only time will heal this."

They drove on in silence, Jassim's mind retracing their conversation and the past weeks. Every one of Bella's moronic questions had produced an answer from him, which she must have recorded in her notebook. It all made a bit more sense now.

Back at work, Jassim stretched his thoughts this way and that, but no matter how hard he tried, he could not shake his thinking straight, could not concentrate on the doing of his job, the proper living of his life. The accident had muddled him enormously, but to place the FBI investigation, the result of a petty, ignorant woman's hatred, on top of that, *and* Salwa's sending money home without telling him, *and* several phone calls from Mr. Hassan Shaheed—

well, that tipped it over the edge, spilled down his perfectly pressed dress shirt. And none of it felt real; it was as if he had wandered into someone else's life. Again, grasping at the flexibility of his workplace, he left early, several hours before his normal departure time, to scramble at fixing his day, his life, his world.

Several hours away that would be documented by Bella. The minute-taker at meetings. The office minute-taker. The minute-minded taker of minutes. Taker of hours. Taker of years past and future, in an innocuous-looking spiral-bound notebook that she kept in her desk, locked up, sealed away, used only for logging his arrival and departure times, his conversations, his moods, his clothing. Inside the front cover was a toll-free number, a number her fingers had already traced several times on the phone, an FBI hotline.

He still drove by the scene of the accident two to five times each day, intrigued by the shrine that had developed. The simple white cross had been replaced by a larger lacquered cross on which was painted Evan's name. Silk roses and plants and stuffed animals and ribbons lasted days, sometimes weeks. Jassim intentionally did not avoid it and in some quiet part of himself hoped to unearth a truth among all the decorations and gifts. Or be forgiven. In the back of his brain was a vague hope that during one of these drives he would come across the body or ghost of Evan Parker and be able to rewind the events, make them unhappen, or at the very least make peace with them.

In the gravel and dust of dawn, morning, afternoon, and evening, he found no truth, no peace, only the constant vision of that young man with his blue sunglasses and his skateboard. It had pushed him away from swimming, had sent him to the farthest corners of the city in the earliest hours of the morning, during work time, even in the evening. Each foray was longer and more detailed than the previous one.

Oddly, the only time he could relax was when he was driving. Daily he traveled, his packed duffel bag ready in case he changed his mind, up and down the streets of Evan's neighborhood and neighborhoods beyond, greedy to see into lives he knew nothing about. Somehow this aspect of American culture had escaped him.

He'd seen the edges of it but had been buffered by a job that had him working with a more educated group of people, by an income that had him living among professionals, white-collar as opposed to blue-. The more he drove and stared and watched through windows and saw people in their yards and looked at their houses, the more fascinated he became, amazed at the years he had spent without ever really seeing. His visits to Penny, while more frequent, had stabilized, had become part of his routine, a welcome debriefing.

Jassim's awareness didn't happen in one lightning change; no one event occurred to peel all those layers from his eyeballs, to remove the bubble-wrap around his consciousness. The movement of his thoughts was gradual, a smooth inclined ride.

Jassim's eyes, for the first time in his life, singled out pickup trucks and pink faces, shaved heads and snotty-nosed children, food stamps, tattered smiles, ill-fitting false teeth, tobacco-stained fingers, and fourteen-hour-shift bloodshot eyes. His eyes doubleclicked on rusted classic cars with engines next to them, cinderblock walls, and forgotten Christmas decorations.

Now, early on Monday afternoon, when he normally would be working, should be working, Jassim drove up and down streets, absorbing all that he saw and trying to calm the panic that had been creeping into him since the FBI had walked into his life. It was so preposterous and so huge that Jassim didn't know what to do with it; swimming was no cure for this kind of pressure. He would have to talk to Salwa, ask her why she had sent so much money home, why she hadn't mentioned it to him. Maybe he could start talking about home, could bring up people he hadn't seen in a while and see whether she volunteered the fact that Hassan Shaheed had called her repeatedly. *Repeatedly* sounded like many, many times. At least seven, maybe as many as twenty. He wished he had asked Agent Noelle James how many times, but he hadn't wanted to show his ignorance, didn't want them to know that he had no idea that Hassan had called even once.

Three o'clock found him pulling into the Denny's parking lot, just as Penny was walking out the door. Just done with her shift. He rolled down the automatic passenger window. "Hello, Penny."

She turned, leaned down to see. "Oh, it's you! Nice car." She looked startled. By the car? By his presence?

"I was in the neighborhood and thought I'd come by and say hello."

"How nice. I was going to run to Wal-Mart and pick up a few things. Do you want to come along?"

Jassim felt the same funny tingling he had felt when Penny referred to him as her "friend" the day he had confessed to killing Evan. "I'd love to. Why don't you get in and I'll drive." It was not a question.

Penny stood, thinking for a moment. "Okay. Just Wal-Mart, and then I've got to get home."

"Absolutely."

She opened the door, sat down, sank into the seat, and looked around. "I've never been in a Mercedes before."

"You are most welcome. Where is Wal-Mart?"

Penny gave him directions and Jassim drove, relaxed and delighted by this new development. Having Penny in the car made him feel safe, attached. When they entered the store, walking closer together than strangers, Jassim realized that in this place he would never have gone to on his own, an establishment with rolled-back prices and rolled-up hope, were all the people from all those neighborhoods. Only here he didn't need to peek in windows, to slow down and try to guess what was going on. Here, at Penny's side, he was welcome and could listen to comments (mostly grouchy, mostly focused on how expensive an item was) and phone conversations ("Hey, babe, I know, I want you too. I've got to pick up some light bulbs and brake fluid now. I'll call you later") as he watched large bodies bursting out of tight clothes, children stuffed into shopping carts, screamed at, slapped, and loved too loudly.

The ways of the poor were new to him, and yes, he assumed that the people shopping in Wal-Mart were poor, all of them. Because why would anyone who could afford not to shop at Wal-Mart come here?

"What do you need?" Jassim asked Penny.

"Kitchen stuff. A frying pan, potholders, that kind of thing."

It was loud and smelled of skin and cleaning chemicals. He walked close to Penny as the tides lapped by him: brown bellies and breasts and piercings and tattoos and stringy hair and done-up hair and more breasts and women in shorts and high heels and men who looked like they'd lived their lives in the engine of a car or muscled and tough as he imagined prisoners to be and old people pushing oxygen tanks and retarded people talking to themselves and too much eyeliner and too much everything.

Coming toward them was a tall woman whose hair was dyed an unnatural color, her breasts enormous, her T-shirt stretching the words *I'm a Virgin*. Jassim's eyes fell on her, not because of her breasts but because something about her was wrong. Maybe she belonged on a tropical island, would have looked right in a skirt, with flowers in her hair. Two small children sat in her shopping cart while her eyes were elsewhere. A moment after she walked past, Jassim turned to look. *This is a very old T-shirt* tidily decorated her back.

As Penny stopped for a moment to look at racks of gauzy spring blouses, his eyes locked on a woman in a blood-red halter dress, her face and hair made up for a party, fuzzy bedroom slippers on her feet. She looked at Jassim and smiled: crooked teeth and lost hope. Women showed more of their selves than men, he decided.

Two swimming breaths and he zeroed in on the faces, not the everything. Porcelain skin puffed up too fat, cheekbones hidden. A woman who would be beautiful if she were not hiding behind sad fat, shuffling along in tired flip-flops that dragged along the linoleum.

By the time they had gotten to the housewares section of the store, one old man had swooshed past them three times, pushing an empty shopping cart, lifting the brim of his stained baseball cap each time he passed.

Jassim and Penny stood side by side and looked down an aisle stacked with affordable pans and boxes of nonstick cookware. He began studying frying pans. Eight inches. Nine inches. Ten inches. Twelve inches. There was no eleven-inch frying pan, and the differ-

ence in size between eight and twelve inches looked to be greater
than four inches, got Jassim measuring with his fingers and com-
paring prices and seeing what the cost of four inches was. He
didn't notice when a woman stood a few feet from him, her hair
covered with a white scarf and her body in a gray dress that
reached the floor.

"*I need one large pan of this size and one smaller, maybe like
this. The sets are nice. Let's see which is cheaper.*" In itself an un-
remarkable conversation, except that it was in Arabic. In unmis-
takable Jordanian Arabic. Jassim glanced at the woman studying
frying pans and the man to whom she was speaking.

In one breath he was in the souq in Amman, a place he
couldn't stand, for the same reason he wouldn't have liked Wal-
Mart if he hadn't been invited to go with Penny: too many poor
people, too many products to sift through, all of questionable quality. Too many people squish-squashing their overworked, coughing
selves together. Whereas Jassim had been eaten by the West, this
woman and her husband had not left home. If they were on the
streets of Amman, no one would glance at them twice, no one
would say, *Hmmm, it looks as though you've been in America for
some time, forgotten the ways you grew up with, perhaps.* No one
would even think that of this couple. It was not necessarily that in
looking at Jassim now, anyone would think that any more than he
or she would have years ago, but now he felt it, felt that he might
not be able to go home. He was so used to this easy American life,
where you could kill a child and the whole family didn't come after
you with demands for justice, or at least an explanation. Where
you could go to work with the same people every day of your life
and know nothing of them. Or they of you. Where your wife could
be pregnant and miscarry and not tell you. Where you could want
not to have children. No question: the West was neater, tidier. One
could control one's life here so much more easily.

"*The set is nice. Three frying pans. I don't need three, though.
I need two, though buying three is only a bit more expensive than
buying the two individually,*" said the woman who had sent him
home with her words.

Penny's voice interrupted. "How about this set?" Pointing

to the same taped-together three pans the Jordanian woman was looking at.

Jassim felt dizzy. "The individual pans are a better buy. They are better quality and have a longer guarantee."

Penny stared at him. He had turned his back to the couple but could feel their eyes on him.

"Are you okay? You look funny. You're not having a panic attack, are you?"

"I'm fine. If you just need one or two frying pans, the individual ones are a better buy." He spoke clearly, hoping the other woman would hear him and take his advice.

"Okay." Penny stood in front of the individual pans, picked up two. "I'm not sure if I want an eight- and a ten- or just one nine-inch."

The Jordanian woman watched her and Penny turned to her, smiling. "He says these ones are good." Her words were loud and slow. "Better quality."

As they walked away, Jassim's heart thumped cruelly and Penny whispered, "I bet people give her a lot of grief these days."

Jassim pretended that he didn't hear her, that he was distracted by boxes of crockpots that were displayed at the end of the aisle. He carried the two frying pans and followed Penny around the store, wishing he had not come, wishing he could be somewhere else with her.

"Could I take you to the Botanical Gardens this Saturday?" he asked, though it was an un-thought-out idea, and after he said it he wished he could take it back. Saturday! How to explain to Salwa that he was busy on Saturday?

"This Saturday? I could meet you there."

Agreed. They went through the checkout line and Jassim paid for Penny's two frying pans, two potholders, one bottle of detergent, and one pair of sneakers. He ignored her objections. Tuned them out as they continued out of the store, into his car, and back to Denny's.

"Look, you really shouldn't pay for my things. That was not why I invited you to come along."

"I don't mind. So I'll meet you on Saturday at eleven?"

"I'll see you then."

As she opened the door, he glanced in the back seat and saw the mugs. "Hang on a sec. I got you something." He leaned back and picked them up by their handles, handed them to her.

"You got these for me?"

But Jassim couldn't lie completely. "I was wandering around a yard sale and I saw them and thought they were pretty."

"You don't strike me as the yard sale type."

Jassim wondered if there was such a thing, if there were people who went to yard sales regularly. "I'm not, but for some reason this one was calling to me." He smiled. "The mugs. The mugs were calling to me. The yard sale was near where Evan lived. That's why I was there."

The door remained open, and Penny sat in the passenger seat, watching Jassim. "Give it time, honey. It will pass with time." She got out, mugs and bags in hand. "Thanks again for the company and for paying for all this. I really wish you hadn't done that."

"It's the least I could do. See you Saturday."

"See you Saturday. Eleven."

Nightly Penny watched the late news as well as the evening news; she had become obsessed by it ever since the Twin Towers had been destroyed. Each time the president spoke about the War on Terror she was outraged, sickened that there were people so sinister that they would want to harm innocent Americans. When he talked about all the American men and women who served for freedom, freedom all around the world, she felt an unspeakable pride. If she had had money, she would have sent it to him; if she had been younger, she would have enlisted, showed all those terrorists what Americans were made of, how they were continuing the great history of this country, getting out there and saving poor people from the oppression of living in their backward countries. As the president said, Americans were bringing democracy to places that knew only tyranny and terror, that didn't have the freedom to choose.

"Isn't your new boyfriend from one of those places?" asked Trini.

"I wish he were my boyfriend. He's from Jordan, but he's so different from those people. That's why he's here."

"How do you know how different he is? That one guy supposedly fit in, went to titty bars and everything."

"What one guy?"

"That terrorist. The main one."

"Well, Jassim is nothing like those people. He's a scientist, and he's been here awhile, and you can tell he's a good person."

"How?"

"Just talking to him. He's got a conscience. He's not some religious freak like them." She was still unsure whether she should tell Trini about this coming Saturday, didn't like to get too personal with her. The television screen was filled with dust and brown as the camera panned over Afghanistan. It then moved to older footage from Iraq. "Sometimes I don't understand why we don't just bomb those places. You know, blow up Osama and all his buddies and be done with it."

"I don't get you, Penny. How can you like that guy and then want to blow up his whole country?"

Penny continued staring at the television. "The one has nothing to do with the other. And he's from Jordan, not Afghanistan. Jassim is a good guy—he's not like them, shouldn't be judged like them. But those people over there, they oppress women and kill each other. They're the ones who should be bombed."

"Hey, Penny, watch yourself with this guy. You don't know what he's into. Men over there can marry four women at once, make them wear those sheets over their whole bodies."

Penny's heart kicked the inside of her chest. She was glad she hadn't brought up Saturday, wished she had her own television. "Trini, he's fine. He's not like those people. He's very respectful and open." Penny looked at her roommate. "But thanks for looking out for me. I really appreciate it."

Penny said goodnight and went to her room. Sometimes watching the news made her nervous, made her want to have a

glass of wine because she couldn't relax. Fighting the urge, she ran
a hot bath for herself, decided to soak away her worries instead.
She shed her sweatpants and T-shirt, bra and panties in a heap and
stepped into the tub. Then, on a whim, she stepped out again, covered herself with a large blue towel, and went to her room. In the
closet she found the bottle of jasmine bath oil that Trini had given
her for Christmas. She took it back with her, deciding that sweet-
smelling relaxation would be just the thing before going to bed.

_ᴄ ᴄ_

Brown habits turned white with practice, groomed to stainless steel
shiny, porcelain smooth: Salwa always called ahead before visiting.
Always can change in a scratch, a graffiti squirt of black, as Tuesday morning found Salwa stranded on Randa's doorstep, ringing
the bell.

"Salwa, what happened?"

Salwa stood on the straw welcome mat trying to rearrange the
letters, the way Jassim would, but all she could find was *cow*.
"Nothing. Why?"

With a pale yellow dishtowel draped over her shoulder and
hair pulled up in a ponytail, Randa looked relaxed. Happy. Welcoming. "Because you're standing at my front door in the middle of
a weekday morning without calling first. Is everything all right?"

"Everything's fine."

"Are you okay?"

"It's nothing, habibti. I just wanted to see you."

Randa squinted her eyes, tilted her head, and listened for truth.
"There's something. Come in." They kissed twice on both cheeks.
"I'm cleaning the kitchen, folding laundry, and watching a Leba-
nese game show." And then in English she added, "*I am Randa,
Mistress of Multitasking.* I'll make tea."

"No. I'm fine."

"Coffee, then. I'll make you Arabic coffee. You can't come over
here unannounced and not have tea or coffee. That would be too
American."

Salwa followed her friend through the family room into the bright kitchen. The television carried the face of a sobbing blond woman loaded with makeup. "That's an ad for one of the soap operas. Her husband is dying," Randa said, pointing at her. "You don't know what you're missing without satellite TV. It's like being home."

Salwa glimpsed home through a window, in the flash of the television screen, in watching her friend pull a small brass *jizwa* off a hook, fill it with water, and put it on the stove. "Randa, are you happy here?"

Randa rested one hand on the counter next to the stove, one hand on a hip. "Salwa, with the deep question that must be answered before she tells me what is wrong. Let's see. Am I happy? I am happy with my children; they are healthy and good, thank God. I am happy to have the opportunity to be at home with them. I am happy my life is safe and predictable. I am happy that my husband is a good man and respects me as his wife and as an independent person. Do I love America? It certainly is easier here than at home. You live your life without being burdened by basic needs, so you can focus on larger things. But American life, as I see it, lacks flavor, that tastiness you find at home. Overall I am happy, but when it comes to some of the smaller details, the ones that don't matter so much but are a large part of what makes life rich, then I am not. Happiness is a luxury, don't you think?"

The two women looked at each other. Randa smiled at her friend and added sugar to the boiling water. "Maybe I gave you more of an answer than you wanted."

"Don't you ever worry about losing yourself here?"

Randa cracked three cardamom pods, ground the seeds with a pestle, and dropped the tiny grains into the water. "No. I keep what is important and the rest is just...what do they say in English? *Topical?*"

"*Superficial.*"

"Yes, *superficial.*" The water bubbled wildly and Randa pulled the pot off the burner and added two spoonfuls of coffee, each heaped to the ceiling. She stirred them in, reached across the continental United States, stretched her arm across the Atlantic until she found Beirut, and put the pot back on the burner, and it boiled, and she stirred in her love for her friend, and it boiled, and she smiled at Salwa, and the coffee boiled away thousands of miles of homesickness, and Randa turned off the burner. "Here's your coffee. Heavy on cardamom, heavy on sugar." Randa took out two fancy demitasses painted red and white (no blue), which she filled to the rim with the thick brown liquid. She then pulled a small tray from the top of the dustless refrigerator and placed the two delicate cups on it. "Let's go sit here," she suggested, gesturing to the couch in the family room and walked ahead to put the tray on the table in front of the TV. They both sat, eyes pulled to the screen.

"Randa, I want to tell you something, but you have to keep it to yourself." Salwa shook inside at the thought of opening the ugliness in herself and showing it to her friend.

"Swear." Randa picked up the remote and muted the television. A thin young man gestured toward a giant gameboard covered with questions.

"I met a man . . ."

"Oh God." Randa's hand covered her mouth, her eyes growing wider.

"There's a man at my work. We've become friends." Was that how it started?

"*Friends is okay,*" Randa said in English, and then switched back to Arabic. "Lovers is another story. God keep catastrophes far from you."

"Let me tell you everything, Randa, and then you tell me what I should do."

Randa nodded.

"After the miscarriage, remember, I felt depressed, sad, all the time. It just seemed to go on and on. There's this guy at work . . ."

"American?"

"Yes. And he was very nice to me, very cheerful, and he would talk to me about simple things and I would forget about the baby, forget about the miscarriage, about Jassim, about all the problems in this country. About all the problems of my marriage. He would just talk about things, stories, people from his world. They were all simple, but it was fun. He would ask me about home and seem so interested. Sometimes we'd have lunch together, or coffee together. Always during those short times together I felt happy. It wasn't deep, just happy. Then one day he kissed me. It was on a Friday, and I spent the weekend swearing to myself that it would never happen again, that I would not allow myself to be close to him in that way, even though a part of me wanted more. We still saw each other at work, of course, and had lunch once or twice, but it was as if I started to see him more clearly. On the one hand he was nice and funny, and on the other hand he would say things that irritated me. I often thought how *immature* he was and what silly notions of marriage and love he had. I would always think, why did I let him kiss me? Why did I kiss him back? Then one day he asked me to dinner. At his house."

"Shame! To his house? Doesn't he know you are married?"

Salwa sipped her coffee, her lips gently resting on the fragile rim of the cup. As the liquid coated her tongue with memories, Salwa stayed put, feet firmly planted, and continued her story. "Yes, he knows. I know too. But I said I'd go. I don't know why. Jassim has been so distant, and I was feeling homesick and empty, and then this Jake waltzed into my office and promised to take it all away. To make me exist again. I think I knew what could happen if I went, and I didn't care. It was almost as if it was going to happen and I just wanted to get it over with. As if I didn't have a choice. He asked me in the afternoon and then he left for the day and I was going to go a couple hours later. I went to Joan, and for some reason when I was there I realized what it was I was about to do and I changed my mind. The problem was that I never got his phone number, because I never wanted to give him mine, and it seemed so rude just not to show up, so I went to his house to tell him I wasn't coming, that I couldn't come."

"But you were there."

"Right. I mean that I couldn't stay. He was very sweet about it, very understanding. He said that we should just be friends and to come in for dinner and then go. Friends, you know."

"But that's not what happened."

"And I don't know how, but I...I...God, Randa, I can barely say it." Not in Arabic. She switched languages, pushed it further away from herself. *"I made love with him."*

"May God keep disasters far from you. *Did he wear a condom?*"

"Yes. And it was very nice. That time was very nice. Romantic." Best to leave it there, to let it stay nice in her memory.

"It wasn't just the one time?"

"No. There was one other time too." Salwa's heart shook at the memory, her palms lay moist in her lap.

"Oh God, Salwa. Did something bad happen?"

"I was showing a house in the foothills. The open house was supposed to run from one to four. Around three or three-thirty, he walked in."

"Who?"

"Jake."

"Jake? That's an awful name. Tell him he has an awful name and he's an awful man. Salwa, what does he think he's doing, inviting you to dinner and then going to your work?"

Randa sat on her couch ready to fight the American Man with his arbitrary borders and sickening sanctions, with his machismo and his rapist's agenda. (Those were the exact thoughts spinning in her brain, but she did not utter them, kept them tucked in her cheek and then spat them into her coffee cup when she was done drinking, rendering the grounds useless for reading.)

"That's what I thought too. Jake walks in around three-thirty. There was a couple at the house, looking around. Jake walks in and acts as though we don't know each other, like he's a prospective buyer. He starts to walk around the house. Eventually the couple leaves and I don't know where he is, and it's making me nervous because I don't know what he's up to and also because the people who own the house are so horrible and the last thing I need with them is problems. So I go around the house calling him." Salwa stopped. The memory grew uglier and uglier as she stepped closer.

"What, Salwa?"

"I went into the guest bedroom, which is beautiful. It is done in brocades and feels luxurious. It has French doors that open onto a fountain and courtyard with a view of the mountains." Trying desperately to focus on the lovely and not the story she was telling.

"Was he in there?"

"Yes, Randa, he was in there. On the bed." Her breath came faster now. "He was naked." More words sat in her throat, but she had to stop, to breathe slowly before she could say them.

"Oh, for shame! How disgusting! Is he crazy?"

"I screamed. He asked me if everyone had gone and I told him they had but that anyone could come at any minute, and he said, no they couldn't. And I told him there was still another hour of the open house. He laughed. He lay there like a naked monkey and laughed. Randa, he took all my signs down. I had signs advertising the open house all around the neighborhood, on the big streets and in front of the house. He had taken them all down. Six of them. I told him to put his clothes on and get out."

"Dear God, please tell me he did."

Salwa's breath kept getting away from her, couldn't keep up with the pace of the story. "I went to lock the front door, put the chain over so even someone with a key couldn't get in. Can you imagine..." She couldn't finish. "It was so disgusting. Disgusting." Here she shook her head, wishing to replace the memory with something more tolerable. "It was like once he touched me, I couldn't stop."

Randa held her friend's hand and waited patiently.

"That was the day before yesterday. I can't stand it. I can't live with myself. I don't know what to do. I can't bathe enough." Nothing would undo it, would take out whatever he had left in her. "Randa, I can't think of anything else, just Jake, and hating myself. And now he says he loves me. That he wants me in his life."

The escaped secret filled the space between them, bound one to the other with the strength of a mythical serpent and entwined the two women together.

Randa took Salwa's hand in her own. "He is a manipulative man, this Jake."

"Randa, that's the thing. I can see all that, and the next minute I wrap my legs around him as if he's a dream. It's as though when he is around I stop thinking. I never knew sex could be like this. It must be like drugs, where you just feel so good and you don't want it ever to end, but then it does and you feel awful and at the same time you think about how you are going to get more. And I swear to you, Randa, I hate myself, feel so disgusted that I cannot look at myself. I want to peel off my skin. I keep thinking that I've lost my mind. What can I be doing?"

Something, whether the five neat piles of clothing stacked with love or her friend's touch, something triggered tears then sobs, and she put her head on Randa's lap and cried and cried while Randa rubbed her back. The tears poured from her eyes and she wailed hysterically, and Randa's eyes welled, but she wouldn't allow them to release their sadness, she was too angry, and Salwa's tears were enough for both of them. The drops puddled at their feet, moved across oceans, and splashed into Lake Tiberias, threatening a flood over the banks of the Jordan, to make up, perhaps, with the tears of one woman for all that had been stolen.

Salwa couldn't speak, just sat up and leaned against the back of the couch, with Randa still holding her hand, squeezing now, saving her friend from being whisked away by the torrents.

"Salwa, listen to me. You need to go home for a little while. You need to be with your mother and sisters." *And your culture, where things like this can't happen.* But this thought she withheld, for not everyone in the room needed to be so forthcoming. "It will help you to see things as they are, and it's been years since you visited. Right now is a good time. Look, a lot has happened in the last few months, and being home will be good for you."

"But what about my job? What about Jassim?"

"At the bank? Your job is a job. You will find another one when you come back—maybe they will even let you keep this one. Maybe it's better they don't. Besides, I thought you wanted to focus on real estate."

"I don't know what I want to do."

"Time apart will be good for both you and Jassim."

Salwa's swollen eyes fixed on home while Randa squinted at today, planned her departure.

"Salwa, you cannot tell Jassim about this Jake person. No matter what. Understand?"

"What happened to 'a lie will come between you'?"

"Another man will come between you even more. Trust me, habibti. Go home. Be yourself. Tell the people at your work that you have a family emergency and go." *While you still can.*

They both knew that Randa was right and Salwa was wrong, even though Salwa lived her dream exactly and Randa bent hers to accommodate others.

And when Salwa finally stopped crying, resolved to fly away and tuck herself into the safety of her true home, she felt no better. The ugliness was simply moister and stickier.

_ᴄᴏ ᴄᴏ_

After lunch, Marcus sat in his office and mulled over whether he could fire Bella. Then his intercom interrupted his thoughts and her voice barged in.

"FBI here to see you, Marcus."

Marcus had not liked either of the agents, thought they both seemed too young for their job. Nonetheless, he welcomed them, invited them to come in. Sit down. Tell him how they were going to ruin Jassim's life and his own business. *Why didn't I get an attorney for myself? What good would it have done?*

"We would like to look at data from the Internet sites Mr. Haddad has looked at over the past few months."

"Why?"

"We want to see if he fits into a pattern, if he is looking at strategic sites."

"Don't you think that if he were going to look at strategic Internet sites, he would do so from home?" Such an obvious question, and yet he felt he was betraying Jassim in asking it.

"Criminals tend not to be very smart."

"Scientists are, and are not often criminals," Marcus countered.

The female agent with the wide bottom spoke. "Are you aware that Mr. Haddad had an accident in which a child was killed?"

"Yes, I am aware of that."

"And are you aware that the child he killed had strong anti-Arab views?"

"Yes." Marcus did his best to keep his face smooth. Fully aware of what the FBI was capable of, the lies, the setups. No, he would not fall into that trap. "What does this have to do with his job?"

"We are investigating all aspects of this case. We believe the man who works for you could be a threat."

"I have known Jassim for years, and I trust him. He is not what you are portraying him to be. Where did you get your information about his behavior?"

"We can't tell you that."

"Well, I can. I know for a fact that my receptionist has been maligning Jassim, has been taking some sort of a personal vendetta out on him. She probably gave you the list of clients Jassim works with, which is why I've had so many calls about you. She, a receptionist with little schooling or real-world experience and a very definite political agenda, is ruining the career of a gifted scientist. And you are allowing it to happen." Blood was pounding behind Marcus's eyes. His words made him angrier, more outraged, more righteous.

The two agents sat in chairs in front of Marcus's desk. These chairs were there for employees to sit in when they came to discuss a project, not for FBI agents. He remembered purchasing them, thinking they made his office seem cozy, a collaborative workshop rather than a boss's office.

The male agent looked smug. "She is not our only source."

"Is it someone from here?" Marcus asked.

"No, it's not someone from here, but obviously we can't give you details."

Marcus said nothing.

"What do you know about Mr. Haddad's wife?"

"She's a lovely woman."

"Is she politically active?"

"I wouldn't know."

Marcus glanced at the business card on his desk, which he had not moved since the first time the agents visited. *Noelle James. Federal Bureau of Investigation.*

"Has Mr. Haddad mentioned anything about the money his wife sent to Jordan on September twelfth?" asked Noelle.

"No, he has not."

"Has he mentioned any of the people that his wife works with as clients?"

"Jassim does not talk much about his personal life."

"Has he ever discussed one of her clients, a retired Marine?"

"No." Marcus was done with this interview. "I would like to know who your other sources are. I want to know if they are clients who have been poisoned by a member of my staff or if they are unconnected to us completely."

"Our other sources are reliable and unconnected with your firm. They have provided detailed information which is consistent with what your receptionist has said."

"What do you want from me?"

"We want to make sure that you are providing all the information you can about Mr. Haddad."

Marcus looked at them with as straight and even an expression as he could muster. Until they left.

We are a private company; I can do as I damn well please.

Before he could think better of it, he called Bella into his office.

"You have worked for our company for just over a year now, and I'm afraid to say that it is not working out."

"Are you firing me?"

"I am."

"Why? I've never been told that I'm not doing a good job."

"I am telling you that now. You may gather your personal belongings and leave the building immediately."

He was sure that if he let her sit in his office she would start crying, and he wasn't willing to allow that to happen. Or, worse, point out that he had no justification for firing her and say that she was going to sue the firm. As soon as she was out the door he realized the stupidity of firing her. Without documentation.

—⁓—

Throughout the day the woman agent's words skated through his thoughts: *She is not our only source . . . a retired Marine . . . detailed information.* Jassim had been in a car accident, killed a boy, and never mentioned it. Now Marcus had Jassim's version, in which he had omitted the boy's anti-Arab feelings. Had he left that out on purpose? A part of Marcus still believed that he wasn't getting the whole story, but another part of him thought that if Jassim had not told him about the accident, then what else might he have failed to mention? Who was the retired Marine? Was this person also a suspect? Then there was the money. Jassim hadn't said a word about sending money. Why wouldn't he tell him if he had nothing to hide?

But this wasn't the bottom line and he knew it. As much as Marcus would like to believe that he himself was shocked and outraged by the accident (which he was), this was not the reason his thinking had darkened. Jassim had been leaving early, coming in late, disappearing in the middle of the day, which probably had nothing to do with the FBI investigation and more to do with his grief. But for Christ's sake, Marcus was trying to run a business. *Jassim had taken advantage of his friendship, had used him.* That was it.

Marcus spent the rest of the day trying to convince himself of this—that he had been wronged and that Jassim was at the root of it, all the while creating documentation to justify firing Bella.

—◌ ◌—

Flip-flops and applesauce, smelly feet and fingernails, sweet little baby grew just right until her mama took up with a man whose name was too big for him. That's when it all started to chip-chop apart, when little pieces of who she was were scattered across the backyard. And she ran and she ran as fast as she could until she found herself face to face with a poison needle and jabbed it into her veins, not caring that its contents would not carry her across the river or even give her a happy high, and saying a final silent prayer for her mother, whose love she knew by heart.

No note, no nothing, just memories and teardrops, lemonade

and plastic pools, all swooshed away in evil winds under a too-bright sky. Left her mother orphaned, so to speak, alone in the world, with no one's love to trust. Until she met the honest Arab man who lied his truths, had to if he wanted her to hear them right. In the matters of importance he was water-clear honest, and it scared her to open her soul to someone from so far away, not because he was foreign, but because if he ever left, the distance would be unmanageable.

There are only so many times you can open yourself up to the world and not get ugly footprints all over your face, dirt smeared across your belly. This was the last time, she promised herself, and if this didn't work she was done, would seal herself off from the universe. Too much squeezing, all life's liquid spreading across the floor from where she'd tried to get her kids back, from where she tried to accept her daughter's death, from where she tried to get away from her crazy-ass husband. She thought it was funny, almost, that although she had been calling him crazy-ass all these years, he had a real adjective to describe him: bipolar. And since he didn't accept the definition, he didn't accept the medication used to treat it, thereby turning her life upside down, shaking all the loose change on the floor, scattered corpses of luscious hope. She had read that in a romance novel once, thought it described her life perfectly. *Scattered corpses of luscious hope.*

Years of grief and nighttime television had taught her to watch closely, to recognize mental illness and peculiar conditions, so when that man had walked in and panicked, she knew, she felt his fear, his nausea. When he came in and sat in the same seat, she recognized that too, as obsessive-compulsive disorder, but then when he came in regularly, when he asked her to meet him on Saturday, in a public place, that was interest. That was hope. There was no mental illness locked in that request, so in the way of foolish humans she buried the voice that told her it was too good to be true, a nice man with a job and a Mercedes taking interest in her, and instead wallowed in the excitement of someone looking at her, looking in her eyes and talking to her like a person, not like a waitress or a derelict mother (which she knew she wasn't, even though she had heard these accusations too many times) or someone he wanted to screw.

How to prepare yourself for the turning point of your life? she wondered.

"I am scared, Trini, I am so scared this won't work," she told her roommate, not able to keep it a secret any longer.

"I don't know why you see so much in that man, honey. Look, no expectations, no disappointments. Take a deep breath and prepare for the worst, and then no matter what, you'll be pleasantly surprised."

The woman held on to this thought throughout the week, did not allow herself to think of the man or his honest face or his Mercedes. Instead she forced herself to accept the possibility that he was married and had five children and wanted to kidnap her to send her to some rich oil sheek. (Is that what they were called?) Yes, that had to be the worst-case scenario. That he was a pimp. But what kind of pimp would invite a woman to the Botanical Gardens? Maybe he really was a terrorist. Maybe he was going to blow them both up, along with the Botanical Gardens. No, that was insane. Maybe he had cancer. Or was going to go back to his home next week. The thoughts were dizzying and endless and exhausting and so she stopped, took his face, and stored it away for a few days. Decided she would deal with it when she had to. But just in case, she called her children to make sure they were doing okay. To make sure they knew their mama loved them. Insisted that she be allowed to speak to them, and was shocked to hear the coldness in Bryson's voice, to be told Bentley was at a friend's house.

"Has something happened?" she asked Sky's stepmother when her own son handed the phone back after only a few words exchanged.

"What's happened is Sky is trying to get his life together. He met a real nice gal, and she reads the Bible with the kids and tells them where you went wrong."

"Where I went wrong? I didn't get drunk and beat anyone up. I didn't stop taking my medication and drive a teenage girl to suicide."

"Now don't put all that on him. We know that Sky's not been the easiest man on earth to live with, but he's getting himself together."

"I want my babies back."

"They're not babies anymore, and they are doing fine here. They're happy and they feel loved. That's what's important."

"Is that what's important? Seems to me what's important is that they have their mother with them to help them get through life and not a bipolar drunk and his Bible-thumping girlfriend. No offense."

Silence on the other end told Penny exactly where Sky's step-mother stood. In a way she didn't blame her; after all, she had been stuck with two children for a few years now, and she probably was ready for them to go. Penny decided that no matter what, she would get herself back there and get her children back. Kidnap them if she had to. And maybe, just maybe, that nice man with the Mercedes could help her somehow.

So much had changed in a matter of days. It was no longer a matter of defending a friend, of standing up for what he believed was right. He was only a partner in the business, and it was out of his hands. Marcus went to the bathroom a third time before asking Jassim to come to his office.

"What's up, Marcus?" Jassim asked, easing into the chair across from Marcus's desk.

In the lifetime of his company, Marcus had fired seven people, all administrative and technical. He had never fired someone he considered to be his equal, nor had he let someone go for such ambiguous reasons as with Jassim. He hated doing it, having to be so decisive about another person's life. Even when things were clear-cut, he liked to give his employees a chance to redeem themselves. If they didn't, if they continued the behavior, he always questioned himself over and over, before, during, and after the firing. If only people had a better sense and could excuse themselves when they were no longer appropriate.

In this case there was no behavior to change. Jassim could not change who he was, and Marcus recognized consciously that in part he was firing him for that reason, though it would be the lost contracts and unreliability on which he would focus.

"Jassim, we've known each other for a long time now."

"We have. Fifteen years." Jassim sat in the chair, with his elbows on the armrest and his thin, clean fingertips spread out and touching one another.

"Which makes doing what I am going to do now that much more difficult."

"What is it that you are going to do now, Marcus?" Jassim's face showed no emotion, which angered Marcus, further convinced him that he didn't know the man in front of him, that Jassim could be hiding anything from him.

"Jassim, lately I have been under a lot of pressure, a lot of pressure. Things are different now."

Jassim let him talk, even though Marcus was sure he must know what he was leading up to.

"Jassim, in the past you have done some of the best work I have seen; you have been a huge asset to this company. Things have changed in the past months, though. Your work is faltering."

"Are you warning me, Marcus?"

Marcus felt sick to his stomach. "I'm letting you go. I have to. We have lost several contracts. Several. These contracts are our livelihood. No contracts, no business."

"And why have we lost these contracts?"

"Because of you."

"Because of negligence on my part?"

Here Marcus had to choose his words carefully. "Jassim, in the past people asked specifically to work with you. Now people are asking not to work with you. If it were my choice alone I would not do it, but it is not my choice. I cannot keep you and pay you for not working."

"Again I will ask you the question, Marcus. Is it because of negligence on my part?"

"To some degree. Look, Jassim, this FBI investigation is scaring off our business. They have talked to every one of the clients you work with, and every one has called me to ask for an explanation. No one will work with you, but it's not just because of the FBI. They say there have been inconsistencies—leaving early, coming in late. Odd behavior."

"Inconsistencies? Odd behavior?"

"Yes, you saying you were in one place when you were actually somewhere else."

"I believe that is my business."

"It is my business when it's on work time, when we are losing contracts because people are scared to have you handle their accounts. When you come in late or vanish for half the afternoon. For God's sake, Jassim, I want to believe you, but you killed a boy and didn't tell me." He hadn't meant to say this. *Stop, slow down.* Words were coming that should not. "As I said, it is not only my decision."

"Ah," said Jassim, shaking his head. "So this goes back to the accident."

"No, it is not because of the accident, but it is an example of an inconsistency, and I, we, cannot run a company based on inconsistencies."

Jassim stood up. "Marcus, I am very saddened by this, sad for the loss of a friendship. You are correct that I didn't tell you about the accident. As I told you, I didn't tell anyone other than the police. I didn't know how to begin."

Marcus felt himself losing ground. *No, do not get sidetracked. Look at the bottom line.* "Jassim, it is not because of the accident that I am firing you." *Why is it, then?* "Bottom line, we're going to lose the business if I don't make an act of good faith to the people we do business with."

"And firing me is your act of good faith."

"Yes." Though he didn't like the way that sounded.

"Marcus, I'm sorry. I have enjoyed working here. I have enjoyed your friendship." Jassim extended his hand, looked into Marcus's face as he shook his hand, and turned toward the door.

"I will have someone escort you out and we will have your things sent to your house."

"You're kidding."

"It's better for everyone, Jassim. I really am sorry."

"May I get my jacket?"

"Of course."

Marcus watched him walk to his office. He could see him through the open door, putting his jacket on and looking around one last time, picking up a photo and putting it down again, glancing at his stacks of articles. He picked up a three-inch pile and came back into Marcus's office.

"Is it okay if I take this?"

"What is it?" Marcus asked.

"These are the articles not directly related to my work that I've been putting aside, which I never have time to read. Random articles about recycling policies in other countries and things like that."

"Why don't you leave them here and I'll have it all sent to you."

"Marcus, you are worried about something, worried that I might be flying the coop with company secrets. Suit yourself." He put the articles down at the edge of Marcus's desk, put his hand in his pocket, and produced a key ring. Coaxed one and then another off the ring and handed him two keys. "Goodbye, Marcus."

Marcus wanted to stop Jassim, to say that he was sorry and this was all a giant misunderstanding, but he could not. He had no words to offer. And so he watched Jassim walk down the hall, watched as Corey followed him out, made sure he was going directly to his car.

And his eyes rested on the top article: "Engineering Mistakes in the Building of the Twin Towers."

─◌ ◌─

Jassim sat in his quiet house, in the recliner facing the silent television, letting the chair swallow him whole, absorb his angles into its hugeness. The nightmare his life had become was now being told by day, under the obscene glare of the sun. Truth lay somewhere under a sordid pile of allegations, unreachable, unfathomable.

He had come to America a simple, focused man who wanted to

expand his knowledge so that he could improve life for others. He had stayed in America to bide his time until he could take his bag of learning home and apply it, until home was ready for him. Until he was ready. No way to see that readiness wouldn't slide up one day, that it required years of hammering and chiseling in preparation. In more than a decade of good citizenship, he had never for a minute imagined that his successes would be crossed out by a government censor's permanent marker, that his mission would be absorbed by his nationality, or that Homeland Security would have anything to do with him. Things like this aren't supposed to happen in America. Americans are pure, simple people, their culture governed by a few basic tenets, not complicated conspiracy theories.

Jassim sat in right angles and parallel lines. Salwa would come home any minute, would find him sitting like this, would ask him what was wrong, and then he could tell her, then it would be easy. Now he had no choice. His secret life, which contained no sin or illegal activity, just weakness, was going to affect her, and she had to know the whole story. Every detail.

The garage door creaked up and down. Jassim remained still, listened as she came into the house from the garage, as she put her keys down, her bag down. He heard the rustling of plastic, which meant she had stopped at the grocery store on the way home. On a normal day he would have gotten up to help, not because she was a woman who couldn't do it herself but because he loved her and that was the way he knew to show it. Today his confusion was so thick that he worried he would get lost in her words and distracted by grocery bags. Might forget to explain exactly what had happened, might not find the right words to tell her, just as he had not found the right words all those weeks ago when he had stolen that boy's life.

The rustling stopped and the refrigerator opened and closed. A fizz of soda being opened, a cabinet door opening and closing, the soda splashing from the can into a sparkling glass held by a beautiful princess's hand. Jassim sat still as his heart lurched, thudded desperately inside his body. He did not take swimming breaths to calm himself; he would let it run its course, let nature be.

The clicking on tile grew louder and stopped.

"Jassim?"

"Salwa."

"Jassim, what's wrong? Did something happen?"

"Yes." (How did she know? How had he known that she would know from the way he sat that something was wrong?)

"What? What happened?"

Though Jassim had rehearsed telling her everything, he had not thought how to begin, and for a moment he was at a loss.

"Are you all right? Is everyone all right at home?"

"Yes. Well, I don't know, actually, but that is not what is wrong."

She sat on the edge of the couch, their knees almost touching. She looked tired. "What is it, then?"

He saw the young girl in her woman's face, returned to that day in the courtyard an eternity ago, when she was so innocent, not yet tainted with American soil, or soiled by American dye, or drowned by American ignorance. (Even now he forgot that she had been born in this country, that she had been drowning since the day of her birth.)

"Salwa, I have to tell you some things. Please don't ask me any questions just yet. I have not lied to you or been unfaithful to you, and that I can swear to on my life and on the life of my mother. I have not provided you with the truth, however, and that is what I have to tell you now."

Jassim looked straight ahead, gazing at the television, and now took two deep swimming breaths. Again he turned to his wife. He spoke slowly and deliberately as he told her about Evan, Evan's mother, not going swimming, becoming obsessed with Evan's world, and finally, most painfully, the changes at work, the investigation. He wanted to lift up each moment of the past few weeks, to make sure she saw all of them clearly.

"Salwa, I feel as though I have lost control of my life, and as a result our lives are about to change for the worse. I don't know what we will do." He was building up to tell her about Marcus, about Marcus's betrayal. Just a few words. It shouldn't be so hard.

Salwa had not moved from her perch at the edge of the couch, her lovely hands holding each other, no surprise or anger register-ing on her face. Jassim wanted her to react to what he had already voiced before he continued, so he sat, his gaze once again resting on the television.

Somehow Salwa was on her knees at his side, taking his hand in hers, stroking his hair, the first bit of volunteered affection in many weeks. Jassim didn't know what to do, so he rested his other hand on hers. "Salwa, I am so sorry for all of this. So sorry for this." His words covered her, caressed her face and body.

She sat up and looked at him, her eyes sparkly and sad. "No, Jassim, I am sorry for you. I am sorry that you have been going through this on your own. You didn't tell me about the boy because I was too obsessed by the miscarriage. I'm sorry."

She was stuck on Evan! He had to move on before he lost his courage.

"...do you see, Jassim? If we had been home and you had hit that boy, his family would have gotten involved from the begin-ning. Here, no one cared until they found out who you were, and now they've made it grounds for a federal investigation. It's crazy —they're not looking at who you are as a person, at all the great work you've done. They're looking at the fact that you're an Arab. Do you think any American would be scrutinized in this way?"

Jassim had not predicted this reaction. In all these convoluted months, he had forgotten Salwa's righteousness, her intrinsic need to fight for what was just. He had to take this opportunity to tell her that Marcus had fired him, a sentence he could say in three words. But she kept talking.

"We have neither of us been honest." She stood up and went out of the room.

Jassim sat, wondering if he should get up and follow her. Was she coming back?

"I have not been forthcoming with you, Jassim," came Salwa's voice a moment later. She held a few pieces of paper, something printed from the computer, and dropped them into his lap.

It was an e-ticket. Tucson, Phoenix, London, Amman. Salwa Haddad. The date was Monday, two days after tomorrow.

Jassim stared. Read and reread the numbers. Read and reread

Salwa's name. Did not laugh as he thought of *Haddad* being *daddah* backward. Or wonder at the irony of her name containing *laws*. He stared in the hope of finding something to say.

"Jassim, I need to go home for a little while, to take a break from here. I was scared that if I told you about it too far ahead of time, you might talk me out of it. I just need to see my family for a little while. So much has changed here." She stopped and then looked at him again. "But I'll stay until this mess gets sorted out."

"Maybe it's time I go home too," he said, though not sure if he meant it. "We could go together."

His eyes fell to the ticket and saw that there was a $200 penalty fee for changing it. His mind wrapped around the concrete number rather than the fact that his wife had bought a ticket a few days ago. Why so sudden, and why had she waited to tell him? How could she have hidden such an important thing? What else had she hidden? Was this because of Hassan? Was she going to see him?

"How long are you planning to stay?"

"I don't know. I thought I'd play it by ear and see, but I'll stay here, Jassim. I'll cancel it and make another one later. It's okay."

"No, Salwa, you should go if you want to," he said, though he didn't mean these words and had difficulty catching his breath at the thought of Salwa gone, at the thought of Salwa sitting at her computer or calling a travel agent and buying a ticket to fly thousands of miles and not feeling the need to tell him. He didn't know what to do. So much was unclear. All of this because she wanted a child? Words dribbled out of his mouth, words that he had not meant to say and was not sure he believed: "Salwa, habibti. I am sorry that I have kept you from having a family. I am ready now. Whether we are here or somewhere else, I am ready for a family. If that is still what you want."

"Jassim, I don't know what I want anymore."

Jassim didn't know either, though he was very clear on what he did not want, which was for Salwa to leave. Yet he wanted her to stay of her own free will, not because he begged her to. "I'll be fine, habibti. You go ahead as planned." Planned by whom? And for how long?

In leaving out what was most on his mind, Jassim realized that they had spent their lives together not saying what mattered most, dancing around the peripheries instead of participating. He had seen in her a passion and excitement for life that had become dulled almost immediately upon their arrival in the United States. What he wanted in her could not exist in America. Could not exist with him, perhaps. And he feared that he could no longer exist in Jordan.

"I told the bank I have a family emergency," said Salwa, shaking Jassim out of his thoughts.

She had told the bank before she told him? More than anything she'd said, this stiffened him. Did all of this have something to do with Hassan? With the money she had sent without telling him? These thoughts swirled in his mind, made him dizzy as he rested on the realization that his wife would be gone in three days and that he had made a date with another woman for tomorrow.

"How long are you going for? A few weeks?"

"I have no idea. I just need to be home. I'm sorry I have not been a better wife."

This statement seemed out of character, and Jassim decided to think about it later. He was sorry too, though he did not see how things could have been any different. Too late he realized that in all of the fuss and confusion, he had somehow not managed to tell her that he had been fired.

Saturday morning, and he was surrounded by jagged edges. Everything in his life had serrated corners that cut into his skin, sliced off layers in bloody chunks. Lately his highs were denser and longer and followed by a spinning-through-hell sensation of crashing, which was exactly what he felt now. He did not eat, barely drank, and was feeling scared and jumpy. Very jumpy.

He had arrived the night before to find police cars and yellow tape.

Manny, the guy who lived downstairs from him, was standing by his front door.

"What happened?" he asked, knowing in his bones what the answer was going to be.

"Drug bust."

"Why do they have the tape around half the complex?"

"Meth lab. Can you fucking believe it? Apparently it's been here for months."

He had always wondered if Manny suspected him.

"They were talking earlier about evacuating the whole place."

He tried to sound casual, an interested bystander. "They arrest anyone?"

"You just missed it. Two guys in handcuffs. Skanky mother-fuckers they were too." Manny had been looking in the direction of the police activity while he talked, but now he turned to face him. "Dealing drugs is evil shit, and I hope they rot in hell for it."

His stomach lurched. Still, he wasn't sure whether Manny was directing this at him or it was just general outrage at the situation. He waited a minute and said goodbye, went upstairs, and found a skinny woman sitting on his doorstep.

"Who the hell are you?" he asked, aware that Manny was still outside, within earshot.

"Barry sent me."

Before she continued talking he shouted, "Who? Who sent you? I don't know you and I don't know any Barry. Police are right over there—why don't you go ask them if they can help you out?"

The woman stood, confused, and huffed down the stairs.

"Do you know Barry?" he heard her ask Manny, and he went inside before he could hear the answer. Bolted the door and fought the thoughts that were shouting in his head. He knew that it was just a matter of time. These thoughts multiplied and divided throughout the night, and by Saturday morning he was exhausted and paranoid.

Problem was that he had run out of his own supply. Not even enough for a bump. And nowhere to get it. So this was it. The big crash. He smoked cigarettes to dull it as he lay on the couch feeling as though he had swallowed the blades of a food processor, every part of his self shaky with a fear that gripped his guts.

Arguments swirled through his brain, with one part of him sighing and saying, *Finally. Now you can move on,* and another saying, *This is a great opportunity for you to set up business for yourself.* And another yelling, *Run.* And another voice, much smaller and sadder, wishing in whispers that things were not so complicated with her. Wishing he could just have her in his life.

And why couldn't he? What was wrong with him? Nothing. There was no reason that they couldn't be together. He would tell her that he wanted this to be a serious relationship, that if she was willing to leave her husband, then he would be there for her. Another voice, his father's, asked, *But what could you possibly offer her? You're still in school, you're a loser drug dealer. You are nothing.*

Slam. He closed this voice off, insisted that it quiet itself while he indulged the idea of the two of them together. Ignored the fact that he had not talked to her since he had explained his feelings.

What are you thinking about her for when you could be arrested? What are you sticking around for? The questions were numbing, the arguments in his head unbearably loud. He actually shook his head to try to make them stop. Run. More business. Run. Together. Police. *Throb, throb.* Smoke another cigarette.

Chapter Fourteen

Jassim awoke from a night of fitful and unconnected dreams; in the last he had been driving a car with Marcus and Bella crowded into the front seat next to him. Marcus held what looked like a golden football and told Jassim that he was going to blow up an old water tower. Jassim had no control over the car as it careened around curves, churning up dust and spinning rocks from its wheels. Suddenly the car came to a jagged stop and Marcus leaped out and ran through a dry wash, tossing the football/bomb impossibly high into the air and catching it, as Bella's voice grated in Jassim's ear that it was now his fault because he had driven him there. "You are responsible for whatever Marcus does," she told him, wagging her finger in his face until he woke up.

Gradually, as he seeped from that confused postdream state into Saturday morning, he realized that Salwa had already slipped away in her silken pajamas, that this was their last weekend together, and that he had made a date with another woman. Five days had passed since Jassim had last seen Penny, had invited her to the Botanical Gardens. And a lifetime. How could so many things have changed in just five days? He lay on his back, terribly awake, jittery and nervous, wishing he could cancel their meeting but paralyzed by the thought. If Salwa were not leaving, it would not seem such a treacherous thing, this meeting another woman for a walk among desert gardens.

"Good morning." Salwa interrupted his thinking.

"Hi, Salwa. You're up early."

"Actually, you're up late—it's already after nine." She went to the closet and reappeared with a blouse and a pair of jeans. "I'm going to shower now." While these words were directed at him, he could see that Salwa had already gone, had already left him as she began the business of preparing herself for departure, her tray table already in the upright position.

Jassim glanced at the clock and turned back to watch her as she let the water run so it would be warm when she stepped in, as she pulled open dresser drawers in search of underwear. In these awful last moments, he couldn't be there, have her so close to him and yet about to leave.

He sat up. "I'm going for a swim."

"Have a nice time, habibi."

Swimming would help get rid of the residual unsettled feeling with which the dream had riddled his body, would better prepare him to tell Penny the whole story.

—m—

For thirty-five blessed minutes he managed to forget about everything, to lose himself in the coolness of the water, in the wetness of it. He noticed no one until he was on his way out, when the pinprick of a voice pointed out that the gift shop was open, walked him past chips and shoelaces and goggles, and plopped him in front of a glass jewelry display, where he found himself staring at dainty necklaces, asking to see that tiny butterfly with iridescent wings. *No, how about that turquoise one?* Yes, something about that delicate pearl and turquoise choker appealed to him.

"I'd like to buy this," he told the clerk, an overweight woman with too much frizzy blond hair and a thick layer of foundation covering her face.

"You have exquisite taste, sir. Did you notice the pendant that centers the necklace? Do you see how it's actually a bead with a flower etched into it? It is so graceful and looks even more beautiful when it's worn."

"Did you make it?"

"Oh no. There's a Thai girl who's a member of the club. She makes all our jewelry on consignment."

Jassim paid for the choker and watched as the clerk, whose fingernails were impossibly long and the color of oranges, removed the tag and gently placed the necklace in a cardboard box, dozens of bright blue and gray eyes nestled in fluffy white cotton. She put the box in a small paper bag and handed it to him. "Turquoise is the stone of friendship and communication," she told him.

Jassim wrapped himself around this thought on his way out. He had always thought of turquoise as a stone used against evil, but he liked that it had this second meaning as well, thought that it was very fitting. He passed the counter, passed Diane. The purchase of the necklace boosted his confidence, had him greet her and ask, "You work Saturdays now?"

"This Saturday. I'm covering for someone. You come here on the weekends too?" Her eyes fell to the bag.

"Sometimes." He wished he hadn't said anything.

Diane was distracted, and his package didn't seem to interest her. "Isn't it so sad about Jack?" She looked into his eyes as she asked this, and Jassim had the feeling he had often had in these past weeks, that he was assumed to have more information than he did. Who was Jack? He looked at her blankly.

"Jack. Jack Franks. Older guy, military haircut. He swims too. Swam. I think he worked with your wife."

Spinning, spinning. Salwa was the banker with whom Jack Franks worked. *He worked with your wife* implied something that was incorrect. Was this something Jack had told Diane? Why had he and Diane been talking about Jassim? "What happened to him?"

"He had a heart attack, poor man. Was in the grocery store and had a heart attack and died. Just like that. I think he was really stressed by something he was working on." Diane studied Jassim's face, peered into his eyes, searching for an answer to something, to Jack's questions, perhaps.

"How awful," said Jassim. And with nothing left to offer her, he walked away from Diane with a feeling of relief, stepped in the dried residue of the puddle her fallen words had left months ago. Damage done. No possibility of slipping further.

Because he had walked away, he couldn't see Diane watching him, her head tipped to the side, as if waiting for secrets to be poured into her ear from above. Perhaps Jack had been right, she thought. *Perhaps things are not what they seem.* And with that thought, the guilt she had felt in indulging Jack's save-the-world-FBI-agent fantasy and telling him about Jassim's recent behavior was completely erased.

—⁂—

When Jassim came home from the pool, he and Salwa moved through the house in odd parallel stirrings, not coming too near each other, not daring to get too close, pointed elbows and hurried steps filling the space of the house.

At 10:30 Salwa was ready to leave for her day of shopping. To buy items she would stuff into suitcases and send through security in only two days' time. "Jassim, do you need anything?"

"No, habibti, your safety. Enjoy. Is Randa going with you?"

"Maybe later. She's got something with the kids, so she may not."

Jassim knew his wife would not be back before evening, and this void, the thought of the house being empty and Salwa being gone the whole day, soon to be gone every day, was more than he could stand. He longed for the Saturdays they had spent shopping aimlessly, and for a moment he thought of inviting himself along, but then he remembered that he had made other plans, that he had asked another woman to meet him. This thought so unsettled him that he blurted, "I am going to meet a client for lunch." Though after he'd said it he thought it sounded like a lie, wished he could have his words back.

"On a Saturday?" she asked.

"I guess that is what is most convenient." Careful not to add *for him.* She didn't know that he had lost his clients, lost his job. He needed time to figure out what to do, and maybe this Saturday away from her, with Penny, would give him the chance to *get a handle on it,* just like before, when Penny had tried to help him come to terms with Evan. *Make peace with those you've hurt.* Is that what she would say this time?

Salwa hesitated before she left, as though there were one more thing she needed to say. Jassim waited, watching his wife and wishing for her and in his deepest self apologizing. She left in silence, and he watched her drive off while her name spilled from his mouth. He remembered the days when she first came to the States and he would stand at the window to watch her go, to catch one last desperate glimpse of her before she was gone.

A few minutes after Salwa had left, he stepped out into the day for the second time, gift box containing the necklace in hand, then safely stowed away in the glove compartment; he settled into his car, headed out to meet Penny at the Botanical Gardens. As he bumped over the potholed lot and parked in front of a thin, drooping eucalyptus tree, his heart thumped wildly, pulsating in his fingertips, pounding in his ears, pushing him with hurried steps to wait for her by the shady entrance. At exactly eleven she walked toward him from the parking lot, wearing jeans and a long-sleeved shirt, a fuzzy pink sweater tied around her waist. He had never seen her in regular clothes before and thought she looked lovely. *Edible* was the first word that came to his mind. Her hair, which he had always seen wrapped up loosely behind her head, was hanging down, long and wispy and wild.

"Hi," he offered, and she smiled like a young girl. Jassim felt her smile throughout his body, thought she was delightful.

"Hi, Jassim. It's weird to see you outside, on a weekend." They stood awkwardly next to each other.

"I needed to talk to you."

Penny looked at him, crossed her arms just in case he was going to try to do something rash, like steal her heart.

"Is that okay?"

She nodded, scared to speak, scared she would say the wrong thing, because she was still not sure what it was he wanted from her.

They walked into the building, to the gift shop, where he paid for their admission, and then out a side door to the gardens. Past the low mustard-colored structures, the walkway looped and turned gently, guiding them in small talk and silence down one shady path after another. They stopped here and there, to marvel at the width of the bamboo stalks in a corner, the delightful fragrance of the herb garden, the thickness of the wall of oleanders that bordered the brick pathway, hid some of the sky. The bricks gave way to dirt corridors and they ambled past an area in which several giant sturdy prickly-pear cacti stretched themselves out of the dry ground, their trunks brown with age and their structure very much like that of trees.

"They look sinister," said Penny. *Like tortured souls coming out of the earth.*

Past statues and sculptures and fountains, through the bird gardens and wildflower gardens they wandered, taking it all in quietly, connected by the loveliness of the day. As they walked through the cactus garden, Jassim's eyes snagged on three small signs that pulled him away from these delicious moments, reminded him of his real life: *A cactus stem has fleshy tissue that will soak up water.* And, *A cactus has a waxy coating to seal in moisture.* Finally, *If you look at many of the cacti here, you will see ribs or bumps (tubercles). These pleated surfaces allow a cactus to expand and store more water during periods of rainfall, and then to contract again during periods of drought.*

He read the last sign through again, committed it to memory, and stored it away for another, more appropriate time. *Ribs and bumps.*

There was a reason Jassim had invited Penny here today; where normally he would have stopped at each plant, studied its name, read each of the signs that explained what and why and how, now, as they circled back through the gardens, he shut out the real world, let it vanish, and zeroed in on Penny, a woman who could offer him freedom from his burdens.

"Penny, I have not been quite honest with you. I mean I have, and in a way I have been more honest with you than I have with anyone else, but not about the particulars of my life."

"You're married."

"I am married."

"I think somehow I knew that."

How did she know that? That was the kind of thing Salwa would say. "My wife is leaving to go home to Jordan the day after tomorrow." Saying it aloud made it worse, etched it into reality. "I don't know how long she will be gone. I am not even sure whether she is leaving me or she is just leaving this country for a while."

"Why are you telling me this?" *Because you want me to be a part of your life,* she hoped absurdly—absurdly because she knew nothing of him.

"Because I can't seem to make sense of it, and you've been such a help for me through this difficult time." There: he had admitted out loud that she had a role in his life.

They walked slowly, their shoulders a few hairs' width apart, their eyes focused on an invisible moving spot on the ground in front of them.

"What is it that you can't make sense of?"

"I can't figure out why she's leaving and why so abruptly." That was it, the suddenness of it. "She has been distant, maybe sad, ever since she miscarried. I feel like I can't reach her." *I feel like she has become someone I don't know.*

"A miscarriage can be a traumatic event in a woman's life. You don't have children?"

"No."

"Well, that could be it. Many women suffer depression after miscarriages. It is like the death of a child." *No, it is nothing compared to the death of a child.*

"Out of the blue she bought a plane ticket home. A one-way ticket." Jassim paused but decided to keep going, to say everything that was on his mind. "I was informed yesterday…" Here he steeled himself, for again, once he spoke it aloud, it would become like Salwa's imminent departure: official, and he would have to accept the reality of it. "I have been asked to leave my job. Our firm has lost three big contracts. It seems because of me. Though not really my work, because I am doing the same job I have always done, but because I am an Arab, though of course they say that has nothing to do with it. I am losing everything I've worked for in my life, in large part because of one petty woman."

"What petty woman?" asked Penny. "Your wife?"

"No, no. There is a receptionist in my office who decided that I was a security threat. She called the FBI, and they apparently opened an investigation. She informed my clients that I am being investigated, and of course no one wants to deal with that." Instead of being overwhelmed by the truth of these words, he heard them clearly and realized that no FBI investigation would be based solely on what Bella had said. Someone else must have reported something. What? And who? A client? A coworker? The stories of the past few months began ricocheting through his head, popping up with no obvious connection to one another.

"And then—this is an aside—I went swimming today, and it seems that a man who knew my wife from her work at the bank was talking about me to the clerk at my health club. Insinuating that he knew my wife better than I am sure he did." *Had Jack Franks been harassing Salwa? Was he somehow at the root of all this?*

"You have had a hell of a few months here." The mothering Penny surfaced again, pushed down the excited girl with the pink sweater still wrapped around her waist. "So what happened between you and your wife?"

"Nothing." He was still stuck on Jack Franks. Maybe Franks had known about Evan. Unlikely, but possible.

"I mean, did you fight, did you argue, did she tell you what was wrong?"

"I think she wanted to have children. Then, after her miscarriage, she seemed so sad all the time, and I think I didn't help her as much as I could because the accident was always on my mind. I don't know." Sad and unhappy. *Had Jack Franks threatened her?*

"Do you love your wife?"

Just as Jassim was ready to release the thought of Jack Franks, to store it away for later, the vision of an angry American father losing his daughter to a Jordanian man *from the sand* flashed through his mind. Could Jack Franks have carried this bitterness all those years and unpacked it that morning in the locker room, all those months ago, when they had first met? Jassim became aware of silence, of Penny watching him. "Sorry. What did you ask me?"

"I asked you if you love your wife."

He pushed Jack Franks away and returned to Penny. "I think so. I'm not sure I know what love is, exactly. I feel affection for her. I want what is best for her. We, my wife and I, seem to be very different people. She could have done so much in her years here, and she didn't really, didn't try to make herself better. I don't understand that."

Penny, whose thumbs had been in her back pockets, now crossed her arms again, in solidarity with Jassim's wife. "So you wanted her to be something and she wanted to be something else and now she's leaving?"

Jassim thought. "I don't think it was like that. It's not that I wanted her to be something else, I just wanted her to take advantage of all the opportunities that she had."

"You wanted her to live the kind of life you would live."

"No. I had no objection to her being a banker. Or even to her selling real estate. It just seems like she could have done more."

Penny's heart thumped but she tried to remain calm, not jagged and jealous, as she imagined an educated, professional, well-dressed woman who also probably drove a fancy expensive car, as she saw the impossible differences between herself and his wife. "Your wife, what is her name?"

"Salwa."

"Gosh, that's a pretty name. Salwa. Maybe it's possible she didn't live up to your expectations of her?"

Jassim was silent. Chewed over these words. Swallowed them. "Yes, I think maybe that is what has happened."

"Do you want her to stay?"

"I did. I don't know; part of me still does. She is a good person. She is a beautiful woman. She is my wife, but we are very different." *Without her, I am lost.*

"And she wants children and you don't."

"She wants children, and actually I don't know that I'd mind anymore. I cannot stay here, though. If my firm has fired me, who is going to hire me? No one in this city."

They sat down on a wooden bench under a mesquite tree, a deformed saguaro standing sentry in the background. "Why didn't you want to have children in the first place?"

"I've been thinking a lot about that. I think it scares me to be so responsible for something so vulnerable and helpless." *And now, how would I possibly provide for a child?*

"Children are the greatest blessing, but they are also the hardest thing in the world to get right," said Penny, lost in memories.

"You have children?" asked Jassim, because until now he had not thought about Penny's life outside Denny's.

"Three."

"How old?"

Penny took a deep breath. "Thirteen, fifteen, and a girl who would have been twenty-one."

Jassim looked at her. "Would have been?"

"My daughter Josie died a couple of years ago."

"I am so sorry." Jassim wanted to touch Penny but couldn't see how, as they sat side by side on the bench, elbows resting on thighs, eyes on the ground, sorrows transferred from one to the other. "How did she die?"

"She OD'ed. Overdosed. On heroin. It was an accident. She was a good kid, not into drugs or anything, but she tried it once. Thought she'd see what it was like, I suppose. Maybe it was a bad batch. I don't know. It doesn't matter, does it? No amount of figuring things out will bring her back."

"How awful. I am so sorry. So very sorry, Penny." Jassim put his hand on her back, surprised at how broad and muscled it felt. "I am glad that you have your two other children to help you."

And because Penny had not come to cry or to dwell on the miseries in her life, she decided to close the door to this conversation. "Yes, my two other children," she said, aware that there was nothing fine in her life except this moment, except sitting under a mesquite tree with a good man whose wife was leaving him. In this moment there was hope. Remote but viable hope. In sharing tragedies, they had knocked down all formality. Partners in anguish.

"Are you hungry?" Jassim asked, taking back his hand.

"Starving."

"Shall we go have lunch?"

Penny agreed, and they walked out of the Botanical Gardens, the ghosts of two children and a baby left playing beneath a shady mesquite tree under the watchful eye of the giant misshapen saguaro.

_ᖇ ᖇ_

Hastily scribbled in invisible ink at the bottom of her list of preparations for leaving America was a reminder to go and say goodbye to Jake. Invisible, because that way no one would know that she planned to do such a foolish thing. As if a reminder were necessary. As if her very reason for leaving America could have slipped her memory, were not clinging onto her brain folds as she walked into one store and out another, making final grabs for the latest electronic this and plastic that. Her credit card burned, exhausted and wishing for a rest after a day of endless swiping. Presents purchased, her trunk filled with the crinkle of dollars spent, she drove to Jake's apartment complex.

She pulled her waxed white SUV into a visitor's slot just to the right of where three men—Mexican, she guessed—were working, two clipping small branches off a mesquite tree and the other, a very short and stocky man, on his hands and knees, bent over a sprinkler connection. It was this man she noticed. His tools were laid out next to him on a square black cloth; two screwdrivers, a wrench, and two objects she could not identify were lined up exactly parallel to one another, Jassim-style. The man was spotless. Kneeling on the grass, digging in the dirt, and spotless. He smiled as she walked by and greeted her with an accented hello.

Something from his broad smile leaped across the sidewalk and entered her; this was not the first time she had seen him. The night her car had been broken into, he had spoken to her. There was no recognition in his face, but she wondered if he knew, or even if he had been responsible.

These thoughts unraveled her as she stepped onto the curvy path that eventually led to Jake's staircase, left swirls of thread all the way up to the landing in front of his apartment. She rang the doorbell, a part of her hoping that Jake would be gone and this item could be crossed off her list. An unaccomplished mission. Her heart pounding, she leaned against the railing for support and, glancing toward her faraway car, saw that all three workers were watching her. Just beyond her irritation, she imagined the miles of desert they must have crossed for the opportunity to trim and mow and prune, the perils they must have endured to have their clear shot at the American Dream.

"It's all a lie!" she wanted to shout. "A huge lie." A lie her parents believed in enough that they had paved her future with the hope of glass slippers and fancy balls, not understanding that her beginning was not humble enough, nor was her heart pure enough, for her to be the princess in any of these stories. That she did not come from a culture of happy endings. That she would have been much better off munching on fava beans from her ceiling basket. She looked at those dark men looking at her and from a distance she could see their sacrifices, the partial loss of self that they too must have agreed to in coming to America, the signing over of the soul. She turned away before she could notice the squiggly red line that spilled from the tidy gardener's black cloth and ran all the way up to her shoe. Her finger pressed the doorbell a second time.

She heard no footsteps from within, no muffled voice, just suddenly was looking at an open door.

"Salwa. I didn't expect you."

Jake, whom she was used to seeing combed and pressed, or tidily nude, wore only boxer shorts. His hair was tousled, and his eyes, though wide open, looked peculiar, creepy.

"Oh, sorry. Sorry, Jake. I didn't mean to wake you."

"I wasn't asleep, Salwa. Come in." His voice grated, sounded irritated, and Salwa now wished she had been more forthcoming from the beginning, wished that she had told him she was leaving when she had given her notice to the bank and had already gone through this goodbye. Why could she never find the rewind button in life? It was so much easier to see how to do the right thing after a bit of time had passed.

Jake stood back from the door so she could enter. The apartment was overly warm and assaulted her with a dirty smell, a mashing in the air of sour perspiration and unclean skin, stale cigarettes and miserable ash piled in heaps on small dishes, clothes left in piles on the floor.

This state of disorder should have been enough to shake any fairy-tale princess back to reality, but Salwa couldn't turn away just yet from the tiniest hope that Petra had somehow twisted Jake's words, that she had lied. The state of disorder that was his apartment overwhelmed her so completely that it blurred her senses and smudged her vision.

"Sorry for the mess. I wasn't expecting company."

"I am sorry. I didn't mean to bother you." *Bother* was not the word. No, *interrupt.* Interrupt? No. *Disturb? Inconvenience?* She scanned her English vocabulary but could not come up with one that fit.

"No bother. Come in. Sit down."

"No. Thanks. I came because I wanted to say goodbye." No, she hadn't wanted to start off with the ending. This was a man with whom she had shared her most private self, and she wanted to honor that somehow, to erase their last encounter and say goodbye properly.

"Goodbye? What? Are you going on a trip or something?"

Go slowly and tell him what you want to say. Without too much detail. "I have some family business to deal with. I can't do this."

"Do what?"

"Be with you. I have to stop." *Because you told Sweeney what we did. Because you see me as an older woman. There is no love in that.*

Jake squinted at her with eyes that seemed terribly distant, that confused her. Something was wrong; maybe her words weren't getting there just right, were being warped and twisted by the same smelly molecules that swarmed around the apartment. He stood, jittery, in front of her and then took her hand, led her awkwardly to the couch, where they sat, where he chattered, with a coarseness to his voice, as though he had to haul it out from the very deepest part of himself.

At first Salwa did not hear his words, was stuck on the voice itself. "Salwa, I want to be with you. Forever. It would be perfect. We could be together, just us. Think how good that would be."

Salwa stared at him. "What are you talking about?"

"I love you, Salwa."

Then why don't you look at me? Why don't you touch me? And then, in a burst of realization, it all made sense. All the hushed conversations at work, the odd sentences here and there, the phone call interruptions, all came together in one. "Do you take drugs, Jake?"

"Salwa, it will be different after this. After today. This is the end. I am starting over. Everything will change. You are everything to me."

These ludicrous statements helped her regain her grounding, made her realize that he was offering a confession to her suspicion. Surely he did not think that after what he had done in the Torreys' house, after he had talked to Sweeney about her, and now after admitting that he was high on drugs, surely he didn't really believe that they would someday be together? "Jake, you are a very nice guy. Really. I have enjoyed knowing you, but I am saying goodbye." In saying these laughable, made-for-TV words, she heard her accent. She stood up. Took one step back.

"Why did you come here?" That odd deep voice. He was almost unrecognizable, his face hidden behind a day's stubble. "No. I know why you came here. You came because you want sex. That's why. That's what all of this has been about. I've cared about you and you've used me."

The ugliness of his statement did not startle her, just added a few feet between them. It was not her English, it was his comprehension of her that was the problem, that had always been the problem. It was so clear to her now. She searched for the rewind button again, her lovely fingers stretching for days and weeks behind her, groping in darkness, but with no luck.

"Well, come on, if that's what you want, then let's do it." He stood up and lurched forward, reached his hand out to take hers. She took one more step back.

"No, Jake. I am saying goodbye."

He stared at her, as if trying to focus on her face rather than understand what she was saying. "What? What the fuck?"

"Jake, I'm going home." She could feel it, the balance of power shifting, and she moved her feet to keep from tipping backward.

Something had changed in his face. "Home?" He had been standing with his arms crossed and teetering a bit, but now he flopped back on the couch and slung a leg over the armrest.

Salwa forced her eyes to remain on his face, not on the opening of his shorts. "Home. Jordan."

"Jesus fucking Christ. Boom. Just like that?" He ran his fingers through his hair again and again, forcing oily clumps into untidy formations.

This must be how movie actors felt. They stood in the middle of a dramatic scene and showed anger, or sadness, or whatever emotion was called for, but inside there was nothing, because it wasn't real. Edging toward the door, looking at Jake, half naked and a mess, she felt no anger, no sadness, no disgust...nothing. Just uneasiness.

"When do you leave?"

"Monday."

"Fuck."

Salwa winced. Twisted her perfect fingers together in search of cleaner words to offer.

"So you're running back to the pigsty?"

Salwa's brain skipped. "Pardon?"

"I said you're running back to the pigsty you came from." He spoke these words clearly and slowly, as if to someone who might not understand the language.

Silence filled Salwa's mouth. Large thumps of blood pumped *Leave* into her brain and feet. In another lifetime she might have argued, spoken her mind, but her mouth stayed shut and she took two more steps backward toward the door, slowly, as if the conversation were perfectly normal and she just wanted to change her position, not inch away from the creature splayed out on the couch. The look on his face, no, the face itself, was not the Jake she knew, the Jake she had been with. Something in him had changed, and she had to leave before she found out what it was. In the middle of a sunny American afternoon, she had to get out of the door into the day, and then she would be safe. Yes. And she would pass the Mexican workers and give them a smile, and then go home and finish packing, try to return her life to normal.

"Goodbye, Jake." Her hand was on the doorknob now. She turned it with her eyes still fixed on him, pulled the door open, and stepped out onto the landing, into the brightness and safety of the day. She turned toward the steps, her right hand on the railing, her eyes on the gardeners less than a minute's walk away. She decided that she would talk to them when she got to her car. Would ask them if they always worked on Saturday, or maybe tell them they were doing a good job, because the plants looked lush and pretty even though they were in the middle of a drought in the desert. Or maybe just tell them they were nosy but in a familiar kind of way.

"Salwa." Jake's voice sounded normal, and she ignored the whisper in her brain to go *quickly* and instead turned around to face him.

"I want you to take this."

The brain, when it is in a state of danger, has odd ways of dissecting and processing the information around it. First Salwa saw Jake standing just outside his door in his boxer shorts, a couple of feet away from her. She saw that he was holding something rectangular that caught the sun. A part of her brain processed that he was giving her a gift, a picture, and that for some reason he was lifting it into the air. In one powerful blink, it came down on her cheek, just below her eye, and she felt as if her face had been sliced with something that was part sledgehammer, part knife. She screamed and bent her head forward, covered her face, caught her blood. Her brain saw, after it happened, that he was holding the Japanese painting, the one lovely thing she had found in his apartment. And as she realized this, that it was the corner of the heavy silver frame that had sliced into her face, she felt a blow again, on the top of her head. She was amazed at the force and the pain. She doubled over in a ball on the landing with her hands over the back of her head, thickly wet, and she felt blows again, on her back, on her side, on her hands. Someone yelled *Stop!* She fell to her side, and the yelling got closer, louder. "Hey, man, stop. Corre! Corre! Lady, run! Just run!"

Salwa turned her head and could see the gardeners below. One of them was holding a cell phone and pointing at the street that ran along the southern side of the apartment building. The man with the orderly tools and the other one were waving at her, the latter with clippers in his hand. "Lady, go!" he kept yelling at her in English. Both men were moving toward the staircase. All three yelled back and forth to each other in Spanish. Frantic yelling.

The thuds on Salwa's body and head kept coming, even as she saw through a haze of red that the stocky man was running toward the stairs, which gave her the courage to move her feet to the top stair below the landing.

Amid the thuds were Jake's strained words, some whispers, some tortured screams.

" ... wanted to love you ..."

Another blow, aimed at the back of her head, sliced at the two first fingers on her left hand and she heard the *pling* of broken glass, the snap of a thread.

"... leaving me now ... "

She pulled herself up by the railing with her right hand and stepped down, one staggering step and then another, her body facing the railing, her head throbbing, pain pinching her hand and face and side.

"Things could have been right between us ... "

She was six or seven stairs from the bottom when she felt tremendous pressure against her right shoulder blade and a push that sent her down the remaining stairs to land on the ground in a folded lump.

"Bitch! Goddamn fucking Arab bitch! You ruined everything!"

Her body rocked back and forth on a dizzy boat in a storm, her limbs too heavy and sick to move. She felt herself being lifted. Heard "Stop, man. Leave her alone."

"Get away. I wouldn't want to hurt you too."

The boat was moving, though she couldn't figure out how, as her feet were so far from the ground. Faster, with quick steps, almost running, which made her head spin more. She found herself lying on the grass, a heavy man leaning over her, talking to her in a soft voice and trying to catch his breath. "You all right? No. You are not all right. You will be okay now. The police is coming." Salwa's face and hand pulsed with a pain she had never before felt. She glanced down, at all the blood, and told herself to focus on the man's words, listen to what he told her, even as she shook and couldn't stop herself, even as her guilty blood trickled between thick blades of grass.

Still breathing heavily, the man knelt next to her, spoke to her quietly. "What is your name?"

Salwa's sweet name fell off her tongue between clattering jaws.

"Salwa? That's beautiful. My name is Esteban. You are going to be okay. The police is coming." As he spoke to her, he daubed at her face with a handkerchief and then held it with pressure on the spot just beneath her eye, where it hurt the most.

Salwa could not move, shook as she felt Esteban's fingers on her face, as she felt her blood being pumped out of her body, spilling into the grass.

"I sure the ambulance will be here soon."

In spite of the staccato way his words came at her and the thickness of his fingers, his gentleness overpowered her. All the years that she had been in America came to this: being saved from her own stupidity by a man who perhaps had risked his life so that he could prune trees and fix sprinkler heads. The sirens came, and Salwa lay bathed in shame; at that moment she would have given the world to have found the rewind button. She would have pressed nine years. And she would never have said yes to Dr. Haddad.

Rocking and tipping and squeezing her eyes closed against noises that seemed to have no connection to her.

"Ma'am," someone kept saying. "Ma'am, do you know if he has a gun in the house? Tiene pistola?"

How could I know such a thing? she wanted to say. *I barely know him. I came to say goodbye. I don't know what happened.* But none of these words came to her broken face.

She opened her eyes. A police officer looked at her and asked quietly, "Do you speak English?"

Salwa opened her mouth to say yes but could not force her voice out.

She moved her eyes to Esteban, to her blood on his white undershirt, on his arms and hands and face. His eyes, as he looked at her, were filled with sadness. "You going to be okay," he told her and again smiled broadly. He held her hand and squeezed, pumping half a continent of courage into her blood, promising her that this was not real, that he could see who she was and not what she had become, and that she had to be strong. For now.

More sirens and more sirens and noises and Salwa closed her eyes, prayed to God as she filtered voices.

"... a meth lab in that apartment too?"

"No, maybe the dealer."

"How many bedrooms is the apartment?"

"One."

"... evacuation?"

"Does he have a gun?"

"I don't think so... attacked her with a picture. Raging. Maybe high."

"... the Guatemalan gardener. Been suspicious for weeks."

"... hospital."

Her eyes stayed closed as she shivered and felt hands move her, lift her again. Where was Esteban taking her now? she wondered. To the hospital, maybe. But she had to go home. How could she go home if she was in the hospital? She had to get up and find Jassim.

⸺ ᘒ ᘒ ⸺

"It's kind of nice being served for a change," said Penny as they walked out of the restaurant together. Arm in arm. Linked outcasts.

Salwa would still be shopping now. Would be filling up her SUV with unnecessary items to take home. Requisite presents. Prerequisites for her return. Jassim twitched a bit as he thought about the hundreds of dollars being spent on things that would probably be discarded shortly after they were received. Hundreds of dollars they could no longer afford. He felt irritated at the thought of his wife carousing about town buying, buying, buying. This scared him, this irritation. He didn't want to be angry with her. He wanted to adore her.

But he didn't, he realized. Had he ever? Somehow, walking next to Penny, he found he could see things more clearly, saw now that his love for Salwa was not as his love for Cornelia had been, was not for an equal, compatible partner. He loved Salwa because in her he saw home, which made her both more precious and a source of resentment. This realization, this seeing, was at once so sad as to twist his stomach and so liberating that he felt he could float in the air. Two entangled kites whose strings had just been snipped, untangled, and now were allowed to float off on their own current of wind. He had married Salwa because he had wished to protect and nurture her. Because he needed her. Quite possibly she had married him for need as well.

It was the lack of this in Penny, a purity of being, that had attracted him. Yes, it was sexual, but it was more than that, gigantic, tidal, and unbearable. In all of Penny's straight talk, he had seen her for who she was, her most basic person, not a tidily manicured person who had accommodated herself to fit in someone else's world. Penny was who Penny was, and she saw him for who he was. This awareness excited Jassim, led him to hold her in front of his car and kiss her quite passionately.

When you are with a woman other than your wife in the middle of the afternoon, where else is there to go? As he held her in his arms, he refused to think beyond this moment. He did not think he should stop because he might be *leading her on,* letting her believe something would be that would not be. For the first time in his memory, Jassim was living for the moment.

In the glove box of his car, next to his cell phone, which showed three missed calls from the Tucson Police Department, a cluster of blue and gray beads waited patiently, but Jassim had forgotten all about it. He stood in the parking lot and kissed a woman with a fuzzy pink sweater wrapped around her waist, while above their heads there floated a kite with a slashed sail and a missing string.

⸻

Though Salwa was able to open one of her eyes, she kept it closed, hoping that she might be able to delay reality a bit longer. Avoid the detectives who had twice tried to ask her questions. Avoid the nurse who came in to check on her. And still she was not sure what was real and what was imagined. She lay alternating between pain, excruciating pain in her face and hand and head, and a groggy, dreamy state where she was watching her life from outside her body.

She woke from one of those faraway trances to feel a hand resting on her leg. Eyes slammed shut, eyelashes locked together, her heart hollowed out.

"Oh Salwa. Habibti, Salwa," came the voice of her husband, her pure sweet husband, who wanted nothing more than to make the world a better place, overflowing in crystal-clear water. Her face ached behind the bandages, and still she did her best to keep her uninjured eye steadily shut, to remain unconscious in his presence.

His hand lingered on her leg, and she imagined him sitting pensively in a chair next to the bed. He was so still and quiet that if it were not for that weight, she would have assumed he had left. No words, no mutterings, just heavy silence and the pressure of his hand against her. She floated away and back and woke to the sound of several voices, but her eyes stayed shut, safely shut.

"...Detective Mills. Has she woken up at all?"

"Not while I've been here."

"We would like to talk to her when she does. Here's my card. I'm sorry, sir, for what you both must be going through."

It occurred to Salwa, who was there and wasn't there, that if they didn't tell Jassim anything, then maybe he knew already. She wouldn't let herself think about it, not ever again. No, it had not happened to her conscious self. She would just forget.

Shuffling and movement and Jassim's voice was next to her ear, his hand caressing the side of her face that was not covered by gauze. "Salwa, I am so sorry it has come to this. For what happened. I feel that I am responsible."

He doesn't know.

"I've not provided for you what you needed, allowed you to be who you wanted. I should have recognized that you would have been better off staying in Jordan. I was selfish to have brought you here. I realized that today. Salwa, I am so sorry. All of this is my fault for being weak, for not being able to tell you what I've done, first killing the boy. And then, Salwa, I've lost my job. Marcus fired me. The FBI investigation, they've fired me."

Eyes burning but still shut, Salwa moved her right hand, hoping to find his, but Jassim must not have been looking and continued talking.

"And I don't know what Jack Franks said to you, if he threatened you or harassed you, but he is dead now, had a heart attack, according to the cheap woman who checks IDs at my health club, so you don't need to worry about him anymore."

Salwa stopped herself from asking Jassim what on earth he was talking about, thought maybe she had slept in the middle of a conversation or that her injuries had forced her to forget some vital bit of information.

"Mr. Haddad," a woman's voice interrupted. The detective's voice.

"Yes?" Jassim moved his face away from Salwa's, rested his hand on her arm.

"Sorry to bother you again, but just to let you know, the standoff has ended."

"Thank God. Why did he do it? Why did he attack her like this?"

"We don't know that yet, sir, but it does seem that drugs were somehow involved."

"My wife isn't involved in drugs."

"That may well be. Sir, this was a crime of passion. Something must have set him off. Perhaps something your wife said—she was only at his apartment for a few minutes."

There was a silence. Salwa held her breath.

"I don't know what you are implying, but my wife is not involved with drugs or with people like that."

"Sir, we don't know anything for sure yet, other than that this guy was high as a kite and that he worked with your wife at the bank. It's possible that she was simply in the wrong place at the wrong time."

"Has he been arrested?"

"Yes, he is currently in police custody."

Just before Salwa decided that she would not ever think about this again, she saw, felt in the deepest part of her soul, that Jassim believed her incapable of any sort of illicit behavior, had defended her blindly. No, she could not think about it anymore, would forget everything that had happened. Muttering words to herself, words to purify herself, words to take her away from this moment, she began to drift again. Away, away, away.

—☙ ❧—

Hassan tiptoed through the darkness from his bedroom to a chair in the farthest corner of the living room. He wore pajama pants, a sweater, and a kaffiyeh against the early morning cold. His bare feet rested on the cold tile floor as he turned his cell phone over in his hand.

Salwa, Salwa, Salwa. My hopes and dreams. My one first love. My perfect beauty. My purest Salwa.

No way for Hassan to know that at the moment he sat, poised to dial Salwa's number, she was lying in an American hospital bed, disfigured and barely conscious. No way for Hassan to know that she was no longer a perfect beauty, nor was she in any way pure.

Hassan could not lose this time in hesitation, and again he scrolled through his directory, clicked on her name, and waited.

"Hi, this is Salwa Haddad. I'm sorry I missed your call..."

"Hi, Salwa. It is I, Hassan. Sorry, I keep missing you. I've tried so many times, and I guess it's God's will that we don't talk together. So I will leave this message, though I would much rather have spoken with you." He paused. "Intizar and I have gotten married. And no, she's not pregnant or anything, but I got offered a job in Qatar, as did she, and it made more sense for us to go married and living together than engaged and living apart."

Hassan paused again.

"Salwa, I am calling to say goodbye, to tell you that I wish you well, wherever you may be, and that I am now going to try and forget you, to live my life with Intizar. God willing, you will be happy in your life."

He paused again, then pressed the button to sever his cellular link with his past. Scrolled down and clicked.

Are you sure you want to delete Salwa Queen of Pajamas?

O.K.

He tiptoed in the darkness back to his new bride.

After

kan
ya ma kan
fee qadeem az-zamaan

They say there was or there wasn't in olden times a story as old
as life, as young as this moment, a story that is yours and is mine.
It happened during half a blink in the lifetime of the earth, a time
when Man walked a frayed tightrope on large, broken feet over an
impossible pit of his greatest fears.

They say that once upon a time a peasant girl was born far
from olive trees and falafel stands in a land where fathers—and
often mothers too—labored so that their children could change
their fates. She was born to parents who were refugees from their
real home, a land snatched away and reworked, a story taken and
rewritten.

What these doting parents didn't know was that when the
mother gave birth out of place to her youngest moon-faced child,
a ghula visited her. The hairy hideous ghula saw the beauty in the
child's face and grew madly jealous, wanted the baby for her own,
but knew she wouldn't get past security, so she took out her wild
ghula threads and began to stitch them under the baby's skin in
all sorts of places—between finger joints, next to her nipples, under
her eyes, at the base of her neck. When the ghula was done, the
baby lay asleep with a thousand and one red threads hanging from

her. The ghula held the ends of the threads together and pulled a skein from under one of her large, dangling breasts. After she secured them, threads to skein, she said some magic ghula words and the threads became invisible.

And so the baby lived as was expected of her. Periodically the ghula would tug at one strand or another and the little girl would feel a pang, a prick, an ache for something else. These pangs and pricks always came at particular times—when an auntie brought gifts of silk pajamas, for example.

One day the son of a martyr crossed the girl's path from behind and tripped on several hundred of the threads. His fall was so great that he severed them from their attachment under her skin, causing her such relief that she fell in love with him in a good and quiet way. The ghula was furious, demanded to know who dared to cross her.

"It is I, Hassan."

The ghula reeled, for ghulas fear no one more than Clever Hassan. She decided to send her ghul brothers to distract him while she bided her time, waiting until she thought the girl would be good and plump before she began to reel her in.

One day a nightingale with deep blue feathers crossed the threshold. "Peace be upon you, auntie," he said, and because he greeted her kindly, she decided not to eat him. Instead she spoke to him in such a gentle way that each night, after he spent his day flying about, he returned to the cave and sang to her before he went to sleep on an oleander stick.

When the ghula thought the girl would be grown and ripe for eating, she began to reel in the remaining threads, pulling the girl away from her familiar world, gently turning the skein a bit more each day.

"What are you doing, auntie?" asked the nightingale one evening.

"I am preparing for a feast."

"What is it you are going to be feasting on, auntie?"

"A young maiden."

"Auntie, that is cruel, you can't do that."

"I can and I will and you cannot stop me."

The nightingale realized she was right.

In preparation for the girl's arrival, the ghula transformed herself into a kindly old woman and turned her slovenly cave into a gleaming villa. The nightingale spent his days flying above the entrance to the cave, hoping that he would be able to warn the girl.

The night the ghula realized what he was trying to do, she turned his oleander stick into a golden cage.

"Auntie, please let me out. A bird is not meant to be trapped in a cage."

"A bird is not meant to betray his master, and I don't trust you," she replied, and transformed his speaking voice into a regular nightingale voice. "There, stay in your cage and look pretty and sing for me in the evenings."

Just then the girl arrived at the door of the villa.

"Peace be upon you," she said, and because she had spoken kindly, the ghula decided not to eat her right away.

"Welcome, my girl. Please make yourself at home."

The nightingale began tweeting with all his might, pacing back and forth across his perch, and the girl went to his cage and admired him. "Auntie, this is a beautiful bird, with such a lovely voice. I know I will be happy here." And she was, finding happiness in the beautiful villa and in her new life. Over time the nightingale forgot that the kindly old lady was actually a ghula who was going to eat the girl, and so he did nothing more than sing his beautiful songs from dawn to dusk.

Many years passed and the girl grew plumper but sadder, longing for her home and yet somehow unable to return. Each time the girl mentioned her homesickness, the old woman offered her a new gift to assuage her sadness, until finally the old woman decided it was time for her ghula self to reappear and her feast to be eaten.

Realizing what was going to happen, the nightingale forced himself to stay awake at night by keeping a seed in his beak, cracking down on it just as he started to nod off to sleep, and tweeting loudly so that the girl couldn't stay asleep for more than a few minutes at a time. *Crack. Tweet. Crack. Tweet.*

After many sleepless nights, the girl said to the old woman,

"Auntie, why does your bird crack seeds and tweet through the night so that I cannot sleep?"

The ghula, who realized that the bird must be trying to save the maiden, covered the golden cage with a thick blanket.

The next night, just as the ghula was about to transform herself for her feast, the girl woke freezing and asked with a sigh, "Oh auntie, how can I sleep when I am so cold?"

"What can I do for you, my dear girl?" asked the old woman.

"Please, make me a fire so that I can warm myself."

The ghula, who was suspicious by nature, thought the girl might be planning something, so when she left the room she hid outside to see what would happen. It was not long before she saw a figure sneak into the girl's room. She guessed that it was Clever Hassan, assumed that he and the girl had been plotting all along. Raging mad that he would dare to come back after all this time and take away what had become rightfully hers, the ghula stormed into the room, ready for a fight. "Thief! Get out of my house!" she screamed, still in her old woman disguise.

Hassan, who after years of patient searching had come across the villa by pure chance, saw the flames coming from the old woman's feet and, given his years of experience with ghuls, understood what must have happened. Even though he was exhausted from years of adventuring, he realized that he was obliged to kill her. He pulled out his knife, raised it high above him so that it glinted in the moonlight, and brought it down into the ghula with all his force.

Unfortunately, even heroes can make mistakes. Just as his knife began its downward journey, the ghula used her magic to pick up the girl and place her as a shield in front of her, so that Hassan's knife plunged not into the body of the ghula but into that of his beloved.

When the knife penetrated the young maiden's skin, it broke the ghula's spell and they were once again in the filthy ghula cave. There in front of Hassan lay the love of his life, rediscovered after many years, crumpled and bleeding, with hundreds of red threads hanging from her, while the ghula had resumed her true form. Hassan slit the ghula's neck in the blink of an eye. Filled with shame and agony, he begged for God's forgiveness, kissed the maiden's forehead, and fled from her disfigured body.

—⁓—

That's it?

Not quite.

Did Hassan kill her?

Yes and no. The cave dissolved, and the nightingale who had been trapped in his golden cage once again found himself standing on an oleander twig. He flew over to the bloodied girl. With his beak he began severing the threads from the girl, one by one, until every thread dangled not from the girl but from the dead ghula, hideous entrails bloodying concrete and burning in the now blazing sun.

So it was a bird who saved her?

Yes and no. Once the nightingale severed the last thread, he transformed into an ordinary man.

Not a handsome prince?

Not a handsome prince. This ordinary man was not so handsome—above average, perhaps, but nothing of the prince-hero type—and had only once before found himself folded over a nearly lifeless body. Years of exercise had left him strong and sound in mind and body, so he lifted up the unconscious and damaged maiden and carried her home across land and sea, hoping that with the proper care she would recover from her wounds.

The End?

The End.

Wait a sec.

What is it?

There's no "they lived happily ever after"?

"Happily ever after" happens only in American fairy tales.

Wasn't this an American fairy tale?

It was and it wasn't.

Acknowledgments

Thanks to the Fulbright Foundation, whose generous grant opened up the world of folklore.

For their help in understanding various aspects of hydrology, from the tangible to the philosophical, and for sharing their time and expertise, I would like to thank Peter Griffiths, Bishara Bisharat, Mohamad Amin Saad, Robert McGill and the folks at Hydrogeophysics, Nadeem Majaj, Joan Blainey, Carla Bitter, and Ali Subah.

For helping me to get the details of the police and paramedic scenes accurate, and for their time and patience, my thanks to firefighter Patricia Brescia, retired detective Marilyn Malone, and Detective Shane Barrett. For their insight into the workings of the FBI and the legal aspect of investigations, my thanks to Cary L. Thornton, Jr., and Nawar Shora.

My gratitude to Joseph Romanov for explaining the details of real estate, and for daily confidence-building and encouragement. To Dale Naasz for his time and thoughts on Mercedes, to Dr. Miguel Arce for answering all questions medical, to Joel Hansen for his technical support and insightful suggestions, to Erik Baker for his attention to detail, and to Anne Ward Abramo for her help with the world of banking.

Thanks to Rebecca Ruiz McGill for gambling and granting me a leave of absence. To Waltraud Nichols for excellent advice along the way and for helpful discussion about small talk and its cultural/anthropological aspects in American society. To Rula Khalidi and

Houri Berberian for their support and detailed reading of the book as it neared completion. To Marwan Mahmoud for sage advice and for absolutely always believing that my stories are important.

To Mahmood Ibrahim, whose passion for water gave me the seed that grew into this story.

My eternal gratitude to my editor, Helene Atwan, who with the keenest eye and great encouragement guided this book to completion; in her I have found my always-wished-for mentor. To the staff of Beacon Press for their integrity, support, and enthusiasm.

To my mother, Margaret Halaby, for encouragement, a lifetime of wordplay, and the laptop that made my four A.M. writing a possibility.

To Raik, Raad, and Rabiah for their enthusiasm about this project, for helping me with my research, and for putting up with endless scenarios and a certain lack of early-morning serenity.

Reading Group Guide

A CONVERSATION WITH LAILA HALABY

Q: What inspired you to become a writer?

A: Writing is something that I've always done—I guess it's how I process life—and I've always loved stories. Something I find particularly interesting is how people communicate with one another and how that communication is perceived—how much miscommunication there actually is, and the effects of those misfires.

Q: Who are your favorite authors, and how have they influenced your writing?

A: I remember reading *Cry, the Beloved Country* by Alan Paton at a fairly early stage and thinking, "Yes, writing can change someone's mind or understanding of a situation." That was very important. I admire Arundhati Roy tremendously, for her courage, perception, and incredible sense of the beauty and agony of life. From Sandra Cisneros and Sherman Alexie, I have learned that you can create nontraditional American characters without apologies and explanations. From Joe Bolton, I learned that you can tell a lyrical story in the space of a poem.

Q: What are your writing habits? Do you have a specific routine? How do you stay disciplined?

A: My ideal writing scenario is three or four hours in the morning, first to write fervently, then reread, then edit, then take a walk to mull it all over, read it one more time, and put it away for the day. When I am writing a scene or something that is functional, I can do it directly on the computer, but if it is poetic or character building or part of the mulling, I have to do it longhand.

A PROFILE OF THE AUTHOR
(INCLUDING A DESCRIPTION OF THE BOOK)

Real People: A Web of Suspicion Ensnares a Jordanian Couple Following Sept. 11 (*Tucson Weekly*, February 1, 2007)

In the days after 9/11, Laila Halaby was dismayed by the depictions of Arabs in the news media.

"I kept reading these awful distortions," says the Tucson author. The daughter of a Jordanian father and an American mother, Halaby is married to a Palestinian. "I had a whole book written filled with normal Arab people I felt I had a responsibility to do something with."

That manuscript, *West of the Jordan,* became Halaby's first published book. A coming-of-age tale of four girl cousins from an imaginary Palestinian village not unlike Halaby's husband's, the book had originally been rejected by numerous publishers. But after 9/11, Halaby tried again, and found a publisher in Beacon Press, a venerable New England institution. . . .

Published in 2003, the apolitical book was well received, even picking up the PEN/Beyond Margins Award given to works by "authors of color." But when Halaby started her next novel, the brand-new *Once in a Promised Land,* she was living in the post-9/11 world. She felt she had no choice but to address it.

"This was a book I would not have written under a different political climate," she says. "What was exploding around the world entered into the tone of it."

Also published by Beacon, the novel tells the story of the Haddads, a well-heeled couple living in Tucson's Foothills. Jassim is a single-minded hydrologist, a Jordanian who got his Ph.D. at the UA and stayed on to expose desert dwellers to the virtues of conservation and rainwater-harvesting. Salwa, his restless younger wife, is also from Jordan, the daughter of displaced Palestinians. Initially attracted to Jassim's passion for science, nine years into the marriage she's having trouble figuring out her own life, trying out banking and real estate, and surreptitiously trying to get pregnant. Weekends, she devotes much of her free time to shopping.

"They're just a couple whose marriage is falling apart," Halaby says.

But their personal misfortunes are compounded by the fallout from 9/11. The novel opens on the morning of Sept. 11, and with the nation (and Tucsonans) terrified of more bombings, it's not long before the couple falls under suspicion. Neither is political or religious, but Salwa has routinely wired money back home, and Jassim has long had access to the city's water supply. Even the lies they've told each other in their marriage begin to count against them.

Writing with a sense of creeping horror, Halaby depicts the Haddads' ordinary activities coming under scrutiny by citizens galvanized by President Bush's call to act as the eyes and ears of the government. It's not long before their comfortable life in the Promised Land is threatened.

Some of the characters who rat them out are obvious bad guys —including a racist ex-military guy by the name of Jack Franks— but Halaby also shows the effects of paranoia on good people. A level-headed hydrologist who heartily admires Jassim eventually succumbs to the whisper campaign.

"Even people who 'get it' fall into the trap," Halaby says.

Tucson's a fairly liberal city, she says, and most of her own family's experiences here after 9/11 were positive.

"We were in a supportive community," she says, and her two sons "were in a school that cherished their Arab identity." Yet people stared at her Middle Eastern husband, and she herself ran into a problem at work related to her "ethnic identity" that "gave me a sense of what it's like to be judged."

Halaby was born in Lebanon, but moved to Tucson with her

mother at the age of five. Her father remained in the Middle East, and Halaby visited frequently as a teen, keeping "a foot here, a foot there. I felt different in both places."

After graduating from Tucson's University High School, Halaby studied Italian literature at Washington University in St. Louis, and picked up a master's in Arabic literature at UCLA. She also won a Fulbright to research folklore in Jordan. Her year there yielded her first manuscript, a collection of Arabic folktales, as yet unpublished, but the structure of the tales also helped shape the new novel. *Once in a Promised Land* recounts several stories outright.

Arabic phrases are sprinkled throughout the book, which also has some scenes in Jordan, but "I speak Arabic like a grandmother," Halaby jokes, "not the language of an educated city person." . . .

The book has already gotten a nod from Barnes & Noble, which named it a Discover Great New Writers selection. The writer Andre Dubus III, author of *House of Sand and Fog*, gave it an enthusiastic blurb, calling it a "deeply resonant tale of our tangled and common humanity." . . .

[Halaby] and her husband moved back to Tucson after their second son, now seven, was born, to enlist her mother's help in raising the boys. Moving to the West Bank, her husband's home, is not really an option, she says, given the restrictions placed on Palestinians by the Israeli government. Her mother-in-law is not permitted to visit Jerusalem, she says, and last summer on a visit home, the family was detained by armed soldiers near the airport.

"There's so much entrenched anger on either side," she sighs. "I wish I had an answer. But allowing open dialogue—and respecting that other cultures are as valid as yours—is the basic premise."

QUESTIONS FOR DISCUSSION

1. Salwa and Jassim find themselves surrounded by hostility after the attacks on the World Trade Center. Did you notice a change

in attitude toward Arabs in the United States after 9/11? Are other groups in your community discriminated against because of their ethnicity or religion? Have you ever been subject to discrimination?

2. Jassim kills a teenage boy in a car accident. What would your reaction be if you hit and killed someone? Would you visit the victim's family, as Jassim did, or avoid them? What if you were the parent of a child who was killed in an accident—would you want to meet the person who was responsible for your child's death?

3. Salwa doesn't tell Jassim that she is pregnant. Why not? How would you have handled this situation?

4. Halaby tells the story from two very different points of view: Salwa's and Jassim's. Is one of them more compelling for you or easier to identify with? Do you find that at different times in the story you are sympathizing or siding with either Salwa or Jassim?

5. Every aspect of Jassim's life is splitting apart: He kills a boy in a car accident, he gets fired from his job as a hydrologist, and his wife is becoming distant and secretive. How does he handle these three crises? If you were in his place, would you have done anything differently?

6. Marcus, Jassim's boss, fires Jassim because his clients are scared off by the FBI investigation and the company is losing contracts. Marcus knows that Jassim is the innocent victim of a witch-hunt but lets him go nonetheless. Do you think he did the right thing?

7. How does Salwa get drawn into the affair with Jake? Can you identify some of Jake's traits or qualities that she is attracted to? Why can't Salwa see the negative side of him that is so obvious to other people (Petra and Randa, for example)?

8. Compare Salwa's affair with Jake to Jassim's relationship with Penny. Are Salwa and Jassim looking for similar things in their extramarital relationships? What is missing in their marriage that they are seeking elsewhere?

9. Arab culture is an integral part of Salwa's and Jassim's identi-

ties, and even though before 9/11 their life in the United States is quite comfortable, it is inevitable that at times they feel misplaced and yearn for the sense of belonging and the warm familiarity of their homelands. Can you point to specific instances when Salwa and Jassim have to reconcile the differences between the Arab and the American cultures or lifestyles? Have you ever had to negotiate between your own culture and a foreign one?

10. When Jake cooks dinner for Salwa, he offers her candy-coated *shumur* (fennel seeds), which "brought back desserts eaten only during Ramadan, brought back home in one tiny burst and then another" (p. 209). Does *shumur* remind you of Proust's madeleine?

11. What do you think happens at the end of the novel? Is Salwa dying? Are Salwa and Jassim reconciled? How do you interpret the folktale?